LED
ASTRAY

A Joe Burgess Mystery

Book Five

Kate Flora

Book and cover design by eBook Prep
www.ebookprep.com

October, 2016
ISBN: 978-1-61417-886-6

ePublishing Works!
www.epublishingworks.com

CHAPTER 1

Burgess wished he could have slapped the little shit silly. He'd just wasted an afternoon with a crucial witness who thought it was okay to play games with the police. Kid calls in a domestic disturbance, they respond, and now that the victim is in a coma, no telling whether she'll pull out of it okay or end up a vegetable, Burgess goes for a follow-up interview and the little shit says he "doesn't want to get involved." Burgess was sick of the lot of them, the assholes who wouldn't do their civic duty because it might take up some of their time. It wasn't like the kid was in any danger. The boyfriend was behind bars and going to stay there. It was just that the kid couldn't be bothered to focus his lazy brain on details. Now that he'd moved home with mama, he wanted to lie on the couch and watch TV.

The sky pissed him off almost as much. The weather couldn't make up its mind to be cloudy or sunny, warm or cold. Like a fickle lover, it raised expectations and dashed hopes. After enduring an endless winter, Portland, Maine was ready for some warmth. Some of the optimists Burgess passed were wearing tee shirts, but just as many were bundled in sweatshirts and looking unhappy. Friday afternoon in May, a weekend on the horizon, and the weatherman was promising more of the same. All his kids had soccer games tomorrow. If he was predicting the weather, he'd put his money on rain. That's what his bad knee said, and his knee was at least as reliable as the talking heads on TV.

It was warm enough in the truck, and he was enjoying the different shades and shapes of gray on gray clouds as he drove over the bridge from South Portland, radio traffic in the background. He was thinking about dinner and Chris's great cooking when dispatch asked for his location. Shots fired down on the waterfront. They couldn't raise the responding officers. Patrol was tied up with a bomb scare at the library. Could he check it out?

"On my way," he said. "Find me some backup." He hit the unmarked's lights and siren, and punched the accelerator.

He knew the place. A location that wasn't really a location. An abandoned warehouse and overgrown parking lot between the railroad tracks and the harbor, lost in a patch of woods beyond a busy commercial yard. The kind of place kids might go to hang out and smoke dope or drink. In warmer weather, the homeless might pitch tents or put up shacks. Place you practically had to walk into. The entrance road had aged into an overgrown track. The spot was one that should be ripe for development but always seemed to be overlooked.

Dispatch had been calm, as they always were, but Burgess had been a cop a long time, and he read a subtle note of concern under the official tone. That, plus the location, plus two officers sent to what might be a gun party, neither of them responding to the radio, their cell phones, or messages to their computers, caused an anxious flare in his cop's gut. Something about this felt very wrong. He'd been out of the truck, interviewing that witness, and missed the initial call.

He sat on his anxiety as he worked his way around the usual stupidity of drivers who couldn't figure out how to get out of his way. Some days it seems like half the population were blind, deaf, or both and never even saw his lights or heard the siren. They just puttered along, chatting on their phones or listening to the thump of their music, while tragedies happened, women and children got savagely beaten, and patients died trying to get to hospitals. Burgess didn't get this modern fascination with screens. So he was a Luddite. A dinosaur. Last week, a mouthy kid had called him "Grampa." Mouthy kid was now sitting in jail and the dinosaur was still working the streets.

Cops responded to plenty of shots fired calls in their careers. If they were good cops, it never got routine. Getting casual about people with guns—or knives, broken bottles, whatever—getting casual about answering any call could get you killed. So he was already reviewing what he knew about the location. Thick woods that afforded plenty of places to hide. A single road in and out. Large, crumbling building—a death trap of a place—with two floors, lots of rooms, a million places for someone to hide. He considered the number of officer-involved shootings lately where the cops had been lured into a trap. Was that what he was heading into? What those two patrol officers had already encountered?

At the back edge of a commercial lot, beyond the employee parking, piles of materials, and some tractor-trailers, there were two marked cars, lights still flashing. He pulled in behind them, shut off his engine, and told dispatch he was on scene. In reality, he was at least two hundred feet away. There were no cars nearby other than the two official ones. He passed the two patrol cars and walked slowly toward the entrance to the road with a sense of déjà vu. Do this job long enough, things circled back around. Maybe fifteen years ago, he'd had a body down here. Unattended death. Homeless guy. Natural causes—if dying of poverty, alcohol, and a lack of medical care was natural. But he hadn't known any of that going in. Just that some kids looking for a place to hang out, get drunk, and scare themselves to death had gotten more than they bargained for. At least they'd called it in.

As he entered the road and the canopy of new green leaves closed around him, the pucker factor clicked in. He didn't like the feeling of this. For the millionth time in his career, he unsnapped his holster and checked that his gun moved easily. Ahead, the empty road made a sharp turn to the left. A rising wind rustled the trees. He felt the first raindrop. Hugging the left side of the curve, he moved slowly forward until he could see around the bend. His heart jumped. Maybe twelve feet ahead, a figure in a blue uniform lay in the road.

Gun out, he scanned the empty road and the thicket of woods. Held his breath and listened. If someone was moving out there, it was masked by the rising wind. Cautiously he crept forward, bent down, and checked the fallen man. Pale face. Reddish hair. Empty eyes staring up at an unseen sky. A huge bloom of blood darkened the man's shirtfront. A rookie. Randy something. He couldn't pull up a name. He checked for a pulse. Found nothing. Kid was prudent. Wearing a vest. He'd done it right, but it hadn't saved him. The shot had caught him in the neck. Still crouching, Burgess saw the sprays of arterial blood like a fine mist over the crumbling tar where the kid had been backing away. Wedding ring on the limp, bloody left hand.

Jesus. God. This was awful. He'd leave it for the crime scene team to figure out what this scene could tell them about the shooter. If he hadn't mucked things up too much checking for life. With shaking fingers, he grabbed his phone and called it in, keying it in clumsily with blood slicked fingers. Said get people here ASAP, with a tent, it was an outdoor scene and rain was starting.

He used his phone to photograph the blood spatter. The body. What looked like a pretty good shoe impression in the blood. Someone who'd walked up to the body after the officer had fallen. It was something, if the rain didn't wash it away. Then he called Terry Kyle and Stan Perry. He'd need his team from personal crimes here as soon as possible.

Where the hell was the backup he'd already asked for, anyway? He knew budget cuts meant they were doing more with less, and a bomb scare at the library would pull personnel from everywhere. But shots fired and officers not responding was serious. In the back of his mind, he made a note. Might this and the bomb scare be related? Later. All those questions were for later.

He didn't want to leave the kid lying in the road like this, but there were two empty patrol cars. There might be another victim. Someone who could be saved. He headed on down the road, staying close to the edge, both to avoid messing up the blood patterns, and to be near trees he might be able to use for cover. They were skimpy things, new growth junk trees—poplar, Norway maple, sumac—but some cover was better than nothing. His whole body was prickly with anticipation, with the sense he might be walking into a trap. That footprint had been headed back toward the parking lot, but a single print didn't mean much, and he didn't have time to study the ground and see if there were more prints heading in that direction.

Gun out, at low ready, he made himself move slowly. He wanted to run. Rush down that road, find the second officer, make something be all right here. He knew better. Rushing was a mistake. Crises could make you careless; make you take foolish chances. An adrenaline shock could make you stop thinking clearly. He needed his head clear for whatever lay down this road.

Normal time had vanished. He was in crime scene time now, that odd combination of being very present and acutely observant, and taking the long view. Slow it down and take as long as it takes. These were the moments when training and experience counted most. When his conscious mind headed into tunnel vision and was only about what was happening right now, about how acutely aware he was of every sound around him and the crunch of his footsteps and how every drop of the rain that was beginning to fall landed on his face like a blow.

He pushed away his rage and sadness about that poor boy lying back there in the road. No time for it now. Emotion clouded perception. Feelings could be postponed until he'd done the job that needed to be done here. The wind was roaring now, tossing the trees and shredding those tender new leaves. Branches snapped and trunks creaked as they were torqued and twisted. Preambles to a rain that was still only random drops. He raised his left arm to shield his face as he plunged on, eyes right, eyes left, eyes forward, fear knotting his gut. It was cold, but he was sweating, he could feel it run down his back under the rigid vest.

The road wound on. Maybe a quarter of a mile on an odometer. A quarter of a century on foot with the potential that a gunman was tracking his every step. Around another curve and the building was in sight. He slid back into the shadows and studied it. Weary red brick with blackened holes where the glass had been punched out of some of the windows. Peeling white paint on the trim. Padlocked sliding doors to sagging loading docks. Last year's weeds and this year's grass pushing up from cracks in the paving.

He checked the windows for signs of movement. Nothing. Listened for any sounds above the wind and got back something that sounded like a moan. He listened harder, cupping his ear, trying to find a direction. Heard what sounded like a mumbled voice somewhere near the building.

He edged forward, hurried across the open space that had once been parking, and moved along the side of the building, gun up and ready. Stopping every few steps to listen. The sound seemed to be growing louder. Then he was at the corner. He darted a quick look around, saw nothing, so he rounded the corner and stopped. The sound was clearer here, where the building blocked some of the wind. A human voice moaning in pain.

The second officer was lying in an open doorway, half in, half out of the building. He was on his back, gun on the ground beside him, both hands clamped to his side. He writhed on the dirty cement, his face twisted in pain. Burgess barely recognized Remy Aucoin.

Kneeling, he put his hand on the young officer's shoulder. "Remy, it's Burgess. We're here. Help is on the way."

He stepped outside, grabbed his phone, and called dispatch. They needed medics and an ambulance. Right now. And Jesus, they needed the ambulance crew to stop short of the body back there in the road. The living trumped the dead, but an emergency kerfuffle of vehicles, personnel, and equipment would destroy much of what that scene might tell them. He was trying to explain that when he saw movement back on the road. He flattened himself against the building, holding his breath as he watched a figure emerge from the trees, gun up, scanning the lot and the building.

Then his breath whistled out in relief. Backup. Detective Terry Kyle.

"Terry. Over here!"

He went back to the doorway and bent over Aucoin, folding up a couple handkerchiefs and pressing them against the oozing wound under the lower edge of the man's vest. "Can you talk, Remy? Can you tell me what happened here?"

Aucoin's eyes were glazed with pain. "I never saw a face. He was across the room. In the dark. Waiting." He grabbed a shuddering breath, and groaned. "God. Joe. It hurts. Am I?"

"You're not dying, Remy. You're going to be okay. They're on their way." When Aucoin didn't respond, Burgess said, "Stay with me, Remy. Okay? Stay with me. I'm right here."

"Nicole," Remy said. "Love her. Tell…"

"I'll tell her, Remy." Whoever Nicole was, he'd find her and tell her. Hoped that Remy would have plenty of times to tell her himself.

Then Burgess saw a grab for control. The cop in Remy wanted to tell the story, in case he didn't make it. "A rifle. One shot. Laughed when I went down. I heard…laugh."

Aucoin went silent. Burgess leaned in, saw that his eyes were closed, his mouth clenched against the pain. "Only if you can, Remy. It's okay."

Aucoin squeezed the words out, one at a time, like they were wrenched from somewhere deep inside him. "It's...not...okay." A shuddering breath as he tried to push on. "Shooter...still...has..."

The last word was barely a whisper. Silence again. He felt Aucoin's body shivering. Shock, blood loss, the effort to speak. He pulled off his coat and draped it over Aucoin. Burgess could feel the effort as Aucoin gathered himself for one last word, filling the pause with a million possibilities.

"...has Vince."

Vince. Lt. Vincent Melia. Burgess's boss and close friend. He felt his heart skip a beat as he went cold all over.

CHAPTER 2

When he got close enough for Burgess to see his face, Kyle looked sick and drained. He flinched when he saw Aucoin. "Jesus, Joe! What is going on here?"

"I've got no answers," Burgess said. "Ambush would be my guess."

Always one to get right down to business, Kyle said, "How can I help? Stan's over at the library. He'll be along when he can get free. I couldn't reach Vince. No one knows where—"

Burgess cut him off. "Remy says the shooter's got him."

Kyle rocked back, his ice blue eyes widening. "Say what?"

"That's all I could get out of him and he had to struggle to tell me that much. So we've gotta search the building. Maybe he's still inside."

Burgess choked back his next thought. Melia or his body. He had a crazy image of Melia's twins back when they were roly poly babies. He shut off the projector. No time for sentiment, for thinking about anything beyond what was happening here. Focus. He needed to focus.

He looked up at Kyle. "We've got help on the way, but I need you...I need someone...down on the road so that ambo doesn't roll right over our crime scene."

"They wouldn't…" Kyle started, then shook his head. Different missions. Different focus. "Shit. Yeah. I'll go head 'em off. But you shouldn't go inside by yourself."

"Not going anywhere yet. I'm not leaving Remy."

God what a clusterfuck this was going to be! He was explosive with frustration. He needed to be in three places right now—here, down on the road with the fallen officer, reading that scene before it got mucked up, and inside looking for Vince. Where he had to be was here until medical help arrived for Aucoin. His gut twisted like he'd swallowed a boa. He'd worked with Aucoin since the man was a rookie. Watched him mature into a really good cop. And now this. He might want to rush inside and look for Melia, but Aucoin was bad. Semi-conscious and in serious pain. He needed to know his people were with him. He needed a familiar face there reassuring him. Burgess believed people came first. The biggest bitch in the world was when you had to choose between people.

"Please tell me we've got backup on the way, Ter?"

Kyle shrugged, an eloquent twist of his thin shoulders. "My man, not only is there no one on first today, mostly we can't even seem to find first. With Melia among the missing, you wanna guess who's in charge at that bomb scene over at the library?"

Burgess might hope for the chief or his deputy, but Kyle's look told him the answer: his arch-nemesis and perennial antagonist, Captain Paul Cote. He shook his head. Just about anyone in the department was more qualified to run a complex scene than Cote, but Cote's self-awareness was about on par with his charity and compassion. His competence ran to CompStat numbers and budget sheets. The only saving grace was that the bomb guys would be there, and they were top notch. And the Special Reaction Team. Guys with plenty of extra training to manage complex scenes. The downside was that SRT was *there* and would be tied up there for who knew how long, when Burgess needed them *here*.

This building was a nightmare. Searching it should be done by a team of heavily armed and armored professionals, not a couple weary old detectives. Not that Kyle wasn't top notch. Or that old. Or that Burgess hadn't searched hundreds of buildings. But they'd be better deployed managing these crime scenes. And praying—Kyle, at least, was good at prayer—they didn't find a third scene and a third victim.

A decade or so later, or so it felt, a competent crew had strapped Aucoin to a gurney and were rolling him away. A saving grace of being police in Maine's largest city—at least they had a great hospital close by, and ER docs who were really good at saving lives. It kept the homicide stats down. It also kept the cop's hopes up. His crime scene people had arrived and were working on the scene where Randy Crossman—Burgess had finally remember the dead rookie's name—lay. He'd called Chris and told her why he wouldn't be home. And Kyle came loping back up the road with Stan Perry in tow.

"Wink and Dani have got it," Kyle said. "Sage is there. They've got the tent up and Rudy is taking his pictures." Wink Devlin and Dani Letorneau were evidence techs. Sage Prentiss the newest member of Burgess's team. And Rudy Carr was their photographer.

Kyle tossed Burgess a raincoat. The rain was really starting to pick up now.

"They're going to need a lot more help before this is done," Burgess muttered.

Not being able to call his lieutenant and get this handled was like an itch he couldn't reach. Focus, he told himself. Focus. Their job now was to *find* Vince. Dammit. He was supposed to be handling this and he couldn't seem to think straight.

"Dani okay?" he asked. Which was stupid because no one was okay with that officer—Christ, Burgess, give him a name—with Randy Crossman lying there with his neck torn open like he'd been attacked by a wild animal. Wild animals were crafty, just like the one they'd soon be hunting. And why was he only concerned for Dani and not Wink? Because she was small and female and he thought he ought to protect her? He *was* a fucking dinosaur.

"We've got a car at the end of the road, holding off the maggots," Stan Perry said, "and patrol is sending some people." His next words echoed something Burgess had wondered. "Why'd he pick this place, Joe? Hardly anybody knows about it." And then, with a wondering shake of his shaved head, Perry answered his own question. "Great fucking place for an ambush, that's why."

Perry was the youngest member of their team, practically a kid. When things got to him, he sometimes let it show. Like now, when he grabbed Burgess's arm and said, "Is Remy gonna be okay?" And, without waiting for an answer, "We're gonna get this fucker, right, Joe? Tell me we're gonna get him."

"Breaking Joe's arm isn't going to help," Kyle said.

"We're gonna get him, Stan. We're absolutely gonna get him. Let's just take this one step at a time." He waved a hand at the building. "First let's figure out how we're going to search this place."

Heads together, they huddled under the eaves, sheltered from the rain while they worked out a plan and checked their flashlights. There wasn't electricity, and the deep gray afternoon was now darkening into evening. Searching with flashlights always amped up the risk. A light in your hand told a lurking bad guy exactly where to shoot. Searching in the dark made things go slower because they couldn't clear a room as fast. In a perfect world, they'd wait. For SRT. For daylight. But Melia might be in the building. Melia and maybe others. Someone else they might save.

Going into a building under these circumstances made your guts writhe and your ass pucker. They had no choice, though. Better to live with the fear, even sick to your stomach and bathed in sweat, than find out later your hesitation had let someone get injured or dead.

They took a moment, then, before they entered, sucking down lungfuls of fresh outside air before they encountered must and rats and damp and old dirty. Places where the homeless had used corners as their latrines. Places where animals had crawled in and died. Become a cop so you can serve and protect and crawl through a world of filth trying to hang on to the hope that one of the people you respected most in the world wasn't lying somewhere in this awful place, bled out like Crossman.

Dammit, Burgess. Focus.

Before they separated, he felt Kyle's hand on his shoulder. "We're all feeling it, Joe."

Kyle always could read his mind.

It was a two-story building. The front end, where they'd entered, a warren of little offices on both floors, the other end a huge open space that had held manufacturing machinery. One by one they cleared the offices on the first floor—a process so slow eons passed, and with every step their anxiety amped up. Stan Perry was practically vibrating with impatience. They all felt it, Perry just wore it more openly. He wanted to break away from slow and cautious and go make something happen. Burgess put a hand on his shoulder. "Easy, Stan."

A few pieces of broken furniture, some battered metal desks. Some stained, mouse-eaten mattresses in a few of the rooms. Piles of trash. Broken glass. Used syringes. Nothing that stood out except one room where someone might be living. It was cleaner than the rest, with a mattress and blanket, a plastic bag with some clothes in one of those wheeled carts like older ladies used for groceries, a camp stove, cooking pot. Some tins of food.

Then they climbed the stairs to the second floor, following several recent-looking sets of footprints in the dust. Each of them, in turn, stepping in Burgess's prints at the far edge of the stairs. Instinctively preserving evidence. If it *was* evidence.

On the fourth step, it became evidence. Evidence of someone falling hard on one knee. Someone who was bleeding. Blood drops on the steps. Blood spatter and a bullet hole in the wall.

They followed that trail of blood, and bloody handprints, as though someone was using a hand for support, the rest of the way up those stairs. The stairwell echoed with their footsteps. With the ragged sound of breathing to keep their stomachs settled and their bodies moving. The starts and stops of anticipation and listening. If the bad guy was still up there, he knew they were coming.

Another row of offices. All the doors were shut. The trail of bloody handprints had stopped. Now there were drag marks in the dust. Confusing drag marks that led to more than one door. One on the right. Another, farther along, on the left.

They fanned out so they became a more difficult target. So that if one of them got shot, the others would have a chance to return fire. So that if someone up here was watching, he could only watch one of them at a time.

Fear scent is a real thing. Right now, the air was thick with it.

They were communicating with hand signals. Burgess on the right. Stan on the left. Kyle behind to cover them.

Those drag marks might be a trick. They still needed to check each room.

Slowly they moved down the hall. Check. Clear. Move on. The door to the room on the right where the drag marks led was locked. The first locked door they'd encountered.

Nothing about this felt right. This bastard was really playing with them.

Burgess hesitated, thinking about bombs and booby traps. Someone inside waiting to shoot. Did he have a choice? What would he tell a rookie? To back off and wait for SRT. To not take unnecessary risks, that part of the job was to go home alive at the end of the day. He thought about Melia's boys. Lincoln, who'd given them such a scare a few months ago. Vince and Gina's terror that they were looking at cancer and might lose him. Their joy when their son had mono, was only very sick and tired, and would live. If

Vince was in there bleeding or dying, and time mattered, and Burgess could do something to save him, would he wait for SRT?

What about his own kids? Dylan, the surprise son he'd so recently acquired, the boy so startlingly like him? Neddy and Nina, finally settled in a safe place after a series of horrific experiences? If he got himself killed, would Chris keep Dylan? He knew she'd never forgive him. If there was an afterlife, she'd reach right into it and tweak him for his stupidity. For being such a macho cop. The problem was that he *was* a macho cop. This was the job he'd signed on for. He hadn't taken an oath to serve and protect only until it got too risky and bathed him in nervous sweat. Seconds ticked off as he vacillated.

Then he said, "Fuck it," and kicked in the door.

An office like the others. Broken window. Battered metal desk. Broken swivel chair behind the desk. Propped up in the chair, his face obscured by drying blood, the front of his once crisp white shirt blown open and dark with more blood, was Melia. On the desk, a crude cardboard tent sign: Lt. Vincent Asshole.

CHAPTER 3

While the meanest, toughest cop in Portland stood there, paralyzed, breathing in the blood-tinged air, Kyle slipped around the desk and checked Melia for signs of a pulse. Then, with a small, twisted smile, he pulled out his phone.

"Alive?" Burgess said.

Kyle nodded as he gave instructions to dispatch, then called Sage Prentiss out at the first crime scene to let him know another ambulance was on the way. Sage said he'd take care of it, and let everyone know. He didn't ask who, or what was up. This was a time for action, not reaction.

All the while, Burgess stood there, staring, ignoring the tears that ran down his face. "You stay with him, Ter," he said. "Stan and I will finish searching the offices."

He didn't want to leave Vince. Not for a minute. But Kyle was clearly more functional than he was, and the search needed to be finished.

"You're his friend. You should be the one…" Kyle shut his mouth.

Perry was already out the door, eager to be away from the horrors of that room, the too-vivid reminder of their mortality. As if Randy Crossman and Remy hadn't been enough. Burgess followed. Backing each other now, feeling far less safe without that third pair of eyes, and Kyle's gun, they finished searching the right side, then came back down the left, slowing when they got to the second set of drag marks. A second locked door. Neither of them wanted to be first one through it or to see what further horrors lay on the other side. But they needed to know.

Perry said, "I'll take this one, Joe," reared back, and slammed his foot into the door. It flew open. They stepped in, gagging as the air currents from the opened door pulled air thick with the scent of blood and feces and urine into their faces, telling them, even before their flashlights illuminated the body, that they were going to see more death. They simultaneously backed out of the room, hands pressed against their mouths.

"Whoops!" Perry said. He ducked across the hall into an empty office and Burgess could hear him being sick.

A quick glance had been enough. Same layout. Crappy metal desk. Broken chair. Man sitting in the chair. Tent sign on the desk. This crudely lettered sign read: Sorry. The man in the chair had a shotgun resting against his chest. And no head.

Perry back up against the wall, his hands over his face. Between spread fingers came a whisper. "Joe. My god! What the fuck is going on here?"

Burgess didn't have any answers.

Leaving Perry to recover his equilibrium, he stepped back into the room, went closer, and moved his light over the body, studying the headless form behind the desk. The position of the gun relative to the body, the arms and legs. The shabby clothing. The scarred, worn, dirty hands. Where the majority of the brain, skull, and blood spatter had gone. Then he stepped back out into the hall. Perry leaned limply against the wall, his face even greener than the flashlight normally made it. Burgess suspected his own looked pretty much the same.

He was beginning feel detached, like this was all happening to someone else. Someone who didn't give a shit about dead and wounded cops and multiple crime scenes, only about finding the asshole who'd done this no matter what it took. Who didn't care about what the woman he loved would say when he didn't come home for twenty-four hours. Or twenty-four days. Or however long this took. A robotic detective Burgess who couldn't think about how all this might scare his kids. Cold detachment was exactly the way to go.

"Crime scene team's gonna have a hell of a night," he told Perry. "And in case you were fooled for even a second, that is not our killer, blowing his head off in a passion of regret. Though I expect we were supposed to think that. More than likely, it's another vic, whoever was living downstairs. Some poor homeless guy who thought he'd found a safe place to squat."

He rested his hand on Perry's shoulder. "Let's finish this side and then update Terry."

Keep him busy. Give him something to do. Get a little space between him and the horrendous sight in that room. Not the first time they'd seen bits of skull and brain blown everywhere, but this was coming on the heels of two gravely injured cops and a dead one. The dead one a kid. A rookie. It was like someone had killed their little brother. Or their kid. Hurt one of them, you hurt them all. He doubted they'd ever have a day that was worse. See worse, maybe. But never so many things that stabbed them in the heart.

They finished checking the offices. No more bodies. No more messages. No more anything but dust and broken glass and cold, dead air. Rain blowing in through broken windows. Outside the howl of the wind.

They went back to Kyle, and Burgess told him what they'd found. Kyle was getting the dead, far-away look he wore when the bad things piled up. He never complained, he just withdrew, like being less present gave him more energy to cope. He'd go dead except for a scary glitter in his eyes. When Kyle looked like that, no one messed with him.

Burgess took off his raincoat, removed the sport coat he'd draped over Remy Aucoin, and tucked it around his lieutenant. Melia was so still. So white. He figured Kyle had explored the injuries. He'd ask later, after Melia was on his way to the hospital. But it sure didn't look good.

"Help is on the way," Kyle said. "You wanna call the chief, or shall I?"

"I'll do it," Burgess said.

He pulled out his phone and went into the hall. Not an easy call to make, telling the chief three of his people were down, one of them dead. But the chief needed to know. And the command staff. And the sergeants and lieutenants needed to know so they could brief the troops. Everyone needed to be extra careful right now. It was too soon to tell what this might be. Was this someone bent on revenge out to kill himself some cops whose blood lust would now be sated? Or the beginning of a series of assaults? Revenge for something real or imagined, who knew? Or a trap set for Melia, which had caught more than the killer had bargained for. That sign—Lt. *Vincent* Asshole—affirmed that the killer knew Melia.

Besides, Melia being here made no sense unless someone had lured him here. Nor did letting himself get caught, or shot, like this. Why the hell was he here? Had working behind a desk made him careless and he'd forgotten the rules? Tell someone where you're going. Call for backup. Don't take stupid chances. Maybe this had seemed innocent. Or so spur of the moment? Aucoin and Crossman hadn't been there as backup, they'd gone in response to that shots fired call. So who had made that 'shots fired' call? An innocent bystander or the bad guy?

A million questions he had no answers to. He had to stop. Right now, running questions would just make his head explode. He had to stay focused. Stay present. Take this one step at a time. The next step was to call the chief. Well, the next step should have been calling his Lieutenant, Vince Melia, who would have notified Captain Cote, and so it would have gone up the food chain. But he couldn't call Melia, and he wouldn't call that fuck-up Cote if his life depended on it. He observed protocol where it was absolutely necessary, but he didn't need Cote posturing and preening. Cote, who didn't have a heart that anyone had ever been able to locate, would call the media before he called the families.

Family. God. Someone was going to have to make a lot of bad phone calls pretty soon. He sure as hell didn't want Cote calling Gina Melia.

Calling the chief would bring a whole lot more people to the scene. Some of them would be helpful. Most of them would just mill around getting in the way and stepping where they shouldn't. That would be especially true if Captain Cote arrived. And arrive he would, because calling the chief would also bring Cote, and wherever Cote went, the media was sure to follow.

Burgess liked his scenes lean. It might make the job harder, or slower, but it meant a handful of quality minds on the task instead of everyone and his brother and sister. And people forgetting to share what they'd learned. Knew. Seen.

The chief should have been gone, but that bomb scare had lengthened everyone's day. He answered his own phone.

"It's Sgt. Burgess," Burgess said. He gave his location, explained the call that had sent him there, and got right to it. "I have some very bad news, sir."

There was an audible sigh on the other end. That bomb scare had probably seemed like enough bad news. "Go on."

"We've got an officer down. Randy Crossman. Gunshot to the neck. Tore out his carotid. We've got techs on scene and an ME on the way."

The chief had schooled himself not to swear, but his first words were unprintable.

"I'm afraid that's not all, sir."

"Christ, Burgess, there's more?"

"Another officer shot, sir. Remy Aucoin. He's on his way to the hospital."

"How's it look?"

"Bad, sir."

"I'll head over there. Unless you need me at the scene. You got enough people? What do you need?"

He'd needed SRT. He needed some answers. He needed to know that Vince was okay. He wasn't given to magical thinking. "Chicf, there's more."

"Jesus, Burgess! More? What the fuck's going on over there?"

"Don't know yet, sir. But there's another wounded officer. It's Vince. Lt. Melia. It's bad. Really bad. We're waiting on an ambulance now. A little complicated. They have to come in right through a crime scene."

Silence. Then, "Vince? Vince has been shot?"

"Yes, sir."

More silence. They were trained to act. React. Take control. It was the same, and different, when it was one of their own. And the chief and Melia were close. "What the fuck was he doing there?"

"No idea, sir. But we'll find out."

"Has anyone called Gina?"

"No one has called anyone. Any of the families. We just cleared the building. Found another body with the head blown off. Pardon the language but it's a shitstorm over here. Be a big help if you could get us more crime scene people. Make sure patrol controls the media. And make some calls to the families."

He felt like a chump, ducking the call to Gina. But she'd ask a thousand questions hc didn't yet have answers to. It was better coming from the Chief or his deputy. They were good with people. With putting the best spin on things. He had no idea how you'd spin this and didn't want to spend his time trying. He had other things to do with his time.

"I'll take care of it," the chief said. "Keep me informed."

"Will do, sir. And if you could…" He hesitated, torn between needing to know and not wanting to. "If you could let me—let us—know how Remy's doing. And Vince, when he gets there. I'd be grateful. And…" Another request that wasn't his call. He'd make it anyway. "Keep as much of this as you can out of the media."

He went back into the room. Perry was leaning against the wall, looking sick. Kyle was kneeling beside Melia. "Terry, step out and call Michelle," he said. "You, too, Stan. Call your girlfriend. Before they hear it on the news. I'll stay with Vince."

They each nodded and stepped out into the hall. Burgess crouched beside his friend, murmuring what they all said to each other at times like this. "Stay with me, Vince. Stay with me. You're going to be okay."

He sent Stan downstairs to wait for the ambulance crew so he could direct them up the stairs. Sent Kyle down to get whatever photos he could of the stairs before many more feet, feet bent on business that didn't involve preserving evidence but rather on preserving life, eliminated what those stairs had to say. Not thinking clearly. Before he was even out of the room, Kyle was on the phone to Dani, pulling her away from Randy Crossman long enough to get those critical photos.

He stayed with Vince, willing every breath in and every breath out to continue. Time felt infinite. Years had passed and there was no sign of that ambulance. Finally, he'd waited long enough. In a situation like this, minutes mattered. Melia was no lightweight, but Burgess was a big guy. And impatience and anger gave him strength. As carefully as if he was lifting Neddy after the boy had fallen asleep on the couch, he slipped his arms under Melia and picked him up.

Melia groaned, and Burgess felt a twinge of guilt. You're never supposed to move an injured person. But this was no time for fucking rules. Bracing the injured man against his body, he pulled his jacket up so it covered Melia's face to protect him from the rain. Then he headed for the stairs. If he met the ambulance on the way, so much the better. If not, he'd drive Melia to the hospital himself.

CHAPTER 4

H e went down the stairs with care, passing Dani, her face fixed and white as she knelt and photographed the blood trail. Passed Kyle, who turned without a word and came with him, opening an umbrella he'd gotten from somewhere and holding it over them. Passed Stan at the door. No one said, "What the fuck are you doing?" because everyone understood.

The road underfoot was soggy from the rain. The night smelled of torn leaves and damp vegetation. The wind threatened to turn the umbrella inside out. Cold rain blew in through his open raincoat. Beside him, Kyle's raincoat snapped like a flag. Both of them getting soaked as Kyle held the umbrella low to shelter Melia. Ahead, the tent and the scene where Crossman lay was illuminated, a brilliant spot in an otherwise black night. The sideways veil of wind-blown rain shimmered like a shower of golden light.

He could feel Melia's labored breathing through his own chest. Ragged and pained. He'd give anything if he could infuse some of his life into the man he carried. Images of Melia flooded his brain. Always impeccable. So competent. Thoughtful. A decent man and a great cop. So ready to have their backs and give them the leeway they needed to do their jobs. It sounded ordinary but was rare. They'd been through so much together, and now this. What the hell had Melia been doing here?

The road ran endlessly onward, that parking lot never getting any closer. A sea of lights flashed at the end like a strobe-lit finish line. In the distance, finally, the sound of an approaching ambulance.

They reached the end of the road at the same time as the ambulance arrived. Shaking and winded, he handed Melia over to the professionals, camera flashes bursting around them in an assault of light as he bent, hands on his knees, trying to catch his breath. Telling his complaining, aging body to just shut it. No time for bad knees or a bad anything else. Maybe a bad, black temper aimed at bad guys. Maybe a bad attitude toward authority and a fierce disgust with reporters looking for their dramatic above the fold image. Otherwise, now that their injured had been sent for care, it was time to focus on the dead.

Then life said, "Not so fast, sonny," as his phone rang and his angry eyes spotted Captain Cote striding toward him across the parking lot. He checked the screen. His son, Dylan. He turned away from Cote's pompous approach and said, "Hello?"

In the strobing light, he saw his hands and clothes wore the blood of three good men.

"Dad. Sorry to interrupt. We just saw…on the news…can you talk?" Dylan's voice broke. Only fifteen, Burgess knew he was trying to be the man of the family for everyone else.

"It's bad," he said. "As bad as it gets. One officer dead, two more wounded, including Vince Melia. But I'm okay. Terry's okay. Stan's okay. I don't know when I'll be home, but I'll be checking in."

He waited, giving his son space to respond. Dylan hadn't grown up with this like most cop's kids. And he knew that Chris would be scared for him and worried about the effect of this on Nina and Neddy. On everyone. His last big case had been hard on his family. He was supposed to be being more careful. He did his best, but the truth was, he had no idea how he could be more careful. Not when stuff like this happened. You get a call and you respond. You can't walk away when you get there because it might be dangerous.

For a moment, he lost the thread of the conversation as he felt the back of his neck prickle, as he raised his head and scanned the dark woods for signs of a shooter. Then he forced himself back to Dylan. Giving false reassurance because that's what they needed. And anyway, he had no idea yet what the truth was.

"I know it's upsetting, when things seem aimed at cops. But I'm okay. You're okay. You're safe. Everyone just be careful, all right?"

"What does that mean, Dad?"

Explaining would take half the night. "Keep an eye on the street. Don't answer the door to strangers. The usual stuff. I don't think you have anything to worry about." A necessary lie. He tried to keep his anxiety from his voice. To sound like he was easy with this. Just another routine case. "We don't know much about the situation yet. We've barely gotten started."

"The news is saying this is someone deliberately killing cops."

"They're just speculating. The news doesn't know its ass from a hole in the ground."

Dylan laughed and Burgess felt a flood of relief. "I've got to go," he said. "I'll call again in a couple hours. See if you can distract Neddy. Keep him away from screens. All the news is going to do is wind everyone up. You don't need that and we don't need that. Can I speak with Chris?"

He heard mumbled voices and then she was on the line. "It's so awful!" she said. He could tell she was on the verge of tears. "Remy? Vince? And some poor boy dead. How can you stand..." She stopped and grabbed a breath. "Sorry. I know. It's your job to stand it. Come home when...if...you can. We'd like to set our beady little eyes on you. And Joe..."

He knew what she'd say. What she'd need. "I'll call you," he said. "I promise. And I'll be careful. I have too many people I love that I need to come home to."

He heard a sob. Then she said, "I love you, Joe."

"I love you." Words it had taken him more than fifty years to be able to say. It felt good, so he said it again. Snatching something positive from this before the next load of crap, in the form of Captain Paul Cote, arrived and needed to be dealt with. Then he disconnected and put his phone away. Turning just as Cote cleared his throat with a self-important rumble and said, "Burgess!" in a peremptory tone.

"Captain."

As usual, Cote was impeccable from his shiny shoes to his large black umbrella. Burgess had mud on his shoes, mud and blood on his clothes, and blood on his hands. He watched Cote's pruny face take it in and disapprove, then waited to see what the opening words would be. Actually, he knew what they would be, and he wasn't wrong.

"I haven't been kept in the loop on this. I need to be updated right now. I've got media all over me and I don't have anything to tell them."

"Haven't got much to tell them yet. We've just been working our way through the building, looking for Lt. Melia. Tell them two officers wounded. One dead. We aren't releasing any names before the families have been notified."

He omitted the headless guy. Not ready to share that detail until they'd had time to examine that scene. They'd long ago learned to keep sensitive information from the captain. He had a dangerous tendency to share it with the press.

Then Burgess swung his racket and batted a question right back, reminding the captain where his concerns ought to be. "Any word on Aucoin's condition yet?"

Cote blinked, like he was surprised. It was absolutely the right question. When a cop is shot, that's what they all focused on. How the cop was doing, how to support the family, and how best to help with the investigation. How best to get the bastard who did it. He made a face and said, "Burgess, I need more than this."

Burgess didn't have time to play the kind of games he'd like to play. Malicious obedience. Another time, he didn't have the dead and dying weighing on him, and an endless night of crime scenes ahead, he'd do the longest, most boring, by-the-book chapter and verse he could.

But it *was* weighing. "As near as we can tell, we've got at least four crime scenes to work in an abandoned warehouse without electricity. We've called in all of our crime scene techs, the medical examiner is en route, and we expect to be working through the night. The chief will be talking to the families, and you can update the press when he gives the okay."

He was trying to think what else he could give Cote that would send the man scurrying back to the cameras when Cote interrupted. "Four crime scenes?"

"At least. Crossman on the road. Aucoin in the doorway. Blood and bullet holes on the stairs. The office upstairs where we found Vince. As we finish going through the building, we may find more."

Let him think that fourth body was still undiscovered. Hell. Let him think whatever he wanted to think, just let him, please God, go talk to the press and leave a bunch of working detectives alone so they could do their work.

Cote nodded, swung without another word, and would have headed away, but Burgess repeated his question. "Aucoin's condition, Captain? What have you heard?"

"Nothing yet."

Burgess knew, from his tone, Cote hadn't even made a call. These were *his* fucking people!

Burgess headed back up the road. Then turned, went back to one of the patrol guys, and said, "See if someone can scare up some coffee, would you?"

Nice hot coffee. It would help. He and Kyle were pretty much soaked through by now, and getting chilled, a situation that wouldn't improve as the night wore on. He stopped at his car for a sweater—somehow his jacket had departed with Melia—and grabbed a bag from his trunk. Search gloves, spare flashlight, disinfecting wipes, bottled water, the gazillion things he'd need in the next few hours. Saw Kyle was doing the same thing.

He wasn't hungry, but if he was going to get through the night ahead, he should probably eat something. Thanks to the influence of a good woman in his life, he now had trail mix, bars, energy drinks, and chocolate in his bag.

Ahead of him on the road he saw a light bobbing along. When he caught up, he found Dr. Lee, the medical examiner, heading toward the Crossman scene. He stopped the man before he ducked inside. "A minute, Doctor? Inside, we've got…"

Obligingly, Lee paused. "Don't tell me you've got another one?" Lee sounded aggrieved, but Burgess knew it was an act. The ME loved the work. Had a clinical fascination with what his skills could uncover.

Burgess nodded. "Yeah. When you're done with Officer Crossman, we've got a guy inside with his head blown off."

Lee's smile came and went in the blink of an eye. "At least this time you're not spoiling my golf game," he said.

"Like I always say, Dr. Lee, don't blame me, blame the bad guys."

"I blame everybody."

Lee probably did. Burgess had worked with him for a few years now, and wasn't sure he understood the man. Sometimes it seemed like they were close, other times, when Burgess pushed for answers, which Burgess always did, Lee would take offense and engage in some of that malicious obedience Burgess always claimed as his own M.O. The place they met on common ground was that they both hated cases involving kids. Before Lee, Burgess had worked with a ME who was so deeply compassionate about victims they always seemed to be on the same page. Every ride with Lee was a bumpy road.

Before going into the tent, Dr. Lee put a hand on his arm. "I'm sorry about this, Sgt. Burgess. It's got to be hard on all of you." He hesitated, then added, "You'll get the man who did this."

Not a flicker of doubt. Burgess appreciated Lee's confidence. And sympathy. Cops don't look to people for kindness. It wasn't a business that saw people at their best. At times like this, he really appreciated it. "Thanks," he said. "Give me a call when you're done here, and we'll lead you to the other guy. It's kind of a warren in there."

"I'll call you," Lee said.

Burgess took another minute to check in with Wink Devlin and Rudy Carr, to see how they were doing. They'd set up a double tent and the ground it sheltered was littered with little evidence markers. Devlin, head of their crime scene team, seemed his usual, unflappable self. Only if you knew him well, as Burgess did after hundreds of scenes, could you see the tension lines around his eyes. Wink would take this personally. These were *his* cops. If there was a scrap of evidence to be found, Wink would find it. On his hands and knees if necessary. He'd work all night and all the following morning. One of those small, gritty Energizer Bunny types.

Burgess headed back to the warehouse, squashing down the muddy road, his wet pants slapping against his legs as he walked. Inside, Dani Letorneau was still making her slow, careful way up the stairs. She was there to photograph, but she was leaving a trail of evidence tents as she went. Someone had brought in lights and a portable generator so she could see what she was doing. More of those waited by the door to help illuminate their work. This mess could use some illumination.

Stan and Terry were just inside the door, waiting for their marching orders. Not that they weren't capable of working a scene by themselves. But on this, they wanted to work together. They wanted to work it right.

"So, you had a chat with the captain," Kyle said. "What did he say about Remy?"

"He hasn't called."

"Why am I not surprised? So it's a good thing that Terry Kyle called, isn't it?"

"And?"

"Sage says he's in surgery. It will be a while before we know anything. He'll get Remy's clothes. The bullets. And Melia's, when he gets there."

"So we wait."

"Yeah, but at least we've got people there. And Remy's uncles, of course, ready to move heaven and earth to ensure their nephew gets the best care." Remy Aucoin's two uncles were both Portland cops.

A crash behind them as Perry kicked something into the wall. "Crime scene, lad," Kyle reminded him. "Anything might be evidence."

"I just wish it was that fucker's head," Perry snarled.

"So do we all," Kyle intoned. "Now, fearless leader, where do we begin?"

Like their fearless leader had any idea. But at this point it was about process, slow, painstaking process. Seeing what the scenes had to tell them while storing up their questions for later. Before they dug in, he said, "In what order were they shot, do you think?"

"Melia. Then, when they responded to the shots fired call, Aucoin. Then Crossman," Kyle said, "right, Stan?"

"Right. Vince was ambushed. Marched up those stairs. At some point he resisted and was shot. We know there was at least one shot on the stairs. My guess would be the head wound? And the guy was good with a rifle."

"One gun or two?" Kyle said.

Stan Perry considered. "Two. At least two," he said. "Plus the shotgun. Pretty close quarters for a rifle on those stairs, so I'm betting that was a handgun. But what on earth was Vince doing here?"

It was the central question.

"What about the guy with no head?" Perry said.

"After Melia, before Aucoin," Kyle said.

"I'm thinking before Melia," Burgess said.

They could do this all night. Speculating, then backing it up with what they'd observed, the evidence they had.

"Let's start with that occupied room. Our shooter might have gotten careless in there if his focus was on Vince."

"Good luck with that," Kyle said. "This is a very organized guy."

"He thinks. I'm hoping he was more arrogant than careful," Burgess said.

Perry was quiet. But Perry quiet was a good thing. Impulsive as he sometimes was, he also had a talent for pondering on things and then suddenly pulling rabbits out of hats. They'd need plenty of rabbits on this one.

"A question," Kyle said. "What makes you think the dead guy upstairs is the one who've been living here?"

Kyle hadn't been with them when they broke down that door. He'd been with Melia, so Burgess explained. "Three things. He's ex-military. The clothes he's wearing are shabby olive drab and camo, just like the ones in the room. Two, the dead guy is a heavy smoker, he's got nicotine stains on his hands. And so was whoever occupied that room. Third, there are blood drops on the floor of the occupied room, and blood drops leading to the room where he was shot."

"Anybody listening would think you were a detective," Kyle said. "Let's check out the room. Maybe we can finally give the guy a name. Headless Guy isn't very respectful."

"Hold on," Burgess said, his carelessness hitting him like a punch in the gut. "If this guy's target was Vince, he's not done yet."

He called the evening shift commander, and asked that someone be assigned to guard Melia's room 24/7. "I want a log, with names and job titles, of everyone who comes near him. Better put people on Aucoin, too." There would be plenty of cops at the hospital, but without officers specifically assigned to guard duty, someone could still get through.

That done, they headed into the gloom of the warehouse, Burgess and Kyle carrying their bags, Perry bringing the lights. Above them, silent except for her camera clicks, Dani Letorneau toiled her patient way up the stairs.

CHAPTER 5

They set up the lights, ready to examine the occupied room. It was cramped and shabby, like the other offices, but the man had been neat and he'd made an effort at creating something homey. The floor had been swept. His cooking stove, food stores, and pots and pans were set up on the desk, which had been pushed against the wall to create a counter. He'd stapled plastic over the broken window. His small store of clothes was clean and folded in the plastic trash bag that lined a metal cart. Two wooden crates made a bedside table, on which there were two books and a half-burned candle.

They were about to plunge in when Perry said, "We should get Dani to photograph this first."

Burgess went to get her. She was almost at the top of the stairs, drooping against the wall. When he got close, he saw that she was crying. When she heard him, she hastily wiped her eyes and looked away.

"It's okay, Dani. It's how we all feel. No one is going to think you're less professional because this bothers you."

When she looked his way, her brown eyes were swimming with tears. "It's just…" She couldn't finish.

He gave her his last handkerchief. He always carried three.

Over the years, he'd covered his city with these little white squares.

She gave him a shaky smile. "One of the famous Burgess handkerchiefs. My first." She buried her face in it and he pulled her against his chest, wrapping his arms around her. "Big girls don't cry," she murmured into his shoulder.

"Humans cry," he said.

He touched the hand that wasn't holding her camera. "You're freezing," he said. "Do you have anything warm in your car?" Almost June and it was still so cold.

She nodded. "I've got a fleece."

"Let's get someone to bring it up here. We've got a long night ahead and we need you."

"I'm okay," she insisted.

Dani always wanted to be tough, which was good, given the scenes she got called into. But Burgess knew it was important to put the living first, to look after his people. Tonight, without Vince here, a lot of that would fall on him. Cote wouldn't think of it and he wasn't sure anyone else would step in to fill Vince's shoes.

"I'll get someone up here who can grab your keys and bring you what you need."

"Coffee would be good."

Coffee would be very good. The coffee he'd asked for should be here by now. They'd kept half an ear on radio traffic, but hadn't paid much attention. He hoped there wasn't another crisis going on in the city that was distracting people. He could imagine their killer creating a series of crises to keep them distracted all night. Especially if he wanted access to the hospital. And Melia.

They needed coffee and they needed more help. He sent Dani to photograph the room while he made some calls. He was putting his phone away when Kyle materialized at his side. Kyle could do that—move so silently he suddenly appeared places.

"You feel it, Joe?" Kyle asked.

Burgess nodded. "I keep thinking maybe he's elsewhere, stirring something up, but the way the hair keeps prickling on my neck? It says he's out there watching."

"Yeah. I'm thinking sniper rifle with a scope? Maybe we should get SRT to do a sweep. Better than a bullet in the head, right? Maybe get a dog in, too?"

Kyle had a knack for articulating what he was thinking. "You want to take care of it?"

Kyle's phone was already out and he was making the call.

Then a patrol sergeant, Kenny Davis, came through the door, carrying a tray of coffee and a bag that might be food. He snagged Dani's keys and said someone would be back with her stuff.

"City quiet tonight?" Burgess asked.

"The usual. Hope it stays that way. Been a bitch of day."

"Tell your people to be extra careful."

The sergeant nodded. "We're feeling it, Joe. Lotta people over at the hospital. You hear anything?"

"Nothing. You?"

Davis shrugged. He'd been on a long time, like Burgess. Days and nights like this amped up the anxiety big time. Raised the risk of someone getting spooked and bad things happening. "Same. Can't decide whether no news is good news or they're just keeping it from us. Dammit. Jesus, Joe. A rookie. That's got the rest of the new kids shit scared."

"We hear anything, we'll get the word out."

Davis headed back out.

Burgess felt uneasy, watching the bobbing flashlight disappear back into the night. If their guy was out there, they were giving him too many targets.

They picked an empty office, and before they unwrapped the food, scrubbed their hands, and the desktop, with antiseptic wipes. Burgess's hands were streaked with blood and it took a while. He drank his rapidly cooling coffee like a thirsty man emerging from the desert and wolfed his blueberry muffin with no semblance of manners. No one was watching. They were all doing the same thing. Dani was no exception. She tore into her muffin like it was an enemy.

The cop's rule: eat when you can. Even if the setting was cold, damp, and disgusting and up above them, a man with no head awaited their attention. It would have been better to get outside, away from this. Sit in a car or grab a moment to warm up in the crime scene van. But no one was going to show up with the van any time soon. It would be down there on the road until that scene was cleared.

Dani photographed and tented the blood drops, barely visible on the dirty gray carpet. Then he and Kyle pulled on gloves and started on the room while Perry took Dani upstairs to start on the room where they'd found Melia. Putting off the headless man as long as they could.

It was a meager lot of possessions and Burgess couldn't help thinking about his friend Reggie. His murdered friend Reggie, who'd come back from a war in Southeast Asia and never been the same again. At least Reggie had had a room. And people who loved him and looked after him. He wondered who this man had had? Going slowly and methodically through everything took so little time. There was a camo backpack beneath the pillow. Inside, discharge papers, some correspondence with the VA, and not much else.

Richard Pelham. Rick, Burgess wondered, or Ricky or Rich? What had people called him? Had anyone bothered to call him anything? There were no cards or letters. Two overseas postings, Iraq and Afghanistan. Diagnosed with post-concussion syndrome. Traumatic brain injury. Living on disability, lucky to get it. This was the kind of invisible injury veterans had to fight to get recognized. So had Pelham been a fighter? Used himself up in that fight and retreated?

And now this. How had this awful thing been done to him with no signs of a struggle? No man who'd served his country should have to live like this, never mind die like this. He imagined the killer's analysis—that Pelham would be the perfect fall guy. Brain damaged and neglected by society, why wouldn't it seem logical that he'd snapped and gone after one of a controlling and neglectful society's most obvious symbols—the police?

Burgess had to step out of the room for a minute. Stand in the dark and breathe in the fetid air and try to get his balance back. No use to Richard Pelham or Randy Crossman if he was indulging himself in what his mother would have called a hissy fit. He recited his mantra: focus. Focus. Trying to keep his repetitions calm when he wanted to yell. Curse. Slam things with his fists. Focus. Slowly. Over and over, until his heart stopped pounding and he could be effective again. Nights like this made him wonder if he was too old for the job and ought to pack it in. Too old and too angry. Nights like this reminded him that when he was doing the job—doing it right—he didn't have time for wondering.

Kyle had finished the room. Nothing in the pockets of Pelham's clothes. Nothing in the books. Nothing else of interest except for a single filtered cigarette stubbed out in an ashtray full of unfiltered butts. It might be nothing. Or it might that arrogance they were hoping for. A killer who figured they'd never notice one butt among so many. Dani'd already photographed the ashtray so Kyle snagged it and bagged it.

Remy Aucoin had been shot as he entered the building. Because of where he was hit and how he fell, they figured the shot had come from inside. Although there had been a fair amount of traffic in and out, making the Aucoin shooting scene hard to work, before they went upstairs, they reenacted the shooting, trying to figure out where the shooter had been standing. Burgess and Kyle were both taller than Aucoin, but now Burgess stood in for Aucoin while Kyle walked back down the office-lined corridor and out into the cavernous open space, looking for signs.

"Here," he said, pulling out one of Dani's little evidence markers and setting it on the floor. His voice echoed in the empty room.

Burgess saw what he'd marked—another half-smoked filtered cigarette. And footprints in the dust on the floor. In a place where there was plenty of accumulated trash, a cigarette and some footprints might not be significant. But this was the only cigarette butt in this area, these the only recent footprints. The office area was carpeted with a dark, moldy stuff that had probably once been gray. Out here the floor was cement. "He's leaving us a lot to work with."

"If these are his. If there was only one of them. If we can find someone to match these up with."

"You're such a freaking optimist, Terry."

"I was feeling optimistic this morning."

"About?"

"Life. Michelle. My kids. That things will be okay and the PMS Queen will finally leave us alone. I looked at my three beautiful women eating breakfast together and I thought wow, this was going to be a good day. It's Friday, I've got the weekend with my family. And now this mess and there will be no fucking weekend."

Kyle was divorced and his ex-wife Wanda—known to his friends as the PMS Queen—was one of the most hateful and vindictive women Burgess had ever known. She'd done everything in her power to sabotage his relationship with his daughters, then, after he fought for and won custody of the girls, she'd tried to destroy his relationship with his new girlfriend Michelle, knowing that—with his crazy schedule—Michelle's presence was the only thing letting him keep his girls. Lately, things had been going okay.

Kyle shook his head. "We should be over at the hospital with Vince."

"Nose to the grindstone," Burgess said. "The sooner we get done here, the sooner we get over there."

"Let's stick up a 'gone fishing' sign, dart over there, and check things out. No one will notice we're gone."

"Wouldn't I love to." Burgess sat on the fear they both shared, based on what they'd seen. Tonight and over their years of policing. That by the time they were done here, it would be all over for Vince and there wouldn't be anything to check out. "We do him more good sticking with this."

Then Kyle put a hand on his arm. They stood together, not saying anything, listening. The wind had died and the rain was slackening, allowing them to hear all the creaks and groans of the building. And something else. Something they maybe weren't really hearing but simply knowing instinctively. Not a crime scene noise. Not a sound from inside the building. The slight rub of a nylon coat against something rough, like bark.

Burgess said, "He's out there," and instinctively dove for the floor, taking Kyle with him, pulling Kyle away from the footprints. Where Kyle's head had been, something smacked into one of the wooden columns that supported the ceiling, sending out a shower of splinters. A yelp from upstairs, then a crash. Perry taking Dani out of the line of fire.

As Kyle touched his head warily, making sure it was still there, Burgess got out his radio. Freakin' SRT was taking their sweet time getting here. And they were needed right now.

It was stone cold. The guy kills Pelham. He kills Melia. Or thinks he has. And then he waits for the cops to respond. Waits like an executioner until Aucoin appears in the doorway. Smoking while he waits. Shoots Aucoin. Then what? Heads down the road, meets Crossman, shoots him. And then? If he'd been waiting in the woods all these hours, he was a scarily patient opponent. If he'd left and returned, then he was bold. Or crazy. Or both. This was not a crime of passion. More like festering hatred, an act of revenge. A dish best served cold.

Search a cop's career and you'll find a bunch of people who blamed the police for ruining the lives they'd wrecked themselves. If they didn't find this guy, or some piece of evidence that led to someone already in the system, it would be like looking for a needle in a haystack.

His mind started running those million questions again. Who had called it in? Could it have been the shooter himself? Should they have searched the woods? Called in a team to search out there while they were looking for Melia and working with things inside the building? Had he already blown this?

"You okay, Ter?"

He heard a muffled sound—Kyle sounded like he was praying—and wished he were a more religious man. Right now, though, while he'd pray for Melia and Aucoin, the rest of his prayers would be calls for bolts of lightning and revenge.

CHAPTER 6

Almost midnight. Dr. Lee had come and gone, authorizing them to send Pelham's body along to the medical examiner's office. Rudy Carr had come up from the scene on the road to take pictures and video and give Dani a break. Added to Burgess's small, but growing body of information was that there was no shotgun wad anywhere in the room where Pelham's body was. That raised a lot more questions. Was this another arrogant mistake—their shooter collecting it instead of leaving it there as evidence that Pelham had taken his own life? Or was this a ha-ha move—the guy letting them know that this wasn't what they'd initially thought and having fun screwing with them? Rubbing their noses in the horror of it. Would there be a shell in the gun? He'd need some sleep before he could do much speculating.

Each of them was dealing with pressure and weariness in his own way. Burgess was plodding, chilled to the bone and so tired he could have stretched out on the dirty floor and slept. His bad knee said carrying Melia all that way had been beyond stupid and he, as usual, was telling his knee to stuff it. Young Stan Perry was getting a second wind and starting to run questions, typing things into his phone faster than Burgess's eye could follow. He'd found a third half-smoked, filtered cigarette in the room where they'd found Melia. There was a creepy leisure in the way the guy had stood and smoked while people were dead and dying.

Kyle, face white and eyes blazing, was a little manic as he directed Wink and Rudy's efforts at the Pelham scene. Dodging a bullet aimed at your head is not conducive to good health and a cheerful outlook.

The chilly air smelled of blood and death. One of those things cops knew—that not only did blood have a distinct scent, so did death. Not decomp, though that could set in fast, but fresh death. A peculiar smell you learned to recognize as a rookie, one that stayed with you always. A smell that had the disturbing power to conjure up other scenes. Now his head, which he needed to have focused on the here and now, was a horror show of ugly images from thirty years on the job.

No one had updated them about Melia or Aucoin. Burgess had gotten so frustrated with their lack of information he'd called the chief. That had gotten him—them—an update that was a whole lot of nothing. Aucoin was out of surgery. Melia still on the table. It was all touch and go, wait and see. Ridiculous, he knew, to think their presence at the hospital could make any difference, but he wanted to be there. They all did. And the chief understood that. If their presence did nothing else, it reminded the public—and the bad guys—that if you messed with one cop, you messed with all the cops. It was also about solidarity, reminding them of their vulnerability and the need to have each other's backs.

Because he didn't have anyone else to ask, he checked with the chief to ensure that both men would be carefully guarded, and got a growled, "You bet your ass they will." *Trust*, he thought, *then verify*. As soon as he got to the hospital, he'd make sure those guards were in place.

He wanted to ask how Gina was doing. Another reason he should be there—Gina needed the people who cared most about her husband there with her. He didn't ask about that. He'd pushed the chief enough already. Just reported the non-news to the others—though he supposed the fact both men were still alive was some kind of good news—and they all went on working.

Outside, in the wet but now quiet night, searchers moving through the woods looked like giant fireflies in the underbrush. Little glimpses of light appearing and disappearing in the dark. Burgess was reminded of nights in his childhood, running through tall grass catching fireflies and putting them in a jar. The jar would sit on his bedroom window until he fell asleep. Then his mother would take the jar and release them. There didn't seem to be many around anymore.

Dani, her lower lip caught between her teeth to keep from crying or screaming, had doggedly recorded the room where they'd found Melia, and was gearing up for the room where Pelham's body lay, when Wink Devlin told her to take a break. Devlin, who always had a proprietary attitude toward her, walked her downstairs and out to the crime scene van. It was warm in there, and had coffee and sandwiches.

When he got back, Devlin looked at their multiple crime scenes and said, "This is gonna take the rest of my life. Or at least until retirement. I'm thinking of retiring tomorrow."

"You can't retire," Burgess said. "Without overtime, Mrs. Wink won't be able to take those fancy cruises she likes."

"Mrs. Wink can come and spend a few evenings doing this. Then maybe she'd get off my case."

"We're all on your case, Wink," Kyle said.

Devlin grinned. "I always thought so." He surveyed the room again, and his weary troops. "Much as I love all-nighters, I think we'll tidy up a bit, send this gentleman on to Augusta, then come back in the morning and look for prints. You got people sitting on the building, Joe?"

Tomorrow, Burgess remembered, was a Saturday. His Saturdays had a different flavor since Chris and the kids came into his life. Domestic. Chaotic. Busy. Surprising. Sports, shopping, family picnics. Homework. Large teenage males and giggling adolescent girls trooping in and out. Neddy and his friends building with Legos or swarming up and down the sidewalk on scooters. Tomorrow he would miss all that.

An hour later, patrol officers were securing the site, and everyone headed home. Or should have headed home, given how dirty and tired they were. In fact, everyone headed over to the hospital, where they joined the anxious, milling crowd in blue drinking coffee and waiting for news.

Stan Perry melted into a crowd of young detectives eager to hear about the scene. Kyle pushed his way through the room, tall, lean, and vibrating with kinetic energy, everyone getting out of the way of his fierce, white face and dangerous glittering eyes. Burgess watched him disappear down a corridor, knowing Kyle was going to find a contact and get some information. He'd be doing the same once he'd checked on Gina.

As soon as he was through the door, Burgess realized his mistake. He'd come straight from the crime scene. Still wore his muddy, blood-spattered clothes. He should have taken the time to change, out of respect for his friends and the job, and because if Cote was there, he'd get no end of grief about how he represented the department. Weariness and worry had made him stupid in another way, too. He'd forgotten about the press. Bad enough that they'd gotten shots of him carrying Melia to the ambulance. Now they'd get him in all his dirty, weary glory once again.

Burgess didn't have a lot of respect for the press, and as they surged around him now, shouting their questions, he brushed them off like annoying bugs with a steady, monotonous repetition of "not now." He shouldered his way through the crowd, looking for Gina Melia, but was stopped by Remy Aucoin's two uncles, Guy and Stephen, who stepped into his path and made it clear they weren't moving. Guy looked determined, Stephen belligerent. The Aucoins were not known for tact. Or for backing down from a good fight.

Between them was a girl—young woman was probably more politically correct, but she looked like a girl to him— just little slip of a thing, barely five feet tall, with a mass of curly dark hair and scared brown eyes. She looked like a strong wind could blow her over. She clung to Guy Aucoin's arm with two clenched hands.

Guy looked him up and down, zeroing in on the blood on Burgess's clothes. "That from our Remy?" he asked.

The girl's sharp inhale stopped him. Aucoin patted the clenched hands and went on, more softly, "You were there with him, Joe?"

When Burgess nodded, he said, "Can you tell us anything? The brass have all clammed up and you know that asswipe Cote doesn't care about anything but his face on the news." He leaned in, aggressive again, and Stephen put a hand on his arm.

"Easy, Guy," he said. "Burgess is one of us, remember?"

Burgess looked at the girl. "Sgt. Burgess," he said, "and you are?"

"His fiancée," she whispered. "Nicole."

"He's a good man," Burgess said. "A good cop. We're all pulling for him."

He shifted his gaze back to the uncles. "What have you heard?"

"That Remy's out of surgery. That was hours ago. And not a word since."

"Let me see what I can find out." Not through official channels. Hospital officials, like cops, were good at the wall of silence. But Burgess had spent a lot of time in this place over the years. He had connections. If Kyle didn't find out something, he would. Given the look on Kyle's face when he disappeared through that door, he figured Kyle would come through. Get information or come back with someone in the know clenched between his teeth like a retriever. Burgess was big and tough and mean, but Kyle, for all his low-key style, was the truly dangerous one.

The uncles parted to let him through. Before he moved on, he bent down so he was at her level, put a hand on the two that were clinging to Guy Aucoin's arm, and said to the girl, "Before we put him in the ambulance, Remy was talking about you. He said to tell you he loves you."

Her "thank you" was half-muffled as she started to sob, turning and flinging herself into Guy Aucoin's arms. Burgess knew Remy's parents had died when he was young, and he'd been raised by his uncles. He hoped for all their sakes that there would be good news. Guy and Stephen were Remy's parents, the girl, if Remy married, would be their beloved daughter.

So many people to worry about made him dizzy. Somewhere, he reminded himself, there was a family who didn't still have hope tonight. A family grieving the loss of a son, a wife grieving the loss of her husband. Was the chief with them? That loss weighed on everyone here. There would be a police funeral. Those were deeply painful affairs. He hoped it would be the only one.

Actually, what made him dizzy was the spinning kaleidoscope of things to be attended to. Here, hoping for the living to keep living and being present for the families. Elsewhere, the dead and the crime scene. The million details and questions that would have to be wrestled into place to start building a picture of this crime—these crimes—and the person, or persons, who'd done it. Right now, he had to keep it at bay and control it like he'd manage a difficult collar. What made it harder was the swirling tide of emotions that kept washing over him, like storm waves hitting a beach, knocking him off kilter and drowning his clarity. Detectives couldn't be emotional and function effectively. No cop was unemotional when three of their own had been targeted. Four, if he counted that bullet aimed at Kyle's head. Was it just luck that he hadn't been shot or was that another ha ha from their bad guy?

He pushed on until he found Gina Melia, wilting in a chair, her face set and white. Gina was his model for the perfect police officer's wife. Understanding when Vince needed to be doing the job; absolutely firm that some family things, even if the city was burning down, were not negotiable. She'd loved them all, fed them all, bullied them all. Tried to marry them off. She ran the house, raised the twins, held down a full-time job, and coached boys' soccer. Gina was family.

The deputy chief sat on one side of her, looking starched and sad, Vince's sister Lainey on the other. Gina popped up when she saw him. "Oh, God! Joe!" She threw herself into his arms. He pressed her tight against his chest as she sobbed into his shoulder. She'd been waiting for someone it was safe to cry with, and he was it. His shirt was dirty and dusty and he was a man badly in need of a shower, but neither of them cared.

The air exploded with flashes as the vultures of the press surrounded them, snapping another headline photo for the morning, until a surge of blue-clad bodies elbowed them back and formed a protective circle around them. Families weren't fodder for reporters.

The Deputy, whose name was Longley, said, "Let me see if we can find someplace more private," and strode off to take care of something he should have done hours ago. If Burgess ran the railroad, things would be different. But then, he'd never wanted to run the railroad, which is why he wasn't a lieutenant or a captain. He needed to be out there getting justice, not inside pushing paper. His fiancée, Chris, though she'd sworn she understood his feelings about his job, was on his case to make a change to something more nine-to-five and desk-bound. It was making things difficult between them.

Gina was still burrowed into his shoulder, still crying, minutes later when Longley came back and told them he'd arranged for a private meeting room where the families could wait. Burgess led Gina there while Longley went to find the Aucoins.

When everyone was settled, and the deputy chief had sent someone for coffee, Burgess excused himself and went to find Kyle. He stopped in the corridor, ignoring the signs everywhere asking people to abstain from cell phone use, and called Chris.

"Joe. You called."

How many times had she said that to him since she'd said it the first time he called her? It never got old. There was something about the way she said, "Joe," that lifted him. Always spiritually, often physically. Her voice did something to him.

"Sorry it's so late."

"Never too late," she said. "Where are you?"

"At the hospital."

"How are they? There's nothing on the news."

"Nobody's saying. Kyle's gone to shake some trees, see what he can learn. Everyone's going nuts here without any information."

"I'm sure." She hesitated. "If you can't get what you need, I can make some calls." Chris was a nurse with many hospital connections.

"If Terry and I strike out, I'll take you up on that. How are the kids?"

"About like you'd expect. Neddy's upset. Nina's upset because Neddy's upset. And Dylan is a rock."

"He shouldn't have to be."

"Maybe it's not a bad thing, Joe. He was so lost when he first arrived. Now he seems to be settling into the big brother role pretty well. I think he likes it. And maybe he can't help himself."

"What do you mean?"

He heard her tiny snort of laughter. "I mean he's your son, dummy. I mean he's just as hardwired to be a caretaker as his father. I confess, it can be a bit daunting to have two great big Burgess males acting like clones, but I'm not complaining."

He spotted Kyle coming toward him. "Terry's back. I need to see what he's learned."

"Go," she said. "But call me again." A pause. "Any idea when you're coming home?"

"Hoping to have breakfast with you all before I dive back in."

"Sounds good, Joe. But what about sleep?"

"Sleep, as we like to say in this business, is overrated."

"Idiot."

"I love you too," he said.

He disconnected and went to meet Kyle. He almost didn't need words. The look on Kyle's face said he was bringing bad news. They met right outside the conference room where Longley had gathered everyone. Before Kyle could speak, Burgess took his arm and led him down the hall. "Longley's got everyone in there," he said. "Let's shape the story before we tell them." Then, knowing Kyle would have checked. "Are there guards in place?"

Kyle nodded and moved on to his news. "It's bad, Joe. Remy may make it. It's one of those 'the next twenty-four hours are critical' things. He's in the ICU and they're hopeful." He stared down at his shoes, and Burgess felt weigh descend on him like someone was coating him with lead.

"Vince? Joe, he's alive, but…the way they're talking…everything's messed up and it was so long 'til we found him…there's so much damage. I think they're gonna come for Gina soon. They're talking last rites."

Kyle could barely get the words out, and when he was done, he leaned against the wall and closed his eyes. Utterly spent. It was not supposed to go this way.

CHAPTER 7

"Vince is a fighter, Terry. He's got too much to live for," Burgess said. "They may think this is the end, but they don't know him like we do."

Kyle didn't move and he didn't open his eyes. "You're just saying that to make me feel better."

He was going to give the flippant answer that he wasn't known for doing things to make people feel better. Then he considered. He *wasn't* just saying this to make Kyle feel better. Deep down, in the part of him that was the cop's gut—the guiding intelligence that worked somewhere beyond sense and training and experience—he felt the truth of it. This *wasn't* over yet.

Was it only because he couldn't imagine this job without Melia? Because he was too old and tired to deal with some young whippersnapper who wouldn't stand between him and the devils of bureaucracy? Because he knew, if the position became vacant, it would likely be filled by someone with more ambition than talent? But he wasn't given to wishful thinking. He closed his own eyes and leaned against the wall beside Kyle, testing his sense of things.

"No, Terry. I'm not saying this to make you feel better. I'm saying it because my gut tells me it's true."

Kyle exhaled like he'd been holding his breath the whole time. "I've got a lot of faith in your gut, Joe."

Often, he and Kyle and Perry stood together like the three musketeers. Tonight, though, Perry had done one of his disappearing acts. He did that sometimes, larking off on some secret mission, and reappearing with some discovery or insight, often after nearly giving them heart failure. As long as he showed up in the morning, when the three of them had to start putting this case together, Burgess was fine with that.

"What do you think, Ter? Meet again at nine? We need some sleep, and we're not going to get it any time soon."

"Works for me. That way I can have breakfast with the girls." Kyle gave it a beat, then said, "But you'll be getting a wake-up call from Cote before seven. You can bet on it."

"Didn't I tell you? I let Nina take those calls now. She's great. She has this 'sweet little girl talking to a mean rude man' routine and refuses to let him speak to me. It really fries his ass, and she loves it."

"What does Chris think?"

"She's certain that I'm committing child abuse, subjecting Nina to Cote's behavior, but she loves it, too."

"Kids," Kyle said. "Who ever would have imagined?"

"Imagined what?"

"Burgess the Monk with a whole passel of kids. It's like having triplets. If triplets arrived all at once but at three different ages. And two of them were teenagers."

Kyle had that exactly right. Last fall, just when Chris had decided she wanted to adopt two foster kids involved in one of his cases, Burgess had discovered he had a fifteen-year-old son from an old relationship. The woman had suddenly moved away and never told him she was pregnant. Almost overnight, his life had gone from being complicated by cases and crime to being further complicated by relationships and family. He was still trying to get the hang of it.

Burgess took out his phone and texted Perry and Sage Prentiss, arranging a meeting for nine a.m. They would form the core group, and draw on other detectives for discrete tasks.

Down the hall, a door opened and a solemn man in a white coat headed toward them. "I'm looking for Mrs. Melia?" he said, cleverly figuring them for cops, not bums, despite their disheveled appearance.

Burgess wondered why, if Kyle's information was right, no one had come for the Aucoins? Hospitals, it seemed, worked in mysterious ways. "She's in the conference room," he said. "We'll come with you."

Kyle went to update the Aucoins while he led the doctor to Gina. She was sitting rigid in her chair, her hands knotted together. Staring at nothing. When she saw the doctor, she flinched and her tense face looked terrified, her bright dark eyes narrowing with anticipation. Burgess was expecting some explanation, some speech of regret or some version of 'brace yourself' couched in medicalese. Instead the man simply introduced himself in a quiet voice, and then said, "I can take you to your husband now." That was all, and the blankness of it was almost more frightening than an explanation.

Gina grabbed Burgess's hand. "Come with me, Joe. Please?"

"Terry would like to come, too, Gina, if that's all right with you."

"He can hold my other hand," she said, stretching it out to Kyle. The three of them followed the doctor out of the room, her grip so tight it was painful. If that was what she needed, Burgess was fine with it.

Like three kids holding hands on the playground, with Vince's sister trailing behind them, they followed the doctor down the hall and through several doors and down corridors to the ICU. Burgess had spent far too much time here when his mother was dying. The place always gave him the creeps. The smells and beeps and level of controlled anxiety always rocketed him back to that time no matter how hard he resisted it.

Hell. He hated this whole place. He and Kyle had tagged it with that line from the Frost poem. It was the place where, when you had to go there, they had to take you in. And you were usually bleeding.

Melia was in a bed in a cubicle, surrounded by an impressive array of beeping and hissing machines. He looked deader than he had when they first thought he was dead. Gina stared at him, silent, but with tears running down her face. Then she turned to the doctor, took his arm, and pulled him out of earshot. "What can you tell me?" she said.

Looking regretful at the bad news he was delivering, the doctor now described Melia's dire condition. She listened attentively, then straightened, tucked her hair back, and shook her head. "No," she said. "You don't know my husband. He is not going to die."

Then, as though contradicting that, she said, "Can you find us a priest?"

The doctor looked confused. Burgess and Kyle weren't. Vince Melia was deeply religious. The doctor might have been thinking last rites. Gina was thinking spiritual comfort and ways to pull him back from the edge.

Burgess looked at the doctor. "Is there someone you can call?"

"Sure." The man strode off like he was glad to get away from them, trailing just the faintest whiff of disdain for ordinary humans who just didn't get it when the doctor proclaimed the end was near. Not much of a bedside manner.

Burgess set a chair next to the bed and steered Gina into it. "Touch him. Hold his hand. Talk to him. It's okay. You won't hurt him and it will remind him of all he has to live for."

His mind was splitting again. He was here with Gina to give her whatever she needed, and he was mentally wandering the corridor outside, looking for those vigilant guards. They'd been there when Kyle checked. Now the chair outside Melia's cubicle was ominously empty.

Kyle, reading his mind again, said, "They were here ten minutes ago. Let's see what's going on."

"Got to check on something," he told Gina. "I'll be right back."

"You do whatever you have to, Joe. I do understand, you know."

"Better than anyone." He figured he might as well tell her. "We want to check on security."

She nodded, and he saw on her face that she did understand, and that she was experiencing a duality of her own. Glad they were doing it. Worried that they thought security was necessary.

"It's what Vince would do."

That got him a faint smile.

"I'll be right back."

He followed Kyle out into the corridor that led to the lounge where families waited. The place Burgess had labeled the desperation lounge. No police officers in the corridor. They checked the lounge. No officer there. Just a handful of miserable-looking people whose eyes flew to the door when they appeared.

"Where's Remy?" he said. "Maybe they're both with him?"

They showed their badges at the desk and were directed to Remy's cubicle. There was another empty chair where someone should have been sitting. No sign of a guard.

"This better not be Cote's doing," Burgess said. Once on a previous case, Captain Cote had decided to save money by pulling the guard off a victim and had nearly gotten her killed.

"Go against the chief's orders? He wouldn't do that, would he?" Kyle said. But his face said that he wouldn't put anything past the man.

"You stay with Remy 'til I get this sorted," Burgess said.

"Yes, Boss."

He gave Kyle his signature 'don't mess with me' look and stepped out into the hall. Not that Kyle would be intimidated. It was a game they played. Burgess was nominally the boss, since he was a sergeant, but Kyle and Perry were both comfortable challenging his orders. Unless he was mad.

Right now, he *was* mad. Mad and nervous. Skin-crawling, watch-your-back nervous. They were dealing with a game-playing monster here. It wasn't safe to take chances. He called Stan Perry. "You still in the hospital?"

"I am."

"Something has happened to the guards on Vince and Remy. Kyle is with Remy. Can you keep an eye on Vince until I figure out what's going on? He's in the ICU."

"Yes, Boss."

Now he was two for two. And about to make his boss—his big boss—mad at him. The deputy was probably still downstairs, but the chief had okayed this and he needed to know directly that something had gone wrong. Passing this to Cote, then the deputy, and on to the chief could take half the night. Or all of what was left of it. If it got past Cote at all.

Before he made the call, he went to the nursing station and asked if anyone knew what had happened to the guards. "I've been in with Officer Aucoin," a woman whose name tag read 'Barbara Huston,' said. "I just left him a minute ago. But maybe five minutes ago, I saw that woman come and send them away."

"What woman?" Burgess said.

"Small. Dark hair. Wearing pediatric scrubs."

"Both guards?"

She nodded.

Burgess felt a surge of panic. Five minutes was a long time. Someone might have gotten in and done something. Trying to keep it out of his voice, he said, "What about Lt. Melia? Has anyone been with him?"

She shook her head, then hesitated. "I really don't know. You can ask his nurse."

The minutes while he waited for the nurse crawled like snails, but all he could do was wait. This was the ICU and patients were the priority. He could stare at the equipment in Melia's room until hell froze over and not know whether something was amiss.

At last she appeared, instantly reading his distress. She put a reassuring hand on his arm. "Barbara said you were concerned about Lt. Melia?"

He nodded.

"I don't know who that woman was. I only saw her back as she was walking away. But I was with the lieutenant until perhaps two minutes before you and his wife arrived." She gave a small, dismissive shrug. "No idea why she sent your officers away. It wasn't anything we did or wanted. But he was not..." A slight hesitation, as though his concern was a judgment about the quality of their care. "He was not alone long enough for someone to harm him."

This time, Burgess thought. He was formulating his next question when she said, "That woman wasn't one of us. I didn't see her ID, but she doesn't work in the ICU. We're a tight team here."

"Could she still have gotten to a patient?"

"We keep a pretty close eye. We spotted her, for example. But if there were an emergency someone might get by."

"How do I plug that gap?" he asked.

She shrugged. "Take names. Check ID's. Call us at the desk if there's a question. Mostly just by being there."

Her gaze swept down the corridor to the chair where a uniformed officer should have been sitting. The chair now occupied by Detective Stan Perry. "We're doing our job. Maybe you should ask why he wasn't doing his? Or who called him away."

A perfect smack down. Living with a nurse, Burgess had heard an earful of how they weren't respected but too often were first in line for blame. He was happy to be smacked down and grateful she and Barbara were doing their jobs.

"Thank you," he said.

She was already walking away.

The chief answered on the first ring. No one was sleeping tonight. This morning. This dead of night.

"Burgess, sir. I'm at the hospital checking up on Vince and Remy, and there's no one guarding either man. We've got a killer out there who's killed twice, wounded two, and taken a shot at Terry Kyle and…"

"Bullshit!" the chief roared. "I specifically instructed…Let me talk to Longley."

"He's in a conference room with the Aucoins."

"I don't know what's going on, Joe. Let me make some calls."

"Yes, sir. I've got them covered for now. But my detectives need some sleep if we're gonna work in the morning."

"I'll take care of it."

Dismissed, Burgess put the phone away. It was almost out of juice. So was he.

Eventually, two things happened. A pair of spiffy, rested patrol officers showed up so he and his team could go home and get some rest, and a furious-looking deputy chief showed up with two shame-faced officers in tow. "You need to talk to these guys, Sergeant," the deputy said. "About why they weren't at their posts guarding our guys."

He hated to leave Gina, but he did her more good working on finding the shooter than sitting here holding her hand. Still, he hesitated until she said, "Go home, Joe. Go catch the bastard." And when he hesitated, she added, "I know you need to talk to me. We can do that in the morning, too."

"Call me if…"

"I'll call you if, Joe. I'll call you. And you call me, okay. No. I guess they don't want phone calls in here. Text me when you want to talk."

He would. He gathered Kyle and Perry and the three of them took the two errant patrol officers down to the conference room to have a little chat. A mini incident room. The deputy said it was theirs as long as they needed it.

Burgess was limping now, his knee absolutely screaming for relief. It did nothing for his disposition. When they passed that rare thing in the hospital, a window, he saw that light was coming into the sky.

CHAPTER 8

The two officers, Brad Kates and Josh Gordini, were so upset by the harm they could have caused, and by the Deputy's reaming, they were practically non-verbal. It wasn't enough. They'd been sloppy when so much was riding on them. They had to understand the awful harm they could have caused. But first, he needed the details. Burgess let them stumble through a few minutes of mea culpas before he bored in.

Gordini, small, dark and wiry, with a reputation as a smart street cop, recovered himself first. "Jesus, shit, Sergeant, she sounded so damned official. I never meant...I mean, I wouldn't have. You've got to believe. I mean Remy. God. He's my friend. But she said...it was an order. From the chief. You know. So I thought..."

He stuttered to a stop and buried his head in his hands, then raised his head and met Burgess's gaze. His eyes were so dark they were almost black, and in that blackness was the fear everyone felt tonight. "Is Remy still...?" Stopped again like a chastened child facing an angry dad.

Kates was memorizing his shoes.

And Burgess *was* angry.

"Back up," he said, "and take us through it, step by step. Never mind what you told Deputy Chief Longley. I need everything you've got."

"A woman in scrubs," Gordini stammered. "Came up to me. She was holding…like…this chart. And wearing a name badge. On a…you know…lanyard, like they do. And she said they had to do some procedures and…" He sputtered to a stop again.

Beside him, Kyle shifted. One eloquent twist of his body that spoke volumes. "Dammit, Gordini," he said, "you're a professional police officer who was supposed to guard—which means stick like glue to—a wounded fellow officer. We're looking for the facts here. Man up, spit them out, and save the excuses for someone who gives a damn. We've got a dead cop here. And a bad guy out there we need to catch before he does this again. An assassin who's targeting cops. So don't waste our time with your poor little feelings, okay!"

Gordini seemed to shrink before their eyes. He swallowed. "I thought she was a nurse," he said. "She had the ID. She had the clipboard. She acted totally professional. She said the chief said it was okay for me and Kates to go get something to eat. Remy wouldn't be alone because they'd be with him doing procedures. It all sounded real to me."

Burgess hoped there was video of this "nurse."

"You get her name?" The orders had been specific. IDs were checked and the names of everyone who went near Aucoin or Melia went on the list.

"Yes, sir." Gordini handed over his list.

"But when she told you that people were coming to do some procedure on Aucoin, you didn't stick around to get their names?"

"No, sir."

"Because?"

"Because…" Gordini swallowed hard. "The chief said it was okay."

"You hear this from the chief?"

A shake of the bowed head.

"You check with Longley, or your sergeant, or anyone with a badge and a rank, who said it was okay to leave?"

Another shake.

"So you took orders from a nurse and left your buddy unguarded?"

Gordini dropped his face into his hands. He made no sound but his shoulders were heaving.

"Kates?"

"Same story, sir." Kates handed over his sheet. A neat list of names and times of everyone who had visited Melia.

"Same nurse? Same name?"

Kates nodded.

He glanced down at the sheet, then turned back to Gordini. "What did she look like, this nurse..." He checked Gordini's sheet. Then Kates's again. "Sheryl Timmons."

"Smallish. Young. Good looking. Very dark hair."

"Big chest?" Kyle said.

"Uh...yeah."

"Had you seen her before, any time, visiting other patients or at the desk? Walking past you?"

Gordini and Kates both shook their heads.

"What was she wearing?"

"Uh...scrubs?"

"Same color as the other nurses were wearing?"

"Uh..." A really long pause. "No."

"That didn't make you wonder?"

"She had the ID badge," Kates said defensively.

"You look at the picture on the badge?"

"Uh...yeah."

Burgess read that "yeah" as meaning not much beyond dark haired and female.

Stan Perry scribbled some quick notes and stood up. Too restless to sit through this. It didn't need three of them, anyway. He'd gotten the essence. "I'll go check on her. See if she works here. And if we can find any video. Call you when it's queued up."

Burgess nodded. Turned back to the officers. "You ask how long the procedure would take?"

"She said fifteen or twenty minutes," Kates said.

Burgess checked his watch. "And that was how long ago?"

"Uh…"

But there was no good answer to this. For some reason, perhaps one that he'd get out of them soon, instead of grabbing coffee or a quick sandwich and rushing back they'd taken their time. He couldn't understand the lack of urgency. The carelessness. These were good cops and this situation was the ultimate cop's nightmare. Then he had an idea.

"Captain Cote asked you to give him an update?"

A nod from Kates.

"Did he ask you to speak to the press?"

Another nod.

Burgess felt the steam coming out of his ears. Cote was a captain. Of course they would have taken the time to speak with him. Of course they would have spoken to the press if he'd asked them to. The biggest of course was that of course, despite the deadly urgency of the situation, Cote would have left two gravely wounded police officers unguarded while their assailant was still on the loose if he thought he had something that would make a good story for the press.

Would the chief ask the right questions and figure this out? Burgess hoped so. More than the job itself, what often wore him down was protecting the job from the very people who were doing it. These guys—kids?—had blown it and they needed to feel the weight of that, but it was Cote who should have known better.

Beside him, he heard a faint sound. Kyle. Growling. Kyle had also figured it out.

"Go back to 109. Write it up. Then go home and get some sleep. Next time, don't be so trusting."

They didn't look at each other and smile, but relief was in the air. They must have thought Burgess was going soft in his old age.

He raised his voice. "The order was don't leave them alone. At all. For anything. Even for a minute. The order was to check the credentials of anyone who came near them, and get the names of everyone on your log sheet. So tell me: what part of that didn't you two understand?"

Both men had risen from their chairs. Now they halted, rigid and waiting. "Pay attention: In this place, someone is always going to try and send you away. They don't want us here, on their turf. They don't get it that someone might dare to enter their hospital and try to harm a patient. But we do. Everyone in this hospital is going to act like we're a pain. That security is inconvenient. And we ignore that and keep our people safe."

He paused, to let that sink in. They should already know it, but people—even cops—could let themselves be cowed by almighty doctors and their minions. This lesson wasn't just for today. Cops practically lived in this place. "You have to stand your ground. You're cops. Your orders come from police personnel, not some pretty nurse with a clipboard or a doctor who's used to being obeyed. Anyone in this place gives you trouble, you say you have to wait for orders and then you call your sergeant. You don't go prancing off for snacks."

Reminding himself they were in a hospital, he lowered his voice. "We've got a guy out there with a sniper rifle who is targeting cops. Through some miracle, two of his victims survived and made it to the hospital. Now they're lying there, fighting for their lives, relying on you to keep them safe. And what do you do? You abandon them. You leave them vulnerable. You leave the door open so anyone can get to them. This is not what we do for each other."

He'd made his point. "You got lucky. But our job is not about luck. Next time, follow orders. If something had happened to Melia or Aucoin on your watch, you would never get over it."

He watched them go, sagging, defeated, knowing that they'd failed. Maybe next time they'd be more careful.

He was already moving on. She had to be bogus, right, this Sheryl Timmons? Bogus or bribed. Had something bad been about to happen, something he and Kyle showing up had forestalled, or was this just another ha-ha from the bad guy? Crying wolf until they let their guard down and then taking another shot at them? But they had let their guard down. Literally. The possibilities made him sick.

Beside him, Kyle said, "What the hell's going on, Joe? Are we becoming a bunch of clowns?"

A text from Perry: There is a nurse named Sheryl Timmons. Not scheduled to work tonight. Let's check the video against her photo. Real or bogus? At Security.

He texted: on our way. Before he went home, he'd stop back upstairs, make sure this pair of guards understood that don't leave, even for a minute, meant don't leave. Or never mind the chain of command, the meanest cop in Portland would be on their asses forever.

They sat in the security office, a file photo of Sheryl Timmons in front of them, and watched the security guy queue up the video, whirring through screens until they had the woman in scrubs who'd identified herself as Sheryl Timmons approaching Gordini. Then they moved through it, frame by frame, as she got closer, then froze it, studied the screen, and then the photo.

"Not the same woman," Perry said. "The woman in the photo is older, heavier, and shorter."

Now they needed a copy of the video, and video from other parts of the hospital that might show their woman entering. Leaving. Changing into scrubs if she hadn't worn them in, and the answer to the all-important question: how had she gotten Sheryl Timmons's ID? Security had an answer that question—Sheryl Timmons had lost her ID a few days earlier and had to get a new one. So talk to Sheryl Timmons went onto their list.

The security chief had been called in, and promised an extra level of security in the ICU. Someone would check the ID of every hospital employee entering, and the IDs of any visitors. A royal pain all around, but it would make it harder for anyone to sneak in. They left Stan Perry conferring with him about what videos to watch and what the timeline was. Good thing Perry didn't need sleep.

Burgess was feeling the weight of a long night and a long day ahead and anxiety about how porous the hospital was. He'd put everything possible in place to keep Melia and Aucoin safe. Still, it depended on everyone being vigilant and doing their jobs. That anxiety would be with him until the shooter was caught.

"Go home, Joe," Kyle said. "Get some sleep."

"As soon as I check on Vince and Remy again."

"Right. I'll come with you."

Burgess made sure the officers on duty understood what had happened. The seriousness of the situation. Then stood by the bedsides, watching the machines that were maintaining life. Remy looked peaceful. Vince still looked like he was circling the drain. Gina beside him, holding his hand, talking to him. She'd aged ten years in the past few hours.

"No sign of a priest, Joe," she said.

"You call yours?"

She seemed surprised, like somehow hospital protocol said they were supposed to use the priest on call. But who thinks clearly in the ICU? She wouldn't leave her husband to make a phone call. Wouldn't leave him all alone.

"Terry and I will sit with him. You go make that call."

She released her husband's hand and stood, so unsteady on her feet that Kyle put an arm around her. "I'll go with her, Joe," he said.

Burgess watched them go, then took Melia's limp hand between his. "You've gotta come back to us, Vince. Everything's going to hell without you."

He watched the still gray face, a tidal wave of emotions slamming down on him. Emotions had no place here. They would spin him and roll him and press him down until he didn't know which way was up. Until he drowned in them, lost his ability to focus and move forward and became as useless as Cote. Like he was fighting undertow, he pressed them back, swimming against them until he surfaced again, grabbed some air, and faced the task ahead. Melia and Aucoin's job was to live. His to find the person who'd done this.

He and Kyle went out into the nearly dawning day.

"We still meeting at nine?" Kyle asked.

It was almost five. "How about nine-thirty?"

He and Kyle moved slowly. Now that he wasn't distracted by human stupidity, his knee hurt like a bastard. They passed a small knot of officers outside the door and were swarmed for details. He told them what he could, then moved on. Someone needed to get on top of this. Be an information officer not for the press or the public but for the police themselves.

Uneasy, he looked back and saw how vulnerable they were. Neat blue targets for someone with a twisted mind and skill with a rifle.

"Terry?" he said, as they got to their cars.

"Yeah?"

"Be careful out there."

"The same right back, Joe." The way Kyle's eyes scanned the surrounding streets and buildings, he knew Kyle was feeling it, too.

Even here at the hospital, a place that was swarming with cops, he had the uneasy feeling their bad guy was watching. It followed him all the way down the street.

CHAPTER 9

He left his shoes at the door and walked quietly through the sleeping house. Sometimes they left him a sandwich or a note, but today, since he was expected for breakfast, they hadn't. He stripped off his filthy clothes, took a quick shower, swallowed some painkillers, and set the alarm for eight. Then he slid into bed.

Sliding into an occupied bed was still a surprise. One of his life's few good surprises. He spooned against Chris's smooth warmth and was asleep in seconds.

At seven, he half-woke to the sound of a phone, and distant voices. If it was important, they'd come and get him. If it was Cote, Nina would handle it.

No one woke him.

At eight, more stunned than rested from a little more than two hours sleep, he dressed his achy body, stuffed three clean white handkerchiefs into his pockets, told his complaining knee to stuff it, and lumbered into the kitchen, a hungry bear emerging from hibernation. His family was gathered around the table, waiting. Elfin nine-year-old Neddy with his quick body and cockscomb of bright red hair. Cautious Nina, about to turn fifteen, slender and lovely, whose porcelain skin and rose-gold hair were attracting way too many boys. His son Dylan, almost 6' 3" and still growing, with his own eyes and hair and mannerisms, already willing to place himself between his family and anyone threatening to harm them.

Chris was at the stove cooking, wearing leggings and one of his flannel shirts, her honey brown hair streaming down her back. She turned and smiled and said a single word. "Joe."

So many promises to honor. To the dead. To the injured. To the citizens of Portland to keep them safe. To his own family. Seeing them made him dizzy and grateful. He was lucky to have them, though with their arrival had come the fear that he couldn't protect them, care for them, attend to them as much as they deserved.

"Blueberry pancakes," Neddy said. "And bacon."

"You want coffee?" Dylan asked, getting up. The boy knew. Cops run on coffee.

"Orange juice?" Nina said.

He was going to sit at the table and let them wait on him. Instead, he detoured to the stove to wrap his arms around Chris. He buried his face in her neck. She smelled of lavender and soap. If he hadn't been due at 109 and they didn't have a kitchen full of kids, he would have skipped breakfast and feasted on her.

"The pancakes will burn," she said, but she leaned back against him and he heard the smile in her voice.

He released her and went to the table. Grabbed his coffee and started the infusion that would eventually open his eyes. "Who was on the phone?"

Nina's grin was impish. "Three guesses and the first two don't count."

"Captain Cote?"

She giggled. "I don't think he likes me much, Joe."

Dylan called him dad. Nina called him Joe. Neddy called him My Joe. Chris called him Joe unless she was really annoyed and then she called him Joseph. "He doesn't like anyone very much. Just his dog. Unless it's a rat. It looks like a rat."

"People do have rats as pets," she said. "But I think he's the rat."

"He say what he wanted?"

"Oh, the usual," she said, unfortunately experienced enough with Cote to know the usual. "He doesn't have any reports. He needs updates. You're not keeping him in the loop."

There was no loop. Or reports. Or anything to update the man about. Unless it was the report on how someone had contrived to leave injured officers unguarded. And that someone else had delayed them even further in getting back to their assignment, putting the vulnerable at risk. Maybe he should write that up and drop it on Cote's desk, with copies to the chief?

"What did you tell him?"

"Oh, the usual. That you'd just gotten to sleep and I wasn't going to disturb you but I'd be happy to take a message."

"And?"

Chris set a plate of pancakes and bacon in front of him, and they all leaned in, eager to watch him eat. Making sure he ate was becoming a family tradition. Not, given his size, that he was likely to starve any time soon, but he was definitely thinner since Chris had come into his life, despite being better fed.

"And he said to have you call when you woke up."

"But not until after you eat," Chris said, putting pancakes before the kids and then herself, and sitting down across from him.

If he couldn't have sleep, he needed food, and this was ambrosia. He tried not to gobble. Setting a good example. "This is nice," he said. "Family breakfast. I'm sorry I have to work today."

"We understand," Dylan said.

Nina nodded and Neddy said, "Maybe you can come to my next soccer game."

Maybe he could. Who knew?

His cell phone rang. He checked the clock. Quarter to nine. Checked the number. Not Cote. A number he didn't recognize. He closed his eyes, hoping it wasn't bad news, and answered.

"It's Lt. Coakley, SRT, Sergeant. Hope I didn't wake you? Didn't catch your bad guy, but we found a couple things in the woods last night you should take a look at."

They made a date for eleven. Burgess finished his breakfast and headed out. The rain and wind had left the world smelling fresh and green, but the sky was still gray and a cool fog had settled in. As he strode to the truck, he saw that a small patch of grass in front had been turned over. Chris and Nina were going to plant a garden.

He hadn't made the phone calls that were pressing on him in front on the kids. Trying to be fully present instead of always halfway out the door, mentally if not physically. Now he felt way behind. He texted Gina Melia to see what was happening. Got back a gloomy "no change. No priest." Called the officer who was guarding Aucoin for an update on Aucoin's condition. No change. Tried to organize his thoughts for the upcoming meeting. It would feel weird— and wrong—to be strategizing about a major case without Melia at the table. His absence would be powerfully present.

His journey from the Explorer to the detective's bay was constantly interrupted by cops wanting updates and offering to help. There was a palpable sense of urgency in the air. An unspoken anxiety. They'd been attacked. Everyone was jumpy, which was okay. He wanted them jumpy if it made them vigilant. What he worried about was it making them careless or trigger happy.

It would be a long day for everyone. There was a funeral to plan. Families to support. There was the same stupid, criminal public who'd be out there doing their usual criminal things, not knowing they were going up against an anxious and angry police department today. If Burgess hadn't had such a revulsion for the ladies and gentlemen of the media, he might have held a press conference.

Suggested they tell the bad guys to lay low for a while. Remind the miscreants that their normal patience with assholes and jerks would absent. There would be no charity or tolerance on the streets today.

Predictably, the receptionist at the desk told him that Captain Cote wanted to see him as soon as he got in. Equally predictably, he moved that request to the bottom of a very long list. Cote would want to know why Burgess needed sleep, and why major progress hadn't been made in the case. Less predictably, the chief wanted to see him. That went right to the top as soon as he'd finished organizing the investigation.

His team, assembled around the table, had all seen better days. Stan Perry was twitchy, ready to go beat some heads in and get some results. He wanted to go and do, not sit and think. Kyle was gloomy, drooping in his chair, whippet thin and angry-eyed. Concerned about their wounded and furious about someone who disposed of other humans as part of their personal agenda. The only one who looked rested was Sage Prentiss, and with a small baby at home, he wasn't getting much rest either. Prentiss was new. An unknown. His strengths not yet revealed. But the chief knew they needed more help.

Burgess ran through what they knew, which was far too little, starting with their surmises about the order in which people had been killed or wounded. "He's a good shot— either sniper training or an experienced hunter. Maybe a night hunter? He's patient and organized. These were executions, not crimes of opportunity, and the choice of location and his ability to lure Melia there suggests a lot of planning. We believe he smokes filtered cigarettes. We've got some good footprints, so we'll get a shoe size. Wink and Dani will go back out there today for fingerprints. Maybe we'll get lucky, he got careless, and he'll be in the system."

"We know this was a man?" Sage asked.

"We think. We don't know," Burgess said.

"You think he acted alone?"

"We don't know, Sage. We don't know an awful lot. Also at this point, we assume that Melia was the target but we have no idea why, or what led him there. We'll go through his messages and his phone records and see if dispatch has anything. It's not like Vince to do this—go someplace like this alone and without telling anyone. Does it suggest he trusted the person he was going to meet? Did he even know he was meeting someone? Was there a distress call of some kind that he responded to, and if so, why him?"

"It's not like Vince," Kyle agreed. "There's something. Some connection, that drew him out there."

"We'll find it," Perry said. "We hear how they're doing?"

"Gina says Vince is the same. No change. Same with Remy."

"The first freakin' twenty-four hours are critical," Kyle said.

How many times had they heard that?

They parceled out the tasks. Kyle was going to track down the guy who'd called in the shots, interview him, then look for other witnesses who might have been working there and seen something. But it was basically a propane depot. Lots of tanks and trucks, the nearest building far from that track into the woods. And it was Saturday, which made tracking down witnesses harder.

Perry was going back to the hospital to see what else surveillance video had turned up, then go talk with Sheryl Timmons. Before she headed over to the warehouse, Dani would have fingerprinted Timmons's locker. Sage was working their other vic, Richard Pelham, looking for background and next of kin.

It didn't matter who took what. They had so little right now, and such a huge case, it was like dismantling a mountain rock by rock.

There was a sharp knock on the door and Guy Aucoin walked in without waiting. His beaky face looked narrower, as though someone had grabbed his sizeable nose and pulled it forward, stretching the flesh taut over his cheekbones. His mouth was just a narrow slit. His eyes were puffy. What was left of his sandy hair was uncombed and he hadn't shaved. He was carrying a tray of coffees and a Dunkin' Donuts bag.

It was hard for any of them to say they were tired or worried or the situation had jumbled the inside of their heads and twisted their guts into knots—cops were supposed to be the rocks for everyone else—so they said it to each other with coffee. With food. With hands laid on each other's shoulders. With small ducks of their heads.

Aucoin slid the coffees onto the table, dropped the bag, and planted his hands on his bony hips. The man had no hips and no ass. Burgess had always wondered how his pants stayed up, even with a belt. Their belts, once all the equipment was added, weighed a ton. "I need to help," he said. "Me and Steve, we've gotta do something here, Joe. You got things that need doing, give us a job." He hesitated. Aucoins tended to bull their way through, not beg, then he said, "Please."

Generally, that would be against the rules. You weren't supposed to work cases where you knew people. But this was different. Work in a city long enough, you knew a lot of people, especially the bad guys. And when a cop was down, the rules changed. Everyone knew the victims. Everyone wanted—needed—to do what they could.

"We get done here, Guy, we'll have plenty for you to do. Gimme your cell and I'll call you."

Aucoin got out his notebook and scribbled on a page. Tore it out and passed it to Burgess. "You damned well…" Checked himself. "Thanks, Joe. We appreciate it."

"Thanks for the coffee, Guy."

Aucoin departed. They shared out coffees and donuts and went on working. An assistant came in with a pink slip. "Autopsies," she said. "Today at three." She'd obviously been crying.

He grabbed the note. Lee was doing them back-to-back. A very long afternoon. This one *would* cut into Lee's golf time, unless he was out there on the course right now. Burgess looked at his crew. "Who's coming with me?"

He hated to take anyone off other tasks, but they liked to have two detectives at an autopsy, just in case one of them got run over by a bus—or shot by a bad guy—before the case came to trial.

"No one," said a voice from the door, which Aucoin hadn't shut on his way out. "It's a waste of personnel."

No one had to look to see who it was. And no one had any doubt that this new arrival would do nothing to advance the investigation.

"Since Lt. Melia is unavailable, someone needed to sit in on your...uh...meeting."

There were more things on their agenda, but nothing anyone wanted to share with Cote. "We're just wrapping up," Burgess said, slapping his folder shut. "But thanks."

He didn't even ask everyone to keep him posted and get him their reports as soon as possible. Asking to be kept posted would bring Cote's whiny demand to be 'kept in the loop' and asking for reports would draw out a string of complaints that would waste his next half hour.

He checked his watch. "Gotta run. Meeting with Lt. Coakley from SRT. He's got some things out at the site he wants me to see."

They all rose, gathered their notes, and filed out past the captain.

"Hold on, Burgess," Cote said. "We have some things to talk about."

Burgess shrugged. "Gotta go see the chief, Paul, and you know he doesn't like to be kept waiting. If you'd like to ride out to the site with me after, walk through with SRT to see what they've found, you're more than welcome."

"I don't have time..."

Burgess nodded and said what he hadn't meant to say. "But you had plenty of time last night to detain the officers who were supposed to be guarding Melia and Aucoin. Just luck, I guess, that nothing went wrong. Luck and the fact that we had it covered."

The captain's pursed duck's ass mouth clenched and opened. Then he thought better of it. "Reports, Burgess. I need your reports. The public has a right…"

Burgess interrupted. "As soon as I can. As I said, if you want to ride with me, I can brief you. But we don't have much yet."

Cote trailed him like toilet paper on his shoe as he stopped at his desk to get his jacket. He changed the subject, shifting the questions back to Cote. "What have you learned about their condition this morning? How's Vince doing?"

Cote loved to brief the press but was always reluctant to share information with his own people. Now, he shook his head. The duck's ass pursed, relaxed, and he said, almost as though the idea pleased him, "It's bad. They had to take him back into surgery."

CHAPTER 10

It felt like his heart skipped, then settled down into a normal rhythm again as he studied Cote's face. A lifetime of studying liars told him what the man had said wasn't true. It was intended to provoke him. He'd heard nothing about this from Gina and she would have called him if Melia's condition had changed.

For the millionth time, in the ugly dance the two of them performed, Burgess suppressed his desire to rearrange Captain Paul Cote's facial features. He had more important things to worry about.

Cote's statement, delivered without emotion, brought back the pressure he kept at bay during their meeting. He thought Melia would survive this. Yet it was so easy to second guess his gut. He relied on it. He trusted it. And he treated it like everything else in his life—something to be trusted yet backed up with facts. He shouldn't be wasting time here, making the brass happy. He needed to be out there finding a killer before he struck again.

You didn't blow off the chief, though, even if you had nothing to say. And the chief, as one of the Aucoins had said about Burgess yesterday, was one of them. He remembered being a cop. Ignoring Cote, who still stood there as though he was waiting to be punched, Burgess limped to the chief's office.

The chief was impeccable. In uniform today, though he wasn't always. A nod to solidarity. To the fact that he was part of the blue line. Burgess figured the man had slept no more than he, but he cleaned up good.

"Sit down, Joe," the chief said.

Burgess took a chair.

"This is a bad business. Without Vince, I'm relying on you to run it. Anything you need, you've got it. Just keep me updated. Directly, not through Captain Cote."

He leaned forward, his sharp eyes boring into Burgess like he could see through clothes and skin and read a man's heart. "Where are we with this?"

Burgess shared what he knew. "It's not much, sir. But everyone's out looking—for witnesses, for whoever was behind that monkey business at the hospital last night. We've got a few bits of evidence that may lead somewhere. Lt. Coakley has some things to show me from the SRT search of the woods last night. Wink and his crew are out looking for prints, and anything we might have missed last night. Autopsies are this afternoon."

"You need more people?"

Burgess shook his head. "I will. But not 'til we've got things for them to do. Maybe by this afternoon, we'll have turned over some rocks, something will have crawled out. If this was directed at Vince—and it looks like it is—we've got a lifetime to paw through, and he can't help us. I'll go by the hospital later, talk to Gina, see if anything was up that she knew about."

He shook his head at the enormity of it. "Our killer is a planner. He's smart. We just have to hope he's not too smart."

The boring eyes moved away, back to the mass of papers on the desk, and his heart started beating again. "One thing, sir? Well. Two."

The chief's nod said, "Go on."

"First, at roll call, supervisors have to emphasize that the risk is still out there. Maybe this was aimed at Vince. That's how it looks. But with three officers down, we have to expect it might be something bigger. Everybody's got to be vigilant."

The chief knew this, but Burgess had to say it.

"And the other thing?" the chief said, "is to be sure Melia and Aucoin are guarded 24/7?"

"Yes, sir. After last night." He didn't finish. The chief wasn't an idiot like Cote.

"It won't happen again."

Burgess, dismissed, rose from his chair. "Updates, Joe," followed him out the door.

He heard it so often it might have been his name. Updates Joe. He wondered what career a man with a name like that might end up in. Was it really Joe Updates? Joe Updates sounded like a man on the make. Updates Joe like a man who made music. He was neither, unless it was the distant music of an investigation falling into place. Clues lining up. Insights flying. Sometimes he heard his victims, especially when they were children. The voices of the dead calling for justice. Screaming out their final traumas. Mourning their stolen lives. Today, the background music was a dirge.

Ten minutes to get down to the crime site. Not enough time for more coffee. He really needed coffee. Coffee would open his eyes and ruin his digestion. The policeman's lot.

There was a paper bag on his hood. A plain brown bag that looked benign enough, but he was on high alert today. There had been a bomb scare yesterday. Why not a bomb today? When he got closer, he could see writing on the bag. Big black letters in marker: Coffe for My Joe. His family, the people he should be looking after, were looking after him.

Lt. Coakley was leaning against his unmarked. Military short hair. Black tactical uniform. Laced black boots.

Asshole aviator sunglasses. But he was a decent guy. He watched Burgess park, then came to meet him and led him down the track and off into the woods. A big square had been marked off with crime scene tape.

"This way," Coakley said, lifting the tape and following a path made by prior footsteps. "Guy must have been out here watching for a while. He left us a bunch of stuff. Shell casings. Half-smoked butts. Gas receipt. An empty Moxie can." As he spoke, he pointed to items in the square. "Even took a leak over there. I spoke with Devlin and Letorneau. They'll photograph this and collect the evidence. But I figured you'd want to see it for yourself."

A Moxie can? That was unusual. Even though Moxie was Maine's own original soft drink, one that tasted a bit like bitter root beer, it wasn't a common choice.

Coakley led Burgess to one of the larger trees. "Now here's the real interesting thing. I probably wouldn't have seen it, especially not at night, but one of our guys, he's a hunter and his dad's a game warden, and he picked up on it right away."

Burgess stared at the tree trunk, not seeing anything. He shook his head. "What is it? Where is it?"

"That's the thing," Coakley said. "It's up there." He pointed to a branch more than five feet off the ground. "Your shooter is tall. Probably a pretty big guy, because those scrapes there, on the bark? My man says that's where something was rubbing, and we speculate that's where he braced his rifle so he could take the shot. Or use the scope."

It was pretty brilliant, someone spotting that at night, never mind in the daytime.

"Your shooter's pretty ballsy," Coakley added. "One of our guys smelled smoke, and one of those butts was still warm, and we never saw him. I'd say he's real comfortable working in the dark, for whatever that's worth. Guess we're all feeling kinda lucky right now none of us got shot."

Burgess was thinking that that creepy feeling he'd had last night was real. Well, he'd known it was real when someone took a shot at Kyle. But even before that, when he was walking down the road. Had the guy been out there tracking him?

He was grateful there weren't more dead or injured. But Coakley was still talking, leading away from where they'd come in. "There used to be a road here along the shoreline. We ran the dog, and he went this way 'til the road petered out and a path led back to Commercial Street. Figure he must have had a vehicle parked out there. Or someone picked him up."

Coakley shrugged. "Found another one of those half-smoked butts there. He's cold, your shooter. Place is crawling with cops and he just walks away, then stops to smoke before he gets in the car and leaves. We've roped it off, but I told Letorneau she'd better get out there sooner than later. Lookie Loos, ya know. They'll mess up a crime scene just to stick their damned noses in things."

"We got someone out there?"

"Yeah." But he didn't sound very confident. Probably not because he didn't trust his people. More like he knew how things could get screwed up. And there probably wasn't a cop in the city who didn't know about last night at the hospital. It didn't exactly make people feel safe.

Burgess was getting that skin crawling feeling again. He didn't know whether it was a sense that the guy was out there again, watching, or just the idea of a killer so cold. Shooting from a distance was one thing. But Melia had been a close shot. Pelham even closer. No way he'd killed Pelham without getting blood on himself. If they found the car, or the clothes, there would be blood. More things went on the to do list. They needed to walk that trail from the woods back to where the scent trail had disappeared. Maybe there was something else there. Maybe he'd discarded his clothes. Dropped something. Left them a tire track. Left a note for Burgess that said: Sergeant Joseph Asshole.

He thanked Coakley and gimped to the building. Chris had bought him a knee brace, which would have helped, but in his fog this morning, he'd forgotten to use it. He was still thinking about blood trails. Assembling what the things they were learning said about their killer.

The other doors to the building had been locked or weren't operational. Aucoin had said he hadn't seen the shooter, but the suspect had to walk right past Aucoin on his way out. Maybe, when they could question him, Aucoin might remember more.

In yesterday's chill, the interior of the building had been unpleasant but bearable. Now, warmed by the sun, it was a fetid meld of the smells of blood, death, rot, mildew, and garbage.

Ever chivalrous, Devlin had Dani working the room where Melia was shot, taking the Pelham scene himself. Rudy Carr and another tech Burgess didn't know toiled in the hallway.

"Anything, Wink?" Burgess asked.

"Maybe. Dani's got some stuff. Ask me again in four hours or so."

"In four hours or so, you and I are going to be in Augusta at the medical examiner's."

"If I live that long. You gonna pick me up? Drive me there so I can catch some z's?"

"Anything for you, Wink." Burgess hesitated. He disliked piling the work on tired people. But that's how this thing would go. "Coakley tell you about that scene in the woods?"

"Oh yeah. And the track along the water. And the place where maybe a car was parked. Dani and the new kid, his name's Charlie, they'll take that when they're done here." He smiled. "Nice to have some kids on the team. They aren't old and tired like us."

Burgess nodded. "Meet you down in the parking lot at two?"

"With bells on." Devlin turned back to his work.

Burgess was moving on, too. He wanted to walk the path the killer had used, see it for himself. The evidence techs would take pictures, but a picture could never capture the thing the way the eye could. Pictures were great for details and narrow focus, recording the position of the body and the location of evidence. The eye saw relationships. Routes in and routes out. The overall geography. He was wondering how the killer knew about this place. Whether the killer was local. When this place had last been used for business or seriously considered for redevelopment? The questions just kept coming.

He checked his watch. The drive to Augusta, the state capitol and the medical examiner's facility, would take about an hour. He had some time before he and Devlin had to leave for the autopsies.

Skirting the area Coakley had lined off with tape, he moved through the woods, following the path the lieutenant believed their shooter had taken when he left the scene, walking the edge and eyeing the ground. Even with all the cops still here at the scene, and visible in the city today, his neck prickled. A long time ago, he'd spent a year in the jungles of Vietnam, fighting an often invisible enemy. He felt the weight of that today, making him take his time and use his senses. All that brought was lingering pain in his knee.

Eventually, the path spilled him out onto an old car track running along the water beside some crumbling buildings and the decaying remnants of wharves until the piece of vacant land running between Commercial Street and the railroad tracks and the water narrowed. He figured he'd gone about a quarter of a mile when a path from the track he was following plunged back into the trees. He followed until it crossed the tracks, and widened into a short road that led to the street.

That small road led nowhere, but it went deep enough into the scraggly woods that a parked car wouldn't be noticed from the street. A uniformed officer guarding the street end of a rectangle of yellow crime scene tape eyed Burgess's approach suspiciously, hand on his gun.

"Police officer," Burgess said loudly, holding up his badge. This was one of his worst fears for today and every day until they caught their shooter—that some nervous cop would jump the gun and shoot someone. He'd prefer it wasn't him.

As he stopped to make sure the officer had understood him, his foot kicked something and sent it skittering against a rock with a clink. As the officer moved toward him, hand off his gun, Burgess bent to search for what he'd kicked.

CHAPTER 11

He was cutting it close, but by the time he got back to his car, Burgess knew he wouldn't make it through the day unless he detoured home for his knee brace. It was the wrong thing to be happy about, but he was glad no one was there, so he didn't have to give updates or try to keep his own worry off his face so he wouldn't worry them.

Braced, and with a handful of painkillers for lunch, he swung back along the waterfront to pick up Wink Devlin.

Devlin was waiting by his car, drooping with weariness. He shoved his gear into the back and fell into the seat beside Burgess like he weighed twice as much as his actual 150. "This is like cleaning out those damned stables in whatever that story was. Too bad we can't divert a river through that shithole and be done."

Devlin's clothes smelled like they'd been stored in a mildewed cellar for a year. He blew his nose. "Allergies. Damned mold gets me every time." He reclined the seat, said, "I'm catching some z's. Wake me when we get there," closed his eyes and just like someone had flipped his off switch, he was asleep.

That was fine with Burgess. He appreciated some time alone with his thoughts. Driving was good for sorting things out. Tourist season hadn't started, so he had plenty of open road and fewer idiots to pay attention to. It was limited access highway, which kept the fight or flight folks—the ones who waited 'til the last minute, then pulled out in front of you—out of his way.

He drove, listening to his stomach rumble and Devlin snore, and wondered if they'd learn anything from the autopsy that would help with the case. He never got his hopes up, but over the years there had been plenty of surprises and a lot of answers. Often, too, they got things from the clothes. He had to go in hoping, because this thing meant too much to too many people, and it was all riding on his team. They were good, but the pressure would be in every face they passed. The whole department was waiting for answers.

Right now he was thinking single shooter. That it was aimed at Vince Melia and that the other victims were just collateral damage. But one thing his years had taught him—taught, reminded, rubbed his face in—was not to let his assumptions get ahead of the facts. Right now, pretty much all he had were assumptions and the grim task of sorting through Melia's cases and his life for facts to connect those assumptions to.

When he got back to Portland, if he was still on his feet, it was time to sit down with Gina Melia and see what she knew. Family members and friends often knew far more than they realized, starting off with the standard, "But I don't know anything" and gradually disclosing critical information. Vince and Gina were close. Some cops never told their spouses anything. They carried the "protect" part of serve and protect to extremes, treating their families like precious entities that had to be protected from the ugliness of the job. Others, like the Melias, shared a lot.

He'd gotten used to seeing people at their worst. Probing their memories when they still wore the blood and shock of attacks on their loved ones or themselves. Like a human tweezer, he'd insert himself into their wounds and probe for splinters of memory and shreds of evidence. It would be harder with a friend, inflicting the necessary pain of remembering. Even harder to take her away from her husband's side for the length of time it would take to do a good interview. But as he often reminded them—and himself—it was a necessary pain.

What were his facts? That the shootings were deliberate. That they were planned. That the shooter's choice of venue probably represented either research or previous familiarity. If the former, maybe someone had seen him around there before, scoping it out. That the shooter was experienced, with either a military or hunting background, or both. The ammunition he'd chosen told them that. A .223 round that had a flat, steady trajectory and limited recoil that wouldn't inhibit subsequent shots. He was confident, even arrogant, regarding other human beings as disposable. Comfortable in the dark. He was tall and the depth of his footprints suggested he was on the heavy side. He smoked and drank Moxie. He liked to play games.

With all that, it should be a cinch, right? If they were to put that description out at a press conference, how many suspects would the public turn in? Hundreds? Dozens? Or, given the level of cooperation they too often saw, none.

Why Vince Melia? Melia had been behind a desk, supervising CID, for the last four years. Did that mean they were looking at someone with a long-held grudge? Someone recently released from prison? The problem with looking for someone with a grudge or a score to settle was the ripples. Catch a bad guy and put him away and other people were affected. Bad guys had family. Girlfriends and lovers. Gangs, cliques, clubs, buddies. Any of them could carry a grudge and blame the cops for messing up their lives.

Despite the painkillers, his head was starting to throb, the effect of not getting enough sleep. He was a high-mileage guy, lacking the resilience of a newer model. He had to remind himself that he brought wisdom and experience to the table, even if he could no longer leap buildings in a single bound. They didn't have the time, but he stopped for coffee anyway. He was no use to anyone if he couldn't watch or assess. He roused Devlin and got him caffeinated as well. By the time they got to the ME's office, they were bright-eyed and bushy tailed.

Lee was doing Pelham first, waiting impatiently as they bagged the clothes his assistant had already removed. They liked to do it themselves, slowly and carefully, but this was Lee's domain. Burgess hoped nothing had been lost. Lee's assistant was a sullen, brooding chap who was far from the sharpest tool in the shed. His own fault, though. He should have planned it better. Said to hell with his knee and arrived earlier.

The body lay naked on the table except for the bags they'd put over Pelham's hands. While Lee rocked from foot to foot, Devlin removed the bags, took his photographs, and swabbed the hands. Devlin didn't give ground when it came to doing his job, no matter who applied the pressure. He consulted with the ME about what else they should collect to get the best information about the ammunition that was used. Plenty of hunters in Maine loaded their own shells. There might be something there. Then he nodded at Lee to continue.

Pelham's body was scarred and malnourished, a sad wreck of what was still a man in his prime. Burgess was angry about the wasted life and the hateful death, and forced his anger away. It wasn't just about Pelham, but about all the forgotten men and women their country had taken service from, damaging them in the process, and then abandoned. He forced his attention back to the process, to Lee's crisp voice recording the details. There were no surprises. No other physical findings. No alternative cause of death.

Wondering about how the killer had gotten Pelham into that chair, Burgess asked if there was any way to tell, from what remained of Pelham's head, whether he had been knocked unconscious before being posed with the gun and executed. Lee said he'd examine the skull remnants and brain tissue, but he was doubtful.

"I've got a kid interning with me, though. Reassembling the skull and looking for premortem damage would be a good project for her." Lee shrugged. "Or it might be too much. Maybe toxicology will turn up something. Tell us if he was drugged. He didn't take very good care of himself, but he was a strong man. Ex-military. I'd say he wouldn't have been taken without a struggle unless he was tricked."

More things for Burgess's list. Was it possible—as the foreign cigarette butt in the ashtray might suggest—that the killer and Pelham had socialized, smoked together, maybe had a drink together? They'd collected the things they'd found in Pelham's room, but what if there had been a bottle? Something the killer had disposed of later, maybe tossed in a corner, or into the woods instead of carrying it away with him. When they were done here, he'd give Dani a call, have her or Charlie take a look around.

The clock ticked on. His knee blazed. One of Lee's virtues was that he was fast. Too fast, Burgess sometimes thought, but the man didn't miss much. In his pocket, his silenced phone vibrated like a forgotten pleasure device. Nothing it had to say to him was likely to bring pleasure, unless it was the message that they'd got the guy. And how likely was that?

Finally, Lee was done with Richard Pelham. He stripped off his gloves. "I'm going to get some coffee. Wink, Joe, you want some?"

Burgess was surprised. Lee was such a machine. The guy never seemed to get tired. But he wasn't about to turn down coffee—or anything that would put off Randy Crossman. Coffee and more painkillers. He was beginning to consider ibuprofen one of the basic food groups.

He nodded. "That would be great. It was a long night."

He paused in the hall to check his phone. Twenty-two messages, of which six were from Cote, looking for those updates. Updates Joe skipped over those and ran through the others. Updates from his team. Calls from reporters looking for an inside track. Nothing from Gina, which he hoped meant Melia was still hanging in. Nothing couldn't wait until he was done here. He texted Kyle and

Perry and Prentiss that they should meet and he'd let them know when he was on the road.

A while back, Burgess had worked the murder of a small, neglected boy. During that investigation, the child had haunted him. Though he'd never known the boy alive, he'd seen images of the boy playing and heard the boy's keening voice, crying out for justice. A voice that resonated in his head until it was almost a scream, growing louder and louder until the case was resolved. Letting the voices of the dead into his head went against the basic investigative rule: don't get emotionally involved. Probably a psychiatrist would tell him he was crazy and suggest drugs or therapy. Burgess disagreed. He'd been on the job long enough to know there were things beyond what you actually know in this world. He was a grounded, "just the facts, ma'am," guy, but sometimes information came from senses beyond the rational.

Just like with the cop's gut—how you grew it and how you learned to trust it—he'd come to trust in intuition, in how he could know things and connect to the victims in ways that weren't simply observation and analysis. As he drank his coffee and made small talk with Devlin and Dr. Lee, he was thinking about Randy Crossman. He'd never known the man, other than casual contact at crime scenes or passing him at 109. But Crossman was a police officer killed doing his job, killed trying to ensure the world was safe for others, and his cry for justice was loud. Had he felt it coming? Sensed something was wrong? Had there been any intuition before that bullet came from the woods and tore through his throat?

He was thinking about Richard Pelham. His life and his cruel, senseless death. The killer treating him like a tool. A device to send a message or confuse investigators. What had that tent sign really meant? Was it possible the killer was sorry about sacrificing Pelham?

Last night had been such a mess. They'd worked hard, tried to do their best, but had they given Pelham his due? Searched carefully enough? What had they found that would help to tell his story and would there be more information when they examined his clothes? He pictured the shabby office that Pelham had made into a room. A neat, solitary man. How had the killer gotten at him? Had the killer been there more than once, perhaps established some kind of trust relationship? How much planning had gone into setting this up?

His skin prickled. Most criminals were dumb or careless. The majority of the homicides and violent injuries they saw were the result of drugs, gangs, alcohol, money, or domestic violence. This killer was different. A planner. By the time they'd analyzed their evidence and developed some theories, he could have cleaned up and disposed of evidence in his possession. Unless he was so arrogant that he didn't expect to get caught, or was one of those calculating looney toons who wanted to get caught. Maybe get into a shootout with the police. Go out in an imagined blazed of glory.

Burgess thought this bad guy didn't want to get caught, but couldn't help toying with them. And if this was aimed at Vince Melia, there was still unfinished business which might draw the shooter out. Business that also kept Melia and his family—his domestic family and his police family—at risk.

He was starting to see it, the vaguest outline of their shooter, like a slowly developing photograph. The thought almost made him smile. Such a dinosaur. How much longer would anyone even understand that image, now that they were living in a digital world?

This late in the day, running on two hours sleep, neither the coffee nor the painkillers were doing much good. He felt foggy and dull and wished he could remove his head, like a helmet, and put it somewhere cold and dark for a while. Officer Randy Crossman deserved better. He should have sent Stan Perry. Perry would still have been bursting with energy. Or Sage Prentiss, though Prentiss hated autopsies. Well, he was here. He'd have to pull himself together and make the best of it.

"Sit a while," Devlin said, another person reading his mind. "I've got to collect his clothes anyway."

It was a kind offer. Burgess could have taken him up on it. But he felt, however useless his presence might be, that Crossman deserved to have a fellow officer with him as he went through this process. He could imagine what Captain Paul Cote would say: "For chrissakes, Burgess, what does it matter? The man is dead." Burgess thought it did matter. That Crossman deserved every courtesy and every attention. There were those who believed that the spirit stayed around the body for a while after death. Burgess wasn't among them. And yet. And yet he felt something. It was important to be there.

He helped Devlin collect the clothes. Carefully. Gently. As though Crossman was injured, not dead. Wondering, as he did, whether the shooter's only contact with Crossman had been from his spot in the woods, more than 200 feet away. Whether he'd only seen the young officer through his scope or his sights as he aimed. Had he watched those dramatic sprays of blood as Crossman's heart beat its last and sent them flying into the late spring air? But there had been those footprints on the road. From before or after? Had he stood over the dead or dying man, and what had his thoughts been?

Wondering. Imagining. Recreating. It didn't sound like what the public supposed detectives did. All those forensic shows that were so popular were making the GP believe that there were always useful forensics—the famous smoking gun—and that detectives relied on their lab techs and their experts for the almost instantaneous results that led them solve crimes. That was so misleading. They might find something here that would be useful. For the most part, though, investigation was a slow, painstaking slog, with a lot of detectives making a lot of phone calls, asking a lot of questions, reading a lot of documents, writing a lot of reports that would fill a meticulously maintained murder book, hoping to find the essential trail of breadcrumbs in the big dark woods.

Cold. Naked. Dead. Except for the torn flesh of his neck, Crossman looked so young and healthy and vulnerable. Burgess recalled his living face—so eager and full of promise. Devlin finished taking his photographs and Dr. Lee stepped up to the table to begin. As the medical examiner carefully inspected the body, then raised his scalpel to begin, Burgess found the words from the prayer to St. Michael the Archangel rising in his mind, almost escaping his lips: *cast into hell, Satan and all the evil spirits, who roam throughout the world seeking the ruin of souls.*

If it had been Vince Melia on the table, he couldn't do this no matter that he would owe his friend the best possible search for justice. He had no idea tears were running down his face until Devlin handed him a handkerchief. Dr. Lee remained tactfully silent as Portland's toughest detective wept.

CHAPTER 12

Finally it was over. The body could be released. Crossman's family could plan a funeral. Crossman's family and his police family. They still had to find a family for Pelham, find someone willing to give him a funeral. That funeral might be delayed to see if they could reconstruct part of his skull.

The days were getting longer as they approached the equinox, and it felt like a gift to emerge from the cave-like interior of the morgue, carrying the bags of clothing and collected evidence, into late afternoon sun.

His phone had been busy, dancing in his pocket. Now, as Devlin dozed, resting up for diving into work when he got back to 109, Burgess got on the road, wishing he could find a way to sleep and drive at the same time, and started returning calls. He told the chief there had been no surprises and that he would be meeting with his team in an hour. Told Gina Melia he would stop by the hospital at seven-thirty if that was okay. Told Chris he wouldn't be home for dinner, but would stop back mid-evening to check in. Told Cote's nine messages nothing.

Knowing there was a long night ahead, and that if they couldn't sleep they needed food, he stopped at their favorite deli for meatloaf sandwiches. The owner's wife made the best meatloaf in town. She liked to look after "her boys" as she called the cops who were her regulars, and even though he hadn't called ahead and it was late in the day, he thought she might be expecting him.

Sure enough. On a day when everything felt heavy and painful, her bright smile when he came through the door was like being bathed in something warm and soothing. "Joseph! I was afraid you wouldn't make it, and I've saved this meatloaf all the day just in case."

"As many sandwiches as it will make, Melina," he said, "and you wouldn't happen to have any cookies left?"

She waved a greasy brown bag and gave him another smile. "If you must work so hard, you must be fed well."

People mattered, and the people in his city, by and large, were good folks who appreciated what the police did for them. Exchanges like this made all the difference. They reminded him who he became a police officer to serve and protect.

"You've made my day," he said. "Mine and Terry's and Stan's."

"You would have said 'and Vince's' if it weren't for this awful business."

He would have. He was impressed, though, by the attention she'd paid. He'd bet if you stopped ten random people on the street, few of them could give the names of the two Portland officers who were fighting for their lives in a local hospital.

"How is he doing? The papers, they don't tell us anything."

"We don't have much to say at this point."

"Yes." Her hands were flying as they talked, making a stack of thick sandwiches. "And then I know from the TV that you must keep things quiet so you can catch the person who did this. But if you see his wife, tell her, please, that we pray for him?" She bundled the wrapped sandwiches and cookies into a plastic carry bag and passed them across the counter, waving away his money.

"This is my contribution, Joseph, to help catch the evil person who did this."

He didn't argue, just grabbed the food, thanked her, and headed for the car. Stan Perry would bring coffee. Hopefully, someone would bring some useful information.

He hoped in vain. It was what they called a "know nothing" day. Despite the hours spent nosing around, asking questions, they didn't have much more than they'd started the day with. Kyle had been unable to talk to the man who'd reported shots fired. According to his aggrieved wife, he'd taken off at dawn to go fishing with his buddies. He didn't carry a cell phone and she had no idea where he'd gone or when he'd be back. When Kyle had asked for the name of the buddies he'd gone fishing with, she'd shrugged and been unhelpful, and when he asked for the names and contact information for her husband's co-workers, she'd casually lit a cigarette and told him to fuck off.

He'd left cranky and frustrated and not too hopeful that the man would call when he returned. Or even get the message. He was going to swing back when they were done and see if the man had returned.

Sage Prentiss had spent a lot of his day on the computer and making phone calls, trying to track down anyone related to Richard Pelham. It being a Saturday made things harder. People weren't sitting in offices, available to take his calls and provide answers. He'd trolled the places the homeless hung out, and the Preble, but no one knew—or admitted to knowing—Pelham. He was truly an invisible man.

Stan Perry had had slightly better luck—he'd gotten some good surveillance video of the woman pretending to be Sheryl Timmons, and security at the hospital had made him copies of the tape and printed off her picture—but no one at the hospital recognized her. He handed the pictures around.

The real Sheryl Timmons was the frazzled mother of three teens and a total space cadet. She thought she'd lost her missing ID at her gym. Or in a parking lot. Or in the grocery store. Or maybe when she was out walking her dog or driving the kids to some sports practice. Or it had fallen out of her car somewhere. She couldn't be sure. All she knew was that it had gone missing a few days earlier and she'd had to get a new one. She didn't think it had been in her locker when it disappeared, but maybe it had.

"She was about as easy to nail down as a bucket of squid," Kyle snarled. "As focused as a camera with the lens cap on. I wouldn't want to be the patients she's looking after."

Burgess deduced from that that Kyle wasn't in a good mood, a deduction which was confirmed when Kyle added that his daughter Lexi had scored two goals in the soccer game he'd missed.

Rocky Jordan, their computer guru, was working on Melia's phones, work and home, but he didn't have anything for them yet. It was maddening, having to wait for information, but it was the job. They were the tortoise and not the hare. Slow and steady won the race while impatience and worry gnawed their insides to bits and made their tempers explode.

They unloaded all the surmises they'd developed as they went through their days. Talked about ballistics. What they knew about the shooter—their suppositions about size and weight and attitude. The shooter's fearless, voyeuristic behavior in waiting around after the police had arrived— waited or left and returned—and whether he'd scoped the place out before. The location was such a good choice. There weren't neighbors to notice, or people driving past.

They moved on, talking about all the things they hoped Devlin and his crew might draw from the crime scene. Along with fingerprints and DNA, there were the spent shells and Moxie can and the shotgun shell. All the things that would become useful to them if only they had a suspect, his gun, and other evidence to match them to.

Tomorrow they'd be pawing through Vince Melia's cases—and his life—looking for someone with a grudge.

In a long-time cop's life, that could be a lot of people. They'd look for threats. Those recently released from jail or the Maine State Prison. Check them for military or hunting backgrounds. As Stan Perry liked to remind them, "A needle in a fucking haystack." Everyone was dragging. Time to get some rest so they'd be useful in the morning.

"Reports," Burgess said. "We need to start writing this stuff down in case the shooter targets us next."

"Yessir, Captain Cote," Perry said, saluting.

They bitched about it, but reports were essential. A record of ground covered. Information that might later link up with other things. Proof that they'd done a careful investigation. Defense attorneys like to claim that the cops had zeroed in on their clients too early and never considered any other possibilities. A record of the dozens, sometimes even hundreds of people interviewed was a good counter to that.

Burgess noted that despite his eagerness to be updated and kept in the loop, Cote hadn't deigned to attend their meeting, even though Burgess had broken down and responded to those nine messages with a text saying when and where they'd be meeting.

Kyle seemed to be elsewhere. He didn't like wasting his days, and today looked like it had been wasted. "You going to the hospital, Joe?" he said.

"When we're done here. Right after I do those aforementioned reports."

"I'll come with."

The only positive thing about their meeting was the sandwiches, which were received with gratitude and vanished so quickly they might never have been there at all. The cookies vanished even faster, leaving a trail of crumbs on the table. What they needed was a different trail of crumbs, one that led to something useful. Or to the bad guy. Then everyone sat in a weary silence, waiting for someone to give them direction. Times like this, food became a substitute for everything they didn't have. The thing that comforted them and kept them going until they got some breaks.

Burgess remembered the little medal in his pocket. He pulled it out and set the clear plastic evidence envelope on the table. "Found this on the road where we suspect our shooter parked his car. Spot where the dog lost his trail."

Kyle leaned in and studied it. "St. Hubert. Hubertus. Patron saint of hunters." A twitch of Kyle grin, and then, "and the patron saint of mathematicians, opticians and metal workers. Archers and dogs. That sure narrows the field."

Kyle knew the oddest things. Sometimes Burgess wondered if Kyle had been reading the encyclopedia when the rest of the guys were out chasing girls. He was always coming out with things like this. Kyle seemed to do okay with the ladies, though, once he got free of the PMS queen. Michelle was gorgeous and good, and she loved Kyle and his kids. The rub there was that she wanted marriage and a baby and his ex-wife had left Kyle gun shy.

"Hunters fits," Perry said, pulling the bag closer. "It's got a freakin' deer on it."

Sage Prentiss rarely spoke. He was the new kid on the block, and had evidently decided the best strategy was to watch, keep his mouth shut, and help where he could. But now he said, "Well, now, this shouldn't be too hard. We're looking for a big man who's very handy with guns, has a grudge against the police, drinks Moxie, and is missing his St. Hubert medal. How many people can that fit?"

Kyle yawned. "You're right, Sage. While we write these tiresome reports, why don't you hop right out there and arrest the son of a bitch. I'd love to be able to sleep in tomorrow."

And that broke up the meeting, the detectives straggling to their desks to write reports. Burgess would get there. First, he detoured down to the crime lab to deliver some sandwiches and cookies. Honoring a rule he and Vince Melia firmly believed—that it was important to look after your people.

* * *

Their first batch of reports done and personally delivered by Burgess to Cote's empty desk, he ordered Perry and Prentiss to go home. Tomorrow, as Scarlet O'Hara had said, was another day. He and Kyle headed over to the hospital.

They checked on Remy first. Found the uncles at his bedside. They all stepped out into the corridor to talk.

"They'll probably move him out of here tomorrow," Guy Aucoin said. "He's doing pretty good. Not talking yet, but mostly they're keeping him down with the painkillers. He wakes up, Joe, you know we'll call you first thing."

"Soon as we can leave him, you gotta given us something to do," Stephen added.

"Come Monday morning when people are back at work, I've got a job for both of you," Burgess said. "We need someone down there at that business, asking questions of everybody. What they've seen, when they saw it, what the guy looked like. You know the drill. It could even be someone who works there. Interview the people there, and find out who comes and goes, who they do business with, who drives those trucks, the whole deal."

"We're on it," Guy said, "aren't we, Steve?"

"Just don't hurt anyone," Kyle added.

Steven Aucoin laughed, a rusty sound like he didn't do it often. "We'd like to hurt *somebody*, that's for sure."

"We all would," Kyle agreed, dropping a hand on Steve's shoulder. It was consolation and a reminder that however much the Aucoin brothers might want revenge for what had happened to their nephew, they shouldn't do anything that might screw up the investigation or subsequent prosecution.

"Don't worry," Guy said. "We find the shooter, we won't kill him. We'll bring him to you." Like his brother, he laughed. "He might be a little worse for wear, though."

Cops had sayings. Among them—don't make me run or I'll hurt you. Sometimes it happened. Guy kills a cop, he's not going to run into warm and fuzzy when he's arrested.

They left the Aucoins to their vigil, passing Remy's fiancée, Nicole, on the way out. Her fiancé might be unconscious, but she'd taken pains with her appearance, as if looking sweet and lovely would call him back to the land of living. People did what they could.

Gina Melia did not look sweet and lovely. She wore the same clothes she'd worn the night before. Her curly hair wasn't combed. She looked ten years older and a decade sadder than when they'd left. Burgess felt a twinge, seeing her like that. Gina was meticulous. Even going off to coach a soccer game, she always looked pretty and pulled together.

She didn't even glance their way when they entered. Maybe, in the intervening hours, she'd gotten used to the constant medical interruptions. Or maybe she was dozing. She didn't move until Burgess was almost beside her and said, "Gina."

Then, in a single fluid motion, she was out of her chair and in his arms, her face buried in his shoulder. "It's so awful," she whispered. "They tell me no change is good. That's he's holding his own. But look at him!"

"Have you eaten anything today?"

He held her tightly against him, felt the shake of her head against his chest.

"Come get something to eat," he said, "Terry will stay with Vince."

"I'm not hungry."

"You take care of him by taking care of yourself, Gina."

Burgess gave her a handkerchief and steered her from the room before she could protest as Kyle slid into her chair and leaned in, already talking to the too still, too dead-looking man in the bed. Burgess stopped at the restroom door. He didn't say anything, and neither did she. She just went through the door. When she came out, her hair was combed and she'd put on lipstick.

"I had no idea I was such a fright, Joe."

She had no idea how beautiful love and the faithful vigil could be. If. No, when Melia opened his eyes, that was what he would see. Not rumpled clothes or uncombed hair.

"You have other things on your mind. Let's get you some dinner and then find a place we can talk."

When she hesitated, he said, "Terry will call us if there's any change. You know he will."

He steered her through the line, grabbing things that were easy to eat—mac and cheese and a big molasses cookie. He didn't even know if she liked cookies, he just knew she probably needed some sugar to keep her going.

He watched her eat like a parent hovering over a child, then led her to the conference room, got her settled in a chair, and turned on his recorder. In an ideal world, he'd do an interview this important at 109, where he could tape it, but right now, their world was far from ideal.

After leading her through the preliminaries—name and address and date of birth—he asked the first important question: "Do you have any idea who did this?"

She shook her head.

"I need voice," he reminded her, "for the tape."

She glared at him, snappish from stress and exhaustion, and said, "You make me feel like a criminal."

He put a hand over hers. "Sorry, Gina. I didn't mean to sound...it's just the way we do things. For the record. Trying to approach all our interviews the same way. For comparison. I—"

"Don't apologize, Joe." She put her other hand on his, making a hand sandwich. "Just do your job. Do what Vince would do."

He nodded. "Do you know of anyone who would want to hurt Vince?"

She started to shake her head, then said, "No."

"Are you aware of anyone threatening him?"

"Nothing that he took seriously. You know. People are always making threats."

"What about making threats against you or the boys?"

"No. I mean, I guess there are always people who are mad at him—at all of you, but nothing in particular. No one. Not lately. And I think I'd know. If there's anything he thinks is significant, he'll tell me, so I can be more careful. Keep an eye out. I expect you do the same with Chris and Terry does it with Michelle."

He didn't think Melia was one of these, but he said, "Some cops keep it to themselves so their families won't be worried."

She looked surprised. "But we're partners, Joe. And you know what that means. I need to know when he's worried. Or what he's stressed about. So I can understand. So I can support him. Recognize when he doesn't need a nagging wife. And…" The shadow of a smile. "When he does."

"You and Vince have an unusually close and trusting relationship. You're real partners, Gina. That's not always the case. I know he confides in you."

Burgess stopped, trying to think how to word this. He needed her to dig into their lives, present and past, to help them find this guy. At the same time, he didn't want to upset her more than she already was. But that was the friend in him, not the cop. The cop knew about necessary pain. So did she.

"I need to know anything he might have said to you, however casual, that might suggest a suspect. An incident. A comment. A threat. An encounter or confrontation."

She nodded uncertainly. "I'll try, Joe."

"Don't worry about an orderly presentation. Just let it flow. We can sort through it later. Give me anything that comes to mind."

She opened her mouth to speak, then closed it. "You know I want to help. I'd do anything…but my brain is like mush right now, Joe. I think you'd better ask me questions."

So he asked questions. About specific threats. About suspicious people. About times when Melia seemed distracted or uneasy. He asked about strange phone calls. Any times when Melia was particularly vigilant or watchful. Cases he'd mentioned where the bad guy had made threats. Anyone driving by or watching the house. Suspicious people or cars on their street. Any encounter that had made her or Vince feel uneasy.

She struggled with her tired and distracted brain and he struggled with impatience. After nearly an hour, he had four names—two of them from before Melia was promoted to lieutenant, one guy in the neighborhood who was a pain in the ass, took offense at everything and was wired enough to hold a grudge and act on it, and a woman with a kid on Gina's soccer team who would move heaven and earth to ensure her kid's success. She and Gina had had words, and she might have a family member who took slights to her personally. That was all, but it gave them a place to start.

She had no idea who he might have gone to meet at that building or why he might have gone there.

By then, Gina was in tears and showing the stress of having been away from her husband for so long. "I'm useless," she sobbed. "I know you need my help to find out who did this, and I'm giving you nothing."

"You're doing fine."

He was supposed to be good at this. But he knew—sometimes the process was just harsh and people too tender. He also knew that often the first interview only primed the pump for a follow-up interview that gained better information. He'd taken her as far as he could tonight.

He shut off the tape. "I'll walk you back. We can try again tomorrow. Maybe you'll remember something. Or you can text me any time."

As they walked down the corridor, he said, "Who's taking care of the boys?"

"Vince's parents. The boys are staying there until...his dad is going to bring them tomorrow. I was trying. I thought. I didn't want them to see...but what if?" She didn't need to finish. What if their father died without their getting a chance to see him and say goodbye?

Then something he should have been thinking about all along hit him like a ton of bricks. He'd made sure Melia and Aucoin were safe, and he knew Gina was safe because she was here with Melia and there was a guard on 24/7.

There were still so many ifs, but among them was this: if this was all aimed at Vince Melia, and the shooter couldn't get at him, what if he tracked down the boys and went after them?

CHAPTER 13

Burgess changed the subject, putting on his blank cop's face until he could get her settled back in the room and make some calls. Gina was a cop's wife, accustomed to reading what her husband might be hiding. He worried that she'd detected his concern when he asked that last question, and hoped she was too distracted by worries of her own.

He knew Melia's parents—where they lived and their phone numbers—so he didn't have to ask for that. Before he left, he asked if there was someone who could bring her some fresh clothes and toiletries. A chore he'd rather not do himself. Right now, sleep was at the top of his to-do list. The sooner the better. He was relieved when she said she'd have a friend go by and pick things up.

They'd barely gotten out the door when Kyle said, "What's up?"

"Vince's boys. I never thought about having someone keeping an eye on the twins." Another thing Melia would have taken care of, if it had been one of them lying there. Wouldn't it be useful if Captain Cote had stepped into the breach, picked up some of those tasks instead of leaving everyone flailing on their own? Cote or one of the other lieutenants.

Kyle nodded. "Think the chief did?"

"Hope, not think."

"You gonna call him?"

Burgess shrugged. Calling the chief was a delicate matter. If the chief had thought of it, he'd be annoyed that Burgess was second-guessing him. If he hadn't thought of it, he'd be annoyed that Burgess was pointing out his mistake. Sometimes you couldn't win.

His mother, who'd been a very wise woman, used to say, "Why do you think you have to win?" In general, she'd been right. The need to win amped up confrontations and caused a lot of unnecessary conflict and stress. But decades as a policeman had given him a different answer: Because someone has to be the champion for the little people. Because if we don't win, the bad guys do.

Right now, the bad guy was ahead 4-0 and the good guys hardly seemed to be in the game. Crap. Sports metaphors. As if this *was* a game.

They went past the anxious knot of officers who would be living at this place until Aucoin and Melia were out of the woods. Here Updates Joe and Silent Kyle had just one name, Yagettim Yet, as they had to stop and answer questions they had few answers to. Maybe it was enough that Remy Aucoin was doing better and Vince Melia was holding on. Yesterday the universal opinion had been that Melia wouldn't make it. Every day, the odds got better. They got lots of hands on shoulders and 'anything I can do,' which were heartfelt and well meant, but the pressure was there.

Saturday night. The city would be hopping, the Old Port crowded with people relishing the return of warmer weather and being able to get out without shoveling or worrying about scraping the windshield or skittering across black ice. Plenty of people meant plenty of trouble. The citizenry of this fine city and surrounding towns wouldn't get it that the cops were on edge. They'd be just as stupid tonight as every other night. If they weren't stupid driving in, alcohol, their buddies, the pursuit of sexy women, and loud music would see that they were on the way out.

He sighed and walked with Kyle to their cars. "You get anything from Gina?" Kyle asked.

"Four names. Nothing that looks very promising, but we'll have to check them out. She can't focus. I figure I've planted the seed, I'll swing back tomorrow, see if she's got anything else."

"Best you can do." Kyle was silent, then he said, "You feel it?"

"The skin-crawling sense that someone has their sights on us? I do. Don't know what we can do about it, though, except keep working 'til we catch this guy."

"I'm thinking of a combat helmet and one of those riot shields. It'll look stupid but I might feel safer." Kyle looked away, speaking to the air. "I know we've got to do the job. But if I get shot..." His words trailed off. Then he whirled around to face Burgess again, his eyes flashing. "If something happens to me, my girls will have to go back to Wanda, and that would put them through hell. Never mind how close they've gotten to Michelle. Wanda would never let her see them again."

Kyle was angry. He'd been angry from the first moment this went down. Someone targeting cops went against the rules they lived by. You couldn't do this job, putting yourself in danger to keep other people safe, if you were always watching your back. The constant vigilance was physically debilitating and a mental distraction from the kind of focus a complex investigation took. "I don't like this, Joe. This shooter is a game player. It feels all wrong."

It did feel wrong. Simply crossing the lot from the hospital door to their cars felt dangerous. Burgess wondered if the brass, sitting in their offices, isolated from the street, understood what it was like out here for officers who were going around feeling like they wore targets on their backs. And how he would tactfully bring that up when he called the chief. He doubted he possessed that much tact.

They reached their cars without getting shot, a routine act that felt like a minor miracle. Burgess dropped into his seat, pulling out his phone to call the chief, then paused a moment to summon some tact and the energy necessary for a complicated call. He'd never had much of the former and was out of the latter. He stared out into the darkening evening, studying the nearby buildings, pushing back against a weariness so great he could barely hold his eyes open. No sense in wasting time driving home. He could just tip his head back and go to sleep. The car was comfortable enough and he was so tired he could have slept on cold bricks. But he'd promised his family he'd come home.

His knee brace was pinching his leg. The pain might help keep him awake but would make it hard to drive. He bent down to adjust it and his phone slipped off his lap into the floor. He muttered an expletive and bent farther. He'd just grabbed it from between his foot and the gas pedal when the driver's window where his head had just been exploded, showering him with fragments of glass.

He felt a biting sensation on his shoulder like he'd been stung by a wasp. Then his door flew open and Kyle, crouched down low, pulled him out onto the ground. Around them, there was a commotion of running feet as the cops gathered by the door dispersed. Some to look for the bad guy. Some to their cars for weapons. All to stop being passive targets for the shooter.

Then Kyle growled, "You okay?" in his ear as he was dragged around to the other side of his car. The difference between concealment and cover. Concealment kept you from being seen. Cover was what kept you from getting shot. On TV they liked to use car doors, which could be pretty useless for stopping bullets. The careful cop preferred an engine block. The cop stunned by a gunshot aimed at his head wasn't thinking clearly and had a head full of nonsense.

Kyle was on his phone, calling it in, asking for SRT. For patrol sergeants and the shift lieutenant. Taking control of chaos.

When they had the engine between themselves and the shooter, Kyle paused between calls to repeat his question, greater urgency in his voice. "Are you okay, Joe? Are you shot?"

Burgess didn't know. Gingerly, he explored his head and his neck. The side of his neck was gritty with bits of glass. Even more gingerly, he touched his shoulder, where he'd felt that wasp sting. His hand came away bloody.

He tried moving his shoulder. It hurt like a bastard but it moved and it didn't feel like anything was broken. Good news. He didn't need something to put him out of commission right now. This asshole wanted to make it personal? Fine. He'd just delivered his latest calling card to the wrong guy.

He was thinking about trajectories and what that hole in his window could tell them about where the guy must have been standing. When they found the spot, would there be more cigarette butts? A Moxie can? What else would the shooter have left them, deliberately or through inadvertence? Was their shooter smart or only arrogant and half smart? Shooting at a cop in front of a mass of other cops didn't feel smart. It felt crazy. Ballsy. But was it "come and get me" or "ha, ha, you can't catch me?"

Kyle repeated his question a third time, raising his voice, the way you did when someone was in shock and not responding. "Are. You. Okay?"

"I'm hit, but it's just a nick, Terry."

If he hadn't bent down, it would have been his head. Saved by a freaking cell phone. He'd called it a nick. It felt like a gouge. Maybe a goddamned trench. It would hurt like hell and slow him down, but it wasn't going to derail him. He was foolishly grateful that it was his left shoulder. Probably something that would need tending and give Chris more reasons to worry about him and pressure him to look for a safer job. Well, screw that.

He loved her and he hated to worry her. To worry any of them. But he and Chris had met on a case. She knew who he was and what he did. And why. Because if everyone stayed home 'cuz it was scary, who would stand between the public and the bad guys? Because when they signed on to be cops, they signed on to do the job themselves but also onto something bigger than themselves. It was that bigger—that sense it wasn't just a job but a calling—that kept them going on when the crazies were shooting at them.

He wasn't mad at Chris. He wasn't mad at himself for not being careful, because there was no way to protect yourself from this except to stay home and when there were bad guys shooting people, the cops couldn't stay home. He was mad at the situation. At someone so evil and determined that he'd decided to terrorize a whole police force. But determined to do what exactly? And why? What was the ultimate goal?

Burgess leaned against his car, the metal cool on his back, feeling his blood running down his arm, thinking about how to get a handle on this. How to get ahead of this guy. What makes someone become a hunter of men? What experiences could tip someone in that direction? What experiences and what pathology? Was this truly aimed at Vince Melia, as they'd been assuming, or at cops in general?

Was he being paranoid to think all of these shootings might be a cover for one of them? Should he be diving into Crossman's life, and Aucoin's? What if this shooter wanted to kill Richard Pelham and the rest was an elaborate misdirection? But Pelham had been such a solitary man. Their shooter could have killed him anytime and no one would have noticed. Unless this was to *make* them notice?

He would hate to have to turn to the World's Greatest for help—working with the FBI was like hitting himself in the head with a hammer and trying to believe he liked it—but he also didn't want any more cops getting hurt.

What he really wanted, at this moment, was for someone higher up the food chain to start taking command of this thing. They weren't called command staff for nothing. In theory, anyway. He'd never had a greater appreciation for his lieutenant, and all the things he did to keep the world running so they could concentrate on catching bad guys.

"I'd offer you a penny for your thoughts, but if the look on your face is any indication, I wouldn't want to hear it," Kyle said. "Let's get you inside and get that shoulder looked at."

"I'm okay, Terry."

"Sure you are. But we're right here. If it needs stitches, you might as well get mended now."

Get mended. How often over the years had one or another of them been here, bleeding? Burgess hated hospitals. Hated doctors. Hated getting stitches, even if he'd had more stitches than a baseball over the years. But Kyle was right. They were here. He let himself be led back inside.

The reports of shots fired at the hospital had gone out over scannerland and, just like the night before, there were news people waiting, looking for a photo and a story. Once again, the wall of blue closed around them so Burgess could make his unwanted trip to the emergency room. If he made the front page two days in a row, Cote would be beside himself.

Kyle was good at working the ER. He got Burgess jumped to the head of the queue, saying they had to get out and catch bad guys, and he snared a doctor in a matter of minutes. Often, even when they got priority, they had to cool their heels, waiting to get stitched up. Burgess had walked out more than once, preferring to bleed through his clothes rather than wait.

The small Indian woman who appeared was one he and Kyle had rescued not long ago from a thug who'd used her as a human shield to escape from police custody. She gave him a shy smile. "My heroes," she said. "What can I do for you today, Sergeant?"

Burgess found himself at a loss for words, suddenly so overwhelmingly tired he could barely sit up.

"He needs mending," Kyle said.

It was just a small injury. He should have been able to shake it off. Did this sudden weakness mean he was hurt worse than he knew? Adrenaline could do that—let you go on functioning while you were flooded with it, then leave you flattened. He sure felt flattened.

While Kyle looked on like a worried dad, the doctor and a nurse removed Burgess's ruined jacket and his shirt, vest, and undershirt, leaving him half-naked and chilled.

He glanced at his shoulder, then looked away. It was ugly and he'd found it always hurt more if he watched. He needed to call Chris. This would be on the news, and, despite his fellow officers' efforts to shield him, there might be pictures of him limping into the hospital, bloody and scowling. She and the kids would be upset. He didn't know where his phone was.

But Kyle, who'd thoughtfully read his mind, was holding out the phone. "Chris wants to talk to you."

They didn't allow phones in the ER. No one said boo when Burgess took the call. "I'm okay," he said.

Chris was crying.

"Chris. I'm okay. It's okay. Really."

"We saw those pictures…on the news."

"I was upright," he said, feeling like he was pushing back against a huge hot air balloon that was collapsing around him. "Please. Don't be so upset. I'm just getting some stitches and I'll be home. I'll be home in less than an hour."

All he heard on the other end were sobs and silence.

Then Dylan was on the phone. "Are you really okay, Dad?"

There was a catch in his son's voice. Not yet sixteen and feeling like he had to be the man of the family. Just like Burgess had been to his mother and sisters. He didn't want that for his son.

"I'm okay. Really. Hold on," he said, "I'll let you talk to the doctor."

She was swabbing his shoulder with something that stung like salt.

He held out the phone to her. "Please. It's my son Dylan. Can you tell him I'm okay?"

She smiled and took the phone. "This is Dr. Sarita Cohen," she said in her lovely lilting English. "With whom am I speaking?"

She listened, then said, "Your father is fine. He is just grazed on the shoulder. I am only giving him a few stitches. Then I am sending him home to you."

Burgess knew that was a lie, but it was kind lie. Her few was more likely six or eight. If he was lucky. But she sounded so cheerful and reassuring. Too bad she wasn't talking to Chris. Christ. Chris was a nurse. She knew he was tough and this was no big deal. She'd seen him after he'd received a shotgun blast and watched him tough his way through that.

"How is he?" Dr. Cohen was saying. "Does grouchy as a bear and explosive as a lit firecracker sound right to you?"

She had a lovely laugh, something he was amazed she could retain, working in a place like this. *We are who we are*, he thought. He never would have guessed from her serious face that she could be like this. Nor from watching her stoicism when an escaping criminal held a blade to her throat.

She listened to Dylan, and her smile grew bigger. "Just like that," she said. "Now I must go and patch him up." She handed the phone back to Kyle, quickly changed her gloves, and picked up a syringe.

"What is it doctors are supposed to say? This will only hurt for a moment? That is a bit of a lie. There will be a stab and a pinch and then pressure and stinging and in the end, it will be for the best, as it will let me work without you writhing and twitching as I sew you up. How is that for truth, Sergeant?"

He meant to grin back at her, and comment that he'd been sewn back together other times without any painkillers and hadn't twitched or writhed. But he felt a little woozy and decided he'd better lie down when she was done stabbing him.

She was delivering the stabs and the pinches when the curtain was drawn back and Captain Cote burst in, already engaged in full-bore complaint.

"Updates, Joe. Is it really too much to ask for updates so I don't have to find out what's going on with my own officers by watching the news?"

Behind him, like poops behind a swimming goldfish, came a gaggle of reporters, eager snapping him in his bloody, half-naked glory.

Enraged, Burgess would have gotten off the table and gone at them if Dr. Cohen hadn't put her hand on his chest, and like he was an unruly puppy, uttered the one word command: "Stay."

Dr. Cohen might have been tiny, but she was tough. She was on her feet and in Cote's face before he could get out a second sentence.

"Out!" she ordered, stopping him in his tracks. "What is the matter with you? I'm treating a police officer for a gunshot wound and you barge in here with the press? Where's your respect? For the badge? For his privacy? Get out right now or I'll call security. And take that rabble with you." She backed Cote to the curtain, waited until he was beyond it, and pulled it in his astonished face.

In that moment, if he wasn't already in love with Chris, Burgess would have fallen head over heels for Dr. Cohen.

CHAPTER 14

One of these days, Burgess was going to lose it with Cote again. He'd done it once when Cote screwed up the case against a child murderer. He'd gone right over the desk and grabbed then Lt. Cote by the throat. And almost lost his job. The man had a facility no one else possessed for pushing his buttons. Not right now, though. First he had a shooter to catch. And he really did need to lie down. Maybe he was losing it, because he was taking a mere scratch like he'd been shot to pieces when usually he took being shot to pieces like a mere scratch.

Perhaps Dr. Cohen was a mind reader, like Kyle, because she was already easing him back onto the gurney before the curtains stopped moving. "Take it easy now, Sergeant. That man is not worth the trouble it would bring."

Detectives were supposed to be opaque. They were the manipulators, the readers of men, the assemblers of complex puzzles. She was seeing into him like he was transparent. Was Kyle seeing this, too? He looked around, but Kyle was gone.

She didn't miss that, either. "I would say he went to—how might you put it?—beat the crap out of that man, but I do not think that is Detective Kyle's way. He beats them like a chess player, maybe?"

It wasn't. And it was. Kyle was probably calling the chief. Doing the job Burgess should have been doing instead of languishing here on the table like some fainting diva. He couldn't stand this. Suppressing his anger, he said, "Sure we can't recruit you for the department? You'd make a fabulous detective."

She shrugged. "I get to be a detective here as well. Yours isn't the only world in which people lie, and try to hide things, you know. Who manipulate for their own ends. Who are sometimes too scared to tell the truth."

She put a cool hand on his lips. "Now please be quiet, so I can finish mending you. Much as I enjoy your company, I have a whole room full of people out there waiting for me."

Neatly put in his place, the meanest man in Portland closed his eyes and drifted, feeling the touch of her hands and the needle tugging through his skin, wondering somewhere out at the edge of consciousness if she'd given him more than just an anesthetic. Then he wasn't lying on a gurney in a hospital cubicle, but was back in his car, in that moment before he dropped his phone, when he was staring at the buildings near the hospital. When something— maybe his sixth sense—saw movement.

Had that same sense made him drop his phone? Had there been some deliberation in that event that was beyond his rational mind, somewhere in his hardwired primitive survival senses? He needed to get back out there and take a second look. See what came back to him. Forgetting where he was and what was being done to him, he started to sit up.

A quick hand stopped him. "A moment more, Sergeant, please?"

If he didn't have a bad guy to catch and a family to reassure, he could have stayed here all night, listening to the music of her voice. After a year of therapy, Neddy had learned to deal with his fears and the demons that life had planted inside his head by going to what he called his "happy place." Burgess thought he might need a happy place, too. Odd, though, to be thinking about finding it in one of the places he'd always detested: the hospital emergency room.

"Done," she said. "Let's get you upright." A hand behind his back and one on his arm, guiding him up.

"Let's get you upright." Chris had said that to him, one of the first times they'd met. Also when he was lying on a hospital gurney. He smiled at the memory of her words and his response: "We get me upright and we both know what will happen."

"Seems I've worked a bit of medical magic," she said.

"I think you have."

He looked around for his clothes. Spotted them on a chair, bloody and torn. He couldn't go out of here wearing those and he wasn't about to leave here wearing scrubs.

But Kyle was back. He held out a black tee shirt. "Not what you would have chosen but it will get you home. I'd have grabbed something from your bag but they've already towed the car."

Damn! He wanted to go sit in the driver's seat and try to recreate that moment. He reached for the shirt. It had a big white band-aid on the front and said, "Yes, I'm feeling better." Not gag a maggot awful, but not something he wanted to be photographed wearing.

Kyle shrugged. "It was all I could find."

"The press will love it."

"The press isn't getting anywhere near you. Besides, you can put it on inside out if you want."

He would have thanked Dr. Cohen but she'd already moved on. Kyle fluttered a little piece of paper. "Your meds," he said. "Must avoid infection."

Moving on himself, Burgess said, "You call the chief?"

"Roger that," Kyle said.

"And?"

"And he said some bureaucratic version of oops, if I read between the lines correctly. And he didn't seem too pissed off at me, since he can barely remember my name. There are definite advantages to being invisible."

Kyle liked being invisible and was good at it. Burgess wanted to be invisible and kept having visibility thrust upon him like some mom making her kid wear an unwanted coat.

"I think I saw something," he said, "just before I dropped my phone."

Kyle cocked an eyebrow. "The shooter?"

Burgess nodded.

"You remember where?"

"Thought I'd sit in the truck and recreate it, hard to do if it's been towed."

"Guess you'll have to make do with the Kylemobile. I know it's not the same. You've gotten spoiled driving around in that big honking Explorer. Not some peonmobile like I drive."

One of their recurrent riffs—Kyle claiming Burgess treated him like a peon and Burgess getting frustrated and denying it. This time, Burgess was too tired to rise to the bait. "Peonmobile will be just fine."

Kyle helped him into the tee shirt, then into his vest. They bundled the ruined clothes into a paper bag—they'd become evidence in the shooting of a police officer—and headed out. Burgess made a mental note to get Wink or Dani to photograph his shoulder. Kyle, who was always thinking about evidence, had already photographed the wound. As had many of those dumb ass reporters with Cote.

They left through another entrance, avoiding the entrance where the press was clustered. They didn't stride across the lot, either, but took a route around the edge, moving slowly and staying where there was shadow or cover. Fool me once, and all that. Burgess felt shot enough for one night.

When they reached Kyle's car, Kyle gave him the keys. Burgess backed it up and moved it into the spot where he'd been parked. He sat there, reliving the weariness, rerunning his thoughts, and scanning the buildings across the street. Nothing. He closed his eyes a moment, feeling the slick plastic of the phone in his hand. Opened his eyes and looked again. Directly across the street was a brick office structure. To its left began a row of old brick buildings. One of them had a small balcony outside a third floor window.

He pointed. "There. The shooter was standing there."

He shut off the car and he and Kyle got out. Too much time had passed for there to be much likelihood that their shooter was still around, but there might be something.

"You want me to call Stan and Sage?"

"Let's just see what we're dealing with first."

What they needed to be dealing with was their families. There was plenty of pressure coming from that direction. Until a cop killer was off the streets, though, the greater pressure was from catching him.

"Oops," Kyle said, when they were standing on the sidewalk in front of the building. "Forgot my helmet and my shield."

"Stress, you know," Burgess agreed. "It can make you forgetful." He pulled out his mini Maglite. Everything that normally lived in his coat was now in his pants pockets, making him feel clumsy and awkward.

They went up the walk and tried the front door. Locked.

Slowly, they circled the building, Burgess going down the driveway that ran along the right side of the building, Kyle along the strip of grass that ran between the building and its neighbor to the left. In the rear was an empty parking lot, dimly illuminated by a vintage gooseneck security light mounted on the building over a back door, and a battered dumpster.

When Burgess tried the knob, the door opened easily.

"Exigent circumstances?" Kyle whispered as they slipped inside.

Searching any building at night has a high pucker factor. Searching a building when there's a killer at large sends anxiety into the stratosphere. They probably should have backed right out and called for SRT. Kyle's imaginary helmet and shield made a lot of sense when you didn't know what might be waiting in the dark. Around a corner, in the next room, in a closet. It also made sense for the detectives who'd searched a primary crime scene to search a secondary scene that they suspected involved the same killer.

Clearing any building is a slow and cautious process. Office buildings have their own risks. All those cubicles and desks where people may be hiding. By the time they reached the third floor and found the room with the balcony, Burgess had sweated through his new tee shirt. Rivulets of sweat ran down his back under the vest. He felt it beading on his face. The anesthetic in his shoulder was already wearing off. Pretty soon it would be a simmering bundle of misery.

A sign on the door said this suite belonged to a psychotherapist, a Dr. J. M. Petrovsky. There were two doors besides the door coming in from the hall. A closet and a small half-bath. Burgess checked those. The window leading to the balcony was partially open, heavy white wood venetian-style blinds rattling in the night wind. Kyle checked the balcony, said, "Clear," and Burgess turned on the lights.

Grimy footprints led away from the window. Aside from the open window and the banging blinds, the office looked undisturbed. A simple room done in soothing tans and mauves with boring framed prints of generic Maine scenes. No hooks for the patients' imaginations unless someone saw the lighthouses as phallic and the beaches as shaped like the curves of breasts or scythes. Burgess curbed his imagination. He had a cynical view of therapists.

"Some good footprints outside, too," Kyle said. "It doesn't look like anyone has been out there in years. And take a look at this."

Burgess stepped across the room, avoiding the footprints. Kyle was pointing to a bloody smear on the window frame. "Big guy," Kyle said, "crawling out through a narrow window. Looks like he got caught on a nail."

Burgess was a big guy and they thought their shooter was even bigger. He compared himself to the opening. "I don't see how a big guy could get through that window."

He and Kyle exchanged looks. The rule was don't let your assumptions get ahead of the facts. They thought they had a fact—that those scrape marks on a tree suggested a tall guy just like the depth of the footprints suggested a heavy one. But what if their killer was messing with them? Or there was more than one shooter?

God but he would like to have something solid in this case. Just one damned thing. Well. One thing was that this guy was a crack shot. Another that he was cold-blooded and calculating.

"Any cigarette butts out there, Terry?"

Kyle stuck his head back out the window, moving his flashlight around.

"Don't see any. You check the bathroom?"

There was a cigarette butt floating in an unflushed toilet. Filtered, like the others. On the wall over the toilet, two smears of dirt. The larger one was where the shooter had planted a hand. The smaller where he'd rested the barrel of his gun. Both on the left side of the toilet. Dirt from the balcony and the window. The guy shoots Burgess and then stops to take leak before leaving. But doesn't stop to flush?

"Thoughtful son of a bitch, isn't he," Kyle said, "leaving us all this evidence. You'd think he wants to get caught."

Burgess stood where the shooter had stood, straddling a set of dirty footprints, and reached for the wall as the shooter had done. His hand would have landed a good ten inches above the smudge on the wall. And on the other side of the tank. Which is also where he would have propped his gun. So maybe their killer was a lefty. It might be game playing, but when a guy braces himself against the wall, it's more often weariness. Or someone who is half-asleep. Or intoxicated. Unsteady for some reason. It made their killer more human, somehow. Still a monstrous human. But human.

He straightened. "Guess we know where Wink and his team are spending part of the day tomorrow. Let's get someone in to sit on this, and then I'm going home."

"Guess I'm driving you, then," Kyle said, reminding him that his ride was over at 109, waiting for the evidence techs. "So I think we'll detour past the drug store and fill your prescriptions."

"You sound more like my mother every day, Ter."

"Sacred duty," Kyle said. "Your mother, may she rest in peace, gave me the job of watching over you—"

"She did not!" Burgess said. "She just told you that I—"

"Could be insanely pigheaded and certain you are right, which, I might point out, was not far off the mark. Anyway, she said to look after you, and in my own small way, I try."

"Screw you, Terry."

"I love you, Joe. You know that. But no thanks. My taste runs in other directions."

They detoured past the dumpster, flipped the lid, and looked inside. On top of a stack of neatly tied white plastic bags was a bloody piece of cloth. And an empty Moxie can. Burgess snagged them, and bagged them, along with a handful of crumpled pieces of paper. Who knew? Maybe the shooter was getting tired of cat and mouse and had left them his name and address? He'd certainly left a signature.

As they climbed into Kyle's car, Burgess was thinking of yet another way Vince Melia's absence handicapped them. Melia would have found Burgess another ride before he finished getting sewn up. He would have understood the importance of keeping Burgess's team mobile. Now he was going to have to go to 109 and scrounge around, see what might be available, something he didn't have time for.

While Kyle drove, Burgess made the phone calls that would put the office building on Devlin's list and get patrol officers to secure the building until it could be processed. A part of him wanted to go back there, just stand in the room, thinking about things, and see what else it had to tell him. But it was late. He was hurting. And there were people waiting for him. Then he made more calls to get a car for the morning.

It was a lot later than the promised "within the hour" when Kyle dropped him at his door. Climbing the stairs felt like he was climbing Katahdin. He was ready to sponge the sticky blood off, take painkillers, and sleep. He walked into a snarl of questions, attention, and anxiety that made him claustrophobic. He took a deep breath, pasted on a smile, and tried to be a family man.

CHAPTER 15

Later, behind closed doors so the kids wouldn't see, Chris sponged off the sticky blood and sweat. Warm hands and warm water, her touch soothing. "I know it's overwhelming," she said. "But you know, this is what other people have been living with all along."

She didn't mean blood or stitches—he had lived with those—but the reality of having to be attentive to a family despite what else was going on in their lives. Most people didn't acquire ready-made families overnight though, the way they had. "On the plus side," she said, "we got to miss diapers. They're all toilet trained and can dress themselves."

Thinking about Nina and Dylan, he said, "Yeah. I'm more worried about them undressing others, or someone wanting to undress them."

"Other people learn to live with that, too."

She ran the washcloth over his face, then dropped it into the sink and ran her fingers over his face instead, her fingers gently brushing the scar, then lingering on his lips, a gesture half erotic, half meant to keep him silent. "I know it bothers you to hear it, but we were worried about you tonight. That's something we all have to learn to live with, too. You worrying about us and us worrying about you and how to strike the right balance."

"I'm a cop," he said. "I was a cop when you met me. I was a cop when you wanted to adopt Nina and Neddy."

"And now you're a dad, too."

That was the dilemma, in a nutshell. He wondered how Kyle did it, going into the same situations he did. Never hesitating, despite carrying the weight of his girls' fate every time. Despite knowing that he risked losing them back to the PMS Queen. Those thoughts led to Vince Melia. Melia had taken that supposedly safer desk job and look what had happened to him. Which led back to the question he couldn't ask his unconscious boss and needed to answer: why had Melia been out at that warehouse without telling anyone where he was going? What had taken him out there? Why had he not thought there was any risk? The fundamental questions that were at the heart of this thing. It wasn't a place where he might have been driving past and seen something. He'd had to deliberately go there. But for what? For whom?

Chris worked her fingers into his hair and massaged his forehead with her thumbs. "You're drifting," she said. "Come to bed."

Her touch felt so good and he was so tired.

She put a hand under his chin, tilted his head up, and kissed him, and that made him want to do more than kiss. He planted his hands where her waist flared to her hips. He'd never been attracted to skinny women and found Chris's generous curves perfect. He pulled her closer and rested his head against her breasts, perched on the divide between lust and sleep.

Before his body could decide, she pulled away. "Come to bed. You need sleep."

"I need you."

"I'm not going anywhere."

Well, that was good to know. But although she wasn't going anywhere, she had backed away from her promise to marry him. She'd accepted his proposal in a moment of intense emotion, when he'd just survived the scariest day of his career. When they were past that moment, she'd begun having second thoughts about the danger his job put him in. Now they were in a frustrating holding pattern. They weren't breaking up but they weren't moving forward. After a lifetime of being commitment phobic, he takes the big step, Chris agrees, and now she was the one resisting commitment.

Life was just a bitch, that was all.

Maybe he should stop obsessing about it and enjoy the here and now. They were still living together. Raising their kids together. Sleeping together. What was his problem, really? But he knew—it was about commitment. About a promise not for today or this week, but for the long haul. About the bigger things that promise meant. For better and for worse. The richness and depth that gave a relationship.

His father had modeled worse and worse and worse. Burgess wanted to craft a new and better course. Yet he understood her reluctance to tie herself to a life where events like this week—and this night—could keep happening.

Tonight was not the time to bring that up. They'd been around and around and found no resolution. He was ready. She wasn't. For now that was what he'd have to live with if he wanted Chris in his life.

Chris and Nina and Neddy. He'd been so angry when she wanted to adopt them. It was enough that he'd been willing to make room for Chris, when being solitary was who he was and how he was. He hadn't seen how sharing his life with three people would be possible. But what it is they say? Life is what happens while you've made other plans? In the midst of trying to sort out how he'd deal with Chris *and* two kids, he'd learned he had a son, and it had become how would he live with four people in his life. How would Chris, who couldn't have kids, deal with his ambivalence about discovering he had one, and how would they blend two damaged kids like Nina and Neddy with an angry boy whose mother had just died and he was being sent to live with a father he'd never known?

Life. As his job often reminded him—it was better than the alternative. An alternative that could have happened just hours ago.

He heard the familiar rattle of a pill bottle, and then she was shoving them into his hand and holding out a glass of water. "Take your meds and come to bed."

"Yes, nurse," he said, following her instructions. If he was going to get himself shot up from time to time, it was a lucky break that his partner was a nurse.

Feeling more like a shambling bear than a romantic partner, he let her pull him to his feet, and lead him to bed. Any lingering romantic notions were gone by the time he'd pulled up the covers. He was asleep the moment his head hit the pillow.

He slept hard and woke feeling already behind to the usual morning bustle of his family. Nina teasing Dylan. Neddy's complaints about feeling left out, and Chris's soft reminders to be quiet and not wake him up. Before he could get his feet on the floor, she appeared with a cup of coffee. "Stan called," she said. "Something about rabbits and hats I couldn't make much sense of, and Terry wants to know when you're getting together."

He sat up and took the coffee. "Thanks. I need this."

"I can tell. A good nurse, you know, we get so we can read our patients."

"Golly, I hope not," he said.

She narrowed her eyes. "You keeping secrets from me, Burgess?"

"To you, I am an open book."

"Right. I just have trouble sometimes keeping track of the pages. The one I'm reading right now is kind of dark and grim."

Her words were tough but while he drank his coffee and tried to get his eyes open, she was checking his wound and her hands on him were gentle. She had the most eloquent hands and voice he'd ever known. Sometimes just a word or a touch made it hard to think about leaving.

He figured she was reading the right page when she said "Just doing my part to make the world a safer place." And then, "I guess you're not going to be around today, huh?"

"Would if I could. No man in his right mind would leave you willingly. But nobody's safe until we get this guy."

"Just so you know...so you don't freak out if you call and can't reach us, we're going on a picnic today. Driving up the coast, exploring things like Fort Edgecomb. We'll probably be back pretty late."

God, she was good. The kids would be distracted and away from the news, and he wouldn't have to spend the day worrying that bad guys might be threatening them while he tried to do his job.

"Thank you," he said.

She gave him one of her sunrise smiles, the ones that lit up rooms. "It's a rare thing, Joe, to find a man who says 'thank you' and 'I'm sorry.' "

He couldn't help himself. He said something totally mushy. "I'll never be able to give you what you deserve."

Totally mushy and totally true. Because, as they both knew, he loved her and he loved his job, and the two were often in competition.

While she went to get his meds—he would take his painkillers and his antibiotics and shut up about it as long as he was around her—he checked his phone and found it on vibrate, with messages beginning to stack up. He couldn't remember whether he'd silenced it or Chris had. Either way, it was okay. Getting some sleep meant he could work effectively today. Before he could start scrolling through the messages, it rang. Kyle.

"I'm outside waiting for you."

"Gimme five," he said, and grabbed some clothes. He almost skipped the vest—it put uncomfortable pressure on his shoulder—but reminded himself that last night someone had shot at him. If he was careless enough to not wear his vest when someone was stalking cops, and then got himself shot, he'd not only leave his family bereft, but all those years of being tough on the younger guys that had earned him his reputation as the meanest cop in Portland would look stupid. You don't want to be remembered for being stupid. He could imagine his tombstone: Good cop but died of stupidity. And he'd deserve it.

His smartass family actually applauded when he walked through the kitchen, but the sarcasm was softened by a hug from Neddy and a bag lunch from Nina. Dylan held back, as befitted a man of almost sixteen. Burgess took a moment to put an arm around his shoulders and say, "Thanks for taking care of everybody last night."

His son didn't say anything, but in his eyes, Burgess saw appreciation. God, he wished his father had done that for him. But his father was too angry to see the people around him.

"Stan's got a rabbit," Kyle said, as he climbed into the car.

"Do tell."

"I told him about that handprint on the wall at the shrink's office."

"While I was home in my footie pj's drinking cocoa and enjoying the ministrations of a private duty nurse?"

"Ministrations?" Kyle said, raising an eyebrow. "That a fancy word for blow job?" He ducked his head. "Excuse me. Mustn't be so rude with respect to a decent woman. And you know, it's almost June, Joe. You can start wearing regular pajamas now."

Burgess stared out at a foggy morning, the kind of clammy gray that makes you sluggish and distorts perception. "Doesn't look like almost June. Looks like almost April. So what's Stan's rabbit?"

"The guy's not tall."

Like they'd surmised last night. But he'd been hoping for a great big jackrabbit. Something they could work with. "And what is the source of this brilliant conclusion?"

"Don't be so cynical, Joe. The kid's trying hard here."

"Sorry. Bad mood this morning. I'm getting too old to get shot. Just can't roll with it like I used to."

"Normal people don't roll with it."

"Since when were we normal people?"

Burgess shifted in his seat. There was no way he was going to get comfortable today, and that did nothing for his lousy mood. He avoided making it worse by not checking his messages to see how many were from Cote. "So. The rabbit?"

"Young Stanley was up early this morning, bright eyed and all that, and he took himself back out to warehouse, to out there in the woods where our shooter was standing, and got down on his hands and knees and crawled around and guess what?"

"He got bitten by a snake?"

"Play the game, Joe."

"He found evidence that the guy was standing on something to make him seem taller?"

"Bingo."

"Unless it was Dani Letorneau standing on something to actually make her taller so she could adequately process that site."

"Golly," Kyle said, as he braked for a guy in a motorized wheelchair who was driving down the middle of the road, "you must be a detective."

"One thing I'm detecting, Ter. You're in a better mood than I am. That mean you got some ministrations last night?"

"Old man," Kyle said, with a totally un-Kyle-like grin. "I get ministrations most nights."

"Call me Old Man again and I'll take you off the case."

"That much more free time to enjoy ministrations. So, do you want to hear about what Stan learned or just be a difficult old fart?"

"Does this mean old fart is different from old man?"

"Shut the fuck up and listen to me."

"You have my full attention, Detective Kyle."

"Dani Letorneau did, indeed, need to stand on something to process the spot where the shooter braced his gun. She used a small stepladder she propped against the tree. Which ladder made a different set of marks than those made by the stool that shooter used."

"You're kidding. A stool? The shooter carried a step stool the site in order to make himself look taller?"

"Perhaps I misspoke. The shooter carried something— Stan thinks a wooden box—to stand on."

"This just gets weirder and weirder."

The morning shift of the homeless who solicited at intersections with their cardboard signs were arriving for work. Burgess imagined a Fagan-like boss somewhere who gave out their assignments, kept the schedules, and handed them their weekly paychecks. He'd often thought the bosses ought to keep tabs on their wardrobes, too. It didn't look sufficiently pathetic to be in nice clothes, and it certainly wasn't smart to smoke, not with what cigarettes cost these days. Too many Mainers were among the working poor, yet very generous. They shouldn't ante up their meager cash to someone who'd smoke or drink it away.

He shifted his thoughts to their shooter and how odd it was to imagine him tromping along by the water's edge, carrying a wooden box and a rifle. Odd, too, with the amount of boat traffic, that no one had noticed him. But maybe the community needed a nudge?

"Stan did good," he said.

"Be sure and tell him."

"I will. So I guess we're meeting this morning?"

"That's what Detective Kyle thinks. And Detective Perry."

"Then who is Detective Sergeant Burgess to disagree?"

As they turned toward 109, he looked down the street toward the harbor. This morning there was no harbor, just a big puffy mass of white, bits of which were breaking off and drifting up the street, like ghosts looking for their lost friends.

They parked in the gloomy garage and walked through the briny air to the building.

Stan Perry was already in the conference room, almost bouncing on his chair with excitement at his rabbit. Burgess grabbed some stuff from his desk and followed Kyle into the room.

"Great job, Stan," Burgess said. "You may have deepened our mystery, but you showed initiative and insight. You keep pulling out rabbits and pretty soon this old fart can retire."

Perry tried to keep it off his face, but his grin broke out. Nothing wrong with that. He should take pleasure in doing good work. And now he'd go out and work that much harder, trying to find them more rabbits.

Burgess looked around for Sage Prentiss. He hadn't called Sage. He hadn't called anybody, but he figured one of the others had.

"His baby is sick. His wife is sick. He couldn't come in today," Perry said. "He's not a happy camper."

Prentiss was working on Richard Pelham, whose life and contacts were still a huge question mark. Burgess took one of those calming breaths, the ones the department's shrink said he was supposed to use when frustration seemed to be getting the better of him. He always said people came first. The challenge was when their tension was between the people who were actual family and the people they worked with, and for. The people in this city. The possibility of their shooter picking off other cops or complicating the picture by moving on to random civilians. They always wanted things to make sense. Often, though, they only made sense looking backward.

He spread his papers out on the table and he and his team went to work. He gave out assignments. Stan Perry got recent cases where Lt. Melia had testified, and recent prison releases. Depending on the numbers, they'd share those out later. Before that, Perry was going to run down that gas station receipt, see if the place had video. Burgess and Kyle split the names he'd gotten from Gina, each taking two. They'd check in by phone in a few hours and see where they stood.

There was nothing from their crime scene people, and Dani and Wink were too busy to join them. That was okay. He'd rather have them in the lab than sitting here being frustrated.

"Before you do anything else, I need those reports," he said. "Just in case someone gets shot."

It wasn't a joke. Two sets of serious eyes fixed on his shoulder. "How bad is it?" Perry asked.

"I'm not allowed to play baseball until it heals," Burgess said.

"That's tough."

"Especially since it's spring and I've got all these athletic kids."

Perry looked away. Thinking about all of their kids, Burgess figured. No one knew what was going on with Perry and his pregnant girlfriend these days. Perry refused to talk about it. But they were still together, and he couldn't help but think about future springs, and how dangerous this job was, and what that meant for raising kids.

Burgess was thinking about Melia's kids. Whether Lincoln was even allowed to play sports yet, or still recovering. And what they were missing while their dad lay on the cusp of death and their mom was glued to his side.

Tortoise, not hare, he reminded himself. He and Kyle had joked on the way about it, but it was the kind of razzing cops did to keep what they were facing at bay. Something as gray and cold and insubstantial as that creeping fog outside lingered in the corners of the room. An enemy they had to beat, one that so far, like fog, they couldn't get a grip on.

CHAPTER 16

In the relative Sunday morning quiet of the detective's bay, Burgess and his team were crouched over keyboards and squinting at screens. One by one, with Stan Perry being first, they finished their homework and were allowed to go out and play. Or chase bad guys. Perry left clutching a handful of printouts. Kyle wasn't far behind, heading out to talk to the two felons Gina Melia had mentioned who had made threats about getting revenge on Melia.

Burgess sat alone, filing their reports and putting together the casebook. Some of that would have fallen to Melia, taking care of the paper so the detectives could go out and beat the bushes for information. He'd never had a clear picture of what Melia did. Now he could see the many ways in which his lieutenant had smoothed the path, soothed the brass, and kept things on track so they could do their jobs.

He copied the reports they'd written to send up to Captain Cote, first carefully checking Perry's reports to be sure that the information about the box, and their shooter's potentially devious behavior, was well hidden in a nest of other information. It was how they'd learned to work. So long as the captain had the habit of spilling critical facts to the press, they would have the habit of burying that information in the midst of other, eye-glazing prose.

Then he looked up the two names Gina had given him, got addresses, and went to see what he was going to be driving today. A Crown Vic so old someone heavier and shorter had worn a shape right into the driver's seat. Shorter and heavier? Maybe the bad guy? But that was a bad joke. Before he left the garage, he called Wink and asked if they could arrange for the window glass people to visit the Explorer as soon as it was processed. He didn't want to be driving this wreck any longer than necessary.

Then he fired it up and headed out into the pearl gray day. The way the fog softened and obscured visibility and distorted sound seemed like a perfect metaphor for his case.

Rufus Radstein, the angry and annoying neighbor, was at home because it was a Sunday. Because it was a Sunday and the cops could find him at home, he was doubly pissed off at being disturbed. Burgess couldn't miss the fact that this was a strongly-held opinion, because Radstein had repeated it three times, at increasing volume, before Burgess even had his foot in the door. Behind Radstein, a small, anxious woman hovered, speaking to her husband in tones so quiet her words couldn't be heard. Burgess thought it wouldn't have mattered what tone she used. Rufus Radstein was all output.

He'd looked Radstein up before driving over here. The man had a folder of complaints an inch thick and lawsuits against several people on the block. His disinterest in social interaction with his neighbors was demonstrated by the fact that he had a solid eight-foot fence around the perimeter of his property, including along the sidewalk, and Burgess counted three motion-activated security lights on the front of the house. Radstein was middle-aged, overweight, and one of those red-haired men with so many freckles it looked like his skin was rusting.

The Radsteins also had a dog. Unsurprisingly, it was a Doberman, clip-eared, chop-tailed, and drooling. Though the woman kept a tight hold on its collar, it looked like it ate unwelcome guests for snacks and was feeling a little peckish.

Ignoring Radstein's bluster, he said, calmly, "Just a few questions for an investigation we're conducting, sir, if you don't mind?"

He already knew Radstein minded, but usually, when the question was put that way, people curbed their tendency to be rude. Not the case with this fellow. "Well, I mind," Radstein snapped. "I'm busy."

If the dining table Burgess could see off to the right was any clue, what the man was busy with was the Sunday papers and his second beer of the day. The rest of a bag of pretzels waited sadly to be finished.

"I know it's a Sunday and you probably have a lot to do. I'll try to be quick."

As Radstein wavered between agreement and shutting the door, he inadvertently opened it wider, and Burgess stepped in. He looked around, then moved toward the sofa. "You don't mind if we sit?" He sat before Radstein could reply, and pulled out his notebook. "Just for the record, sir, because I have to write reports about any interviews I conduct, may I have your full name and date of birth?"

Radstein thumped into a chair across from him and gave up the answer like a troll who suspected Burgess was stealing his gold. The little woman took another chair, perching on the edge of it, her hand still firmly on the dog's collar. Burgess turned to her. "And ma'am? Your name, if I could, and date of birth?"

Her name was Lucille, a nice old-fashion name, and he doubted that people called her Lucy. She had a slight build, a thin face with a narrow nose that would have been pretty if it were softer, and well-cut dark hair.

"Now, Mr. and Mrs. Radstein, I expect you're aware of the recent, tragic attack on your neighbor, Lt. Vincent Melia?"

Radstein snorted.

His wife said, "So awful, officer. Will he be all right?"

Burgess shrugged. "We really don't know yet, ma'am. What we're trying to figure out right now is whether anyone on this street might have noticed anything suspicious prior to the attack on Lt. Melia." He gave it a moment and got the expected response from Radstein.

"I don't know how the hell you think we could have seen anything. Didn't you notice the goddamned fence out there?" A snort, then, "I thought cops were trained to be observant."

"It does appear, sir, that you are concerned about security. That's one reason we're talking to you—because your setup here suggests that you are particularly vigilant about inappropriate activity in your neighborhood. Because you're likely to be someone who'd notice if anyone didn't belong, was behaving suspiciously, or seemed to be studying the houses."

He was looking at Radstein, but from the corner his eye, he saw her suddenly stiffen. She'd seen something. Or knew something. The question was whether he could draw it out without her husband stopping her.

"We mind our own business, and like other people to mind theirs."

"Admirable," Burgess agreed. "We'd have a lot less work if more people embraced that philosophy. But as to my question, have you, over the past few weeks, noticed anyone parked on the street who didn't seem to belong?"

Radstein shook his head. "Too many people coming and going to keep track. Spring cleanups and people having work done on their houses." He shrugged. "Nothing beyond that." Even if he had seen something, he fell squarely into a category they saw all too often—those who wouldn't cooperate with an investigation out of pure disagreeableness.

"What about in the evenings? Times when workmen wouldn't normally be about? Have you seen anything then? Strange cars or trucks or vans?"

"No."

Radstein had, though. Burgess was sure of it.

"What about someone sitting in a parked car for an unusual period of time?"

Radstein shook his head.

"What about someone driving past multiple times, or seeming to slow down near Lt. Melia's house?"

"Nope. Nothing like that. Now, if you're done, I'd like—"

Ignoring the obvious invitation to leave, Burgess shifted his attention to Lucille Radstein. "What about you, Mrs. Radstein? What have you noticed?"

Putting it to her that she *had* noticed something, he just needed to know what.

She looked a little nervously at her husband, but he was looking longingly back toward the dining room and the waiting beer that was getting warm. "Well, I did…" she hesitated. "It's probably nothing, officer…"

Her voice was so soft Burgess had to lean toward her to hear, and when he did, the dog gave a menacing growl.

"Baby, hush," she said. The dog quieted but it remained alert.

Baby was the world's most inappropriate name for that beast. "You were saying, ma'am?" Burgess nudged.

"Last week, I was coming back from choir practice, and there was this car parked across the street. Well…I mean not directly across…but down a few houses. Between us and the Melias. And normally, a parked car, it's not something I'd pay attention to, only it was kind of funny looking."

He waited to see if she'd go on, but she'd stopped speaking. "Funny looking in what way, ma'am?"

She looked at her husband, as though she was asking permission.

"Dammit, Lucille, will you just tell the man what he wants to know so he'll get out of our goddamned house and I can finish my fucking beer?"

Lucille Radstein looked down at her lap, then across at Burgess. "It was one of those mean looking cars."

"Mean looking in what way, ma'am? Like a muscle car?

Like something an aggressive driver might have?"

She shook her head. Between intimidation by her husband, and her nervousness at talking to a police officer, this was going to be like pulling teeth. He'd just have to take it one step at a time.

"Was it a sedan, ma'am?"

She tilted her head quizzically.

"A car," he explained. "Not a truck or a van or an SUV."

She considered. "Yes. I guess you'd call it a sedan, only when I think sedan I think family car, and it didn't look like a family car. It looked like the kind of car someone who was always angry might drive…"

"For shit's sake, Lucille," her husband interrupted. "You sound like a moron. What she means is that it was like one of those Dodge Chargers."

Burgess nodded. He'd now discovered another way to get information from Radstein. Aggravate the heck out of him. Well, Burgess was good at that.

"What else can you tell me about the car?" he said.

"It was black, and it wasn't a smooth, shiny black like maybe it once was, but a kind of flat black, like it had been sprayed with spray paint by an amateur, you know," she said, "or how a car looks when it's in the middle of being repainted but there's only a base coat on it or something."

She looked at her husband. "Have I got that right, Rufus?"

"Yeah. You got that right." He went back to eyeing the beer.

Burgess couldn't figure out why the man didn't just go get it and bring it back in here and drink it. "Anything else you can tell me about the car?"

"It had those really dark windows, like I saw when we drove down to Florida once, so you couldn't really see inside. It just looked…I don't know…sinister."

Burgess nodded, frustrated by the slowness of her responses. There was something else coming. He just had to be patient. "What else did you notice about the car?"

"The white door?" She said it like a question. Like he knew the answer and was testing her.

"Do you remember which door?" If she'd just been driving past it on the street, depending on how it was parked, she might not have seen the passenger door. But if she'd been out walking the dog?

"Passenger side."

"Could you tell if there was anyone in the car?"

"Somebody. I couldn't see much, though. I couldn't even tell it if was a man. But it sure looked like a man's car."

"I don't suppose you noticed the license number?" It was a long shot, but long shots had paid off before.

She shook her head.

"What time of day did you see it?"

"Around eight, maybe? That's when I usually take Baby around the block."

"Did you see this car more than once?"

Another shake. "Just the once." She turned to her husband. "Rufus, did you see it another time, or just that once?"

Her husband gave her an angry look. He didn't want to be involved in this. But Burgess already knew he'd seen it, because of the certainty with which he'd ID'd the make and model. "More than that one time, Mr. Radstein?" he asked.

Radstein pursed his lips like he was trying to physically hold back words that might show he was cooperating. Then he almost spat as he said, "Two times. That night and one other time."

"When were these times?"

Lucille Radstein took the question. "The time we both saw it was what? A Wednesday, because when I came back from choir practice, I saw it. And it was still there when I went out to walk Baby, so I made Rufus go out and take a look. Not this past Wednesday, but the Wednesday before that." She gave a decisive nod. "I didn't see it that second time, only Rufus did, and he told me about it."

"Mr. Radstein?"

"She was out to choir practice and Baby was restless and couldn't wait for her to get home, so I took him out. And it was there again, in that same place. That's all I can tell you."

Burgess thought there was plenty more that Radstein could have told. He was the type to go up and bang on car windows. The type to write down license plates and call the cops in a heartbeat if anything in his neighborhood seemed off. Burgess could check with dispatch. Maybe Radstein had called it in. Or maybe he was just as happy to have someone out there who seemed to be bent on making trouble for the Melias. Radstein was a type—the type who thought the police should be at his beck and call but was affronted by the idea of helping them.

He wanted to interview Radstein about whether he had guns, and his whereabouts on the night of the shooting, but right now, he was getting something useful that could be augmented by doing a canvass of the street. He might save his next set of questions for a follow up visit.

"How long have you lived in the neighborhood," he asked.

"We've been here, what is it, Rufus? Nineteen years?"

Her husband nodded.

The Melias had been here about thirteen. "You and Lt. Melia were neighbors. Did you know him well?"

"We keep to ourselves," Radstein said. "We like it that way."

"Ever have any run-ins with him?"

Radstein shifted on his chair and glared at Burgess. "The hell's that supposed to mean?"

"Was your relationship cordial?"

"Not your business," the man said. "Now, I think—"

"When cops are shot and killed, everything about their lives becomes our business. I think you know that. So I'll repeat my question. Was your relationship cordial?"

"That fucker had the nerve to come into my home and talk to me about being civil to my neighbors. Like I'm the one just moved in, and not those folks next door with a passel of noisy brats or that whore across the street with a whole line of men coming in and out of there. Why we had to put up the fence. We're just decent folks who like our peace and quiet, which is something most of them..." He waved a dismissive hand toward the front of his house, "...have never heard of."

"Tell me about Lt. Melia coming to the house."

"Nothing to tell," Radstein said quickly. "He got in my face, which no one should ever do in a man's home, and told me that I was driving my truck too fast for a residential neighborhood, and that steering it toward kids playing in the street or blasting my horn at kids on the sidewalk was not necessary. Told me not to use Baby to intimidate people. He said we all had to live together and asked me could I try and be more neighborly."

The sound he made could only be called a snarl. The dog started when he did, and growled in response. Burgess thought they made a good pair.

"It ain't me needs to learn to be neighborly. It's them. Man's got a right to drive down the street. Walk down the sidewalk with his dog. Be peaceful in his own home, without a whole lot of crap from the people around him. That's what I told him and then I shut the door in his face."

Burgess figured the kids in the neighborhood were scared of Baby, and that Radstein enjoyed that. Used his attitude, his animal, and his vehicle as weapons in his war against his neighbors.

"Other than the one time that irritated you, did you have any conflicts or disagreements with Lt. Melia?"

Lucille Radstein sat with the back of her hand pressed against her lips like she was holding something back. He'd never get it out of her in front of her husband, though. Maybe he'd have to catch her after choir practice. He waited for Radstein's answer.

Instead of answering, Radstein levered himself out of his chair and launched himself across the room toward his waiting beer. "I've had enough of this," he bellowed. "I guess you ain't figured this out yet, but I don't give a good shit what happened to holier than thou Lt. Vincent Melia. I hope the fucker dies. And now it is time for you to leave."

Burgess would have figured she'd be used to it, after at least nineteen years with the man, but Lucille Radstein gasped when her husband said that. Just a gasp, then she gave a glance toward the dining room and pressed her hand more tightly against her mouth.

"I'll just see you out," she said.

At the door, Burgess said, "If you're inclined, as a church-going woman, you might add the lieutenant to your prayers."

"I am," she said in that impossibly low voice, "and I will. I might go to evening services tonight and do just that. We go to the New Community Church."

Almost like she was inviting him to meet her there. Though she'd said 'we' he figured she meant 'I.' Her husband hardly looked like the church-going type. "You take care, ma'am," he said, "and thank you for the information about that car."

She didn't say she was happy to help, maybe because her husband had finished his beer and his glare said he didn't want to wait long for her to bring him another. What was a nice woman like her doing with a man like that? Despite his years as a cop, people's domestic arrangements were still a mystery.

He went down the path and let himself out through the fence, then paused in the street, trying to see if there was a security camera. He didn't spot one, but he wasn't ruling it out. The fence and motion-sensor lights said Radstein was the security camera type.

If pure cussedness was enough, he would have arrested Radstein on the spot. The man could have done it. He carried enough hate and anger in him to fuel a whole lot of bad.

He got in the car, trying to find a comfortable spot in the misshapen seat, treated himself to some painkillers, as though medicine could erase the man's hateful words, and looked up the address for the next place he had to be.

CHAPTER 17

The weather hadn't improved while he was interviewing the Radsteins, but gone in the opposite direction. As sometimes happened in his charming city by the sea, the fog had thickened into a clammy soup that left his skin feeling slimy in his short trip to the car. He couldn't see from where he was parked to the end of the street, and it was a short street.

Ordinarily, a late May Sunday wasn't a great day to ask the patrol commander to organize a canvass of the neighborhood. The ranks tended to be thinner on weekends and people tended to be out recreating. Good weather could also bring out the bad actors. Burgess imagined them rolling out of fusty beds, scratching their bellies with visions of larceny dancing in their heads, and reaching for their guns. But requesting officers to go house to house on Melia's street, asking about a strange car that had been parking there, was different. Everyone, with a few ex-felon exceptions and Radstein, wanted the shooter caught. Cops would be relieved when they didn't have to watch their backs. And a Sunday when the weather was crappy was a good day to find people at home.

He made the calls that would set things in motion, knowing that within the hour he'd hear from Captain Cote about his use of resources. Again, no Melia in the middle to take the flak. There was a line from an old song he vaguely remembered, something about you don't know what you've got until it's gone. He'd stop at the hospital later, stand by Melia's bed and say thank you. The man had better recover. He was an unsung but vital asset to crime fighting in this city.

Then he went to visit Gina's unhappy soccer mom.

At first glance, Madelyn—"call me Maddie, Sergeant, please"—Morris seemed like a delightful person. She opened the door with a flourish, greeted him with a smile, and ushered him into a pleasant living room with an instant offer of coffee or something cold to drink. But police detectives don't just go on first impressions. He'd read Ted Bundy was reportedly quite charming.

Burgess accepted the coffee, took out his notebook, and settled in to see what the woman was really about. Maddie Morris was a substantial woman. Crisp, short, frosted blond hair. Not fat, but large-framed, well-muscled, and strong. More athletic than feminine, despite her white capris, melon-colored twinset, and melon running shoes. He figured she was maybe 5' 10" to his 6' 3". She asked him how he liked his coffee and whether he'd like a slice of coffee cake. Oh yes, please. It smelled wonderful.

She delivered it, and dropped into a chair across from him with a slice of cake for herself. She dug into her own slice with an exuberance that said she enjoyed her own cooking. "This is so terrible for those poor boys," she said. "I was going to go by later and drop off one of these coffee cakes. It's my grandmother's recipe. Is there any news about Lt. Melia's condition?"

"No change," he said. "But we're hopeful."

More than he normally would have said but he was on good behavior today. Trying to charm a bit of information out of people. Chris would have laughed to hear him say that, but he could be nice if he had to. Chris also liked to call him a grouchy bear. Her current nickname for him was "Mudgy," which was short for curmudgeon, a label he frankly hated. He sure could be a grouchy bear, but right now he was being a different bear. A sad bear. A weary, hunched lump of a bear worried about a colleague and looking for help from anyone who might provide it.

"So, Maddie, we're trying to get a handle on people who might have had a grudge against Lt. Melia, or against his family. Something that can help us explain what happened—"

She didn't let him finish, but said, "Of course it's some criminal, Detective, isn't it? Someone from his career who carries a grudge?"

"We're looking into that, Maddie. But in a situation like this, where we don't have witnesses or obvious suspects, we cast a wide net. We look at all the possibilities. One of those possibilities, of course, is his personal life. Someone angry at the Melia family, for example."

"Oh, I doubt that, Detective. They're such nice people."

She hadn't shown herself as difficult yet, but Gina Melia was tolerant and fair-minded, and she wasn't given to exaggeration. Even in her exhausted and worried state, she'd had some reasonable basis for suggesting Maddie Morris. Difficult people, he knew, rarely regarded themselves as difficult or saw that they created problems and conflicts. In their world views, they were victims who had to fight back to hold their rightful places and get what they were due.

"They are nice people," he agreed. "But Vince can sometimes be a bit fierce, I've heard, and Gina has a reputation for being a tyrant on the soccer field."

He sure hoped that would never get back to Gina, but he had to give this woman some hooks.

She looked thoughtful. "I've honestly never seen him fierce, Detective. He's very patient with those boys, and they can be a real handful."

Burgess's observation had been that Lucas and Lincoln, the Melia twins, despite plenty of youthful exuberance, were about the best behaved kids he'd ever seen.

"Boys," he said. "They sure can get exuberant."

"That's one way to put it."

He cocked his head toward her and waited.

"That Lincoln is such a bully, and his brother Lucas just does whatever Lincoln does, so it's bullying in stereo."

"I thought Lincoln has been pretty sick."

She tossed that off with a shrug. "Lucas makes up for it when his twin isn't there."

"And you have a son who's been bullied?"

"I sure do. And I'm afraid that I don't share the general impression of Gina as tough but fair. She's anything but when it comes to those boys."

Now they were getting somewhere.

"Plays favorites, does she? I imagine it's hard for coaches to avoid that."

"It's not hard. She just thinks her boys are better, so she gives them more playing time."

"You've heard other parents complain?"

She tipped her head and he thought she looked like a raptor about to peck at some prey. Something in her look made him uneasy. "Oh. You know. They don't come right out and say it. But if you read body language, it's absolutely there."

"And that has made your son unhappy? What's your son's name, anyway?"

"Peter. And actually, officer, it's made *me* unhappy. I hate to see Peter slighted. You know how sensitive children can be. He'd never complain. Boys, you know, they have such a code of sucking it up. But that doesn't mean *I* have to take it lying down. A mother's job is to protect her children."

She shrugged and tipped her head again, like that let her see him better, and he felt an uneasy urge to move out of striking range. "But I still don't understand why you want to talk to me? Or what Gina has to do with this. She wasn't shot at."

Pleasant, well-groomed, well-spoken, yet there was something there, in the strength of her tensed neck and the purse of her mouth. A coiled energy that he could feel her restraining.

"We're talking to a lot of people who knew them. Gina mentioned that you are an observant person, which not everyone is, believe me. And you're usually there at the games, so she thought you might have noticed something. A conflict. Someone looking aggrieved who might be willing to act on it. Or heard something."

"Among the other parents? Not really. As I said, it's there in their faces but no one is willing to act on it. It's too bad. You know people are so eager to have their children play sports, but few of them are willing to coach. So even if Gina Melia is far from ideal, I guess they figure she's better than nothing."

"Have you ever thought about coaching yourself?"

There was an awkward silence. He realized he'd asked a question she didn't want to answer, and had already guessed the answer: she'd been a coach, maybe when her son was younger, and had been asked to stop. Perhaps even had her team taken away from her.

While she regained her composure, he looked around the room. There were lots of family photos. A man, Maddie, and a child. They marched around the room. Then, at some point, the pictures showed two people instead of three. The man had disappeared.

Divorced or widowed? "What about your husband?" he said. "Has he been concerned about Gina's coaching style and its effect on Peter?"

"I don't have a husband, officer. He was killed in an auto accident three years ago. I'm afraid that's one reason I'm a bit overprotective. Peter doesn't have another parent to take his side. He has no father to teach him how to fight back. Show him the ways of a man's world."

His own son had, and hadn't, had that. Raised by a stepfather who favored his own children and always seemed slightly resentful of the little boy his wife had brought to the marriage.

"I'm sorry for your loss, ma'am. I have a son. He's fifteen. And he's lost his mother. Losing a parent is hard on our boys."

Again, something he wouldn't normally reveal. He wasn't sure why he'd said it. Maybe his sense that he was losing her. That she was about to terminate the interview while he was sure there something to be learned here.

Burgess changed the subject. He wanted to ask about her whereabouts the day of the shooting and about her familiarity with guns, but he'd have to come at it indirectly. There was nothing about the house, or the photographs, that suggested hunting, or guns, but a responsible mother would have any guns locked up. For that matter, there was nothing about the house that suggested a child lived there. No discarded, untied shoes by the door. No clothes, no games or toys, sports equipment, drawings, or books. She might be a fierce advocate for her son, but in his own home, his presence was invisible.

"Getting back to an earlier question," he said, "beyond the behavior of the parents on the sidelines, have you ever noticed anyone at games or practices who didn't seem to belong? Someone who might have been watching the Melias rather than the players?"

It was too broad a question, but he couldn't find a more subtle way to ask it. Not when he sensed she was restless and would soon want him gone. He had to draw her back in. He sipped his very good coffee while he waited for her answer.

"That's an odd question, Detective," she said, "but you know…actually there *was* someone like that. Once. No. Twice. I noticed him because he didn't seem to belong there. Well. I say him, but actually, it was a couple. A man and a woman. The right ages to have a child on the team. But I know the boys and their parents, and they weren't parents. The first time I saw them, I just thought that maybe they were new to the area and had a son who played soccer and were checking out the teams and the coaches. You know how competitive parents can be—"

She broke off, tipping her head again. This time because she was remembering, and that was something people sometimes did when they were remembering. And something people did when they were making up memories. Burgess waited.

"When I say they didn't seem to belong, I guess I'll label myself as a snob if I put it this way—but they didn't look like the rest of us. There was something about them."

She tapped a thoughtful finger against her lips. "It wasn't just the way they were dressed, which was, I don't know exactly how to describe it, kind of outdoorsy." She looked down at her hands, a slight color flushing her face. "Most of us come from work, or running errands, and so even though we're on a soccer field, we look…uh…well, L.L. Bean-ish, if not businessy…and they looked liked they'd come from a different kind of work. Physical work. They both wore those tan work boots and…"

Another hesitation. Burgess waited impatiently. This could be nothing. Or it could be something. He bit back his urgent, "Just spit it out," and sipped his coffee like someone who had all the time in the world, not someone whose gunshot wound was getting red hot with pain and who had a friend in coma who might never wake up. What had Shakespeare written? All the world's a stage and we are the actors. Cops were definitely actors. The grouchy bear kept his sad bear face on.

"I can't recall the name," she said, finally. "But you know them. Those…please excuse me for saying this…but those baby-shit brownish workpants and jackets. Like they'd just come from a construction site. Or like they were carpenters."

"Both of them? The man and the woman?"

"Both. Almost like it was a uniform. But you see a lot of people around dressed like that."

"Can you describe them?"

She shook her head. "Those clothes, you know, I guess they're padded or lined or something. They make everyone look bulky and square. So they kind of…I don't know. Looked alike, I guess. More like relatives than a couple. He was maybe my height. She was shorter. And they both had dark hair, what you could see of it, because they were both wearing hats. Caps. Baseball caps. And those brown clothes."

"And you think they might have been watching the Melias, rather than the players?"

Another hesitation. "She definitely was. Which is why I noticed. Because what mom comes to a soccer field and stares at the coach? At the coach's husband, maybe?" A quick nod of her head. "Vince Melia is a darned good looking man, so I suppose a woman might stare at him. Only it wasn't that kind of a stare, if you know what I mean? It wasn't a woman admiring a good-looking man, it was assessing. Like she was looking at a purchase. Or like she was judging him. Does that make any sense?"

He nodded. "Gina was right. You are a good observer. So you saw them just those two times?"

She nodded.

"Do you remember when it was that you saw them?"

She considered. "Maybe two weeks ago. Or three. Or maybe one time each week." She shrugged. "Sorry. I wish I could be more definite, but I just don't remember. If I could tie it to something…hold on and let me look at the calendar. I've got Peter's practice schedule."

She stood quickly and disappeared into what he assumed was the kitchen. She was being helpful. Cooperative. Informative. But he still had that uneasy feeling. He didn't like having her out of his sight. He picked up his cup and his plate and followed her.

She was standing at the counter, stuffing a piece of coffee cake into her mouth. She turned, surprised, when he came in, then picked up a napkin, swiped away some crumbs, and gave him a rueful smile. "Caught me," she said. "I confess. I'm addicted to sugar. Which is why I never make this cake. But once I was making one for them, I made one for me."

For me? Not for us?

Her kitchen was as pleasant, neat, and childless as the rest of the house. No photos on the refrigerator. No fliers from school. No drawings. No magnets a kid had made at school or camp. There was a dramatic black and white photo of a much younger Maddie Morris, on skis, aiming a rifle at something in the distance. That answered the gun question.

She saw what he was looking at. "Twenty years and thirty-five pounds ago, I was a biathlete. I guess some of my frustration with Gina is my own competitiveness. It made me a rotten coach. Maybe makes me a rotten mom, sometimes. Peter certainly thinks so."

"Where is Peter today?"

"Where he always is. With his father's parents. I travel a lot for work. They stay put. So Peter mostly lives with them." Her tone was defeated, as though Burgess had now learned her sad secret—her son had rejected her as a mother. "We get along much better now that he lives with them. It breaks my heart, but he's happier, and that's really what counts, isn't it?"

Burgess imagined the pain of letting your son reject you, believing it was the best course for him. Maybe that's what he'd been reading from the room all this time. But he wasn't sure. What the younger guys called their "spidey sense" was still telling him there was more going on here. He wasn't going to learn it today. Having made her confession, Maddie Morris now wanted him gone.

He had one last question before he complied. "You were going to check your calendar?" he reminded her. "See if you could recall the dates you saw that couple?"

She swung around to the calendar, fast on her feet, and studied it. "Two weeks ago, at the Monday practice. And the week before that, on Thursday."

"Thank you for your time," he said. "And the delicious cake. I have a sweet tooth, too."

A lie. If he had anything, it was a meat tooth. A dark, carnivorous desire to bite into something rare and bloody. But she smiled at that, and showed him to the door.

He headed down the walk to his ride, feeling like a bear, like he was lumbering instead of walking. Wondering if she was standing behind her closed door thinking that she'd done a good acting job. Was the world her stage, too?

As he settled into the car's seat, a seat so worn into someone else's shape it felt like he was wearing another person's clothes, the thought struck him. Something so obvious he couldn't believe he hadn't wondered about it before. Remy Aucoin had said "he," but he hadn't gotten a good look at the shooter. The height and the depth and size of the footprints said they were looking at a man. But Stan Perry's box said they might be all wrong.

It felt like a man's crime, but increasingly women were making crime an equal opportunity field of endeavor. What if their shooter wasn't a man? What if it was a woman? But then what did the handprints on that bathroom wall and the un-flushed toilet mean? And the seat had been up. What if there were two shooters? They'd seen one set of footprints, but what if that's because they were only looking for one set?

Maybe Maddie Morris's mystery couple were the shooters, and they were working together?

CHAPTER 18

The painkillers he'd taken after his visit to the Radsteins didn't seem to be doing any good. His shoulder was giving off waves of heat and glowering at him like a malevolent presence. He was definitely not a happy camper. The cake and coffee had given him a useful infusion of sugar and caffeine but, like a cranky toddler, what he needed was a nap. There were no naps in his immediate future.

He figured if he couldn't rest, he'd go bother people instead. Stop at 109 and see if Wink and Dani, or the new guy, Charlie, had come up with anything. See when he could get his truck back and stop driving this uncomfortable ride. Call Perry and Kyle and see what they'd come up with. First, though, he decided to go by the hospital and see how Melia was doing. Check in with Gina and see if she'd noticed the strange car on her street or the odd couple at her soccer games. Or remembered something else.

He'd turned his phone off during his interview with Maddie Morris. Now he turned it back on. What he hoped for was a fingerprint match. A name. Something that would put them on a solid track. He was unsurprised to find that Captain Cote had left him three messages. He figured he might as well get it over with, so he hit call back, and, also unsurprised, reached Cote's voicemail. The captain's MO was not communication, but creating the ability to say, "Look, I called you three times."

"It's Burgess," he said. "Returning your call."

Then he put the recalcitrant heap in gear and headed to the hospital, listening to his other messages as he drove. Kyle wanted to meet up. Perry was going to take a meal break—read a break to see his girlfriend, Lily—and would have his phone off for the next hour. Dani Letorneau had a question and wanted to know if he was coming in, and as an inducement, she said Wink had processed the car. He could have it back, but he'd have to drive with no window or wait 'til it was replaced.

Great news. He'd take cold air over this wreck any day. The smell of fast food had so permeated the seat that when he shifted in a futile effort to make his shoulder more comfortable, it gave off stomach-turning waves of old French fry grease, bitter coffee, and cheap gentlemen's cologne.

The fog had thickened so much he needed headlights to drive and wipers to see. Sometimes fog was local, socking in Portland while farther up the coast it was sunny. He hoped that was the case today, otherwise Chris and the kids were ~~going~~ having a miserable outing.

He parked in one of the few spaces by the emergency entrance—one of the last remaining perks a police officer still enjoyed—and headed inside. Mercifully, given that his grouchy bear persona was ascendant, he didn't encounter any reporters, though there was still a strong blue presence.

The first thing he did was ensure the requisite guards were in place—they were—but somehow that didn't give him the vague comfort it should have.

The place did its usual number on him. Everything about it—the cold glare of the lights, the sotto voce hum of machines and the incessant beeps of monitors—could flip him back to a whole list of bad times he'd spent here, top place on that list being his mother's miserable and unnecessary death. The place pushed his buttons in a way few places could. However nice Dr. Cohen had been last night, this was definitely not his happy place.

Gina was right where he'd left her last night—sitting beside her husband's bed, holding his hand. At least someone had brought her fresh clothes and it looked like she'd showered. Melia looked unchanged, too. Both of them frozen in a tableau of wait and hope that hurt his heart.

Like last night, she stood and stepped into his arms, burying her face in his shoulder and staying there. There weren't too many sources of comfort in an ICU. He wrapped his arms around her and held her tight.

Finally, she raised her head and stepped away. "You got shot," she said.

Not 'are you okay?' or 'what happened?' Just an acknowledgment of their current craziness. That everyone was getting shot, and those who could still get out and do, got out and did.

"Couple things I need to ask you about," he said. "Following on my interviews with some of those names you gave me. Think you could step away for a few minutes?"

She looked at the clock on the wall. "I've got a few minutes. My parents are bringing the boys in half an hour."

"Just down to the waiting room is fine. We don't have to go far."

Before they left the room, he stepped closer to the bed and put his hand on Melia's arm. "I never knew how much you did for us, Vince. So please, wake up, get up, and come back to work. We can't do this without you."

When he turned, Gina had tears running down her face. "Hell of an inducement," she said. "That ought to snap him right back."

He led her down the hall to the lounge of despair, surprised to find it empty. They sat, Burgess in a chair, Gina at right angles to him, perched on the edge of a sofa. She looked diminished by all this. Nevertheless, she squared her shoulders and waited.

"Have you eaten anything today?" he asked.

She smiled. "Nobody, looking at you, would think the word 'nurturing,' but you're always about other people, aren't you?"

He didn't answer, so she continued. "Vince's sister was in this morning. She brought these terribly unhealthy and rather delicious croissant breakfast sandwiches from Dunkin' Donuts. So yes. I've eaten. Thanks."

"I spoke with your neighbors, Rufus and Lucille Radstein, this morning."

"I'll bet that was a treat."

"It was interesting. Getting anything out of him was like pulling teeth. The man couldn't wait to get back to beer and the sports page. But they did tell me one interesting thing. She said, and he corroborated, that there had been an unusual-looking car parked on your street a couple of times in the last few weeks, between their house and yours. Black Dodge Charger with a homemade paint job and a white passenger door. You ever see it parked there?"

She shook her head. "But I'm not a very good observer, Joe. I'm always running. Wherever I am, my mind is always moving on to the next thing. Where I have to be, what I have to do. Who needs to be picked up, or has a doctor's appointment, or needs new shoes."

She shrugged. "They always need new shoes and lately, there have been a lot of doctor's appointments. So unless Vince told me to be on the watch for something, I could step on a bad guy and hardly notice."

She looked down at her hands, shoulders bowed, a humble gesture, like she was feeling guilty at not having observed something that might be important to this investigation. "Vince is training the twins, though, so maybe one of them noticed it. I'll…I ask when they're here…if I get the chance. I don't know if the timing will be right. It's going to be such a shock."

"When you can, Gina. When you can."

He gave it a moment, then moved on to his next question, trying to get it out quickly. He could feel her moving away, into prep mode, into anticipating what she'd need to do to help her boys through the upcoming visit.

"I also spoke with Maddie Morris, and she said something interesting. She mentioned seeing a couple at two of your soccer games, watching the boys playing, even though they don't have a child on the team. She described them as mid-to late thirties, and dressed in brown Carhartt work clothes and work boots. You have any idea who they might be?"

"Sorry, Joe." She shook her head. "When I'm coaching, a crevasse could open up behind me and I'd never see it. All my focus is on my boys and on the game. I can give you the names of some other parents. You could check with them, see if they noticed something. It is odd, though, isn't it? People don't generally just watch anonymous middle school soccer teams. Could have been a relative, though. Aunt and Uncle or something."

A brief smile. "Maddie would notice the clothes, wouldn't she? And the work boots. She's got kind of a thing about footwear. And, though I shouldn't say this— about class."

"I got that," he said. "Sad about her son not living with her, though."

"Sad for her," Gina said. "I think not so sad for him. She didn't mean to, I'm sure, but she was whipsawing that poor boy in two directions—being so overprotective he couldn't breathe without her, and at the same time turning him into her little husband. When the dad's family stepped in and offered to help, it was a blessing. Even a blessing for Maddie, though she may not realize it for a long time. She did not need her entire life wrapped around one boy."

She fell silent, thinking about the possibility of more fatherless boys, then swiped at her tears and stood up. "I've tried to think of anyone else you might want to take a look at. Haven't come up with anyone, though. But I'll keep thinking. How are things going?"

Meaning—did you catch the bastard yet? He shook his head. "It's early times, Gina. We're all working on it."

"The first twenty-four hours are critical," she said, half in irony, half in truth. "Funny how that's true in medicine and in police work."

"Vince is still with us," he said. "How about the *next* twenty-four hours are critical. You tell that man to rally, and I'll tell his guys to go find the shooter."

"Deal," she said. "Walk me back?"

She stood and headed for the door, then stopped. "If it had been just a guy, lurking around, and not a couple, then I might think pedophile. Despite what I said about concentrating on the game, we're always on the lookout for them, and kids' sports practices are a big attraction. An exception to what I said before. But you know that."

She stared at a bland painting without seeing it. "I suppose they could work in teams. As couples. Sick as that seems."

He walked her back, watching her steps falter as she got closer to the room. "About the boys? Just deal straight with them, Gina. Vince always has. Tell them it's bad. Tell them we're hopeful."

He smiled. "Tell 'em Joe Burgess says their dad is going to be okay."

Her eyes widened. "You really believe that, don't you?"

"I do."

She swiped at some tears again. "Cop's gut? Vince always says you've got the best instincts he's ever seen."

Melia had never told him that. But then, it wasn't the kind of thing they did. Support, yes. Compliments? Not so much. You were supposed to be there for each other, but beyond that, it was about doing the job, not being praised for doing the job.

He thought he'd stop and see how Remy Aucoin was doing before he headed back to 109. Before he left, though, he said something that wasn't going to make her feel good. "What you said about being so wrapped up in things that you're not observant? You can't do that right now, Gina. However much this consumes you, you have to keep your eyes open. We've got people watching, sure, but everyone needs to have eyes on this. The shooter is clever."

"I don't know—" she began. "I don't want—"

She faltered. "I want to say that I shouldn't have to do this. He's done enough harm already. He should leave us alone."

"He should always have left you alone. But that's not the reality right now."

"I thought you came here to comfort me, Joe."

He was feeling like a sad bear again. "I came here to look after you, Gina. Keep you safe. You and the boys. To do what Vince can't do right now. Part of that is reminding you to be vigilant."

Shoot. He'd gone too far. He'd mentioned the boys. Because they were on his mind. On her mind. This wasn't how he wanted the conversation to go. His mistake was immediately apparent. She turned away, burying her face in her hands. She didn't make a sound but her shoulders told him she was sobbing.

"Gina. I'm sorry. I didn't mean…"

"Don't, Joe," she said. "You're right. It's just that I don't know how much I can take right now. How much more bad stuff. I just want…"

What they both wanted.

"I need a few minutes," she said. "I've got to pull myself together."

Nothing more he could do. He couldn't watch over her and the boys, he had a killer to catch. All the other cops and family of his own to worry about. He left her and went to see Aucoin.

Remy Aucoin was out of the ICU, which was the good news, but in so much pain they were keeping him heavily medicated. Burgess sat with him for a while, the uncles and the fiancée having tactfully departed so he could have Aucoin to himself, but there wasn't anything to be gotten here. Not yet. On TV, cops were always pulling people back from the brink to interview them. In real life, it often wasn't that simple. Subjecting a wounded colleague to excruciating pain so he could get some answers? Burgess wasn't ready to go there yet. Maybe when he had more to ask about.

Time to go back to 109. Trade his hateful ride for the truck. See what Dani had for him. Whether someone else had turned over any rocks today and found a lurking bad guy. Get addresses for the parents whose names he'd gotten from Gina. Later, he'd go and catch Lucille Radstein after evening services, see what it was she didn't want to tell him in front of her husband.

The few short steps from the entrance to his car were the length of a football field and made the hair on his neck prickle. There was no visibility. If someone was lurking out there with a gun, he'd never see it. He wasn't sure whether that made him safer or whether the gunman was also hampered. Was there such a thing as a fog scope?

He made it back to the car without getting shot again but had to take a moment to remember how to breathe. He hated letting the bad guy—guys? Gals?—mess with his head like this, and knew it was deliberate. He imagined the bastard laughing up his sleeve as he watched a city full of cops mincing and cringing, afraid to go out and do their jobs.

Something the bad guy might not be taking into account though—some cops, when you messed with them, just got mad and had more reasons to get even.

CHAPTER 19

Dani Letorneau was wearing a lab coat over soccer shorts and tee-shirt, still wearing her shin guards, her shiny brown hair pulled back in a thick braid. She grinned at his look of surprise. "Couldn't let my team down, Joe, and I didn't have time to change." Then, her grin getting bigger, she said, "Nobody who cares about my professional image is going to be around today. It's Sunday. I read somewhere it's supposed to be a day of rest."

"You look cute," he said. "I hope that's not a sexist comment? You know this being the father of a daughter is pretty new to me, and anyway, I'm a dinosaur."

"You *are* a dinosaur," she agreed. "And it probably is sexist, and I really don't care."

"About that day of rest thing?" Burgess said. "You are taking care of yourself, right?" He'd never known she played soccer. How had he missed that during their years of working together? Maybe because there was so little time for small talk when the cases were hot. He wasn't much for small talk anyway.

"Do I look exhausted and draggy to you?"

She looked pink from exertion and otherwise pretty perfect. "I expect the only appropriate thing I can say is 'you look very professional.' It's those shin guards. Very intimidating. They suggest you could run after bad guys. I'm thinking of adding them to my own look."

That made her laugh aloud, and brought Wink Devlin from the other room. "We've got no time for fun and games, Burgess, so stop distracting her."

"She said she had something for me, Wink."

"I keep telling her she should find a different way of putting it, that calling guys up and saying she has something for them isn't ladylike, but she just won't listen."

"I *do* have something for him, Wink. That's why he's here. And if I stuck to being ladylike, I could never work around you guys."

Wink snorted. "It was anyone else, I'd think he was here just to stare at you in those shorts, but Burgess doesn't notice whether we're male or female, he just wants results."

Burgess thought that if it were Wink in soccer shorts and shin guards, he'd probably notice the hairy, bandy legs, but he kept his mouth shut. Wink and his team were vital, talented, and hardworking. Besides, it *was* a Sunday and it *was* supposed to be a day of rest. They'd rest when they had their shooter, and let the folks upstairs bitch about the overtime then.

"So what have you got for me?"

She made a face. "It's a small thing, really. And I could be all wrong, because actually, it's kind of a crazy idea. I was just…I don't know…kind of following my cop's gut." Another quick grin. "It's catching, working around you guys all the time."

As if sensing his impatience, she got to the point. "I was looking at the footwear impressions—out on the road, and inside the building. I took some impressions and a lot of photographs. And something seemed strange. Off, somehow, you know. So I went back out there this morning, before the game, walked the road, walked through the building again, and then walked that track down to where the car was parked."

Burgess shifted and Dani held up a hand. "Don't rush me, Joe. I need to walk you through this. So here's the thing. All of those footwear impressions are the same size, and they're all from the same shoes. Or rather, they're all from the same brand and size of shoe, but—and yeah, I know this is gonna sound weird—I think you've got two different people out there."

She shrugged, like she expected him to say she was crazy. Only it matched up with what he'd been thinking. Or hearing. Like things might slowly be coming together, if he gave it time and kept collecting pieces.

"Why do you think it's two people?"

She held up two fingers. "Two things. First, because the depth of the impressions is so different—it's like someone kept gaining and losing weight—sinking into that mud and then skimming along the top of it. How does someone do that?"

She looked at him, a little defensive, still not certain that he wasn't going to call her crazy. "And second, while these shoes are too new to have wear patterns, the way the feet strikes the ground is different. You know how, with running shoes, they can look at the way your shoe wears to see what kind of runner you are? Well, you can sort of do that with the impressions, too. One of these people was heavy-footed, probably a hefty person. The other is lighter, and walks on—okay, I want to say this, despite the shoes being men's size 10 ½—I want to say that *she* is lighter on her feet and sort of walks on her toes."

She took Burgess's arm and pulled him over to a bench, where she had photos laid out. "Look at this." Pointing to the first photograph. "And this." Tracing a finger over a second. "See the difference?"

It was so subtle he might not have seen it if she hadn't pointed it out. And if Maddie Morris hadn't mentioned the out-of-place couple, he might still have blown it off. Their shooter or shooters were definitely going to a lot of trouble to throw them off. He wondered why? Was it just a game they were playing with the police, or were they paying a lot of attention to not getting caught?

He considered. If the aim had been to get Melia, or just to shoot some cops, then why keep shooting? Why target him at the hospital? Had he been deliberately targeted or was he just a target of opportunity?

He thought it was deliberate—given that sea of milling blue-clad officers by the hospital door, the shooter could have had a choice of victim, or many victims. But he'd been the one who was shot. Not them, and not Kyle, who'd been right beside him.

And why kill Pelham? Or try to make it look like suicide and then go on killing? He wished he had a profiler in his pocket. He wished he had some answers instead of these endless questions.

Tortoise, he reminded himself. Not hare.

Wink was smiling like a proud dad. He did that a lot around Dani. He was very proud of her work and very protective of her. Now he switched his gaze to Burgess, a challenge on his face, daring Burgess to say anything negative about Dani's theory.

Burgess nodded. "This is great, Dani. It matches up with something else we're looking at. With a couple things. Like the impressions made by that box that Perry found, those prints on the wall at that shrink's office, and something a witness told me today. Now if we only had a person—people—to match this up with."

"You'll find them, Joe."

If she'd been a healthy pink before, now she absolutely glowing. People didn't expect compliments from him. Confirmation was enough.

"Gotta get back to work," she said. "Go catch bad guys. And gals. And by the way, your window's been fixed."

Dismissed, Burgess went to the detective's bay to see what had landed on his desk while he was out, and get ready for his team meeting. Before he dug into the sea of pink message slips on his desk, he called Chris.

"Hey, you," she said when she answered.

"How's the weather up there?" he said.

"Gorgeous. Warm. Sunny. We're having a blast. Dylan thinks he wants to take up surfing. Neddy is planning a bird bone collection, and Nina is thinking about bathing suits. We have to be having a better day than you are."

"You've got that right. Though there was a very nice coffee cake in there somewhere. Homemade."

"Don't try to guilt me, Joe. You really wouldn't like the results if I took up baking. Maybe Nina will make you something. She and Dylan are talking fish tacos. You coming home for dinner?"

"That's my plan."

"I know all about you and your plans."

Alone in the detective's bay, he smiled. She did know about him and his plans. And about how often his plans went awry. How when he slipped into bed beside her, no matter how late it was or how tired he was, being with her made everything better and gave him very specific plans. Especially when she wore his favorite blue nightgown, which had the magical ability to cover everything yet gave him complete access to all the secret parts of her body.

Man, if middle-aged male detectives had hot flashes, he'd be having one now. Or whatever what was coming over him was called. Yeah. Okay. He was cop and knew all the words. The nice ones and the rude ones. And every piece of slang. He just wouldn't connect those in his mind with Chris.

"I wasn't thinking about dinner," he admitted. "I was thinking of you."

"You are bad, Joe Burgess. We have a family now. We have to set a good example."

"Am setting a good example," he grunted. "Of domestic happiness. Of good, healthy, loving sex."

"Idiot."

He decided not to explore how being frankly in love with her and finding her sexy made him an idiot. Not that he got the chance.

"Gotta go," she said. "Neddy is unearthing a seagull skeleton with a lot of clinging flesh. While we may want to encourage his budding interest in forensic science, we are *not* bringing that home."

"Jeez, Chris. My mom would have let me…"

"She spoiled you," Chris said, and disconnected.

Burgess thought about that. About a childhood with an exhausted mother who toiled to clean other people's houses, a violent father who beat his mother and terrified them all until Burgess was big enough to make him stop. About babysitting and doing neighborhood chores to put dinner on the table for his little sisters. He didn't think he'd been spoiled, except by his late night access to his mother's ability to observe the world. While the household slept, they had peeped out the windows, or gone out into the night, listening and seeing. Maybe Chris meant something different. Maybe she meant his mother had spoiled him for any job other than detective because she'd taught him to observe.

He snatched up a handful of pink slips. It was rare, but sometimes in the muddle of quotidian details and confessions from the crazies, one of these small pink squares held a piece of vital information. So while his instinct might be to crumple them into a ball and toss them in the trash, experience slowed him down and made him careful. Now he took a few minutes, slowing his impatient rush forward, and read through them, sorting them into piles.

Nothing went into the urgent pile. A lot of things in the "get to it when I can" pile. Most of it he crumbled and threw in the trash. In the end, he was left with only one thing that seemed interesting—an older patrol officer wanted to talk to him about a field identification card. FIDs were something they'd used for years to record observations. People parked where they shouldn't be. A lot of comings and goings from a particular house or vacant building, including license plates or physical descriptions. They were now being phased out, both because of the increased use of computers for reporting, and because of so many people wanting to look over their shoulders, looking for signs that they were profiling or targeting particular groups.

But this guy was old school. He might use the computer in his cruiser, but he also kept notes to himself—even if they didn't go into computer files—about things he saw as he drove the city. Friday night's shooting had sent him looking through his cards and he had something he thought Burgess might like to see. Burgess reached for the phone. And went to voice mail.

He left a message, feeling like a kid who'd been promised an ice cream cone and was now told he'd have to wait while daddy mowed the lawn. Impatient and petulant. There was no one around to see. No Kyle to bitch to. He wanted to kick a wastebasket, but it would just make a mess he'd have to pick up, and both his knee and shoulder argued against that.

He walked to the other end of the room, and went into Melia's office, staring at the empty chair as though the power of suggestion could put his lieutenant back in it. Then he picked up Melia's pink slips and thumbed through them. A bigger mass of administrative BS than in his own stack. He'd always known he didn't want the job, but this case was really bringing that home. Better that the younger, more socially adept guy should have the job, so Burgess could go out and stick his foot in people's doors and bull his way into their houses.

Hard on his shoes, but driving a desk would be harder on his temper.

Nothing in Melia's messages that might be helpful, so he went back to his computer and looked up the names Gina had given him. Wrote their addresses in his book. Glared at the clock. Thought about the patrol officers canvassing Melia's street, and whether they'd turn up anything.

Then he picked up his file and went into the conference room, which they were now using as an incident room. Laying out the reports and the photos that they had reminded him that he still didn't know about the call to Dispatch about shots fired. What time it had come in and what had been done in response. Nor about who had called it in. Who had he assigned that to? Prentiss? He couldn't recall and wondered if he was losing his grip on this thing.

Then he remembered. Kyle had this one. This was guy who'd gone fishing and his wife couldn't reach him. Kyle had gone back again in the evening, and neither the guy nor his wife was home. He assumed Kyle would follow up on that today, maybe bring something useful to their meeting.

He had too many questions and not enough answers. He went to look for Rocky Jordan, their computer guy who was supposed to be working on Melia's cell phone calls. His space was dark. His screen was dark. And he'd produced no paperwork for Burgess. Tomorrow, they'd do the official request to the phone company for those records, but Rocky should have been able to work with the phone itself.

Wherever the hell the phone was.

You want to commit a crime and give the police a hard time? Definitely do it on a Friday afternoon or evening, when no one could get a damned answer to anything.

His phone rang. Kyle, checking in. "We meeting, Joe?"

"I thought we were getting together again around four." He glanced at the clock. It was almost four.

Kyle sighed. "I've got to—" He shut himself down. "I'm on my way. Let's make it quick."

And Kyle was gone.

Burgess called Stan Perry. Got an abrupt, "I know. I know. I'm just pulling into the garage."

They were going to have a hell of a meeting, everyone in a mood like this. But why shouldn't they be angry?

Knowing it was a stupid thing to do, Burgess did kick the wastebasket. It spilled a trail of popcorn, part of a slice of pizza, and an ooze of Dr. Pepper onto the carpet. The smell of fake butter and rancid green peppers turned his stomach. He held his breath as he bent and scooped it back in, his knee screaming that he was the dumbest bastard who'd ever walked the earth.

Kyle and Perry came through the door as Burgess's phone rang. The officer who'd mentioned the field identification card, calling back. "Burgess? Bill Thornton. Got a minute? I think I maybe saw your shooters."

CHAPTER 20

Burgess wanted Thornton's information. Badly. And again he didn't want it. He wanted to delay the moment, some deep-seated instinct telling him it was going to screw with his head, and with their investigation, and make the picture even muddier than it already was. But the guy had called, and everyone wanted to help.

"You working tonight?"

"Nah. Home with a beer, watching the TV. You want me to come in? Bring it to you?"

He could get the information over the phone, but there might be more. There might be things that Thornton had seen and remembered that hadn't gone on the cards.

"Just one beer?" Burgess asked. He wasn't going to ask an officer who'd been enjoying a few beers on his day off to drive.

"So far."

"Do you mind driving in? I've got my team here, they could all hear it. But I can come to you if that's easier."

"Four grandkids in the house, I'm happy to come to you," Thornton said. "Be there in ten."

Burgess disconnected and followed Kyle and Perry into the conference room. They looked at the bulletin board just like he had. Disappointed. Frowning. Like it should have sorted itself into some new order by now. Magically rearranged itself to give them some clarity. Cops might not be given to magical thinking but that didn't mean they didn't long for a bit of magic sometimes.

"What a crap day," Perry said, throwing himself into a chair, "sifting through batches of bad guys. Thought I might get lucky with that gas receipt Dani found. But hell no. Kid working at the gas station was able to confirm the gas receipt was theirs—which didn't take a whole lotta smarts—and that's shit all I got. The regular guy who worked on Friday was called away for a sick mom. They don't know when he'll be back. Don't have a phone number for him. And their surveillance system was busted on Friday so they got nothin' for that day."

He looked bruised and tired. Burgess remembered that he'd been back out at the scene early in the morning, pulling rabbits out of hats. Was reminded that even Stan Perry wasn't a kid anymore. And stuff like this took a toll on all of them.

"I second that," Kyle said. "Anyone get anything today?"

"Maybe," Burgess said.

They perked up and leaned in as he told them about the suspicious car on Melia's street and the odd couple at Gina's soccer practices. "And Dani may have pulled out a rabbit of her own."

"Do tell?" Perry said, but he looked aggrieved, like he thought producing rabbits was his own private trick.

Burgess described her theory about maybe they were looking at two people in the same shoes, a lighter one who walked on her toes and a heavier one who left deeper footprints in the late spring mud.

"Maybe she was our fake nurse at the hospital?" Perry suggested. "Maybe we should take those prints from the security cameras and show them to your wit?"

It was a good idea. Burgess couldn't believe he hadn't thought of it.

"Now if only someone else on the street saw that car. That couple—the Radsteins—are more than a little bit strange. I wouldn't put it past him to invent a story about a car, just to jerk us around. He's that type. Has a real hard on for Vince," Burgess said. "But his wife brought it up. She doesn't seem like a game player, but she's totally under his thumb. I just don't know if she'd lie for him."

Maybe he'd get a better feel tonight when he caught up with her after church.

"Anything from the canvass?" Kyle asked.

"Nothing that's been shared with me. But you know how they operate. They'll wait for the thing to be done, then give us their results."

Kyle leaned back, looking sour.

Hoping to cheer him up, because Kyle sour was rare and concerning, Burgess told them about Thornton and how he might have spotted the shooters. "He should be here in a minute. We can hope maybe he's got something. A make and model. License number. Descriptions. Anything would put us ahead at this point."

He changed the subject. "Anything in the recent cases, Stan?"

"Not so's you'd notice," Perry said. "I ran down five scumbags today. Two of them had scumbag alibis, read scumbag girlfriends who'd vouch for them. The other three weren't where their parole officers said they'd be. Isn't that a big surprise?"

He tipped back in his chair. "I'm liking the two shooters thing. But who? Why? And where the fuck are we going to find them?"

"Terry, anything from those names Gina gave us?"

"I think there's an epidemic of stupidity in the city right now."

Kyle was definitely off. Usually he was stoic. Silent. Burgess thought he needed to get his friend alone and find out what was really going on. Maybe something with Michelle? With the girls? He normally shrugged off fear like it was just another annoyance that life dished up.

Thornton's ten minutes stretched to fifteen, then to twenty. They could only stretch their next to nothing out so far. Kyle and Perry had wanted the meeting short and were itching to be gone and Burgess was getting nervous. The mind has a way of filling a void with the worst case scenarios, and right now, it didn't take much to conjure up images of more cops shot. Of killers so bold they'd set up right at the police station and pick off officers as they pulled in or out of the garage.

He'd just about stopped breathing when Thornton came through the door. A heavy man with a big mustache and a belly that stretched his Seadogs t-shirt. He entered without knocking and skidded to a stop when he saw all three of them looking at him like they were starving and he was dinner.

"We were worried," Burgess said.

"Wife didn't want me to leave. She's not that much more keen than I am about all those kids around. Our kids think we were put on this earth to babysit for them. Like we didn't already do that. And that damned fog didn't help. Can't see two feet in front of the car."

Thornton fumbled a battered card out of his pocket and dropped into a chair. "I don't know if this is anything, but it was down where that shooting happened and it was weird as shit."

He handed the card to Burgess.

"A week ago," he said, "I was patrolling down in the Old Port. This bunch of kids got into a car and took off down Commercial Street. It looked like they'd been drinking and there were four guys and one girl in the car, so I followed them, figured I'd just keep an eye on things, stop them if it looked like they couldn't handle the drive. You know. Like we do."

He ran a hand over a graying crewcut. "They slowed down, out by the gas place, and I thought maybe they were heading toward that parking lot. Not much going on there at night. It can be a pretty good place to pull in and drink, and we've been asked to keep an eye on it. But they kept on going, 'til they got to this little road, doesn't go anywhere, just down to the tracks and then to the water.

Another place we find kids parking. This time, they did pull in. So I pulled over…"

He hesitated, waved a hand at the card. "I got their license there, on the car, it was a beat up old Toyota. Kind of a tan color. Anyway, that's not what this is about. So I gave them a few minutes, see if they were going to stay there. Then, I was going to get out, shine a little light on 'em, see what they were up to. Only just as I was about to get out of the cruiser, their car came backing out of that road like the devil was after 'em, and took off back toward the Old Port. Before I could get back in and take off after them, another vehicle came out of that road. Big mother black pick-up, woman at the wheel and the guy in the passenger seat waving a gun out the window. Headed off in the other direction."

He paused for breath, getting out of breath just telling it.

"I hit the lights and siren took off after 'em, and damned if this old lady didn't pull right out in my path, never mind my lights, and I had to slam on my brakes to keep from hitting her. I tell you—that truck? I've never seen anyone drive so fast as that here in the city in my life and I've seen plenty of stupid stuff. And the thing was that when she spotted me, she turned her lights off. Black truck. Black night, and shit, they just disappeared."

"But you got their license number?" Burgess said, hopefully.

"I got a partial, Joe, but I couldn't get it all before she turned the lights out. What I got's on the card."

"Maine license?" Kyle asked.

"Yeah."

"Got a make on that truck?"

"Ford."

Burgess looked at the card. Black Ford truck and HOT. He didn't know if it would be enough. And shit, yeah, just like he'd figured, if the people parked on the Melia's street were the same as these folks, they were switching up vehicles just to keep the game interesting. It did confirm, if this was the shooter or shooters, that they had scoped out the place in advance.

"What day was this?"

"Last Monday, I think. Date's on the card. I know these days they want us to put all that stuff in the computer, but I've put stuff in before and then I can never find it again. Most of the stuff I write down, I do it because I might need it. So I still use the cards."

Burgess was glad he did.

"This could be something, Bill. Thanks."

"I sure hope so. I'm getting a crick in my neck swiveling my head around when I'm out there, watching for the next bullet. Out on patrol, we're jumpy as crickets. My wife says I should take some vacation days 'til you catch this bastard."

"Kind of what we all want to do," Burgess said. "But someone's gotta get out there and catch him."

"Or them," Thornton said.

"That's what we're thinking, too, but I'd appreciate if it you didn't share that around."

Thornton dropped his eyes to the floor in the direction of Captain Cote's office. "Yeah, I don't guess you'd like that to get around. That'd be a hell of a press conference. You'd have to kill him this time, Joe."

The perils of having a reputation. Burgess's attack on Cote was the stuff of departmental legend and there were way too many people who wanted a repeat.

"Trying to avoid that, Bill."

Thornton grinned. "Yeah. I've heard that, too." He rose and headed for the door. "Good luck. I'll keep an eye out. You never know what you'll see out there. And I'll ask the other guys on my shift, see if anyone else has seen them."

"Appreciate it. Thanks for coming in."

When the man was gone, Burgess put his head in his hands. "This is like building a fucking elephant by committee," he said.

"Go home, Joe. Get some rest," Kyle said. "You just got shot up, remember?"

"Can hardly forget when it hurts like hot hell every time I move."

He looked at Kyle, already half way to the door, and Stan right behind him.

"Be careful out there, okay? You guys going straight home?"

Stan said yes. Kyle shook his head no. "Wish I could, but there's the guy who called in those shots. Gonna go by his house and see if he's home. I'm getting nowhere with the phone. Don't even know if his wife gave him my messages. I was married to her, I'd go fishing, too. Go fishing for the rest of my life."

Not entirely true. Kyle had been married to the bitch from hell and he'd been so patient during the marriage and after the divorce Burgess was ready to put him up for sainthood. Instead, he'd helped Kyle get a tough lawyer and win custody of his girls. A good result, but now Kyle felt like he had to be the perfect father.

Sometimes it seemed like they couldn't win.

"We're wearing our vests, dad," Perry said.

"And daddy is very glad you are."

"Be careful out there," he said again. He felt like their father sometimes, especially Stan Perry's dad. Perry had an unsettling tendency to go off on his own and get into trouble. Burgess thought that was getting better, but in this case, it just couldn't happen. He had no time or energy to pull Perry's ass out of some peripheral fire. Perry got out of line this time and he was off the team no matter how good he was at pulling rabbits out of hats. There was too much riding on this.

He watched them go, unable to shake the creepy feeling that something bad was going to happen tonight. He wondered how many officers in the city felt like Bill Thornton? Figured they'd just go on vacation until the bad guy was caught.

Burgess and his team couldn't all go on vacation until this thing was over, because it was their job to make it be over.

He stared out the window at a world so fogged in he could barely see the streetlights below. Wondered if some of the newer night vision devices might be able to see through fog? If their shooters had the means to ante up for thermal imaging technology?

His skin crawled as he considered the possibilities. Cops got used to working in the dark. It was a part of the job. Dark buildings, dark alleys, unlit parking lots. Those childhood monsters that lurked in the closets and under the bed had to be put to rest, but there was still something about darkness. It was not for nothing that Satan and evil were always associated with the dark. Things could happen in the dark. People could reach you. He and Chris might tell Neddy he was perfectly safe when he had nightmares, but things you couldn't see could be out there in the dark and they often were dangerous.

Fog just made it that much more complicated. Even if you'd learned to tune your senses to the dark and use your ears as much as your eyes, all of that got distorted in the fog. Sounds were muted, muffled, seemed to come from the wrong places. It was disorienting. If you wore glasses, it instantly blinded you. If you used your flashlight, you got back a blinding curtain of light.

He checked his watch. He had time to run the plate number for those kids Thornton had been following, then grab some food before his rendezvous with Lucille Radstein. He'd leave the partial plate on that black Ford for Rocky Jordan. Rocky had a way of coaxing useful things out of a computer, while Burgess was more likely to stab a keyboard in frustration. He was a go out and do kind of guy. More leather on the ground than eyes on the screen.

He ran the plate from the Toyota through his computer and pulled up an address. Added it to his notebook. Called Wink and left a message—was there any way, from the stuff they'd collected, to tell whether there was a female involved before the DNA came back?

Then he leaned back in his chair and closed his eyes. He was beat. His shoulder screamed like a toddler throwing a tantrum. He was consumed by worry about the cops out on Portland's streets tonight.

After a minute, he shoved back his chair. Never mind that his to do list was endless. He needed to go home and set eyes on his family. Refill the well of good stuff before he plunged back into the dark pool of the bad.

He grabbed the keys Dani had left on his desk, went down to the garage, and got into the Explorer. It was like being back with an old friend.

"Home, Trigger," he said, and pulled out of the garage.

He found them just spilling out of the car. Dylan with windblown hair and skin burned red by the sun, looking handsome, healthy and content and not at all like the sullen teen who'd arrived back in November. Nina was next, neat and impeccable in denim shorts and a sweatshirt, her bright hair held back by a bandana. She sketched a little wave as she passed. "Hey, Joe."

Chris slammed the driver's door, clutching a tote bag and a bunch of fast food trash. She was also sunburned, smudged with dirt and something that looked like mustard.

God, they all looked so good to him.

Last out, Neddy jumped down and danced around them, dirty and smelling suspiciously like something dead. He was holding a plastic bag which he immediately held out for inspection.

"Joe! My Joe. Look what I found."

The stench gave it away. No matter what Chris said, Neddy had brought home that dead bird for his bones collection.

"That is not coming inside," Burgess said. "Let's put it in the garage until we figure out what to do with it."

"But it's for my—"

"Garage," Burgess said. "No buts."

Chris was smiling as she watched. Then her eyes shifted to Dylan and Nina, heading inside, Dylan saying something and Nina laughing, and her smile got bigger.

"You love it, don't you?" he said.

"Love what? Getting sunburned and bringing home decomposing birds? Getting mustard on my favorite shirt?"

"Being a mother. Having a family."

She considered that, like she'd never thought about whether it made her happy before, then nodded. "I never thought…never imagined…but you're right. Two years ago I had a job, and that was about it. And now I have it all. I have you and I have them and hard as it is sometimes, it feels just right."

As Neddy came out of the garage empty handed and scampered into the house, Burgess stepped toward her and opened his arms. She stepped into his embrace, nuzzling her head into his good shoulder.

"I never thought I was entitled to be this happy."

"Why shouldn't you be happy?" he said. "Who decides?" Realizing as he said it that he'd rarely thought about being happy himself. Or what he was entitled to. Usually, when he heard the word entitled it was followed by "to an attorney." Happy was rarely on his radar screen.

As he held her, in no hurry to go inside, he heard something in the night. Just the slightest crunch of feet on winter's leftover sand. Could be anything. Just a neighbor walking. But people didn't usually go walking in fog like this. And he knew the rhythms of his neighborhood.

He stepped back, keeping an arm around her, and steered her toward the door. "Got anything you could feed a hungry man?"

As he'd hoped, it tripped her right into nurturing mode. "We had Burger King," she said, "but I've got food. Come on in. I'll fix you something."

"Just gonna grab something from the car," he said.

He breathed more easily the minute she was through the door. Then he unsnapped his gun and listened.

CHAPTER 21

H e stood, her car and his between him and the street, and listened. Nothing. He waited, hand on his gun, as the fog licked his face and neck, leaving him wet and sticky.

Nothing.

Then he heard it again. The scrape of a foot shifting slightly.

This was definitely wrong. If someone was walking, they'd keep walking, they wouldn't stop and stand around on a night like this.

There were streetlights, but the fog had turned them into little cones of light that didn't reach the ground, providing no illumination for the sidewalk or the street.

He held his breath and listened. Another crunch. Quietly, he got out his flashlight, the small LED one that fit in his pocket. The narrow beam worked better in fog. He found the switch. Then the steps crunched again and something rustled. He muffled his breath with his sleeve and inched toward the street.

Another crunch. He darted forward, pulling his gun with his right hand as he snapped on the light with his left. Close enough so it should give him some visibility. "Freeze, Police," he commanded.

The startled raccoon did as he'd instructed, its eyes gleaming at him out of the darkness. Then, with a hiss and a show of sharp teeth, it turned and scuttled away.

He snapped off the flashlight, holstered his gun, and went inside, letting his breathing settle, his heart rate return to normal.

Chris was bustling in the kitchen, pulling things out of the refrigerator. From the other room, he heard the TV and the kids laughing.

"You mind getting Neddy into the shower while I fix this?" she said. "He smells a little ripe. And be sure you take his clothes and put them in the washer. Otherwise, he'll put them right back on again."

Getting Neddy to take a shower could be a challenge. He loved his dirt in the way that young boys did, cherishing it as the emblems of how he'd spent his day. So Burgess started the shower first, then snatched the boy off the couch and dragged him, screaming in mock protest, to the bathroom. Tonight, though, he didn't get the usual protests. Neddy had so much to report and was so busy giving a running commentary on his day that he hardly noticed when his filthy clothes were pulled off. He didn't even stop talking when he was in the shower.

"Hit the pause button, kiddo," Burgess said. "I've got to put these clothes in the washer or Chris will kill me."

"Can I have the Batman pajamas?"

"Sure."

Burgess dumped the filthy clothes in the washer, then went to find the Batman pajamas. He carried them into the bathroom, closed the lid, and sat on the toilet. "Press play," he said.

Burgess sat in the truck in his driveway, fog drifting in through the window he'd opened to get some cold air to keep him awake. He wanted to go back out into the night like he wanted to be rubbed from head to toe with steel wool, but his day wasn't done. Time at home had pulled him in two directions. Amped up his need to find their shooter and make the city safe again, and amped up his desire to be at home, enjoying the warmth and the laughter, Neddy's silliness and Chris's smile. The meatloaf sandwich had been an added inducement. For a moment, sitting at the table in the midst of all that domesticity, he'd felt the temptation of a desk job, something nine to five that would give him more time for this.

But he knew himself better. Give him a month driving a desk and he'd be out of his mind. He'd been confined to his desk before. It was one of the things Cote had tried to do to him to make him lose it. Shut him out of an investigation, make him take a few days off when they were close to finding a child's killer. It hadn't worked. Burgess was too bullheaded. Luckily, his bullheadedness had created breakthroughs that had let them solve the case. Otherwise, Cote might have won.

Burgess didn't like to let bad guys—inside or outside of the department—win. That wasn't the game he played.

Chris hadn't let him leave before personally ensuring that he'd taken his meds. All those decades as a tough loner. Kyle had called it his "monkish existence." Burgess still wasn't sure how he felt about being taken care of. He liked it. He feared it. He feared the way it might make him soft. Make him let down his guard if he wasn't living on the edge all the time. He feared the way concern for his family split his mind, might distract him from the kind of clear, analytical focus he needed to catch bad guys.

He was used to coming home to empty space, to a place where he could think without distractions. He needed that kind of emptiness. Now he had to find it elsewhere. He couldn't make his family magically disappear nor tune them out like they weren't there. Kyle said he'd get used to it. That it was an adjustment that they all learned to make.

Thinking about the adjustments and family brought him to Vince Melia, and that brought him back to his resolve. Centered him. Melia was coming back to them, and Burgess needed to be sure that he was coming back to a world where order had been restored, a place where they didn't need to worry about themselves, or their families, becoming the targets.

He backed out of the driveway and headed for the New Community Church and what he hoped was a productive chat with Lucille Radstein.

The church lot was pretty full for such an awful night. Maybe because the day's bad weather had forced everyone to stay inside, they all had cabin fever and that had brought them out. He wondered, irreverently, if they were praying for better weather. After the winter they'd had, Mainers were desperate for some sun and mild.

He parked where he could watch the door, waiting for the service to end and people to come out. Finally, with a spill of light and the final chords of a hymn, the congregation emerged, pulling on raincoats and opening umbrellas. The last person out was Lucille Radstein. She paused in the doorway and looked around. Looking for him?

He got out of the truck and went to meet her.

"Detective," she said, still in that impossibly low voice. "I wasn't sure you'd get my message. I mean, understand that I wanted to talk with you further, without upsetting Rufus."

"I'm here," he said. "What would you like to do? We could sit in my truck."

She shook her head. "Someone would see. Someone might talk. It might get back to Rufus. Do you know Payson Park?"

He did.

"I'll meet you there."

It felt wrong, somehow. He didn't think she was setting him up. Maybe she was just paranoid from living with that husband for nineteen years. He got back in the truck, waited until she'd pulled out, then pulled out behind her, leaving enough distance so no one who might be watching—as if anyone could watch on a night like this— would think they were together.

They wound through invisible streets until the sign for the park loomed up. She put on her blinker and turned in and Burgess followed.

He parked and waited and a moment later, she appeared out of the gloom, opened his passenger door, and climbed in.

"I'm sorry about all this cloak and dagger business. It's just...I'm just...well, maybe I don't need to explain, since you've met Rufus. But while Rufus doesn't like Vince and Gina, or anyone else for that matter besides his buddies down at the VFW, I like them. They're good neighbors. Vince has been very kind to me. I just don't let on to Rufus that we have different opinions of them."

She broke off, and Burgess filled in the blank—that Rufus thought he was in control but there was a lot of stuff Rufus didn't know about. VFW. Veterans of Foreign Wars. Burgess wasn't surprised to learn Radstein was a veteran, and wondered which war he'd served in. Maybe that's where the paranoia came from?

"They're good people," he said.

"Yes. They are. Which is why I'm sitting here. It's a small thing, I'm afraid. I hope you won't be disappointed that I'm not bringing you more. All I really have is this. The windows in that car I mentioned were tinted and pretty dark, but I could see a little bit, and what I saw were two people sitting in that car, a man in the passenger seat and a woman at the wheel. And I've got this."

She dug around in her purse and pulled out a manila folder, which she handed to him. "Rufus didn't mention this, either, because he doesn't like people knowing things about him, but we do have surveillance cameras. I couldn't bring you the disks. He's paranoid enough that he'd know if one was gone, so I printed a couple screen shots for you."

He put on the dome light and opened the folder, wondering how Rufus wouldn't know she'd made copies, or why she could print these but couldn't make a copy of the disk, but he didn't ask. Maybe Rufus didn't keep spare disks in the house and controlled her spending. He'd seen controlling guys before. She was taking a big risk, meeting him at all. And he figured she had her reasons.

The pictures weren't great, but they did show the hood of a dark car, and two people sitting inside. Not well enough to make out features, but he could get hair color and relative size. Dark hair. Similar in size. And make out enough of the heavy sweatshirts they wore to see that this might be Maddie Morris's blue collar couple.

"Your camera didn't catch the license plate?"

"It didn't."

"Do you know when this was recorded? What day? I think Rufus said he'd seen the car twice."

"The earlier time."

"I appreciate this," he said, closing the folder and putting it on the backseat. "You don't think your husband would be willing to share the rest of the surveillance video with us?"

"He won't."

Thinking about what Bill Thornton had told them earlier tonight, he said, "We've also heard about a couple resembling these two being seen in a big Ford truck. You haven't noticed this couple in a truck near the Melia's house, have you?"

She was sort of cowering against the door, and she visibly shivered when he asked about the truck. He thought that doing as much as she'd done had been a huge act of bravery. Maybe he was asking too much, keeping her here any longer, but he had to know.

She bit the end of her thumb as she considered. "Like Rufus's truck?"

He realized he didn't know what Rufus drove. Whatever it was had been in a garage when he visited, only her small beige Corolla was in the driveway. Something he'd have to look up. Was she trying to tell him something?

"I haven't seen his truck, Mrs. Radstein. But this was described as big and black and shiny with a lot of flashy chrome. Rufus have a truck like that?"

"He has a black Ford pickup. It's just…you know. A truck."

"Have you seen any trucks like the witness described on your street? Black with lots of custom chrome?"

She shook her head. She looked exhausted, like it had taken a tremendous effort to take the chance to tell him this much. He might think there was more to be learned, but he had to respect her limits. If she'd come to him once, she might approach him again if she decided there was more she could share.

He realized how little he knew about them. His earlier questions had been focused on what they might have seen. "What kind of work does Rufus do?"

"Custom bodywork. He has a shop out on Warren Avenue. He's very good at it. People come from all over."

Proud of that, he thought. "And do you work outside the home?"

She nodded. "I'm a legal assistant." She named one of the bigger firms in town. He was surprised. Legal assistants made decent money and often had a lot of responsibility. Odd that someone who could hold a job like that would let herself be so controlled in her own home. People's domestic arrangements again. It was a puzzle. Maybe she liked the security. Maybe she was so controlled she didn't even know there was something different out there.

"Thank you," he said. "I know this was difficult for you."

"It was."

She paused, her hand on the door handle, as though there was something else she wanted to say. Staring out into the night like there was something to be seen there. Then she shook her head and slid out, leaving Burgess puzzling over what had been left unsaid.

He waited until her taillights had disappeared in the fog, then drove himself to a place that felt safer, where there was more light and people around. He parked and opened the folder again, studying the pictures. Wondering what she was still holding back and what had made her so uneasy. Why she'd kept looking around like she was expecting her angry husband to materialize out of the darkness.

Despite her claim that these were strangers, he wondered if this couple had some connection to the Radsteins? Maybe their children? The woman in the picture was sharp featured and dark, like her. He realized he had no idea whether they even had children. There certainly had been no sign of children in the house. Children or grandchildren. But they weren't young. There might be children from a prior marriage, or even from this marriage long gone from the house. He'd assumed nineteen years in the house meant nineteen years of marriage, but he had no basis for that assumption.

But if these people were related, she wouldn't have needed the pictures, she could have just identified them. She would have known what they were doing there. And wouldn't have turned them in. Unless she was trying to steer him toward something involving her own family that she couldn't bring herself to reveal?

Was the feeling he'd gotten tonight just her fear or a sense that he wasn't getting the whole story? Were these photos genuine information? Could they be someone on the street that the Radsteins disliked? Rufus Radstein was still high on his suspect list, despite the grudging cooperation. He wished he knew more about them.

Everything he learned brought its own set of questions, like trying to solve a puzzle wearing kaleidoscope glasses, so every individual piece fragmented into its own complex picture.

He was getting a headache again, and fighting pain all day was taking the starch out of him. It was only nine p.m. and felt like it was way past his bedtime. Bed would have to wait. He still had to talk to the kid who'd been scared by a gun-waving guy in a big black truck.

CHAPTER 22

The license plate Thornton had recorded belonged to a ten-year-old tan Toyota registered to a twenty-year-old man named Jared Laukka. After an excruciatingly slow twenty minute drive through the fog that should have taken ten, Burgess pulled up in front of a nice looking colonial on a quiet street. He figured that Laukka still lived with his parents. There weren't many kids that age in Portland who could own a house like this.

He hadn't called ahead. Far too often, warning people of his impending arrival meant the doors were locked and the lights were off, or everyone had developed a sudden need to depart for other locations. It was a hazard of the job. The tan Toyota was parked in a driveway already occupied by a Volvo and a BMW. Having had too much experience with people who tried to drive away when he came to call, Burgess parked his truck across the end of the driveway, blocking the Toyota. And smiled. There were lots of lights on inside.

He crunched up the drive and rang the bell, taking the moment before the door was opened to banish the angry bear and put on his sad bear. The woman who answered the door would have been pretty if her mouth hadn't folded in permanent lines of disapproval. She didn't look like she cared what kind of a bear he was, she simply didn't like bears on her doorstep.

She opened the door without a word of greeting and then stood there, tight-lipped, waiting for him to state his business. This would probably be another place where his charm was wasted. He took a step closer, standing tall and intimidating, flipped out his badge, and said, "Detective Sergeant Burgess. Portland police. I'm looking for Jared."

She took a step backward, sucking in a shocked breath as she prepared to deny that her son was home. "Jared isn't…"

It was a sad truth. Everyone lied, even decent mothers who otherwise considered themselves good citizens. But Burgess had done this dance many times, and as she moved backward, retreating from the open door, he moved forward. "Don't tell me he isn't here, ma'am. I see his car outside. I need to talk to him about something that happened last week."

"I'll get my husband," she said, turning and disappearing into the house. His mother would have been shocked by her rudeness. Occasionally he got blindsided, but Burgess was hard to shock. He stepped into the foyer and closed the door behind him, listening to her departing footsteps. Fetching her husband, he noted, not her son. As though producing the authoritative male of the household would get this annoying flatfoot off their stoop. Many had tried. Few had succeeded.

Somewhere in the house a TV was on, some comedy show, he assumed, from the amount of laughter he could hear. Beyond that, fainter, the rumble of rap music. He didn't get rap music. Maybe sometime, when he wasn't out chasing bad guys and getting shot up, he'd get Dylan to give him a tutorial. His son was pretty good at explaining the attraction of different types of music to the dinosaurs of Burgess's generation.

What he could see of the house was pretty in a bland, furniture-store display way. The kind of décor where the art matched the paint colors and was intended to produce no response in a viewer. The air was scented with something artificial and cloying, one of those nasty plug-in scents that people think enhance the ambiance of their dwellings. This one smelled like one of those candle stores that catered to tourists, vanilla warring with pine warring with cinnamon with notes of bathroom cleaner.

As he stood, he felt like someone was pouring lead over him. Soon he'd be too heavy to move. His wound was like an evil imp on his shoulder, whispering to him how much it really wanted to get out of here and go lie down somewhere. His clothes felt tight and hc thought he might be oozing through Chris's carefully applied bandages. He'd better not be. This was his last sport coat and he didn't have time for shopping.

After a wait so long he could have knitted an afghan, the woman returned with an attractive, well kept, but peevish-looking man with stiff sprayed hair and gold wire-rimmed glasses. The man squared off, like this was Main Street and it was High Noon, and said, "Now just what is this about?"

No introduction. Burgess's forays among the wealthier denizens of this city had taught him that manners and money did not necessarily go together. In fact, there was almost a negative correlation. He put on his best expression of surprise and said, "Jared Laukka?"

The man blinked like a goosed owl behind his glasses, then shook his head.

Burgess went through the badging and intro again. "Detective Sergeant Burgess, Portland police. I'm here to see Jared Laukka."

Then he waited.

"What's this about, Officer?"

"Detective Sergeant," Burgess said. "Is Jared Laukka here?"

"I'm his father. You can talk to me," the man said.

"You saying you're the person who was driving Jared's car last Saturday night, speeding along Commercial Street with three other males and a female in the car?"

The owl blinked and didn't answer.

Burgess was losing patience. "Is Jared here?"

Somewhere in the house, a door slammed, then he heard a car door slam, an engine start, an engine stop, and the car door slam again. Jared's attempt to escape had been foiled by a wily flatfoot.

Burgess tilted his head toward the driveway. "That Jared out there?"

Once again, the owl blinked, like he was supposed to have stalled this annoying cop so his son could make a getaway. Like that was an intelligent way to deal with the police? Obviously, the man had little experience with cops.

"He's not going anywhere," Burgess said, "since my car is parked behind his. So why don't we stop playing silly games, bring the boy back inside, and let me ask him a few simple questions."

"About what?" the owl said. But the authoritative voice had gone squeaky.

"Your son is an adult. If it's all right with him, you're welcome to sit in on the interview, but I need to speak with Jared."

Burgess felt a wave of cool air as the door behind him opened, and a tall, skinny male with fogged up glasses, gelled blond hair, and a clone of his father's peevish expression stomped in. "You're parked behind my car," he said. He didn't even preface it with "Excuse me." The owlet doesn't fall far from the owl.

Burgess swung toward him, an abrupt move designed to put the kid off balance. "Jared Laukka?"

"Yeah."

Burgess flashed his badge a third time. "Detective Sergeant Burgess, Portland police. I have some questions about an incident last Monday night on Commercial Street."

"There was no incident," the kid said, casting a nervous glance toward his father.

"The patrol officer who was following you said there was an incident," Burgess said. "Do you mind if we sit? Been kind of a long day."

"Here is fine," the owl said, and went straight to the top of Burgess's shit list. Cops had their ways of dealing with the self-important. This guy had better not speed, run a red light, fail to use his blinker, or do anything else in this city, or he was going to find himself seeing a whole lot of flashing blue lights in his rearview. Burgess was a patient man, or at least an impatient man well-schooled in patience, but he didn't need this. Not with some guy out there shooting cops. Shooting him.

These stupid, self-centered pretty people in their nice house with their nice cars and nice lives thought crime didn't matter to them. Well, keeping the city safe and civil mattered to everyone. The angry bear must be peeping through, because now the man took a step backward.

Letting his temper get the better of him, Burgess said, "Never mind. I'll send patrol to pick him up and bring him down to 109 in the morning, since that seems to be more convenient for you. Many people prefer a quiet interview at home, but I see you're not among them."

He put his badge away and turned, reaching for the knob.

"Wait," the man with no name said, "wait. You're right. It would be better to get it over with tonight."

When Burgess turned, the man made a sweeping gesture with his hand toward a room behind them. "We can go in the family room." He hesitated, perhaps finally remembering his manners. "Can we get you anything? Coffee? Or maybe a cold drink? We've got some seltzer with lime." The man with no name looked at the woman with no name. "Do we have anything else to offer the detective, Alyce?"

She practically hissed out her reply. "Maybe he'd like a single malt Scotch?"

"Kind of you to offer, ma'am," Burgess said, "but I'm working. Some of that seltzer would be nice, if it isn't too much trouble."

She stomped off without replying. Mad at him for threatening her son, and mad at her husband for not throwing Burgess out.

Burgess followed the Laukka men into the family room, and waited until they were seated on the couch. Then he took a chair across from them and took out his notebook.

He looked at the kid. "Are you Jared Laukka?"

The kid nodded.

"Were you in the Old Port last Monday night with some friends?"

The kid shrugged. Burgess didn't know what the shrug was about. Maybe that they weren't friends?

He raised his voice. "Were you in the Old Port last Monday?"

Got a sullen, "Yeah."

"Were you with other people?"

Another yeah.

"Can you give me their names, please? Phone numbers and where they live, if you know."

Jared coughed up two names—Jimmy Partridge and Cleon O'Dell, one address, and two phone numbers. Burgess waited, pen poised, but that was all Jared was giving up.

"Patrol says there were four people with you in the car. Three guys and a girl. So who else was there?"

Jared cast a quick glance at his father, and shrugged.

"Who else was with you in the car," Burgess repeated. He wanted all the witnesses, in case one of them was a better observer, and to corroborate each other's stories.

"I don't remember."

"I see. Well, maybe one of these other people will remember." He made a show of making a note. "Now, while you were traveling on Commercial Street, you pulled into a side road down past that cluster of buildings on the right, didn't you? A little road running down into the woods?"

Palpable tension was coming off the man with no name, waiting to hear what it was his son had done that brought the police to their doorstep. Burgess kind of enjoyed stringing this out, a little payback for their rude reception, but the clock was running, and he wanted to get home to bed. He would have liked that seltzer with lime, though. All this talking made him thirsty.

"Yeah. We did."

"Why did you do that?"

"O'Dell had had too much beer and he wanted to take a leak."

What Burgess thought was really going on was four guys who had an intoxicated girl in the car, looking for a chance to score. But Jared wasn't going to tell him that.

"So, did he?"

"Did he what?"

"Did O'Dell take a leak?"

Jared's head came up, chin jutting belligerently. "So what if he did? Is taking a leak some kind of a crime?"

"Depends on where you do it," Burgess said. "Sometimes it becomes indecent exposure. But I'm just looking for information here. Establishing a timeline. So, you pulled into the road and then what?"

Jared hesitated and Burgess thought it was a combination of not wanting to relive something scary and a macho desire not to admit that he'd been scared. "Then there was this big mother truck coming right at us with two maniacs inside. I mean, that road doesn't go anywhere."

"Tell me about the truck."

"It was black. And shiny. Had a lot of chrome on it. Not like a regular truck, you know, but like some custom job. And it was moving fast, coming right at us. O'Dell was out of the car, so like, I couldn't just put it in reverse and back up. And while I'm waiting for him to get back in, him and the girl, the driver starts blowing the horn and they came up until they were right on our bumper and that's when I saw the gun."

"The what?" his father said.

"The gun. The guy was waving this fucking gun around, like he was saying if we didn't get out of his way right then, he was going to shoot us."

"Walk me through it," Burgess said.

"I couldn't wait for O'Dell, I just jammed it into reverse and started backing up, and O'Dell and the girl were chasing after us. I thought, honestly I thought that truck was going to run them down, but she was screaming and I slowed and they jumped in and we just kept reversing…it felt like forever and that damned monster truck kept coming. I don't know if he fired that gun or not, I couldn't hear over my engine and his. Then we got out to the road and I just took off, back toward the Old Port, thinking maybe I could find a cop…and the truck took off the other way and a second later there was a cop right after them."

Jared stopped his narrative and sucked down some air. He didn't look peevish now. He looked shaken. More like the kid he'd been than the man he was becoming. "I was scared like I've never been scared. I was sure they were going to kill me. Kill all of us."

"Can you tell me anything about the people in that truck?"

The kid shook his head. "Not much. There were two of them. A man…he had the gun…and a woman driving. He was a big guy. Dark hair, longish, mustache, wearing a baseball cap turned backward. I think he had on a sweatshirt, but I'm not sure."

"And the driver?"

"She was kinda smallish. You know, not big and bulky like him, but she drove that truck like a pro. Dark hair, thin face, really pale skin. They kind of looked alike, the two of them, you know? Both with those dark sweatshirts and dark hair and kind of pointy noses. Her face is kind of imprinted on me, because she was right there in front of me, driving me back, so we were kind of staring at each other, you know?"

Reluctant as hell to cooperate, but the kid was a good witness, now that he was talking.

"You didn't happen to notice the license plate?"

"Not all of it. A couple of the letters, I think, were TDO. Maybe it was a vanity plate. I wasn't paying attention. I was just trying to get us all out of there and not get us killed."

"You notice anything about the gun? Was it a long gun...a rifle...or a handgun?"

"Handgun. Big. Black. Detective, I don't know anything about guns."

"You're doing great, Jared. Just great. This is very helpful information."

"What the fuck!" the man with no name said. "You're barging in at this hour on a Sunday night because you wanted to ask about a freaking truck?"

"Dad," Jared said, "it's okay. Really. It's okay."

Burgess was warming to the kid. Once he'd gotten past his parents' unnecessary defense line, he was doing okay. Not entirely his fault that he'd been raised to be peevish. That was nurture. With luck, he'd find his nature when he stopped living at home.

"It's not about a truck," Burgess said. "It's about who was in that truck. You've heard about the shootings the other night. We've got two people dead, one of them a police officer, and three more officers wounded. The people Jared saw in that truck may be involved. Your son may be a crucial witness in a multiple homicide case."

He turned back to Jared. "You think your friends might have noticed anything else?"

Jared shrugged. "I can't say. It all happened so fast. We were all just trying to get out of there alive, and that girl wouldn't stop screaming, but Jimmy, he was in front with me, he's kind of an artist. You know, like those ones who do the police drawings on TV and stuff? He might be able to do a drawing. I say might. Jimmy's funny. Sometimes he'll do stuff for you and sometimes he'll just blow you off. I don't mean you, Detective, I mean anybody. But you can try."

Burgess had one more thing he wanted to ask Jared. He wanted to show the kid the surveillance picture from the hospital of the woman who had pretended to be Sheryl Timmons. He worried that if he went out the door, he might not get back in.

"I want to get my briefcase from my truck and show you a photograph, see if you recognize the woman. Would that be okay?"

He watched Jared teetering between relief and a desire to see Burgess gone, and curiosity about whether he might get to play an important role in solving one of Portland's worst crimes. He came down on the side of cooperation. "Sure," he said. "Sure. Go get it."

He cast a look at his father. "That's okay, dad, isn't it?"

Reluctantly, his father nodded and Burgess went to get the picture. He just hoped that when he got back to the door, he wouldn't find it locked, and the lights inside turned out.

CHAPTER 23

Even here in this carefully tended neighborhood, the walk felt slimy underfoot in the way dirty old bricks might. Down in the Old Port, there were some cobblestone streets that seemed permanently slicked with beer and vomit. Here, everything was scrubbed clean, but the briny fog touched rich and poor alike. He unlocked the Explorer, leaned in, and took the folder with the pictures Perry had gotten at the hospital from his briefcase.

His phone buzzed in his pocket. He took it out and checked the number. Kyle.

"Hey, Terry. What's up?"

"You got a few minutes?" Kyle sounded agitated.

"For?"

"That guy who called the shots in? Without much help from the wife, I've tracked him to the VFW, where he's drinking with some buddies. Figured I'd rather go in with someone to watch my back. These guys are usually pussycats, but after an evening of drinking, they can be a bit irascible. So, can you back me?"

"Fifteen minutes," Burgess said. "Gotta show a wit Stan's photos from the hospital. Of that fake nurse?"

"I'll be in the parking lot."

He put his phone away and went back to the house. The door was closed, so he rang the bell. And waited. If they made him knit another fucking afghan, there would be hell to pay. He'd only gotten half way through a baby blanket when Jared swung the door open. His cheeks were pink with something—emotion or anger, and he was holding a glass of seltzer with a neat slice of lime.

"Sorry," he said, and led the way back to the family room.

The man with no name was gone. "My mom and dad," he explained. "Well, uh…they were sorta in the middle of a fight when you showed up. I guess they've gone off to finish it."

Burgess took the glass and had a long drink. Just water with bubbles and lime, but it was delicious. Sometimes it was the little things that got you through a day, changed the tenor of an interview. Jared slid a coaster toward him across the smooth dark wood and Burgess parked the glass. "Thanks. I needed that."

He opened the folder and spread out three photos. He should have done a proper ID, maybe a six-pack of photos to see if Jared picked anyone out, but he had other wits, and he planned to find these people and do a formal line-up. Yeah. He planned to find these people.

Jared bent over the photos and Burgess waited. He had places to be, but the kid was cooperating, and it had been a pretty tense situation. The kid might not have had enough clarity to recognize the woman. But then Jared raised his head and gave an affirmative nod. "Yeah. That's her. The woman from the truck. You can even see the little stud in her nose."

Burgess hadn't seen the little stud in her nose, and no one on his team had pointed it out. But for these kids, nose studs were a common accessory, and though it was tiny, it was something Jared would be familiar with.

"A nose stud? You're sure?"

"She was right on top me, Detective. Like we were face-to-face staring at each other. It was tiny, but I could see it.

A nose stud and three earrings in one ear, and a slight chip in her front tooth." He ducked his head. "I know it sounds weird, like how could I possibly see all that, but I thought I was going to die, and somehow…I can't describe it, but it really amplified my vision or something."

Burgess understood pretty well. Eyewitness testimony could be totally off the wall, but there were also those moments of incredible clarity in the midst of awful fear that imbedded things in memory.

He took out a card and gave it to Jared. "Thank you. You've been a great help tonight. If you think of anything else, however small, please call me."

He drained his glass and landed it on the coaster again, then nodded toward the ceiling and the faint rumble of angry voices. "I hope they work it out, whatever it is."

Jared shrugged. "It's chronic. Soon as I finish school, I'm moving out. When they don't have anything else to fight about, they fight about me. You coming here tonight…that'll take them through the rest of the week. She thinks he's too soft on me. He thinks she's too hard. And I think they're both a pain in the ass who should get lives of their own and stop worrying about mine."

Burgess stood. "I hope that girl wasn't under sixteen," he said.

Jared did his father's goosed owl thing. Then he shrugged. "That wasn't me. That was O'Dell."

"You were there. You were driving. Anything happened…and there was a cop following you, you know, that's how I found you…you'd be in it, too. You don't need to take chances like that."

In the kid's surprised nod he could almost hear a faint "Thanks, dad." But he knew. Kids could be stupid. Even good kids could be stupid. Something he needed to talk to Dylan and Nina about. But not tonight.

As he drove out Forest Avenue to meet Kyle, he reviewed what he'd learned tonight from Lucille Radstein and Jared Laukka. Lucille hadn't mentioned the mustache.

Nor had Maddie Morris when she described the couple she'd seen at soccer. Neither of them had mentioned the nose stud, or that the man was a lot bigger than the woman. Was it an oversight, or was the number of players on the bad guys team getting larger? A question for the board but not one he could answer tonight. Tomorrow, he'd find Maddie Morris and stop in to see Lucille at work and show them the surveillance photos of the false Sheryl Timmons.

He sighed, wishing he knew whether they were getting anywhere, then shifted his attention to driving, which was still like navigating through pea soup. As fast as his wipers slapped the stuff away, it coated the windshield again, and the warming air outside made the inside of his windshield fog up as well. He felt like the environment tonight perfectly mirror his internal environment—brief moments of clarity obscured by a lot of confusion.

Finally, his turn loomed up and he pulled into the VFW lot. Found Kyle idling in the back. Almost ten on a Sunday night, there were still a lot of cars in the lot.

He got out and slid into Kyle's car. "How you want to do this?"

"We can just go in," Kyle said. "You are a veteran, after all. Scope things out, then move in on this guy and cut him out of the herd. Hope he's not so drunk he won't be coherent. Guy's name is Kendall Whorter. I was by his place earlier, and man, in the world of bitch wives, his is vying for best in show." Kyle ducked his head. "And I'm kind of an authority on bitch wives."

"Speaking of wives," Burgess said.

"I'm going to marry her," Kyle said. "I'm just not ready yet."

"I was thinking about young Stanley. Think he's gonna wait 'til the baby comes? Lily seems like the kind of decent girl who'd like a ring before she gives birth."

"Haven't got a read on that," Kyle said. "After that business with the Iron Angels, I thought he was ready to jump. They're still together, which is something, given what a horn dog that boy has been. Guess we'll just have to wait and see. At least his disposition has improved. And he loves pulling rabbits out of hats."

"We could use some rabbits. I might have gotten something tonight, following up on Thornton's tip."

Kyle opened his door. "Let's go see if we can get something else. Getting tired of watching my back. Makes it awfully hard to drive."

"Try getting shot," Burgess said, climbing out.

"No thanks. Really. I'd rather not. The girls are freaked out enough already. How are your kids doing?"

"Neddy is oblivious. Nina disappears into her music. Dylan is trying to be the man of the family when I'm not home. Pretty soon he's going to be conducting emergency drills and start asking for a gun. I don't know how you've done this."

"Honestly? Neither do I. I just take it day to day."

Burgess thought about the time when Kyle's ex had threatened to take their girls to Texas and Kyle had taken refuge in a bottle, proving himself exactly the kind of unreliable man his wife claimed he was before Burgess knocked some sense into him. He skimmed over Chris's refusal to marry him. Life wasn't easy or fair. Maybe the best they could do was take it day to day.

They crossed the gravel lot and went inside. The bar was dark and warm and smelled of old beer and cigarettes and burned coffee. Knots of men were gathered at tables or on stools at the bar. There was some country music in the background, and the hum of voices. Burgess paused in the doorway, caught by a momentary desire to belly up to the bar, eat a burger and fries, take his time sipping hot, sweet bourbon in the company of men whose memories matched his.

Ahead of him, Kyle was scanning the crowd, looking for Kendall Whorter. Then he moved forward, aiming for a table in the corner where four men were sitting. *First Gulf War*, Burgess thought. Whorter, facing toward them, was a heavy, genial-looking man with a fireman's mustache and a plaid flannel shirt straining at the buttons. His hands waved like twin flags as he illustrated a story he was telling.

Burgess followed Kyle to the table, hanging back a little, as Kyle made the approach. If Burgess was a bear, Kyle was greyhound, or maybe a wolf. Something lean and fierce and always a little wary. Kyle also moved faster than most people. While another cop might have fumbled out a badge, Kyle's was out of his coat and in his hand without the motion being visible.

"Kendall Whorter?" he said, his voice low so it didn't carry to the rest of the room.

Puzzled, Whorter nodded.

"Detective Kyle, Portland police. About those shots you heard and called in on Friday? Did your wife tell you we've been looking for you?"

Whorter shook his head. "'Bout the only thing my wife bothers to tell me anymore is what a piece of shit I am. You spoke to her, maybe you guessed that?"

He grinned at the other men, who nodded in agreement. Evidently Mrs. Whorter had a reputation.

Kyle nodded toward an empty table. "Wondered if we might speak with you for a minute?" Phrased as a question, meant, and understood, as an order. Whorter pushed back his chair, said, "Later, fellas," to his buddies, and followed Kyle. Burgess followed them.

Kyle was in a chair, notebook out, before Whorter was seated. Kyle clicked his pen and said, "Tell me about Friday afternoon."

"Ain't much to tell," Whorter said. "I was out there at the gas works, making a delivery. Thought I'd have a smoke and ya know…there's about a gazillion signs around there about not smoking, so I went over to the far end of that parking lot, over to that woods road, goes into the old factory there. It's where everyone goes, wants to smoke, you can tell 'cuz the ground there, it's covered with butts. So I'm just standing there…"

He stopped, his eyes going unfocused, while he tried to remember. Then he said, "I gotta back this up a bit. What I was delivering was some building materials, ya know, for some repairs they was doing to one of them buildings down there. And I guess my people had fucked it up. At least, that's what the foreman who'd ordered the stuff said. So it wasn't just one of them quick in and out things, never mind that I had other places to be and other people waitin'. But you know how some people can be. Can't wait 'til Monday even if they ain't gonna use the stuff 'til then, because being right is so fuckin' important."

Another pause. The imp of pain was making Burgess impatient, but Kyle was like a statue. A man with all the time in the world for someone who was willing to give them the whole story. Whorter tapped out a cigarette and lit it with a give-away gas station lighter. Hot pink. Seemed like an odd choice for a guy like Whorter but maybe pink made them harder to lose. When the cancer stick was lit, and Whorter had experienced the ecstasy of that first puff, he went on.

"What I'm tryin' to say is that I was there for a while, cooling my heels while my boss and this contractor worked it out over the phone. So I saw that car, looked like an unmarked, arrive and that guy in the suit heading into the woods."

Melia.

"Got any idea what time that was?" Kyle asked.

Whorter considered. "Two. Two-thirty. Around then. Because I remember looking at my watch and the rest of my load and wondering how long it was gonna be before those two assholes got things sorted out and I could go make my next delivery."

"When did you hear the shots?"

"That'd be around three. When I got sicka waiting on those guys and went to have a smoke. First there was just the one shot. I thought I'd heard a shot but it coulda been a backfire. I looked back over the parking lot to see if anyone else had noticed it, but that construction boss was still on the phone and my boss hadn't called me to say I could unload what I'd brought and leave, so I lit up another—nothin' better to do—and that's when I heard the second shot."

The shot downstairs and then the one when Melia was in the chair? Or maybe Melia was shot and then propped in the chair.

"About how long between those two shots?"

"Between them two?" Whorter considered. "I'd say maybe about five minutes. Five. Seven. Not long but it wasn't no double tap. So I called it in and then my boss called and said to unload what I'd brought. I was doing that when the first cop car came. Ya know, the first guy was in a suit, and this guy, he was in uniform. He parked and headed down that road."

Aucoin, Burgess figured. He'd had time to reach the building, while Randy Crossman was gunned down on the road. He felt a flare of anger as he thought of that senseless death. Just a kid doing his job. His anger was rising but his impatience was gone. Whorter was a cop's dream witness.

"You hear any more shots?" Kyle asked.

"Yeah. I didn't call them in 'cuz I'd already called in the earlier ones. But a while after that first uniformed cop walked down the road, I heard another one. I dunno. Guess I figured he'd found a bad guy. And that if he had, place was gonna be swarmin' with cops and the road would be blocked and I'd better get out while I could."

Burgess liked Kendall Whorter. Just a straight shooter who let it all hang out. Quite a contrast to Jared Laukka's family. It took all kinds to make a world.

"Did you see the second police car arrive?" he asked.

"Yeah. He came tearing in just as I finished unloading."

"Just those three shots? That's all you heard?" Kyle asked.

Whorter shook his head. "There was a fourth one, just as I was leaving."

"Rifle shots? Shotgun? Can you tell the difference?" Kyle asked.

Whorter looked around the room. "We're sitting in a VFW and you're asking me that?" He grinned and said, "Rifle."

So none of those shots was Pelham. Burgess made a mental note to check the file, see if they knew how long

Richard Pelham had been dead. Think about who might have been around to hear that shot.

"But you didn't talk to those police officers you saw drive in, tell them what you'd heard?" Kyle asked.

"Maybe I should of, but I was back over by my truck, finishin' up, and you know how far it is across that lot. Anyways, that second guy was out of the car and away almost before I'd seen him. I'd of had to chase after him. Which, I'm sorry to say, given what happened out there, that I don't guess I'd of liked to do. Not..." His eyes took in the room again, "that I'm any kind of a coward."

It wasn't the kind of thing they asked of civilians anyway. "Do you think, given the distance across that lot, that anyone at the gas works or working that construction project might have heard the shots?" Burgess said, thinking that in the morning the Aucoin brothers would be checking that out.

"I dunno. They seemed pretty loud to me, them shots. Loud and outta place. But a lotta people, a chopper could land right beside them and they'd go right on yakking, so you'd have to ask them. Guys sawing and hammering, they might not of heard. I was just about on my way out then, when I heard that fourth shot, so I don't know if there was any more shooting. Places to go. Stuff to do. I had to be done by five because we had to go to my bitch wife's bitch mother's for dinner and we couldn't be late or I'd never hear the end of it. And I had the radio on."

He paused. "You ever get a call about shots fired out by my place, figure it's me, putting an end to my misery."

Kyle nodded. "We like to suggest less radical solutions, Mr. Whorter."

Whorter snorted. "Less radical solutions. I like that. Least, this time of year, I've got fishing. Them fish never argue and they never talk back. I ain't never been nagged by a fish. Fought with a few of 'em, though."

"You see anyone else coming or going who didn't look like they belonged there. Belong to that business?" Kyle said.

"I didn't notice anyone other than them cops."

But Whorter was a good observer, a person who drove all day and knew what was normal and what was not. Now he hesitated.

"There was that girl in the truck," he said. "Only she wasn't in the lot. I passed her up on the road as I was leaving. So she could have been anybody, doing anything. I only noticed her because she didn't look like she belonged in a truck like that."

"A truck like what?" Burgess said.

"Big ass black Ford F-150 pickup with a shitload of custom chrome. Mostly them are driven by guys. Guys who put their whole paychecks into 'em. And more besides. She was a little thing, could barely see over the wheel, but she pulled outta that side road and took off like a bat outta hell. You know them things ain't the easiest to drive."

"I don't suppose you noticed the license?" Burgess said.

Whorter shrugged. "Nope. All's I can say is it was a vanity plate. Ya know. Some stupid thing or other. I kinda think it had the word dog in it. Top Dog, maybe?"

Whorter might be just a guy who drove a delivery truck and was grabbing a smoke, but he was a heck of a good witness, because he was looking around him while he went through his day. And he'd called in those shots, which no one else had bothered to do. The irony being that if he hadn't, Aucoin wouldn't have gotten shot and Crossman wouldn't have died. But Melia would have.

A crappy set of choices.

Kyle looked at him. "You got any more questions, Joe?"

Burgess considered. "Two. You say you saw the guy in the suit who came in the unmarked arrive. Did he seem to be in a hurry?"

"If you mean was he driving fast, then no. But if you mean did he seem uptight like he was maybe heading into something bad? Like if he was nervous, then yeah. You know how people are—they kinda lean into it, like they don't wanna go so they have to kinda drive themselves to do it? He looked like he was bracing himself for something he didn't wanna do but he had to." Whorter hesitated. "Like when you go out on a mission that you know could go bad, but you haven't got a choice?"

Burgess could picture it. He'd seen Melia heading for the chief's office just like that many times. "You get a good enough look at that girl in the truck so you could describe her?"

"Nah. It was only for a second. Dark haired. Small. That's all I can tell you."

"That's it for me, Terry," he said. "You have more questions?"

Kyle shook his head. "You've been a great help, Mr. Whorter. We appreciate it. There's just one more thing." One of Kyle's rare smiles, and then, "Please don't shoot your wife."

"Wasn't planning to," Whorter said, getting up and stretching, entirely comfortable having a chat with the police. "More like shooting myself. But not while the fishin's this good. I got me three of the prettiest little brownies you've ever seen yesterday. We had 'em for breakfast this morning."

They left Whorter and headed out into the night, now carrying a lot more stuff to assess in the morning, and a new list of people to see and things to do. Right at the top would be finding that truck.

CHAPTER 24

W hen he got home, Chris was in the living room, the room dark except for the pool of light she sat in, reading a book. Otherwise, the house was quiet. She was wearing a blue robe and he noticed that the toenails of the feet she had tucked up beside her were a matching blue. She saw where his gaze was going and smiled. "Nina thought I needed a little tarting up."

He dropped into a chair, wanting to be good company and companionable, but feeling like he was running on empty. Sometimes it was like she could read his mind, because she looked up from her book and said, "Don't worry about it. I don't need conversation. I just like having you here."

"Long day," he said. "I think that sandwich saved my life."

She smiled.

Watching her smile always did him in. It would start small, like the edge of a rising sun peeping over the horizon, and then broaden until her whole face was alight with it. He'd never understand why her first husband had let her go. Why anyone would let a woman like her go. She was like a fire he could sit by and be warmed. He'd never stop regretting that his mother didn't get to meet her. She would have loved Chris. She would have been so comforted by the idea that he had a good woman in his life.

"Alana called," she said.

His breath caught. He had nothing to give to a troubled ex-hooker right now, and Alana was just a walking ball of emotions. She was so needy dealing her was draining when he was at the top of his game.

Chris held up her hands in a calming gesture. "It's okay, Joe. She's not in trouble. She saw you'd been shot and she was worried about you. I told her you were out chasing bad guys and she said it would take more than one bullet to keep you down."

She watched closely until he relaxed, then said, "I told her when this is over she should come to dinner. She wants to meet the kids."

"That will be an interesting event."

He wondered how he'd explain his relationship with Alana to his kids. He'd met Alana Black when he'd found her beaten and bloody in a city park, victim of a message delivered by some rival hookers who thought her sexy beauty was ruining their business. Only sixteen—and so scared and alone. He'd taken her to the hospital and then to his sister's to recover. It had taken longer to get her off the streets, but as far as he knew, she'd completed a massage therapy program and was using her skills at reading people's bodies and what they needed in a more socially acceptable way. It had been a while since he'd checked in, though. He'd been kind of busy.

Sixteen, he thought. Dylan's age. He'd expected a lot of her. No wonder she'd backslid. Had trouble taking charge of her life.

"Hello?" Chris said, a teasing note in her voice. "I heard you've been shot. How are you doing?"

"I could use a little care," he said.

That got him another smile.

"I know a good nurse," she said.

"I know a good nurse, too. I wonder if she's available?"

"I think she might be." Chris closed her book, stood, and held out her hand. "Let's go see what we can do."

He hung up his coat while she got out her supplies. Then he sat on the edge of the bed while she helped him out of his shirt, his vest, and his tee shirt, her hands warm and gentle. "This is going to hurt," she said, pulling off the bandage. She inspected the wound. "Looks okay, Joe. I was afraid you'd go out there and pop some stitches."

"Tried to stay out of trouble," he said, wrapping his arms around her waist and pulling her against him.

"I am trying to provide medical care," she said.

"I'm trying to get cared for so I can take you to bed."

"Really?" she said, tearing open some packages and laying gauze pads over the wound. "I thought guys your age were supposed to be slowing down?"

"And I thought women were supposed to like guys who went slower."

Outside the bedroom door, a floorboard creaked. Then there was a cautious knock on the door. "We're decent," Chris said.

Burgess didn't think his exposed torso was very decent, but he was at a point where he couldn't scramble around for clothing.

The door opened and Nina stuck her head in. "Do we have any glue sticks? I need one for a project."

"Try the second drawer in the living room desk," Chris said. "I think I saw one there."

"Thanks," Nina said, but she didn't go. "Does it hurt a lot, Joe?"

He considered a range of replies. His normal response was "I've had worse," but he figured that while he wanted to strike a careful balance about not worrying his family, he also believed in telling the truth. "It's pretty sore," he said.

"Good thing you've got Chris," she said. A hesitation. "We've got Chris." And she left, closing the door quietly behind her.

"I think I like having a daughter," he said. "Kyle says it's the best."

"That wasn't about a glue stick," Chris said. "It's about needing to see you. Needing to know you're okay. When she's doing okay, it's easy to forget that this is a little girl who saw her dad kill her mother. Who blames herself for almost getting her little brother killed because she made a bad decision. She doesn't think she's worthy of love, or of having a family. We have to remember that."

God. He was better at remembering his care-taking duties with strangers than with his own family. Nina was right. They were all lucky they had Chris.

"I like having a family," he said.

She smiled and finished her ministrations. The word ministrations brought back Kyle's remark. Burgess might be an ugly, angry, sad old bear, but somehow ministrations always put him in a better frame of mind.

He finished undressing. "In the mood for some ministrations?" he said.

"I could be persuaded."

And she was.

After, like the lout that he was, he fell asleep. A dreamless sleep at first, but that never lasted. Around two he woke from a dream where he was being chased down an endless road by a monster black truck decked out with absurd amounts of chrome, including a massive set of chrome wings. He knew where this was going. One bad dream would follow another and pretty soon he'd been back in the worst of the dreams—the murder of little Kristen Marks. It was where his bad dreams always went, right to the body of the little girl for whom he hadn't been able to get justice.

He got up and went into the kitchen. He wasn't hungry but still clung to the myth his own life had disproven numerous times that maybe if he drank some warm milk he'd be able to get back to sleep. He took out the milk and a coffee mug. Then shook his head and put it away. Got out the Jack Daniels and poured a short drink. He sat in the living room in the dark and did a little self-medicating. His shrink had made it clear that this was a bad course, but sometimes it was the only course.

Forty minutes later, he was able to go back to bed and sleep. He woke with a head full of lists and the surprising realization that he'd never gotten a call back from Captain Cote. He lay there listening to the usual Monday morning chaos. Neddy wanted to take his decomposed seagull to school. Nina couldn't find her favorite shirt. Dylan had forgotten to print out his homework. With amazing calm and grace, Chris sorted them, fed them, calmed them, and appeared by his bedside with a smile. "Got time to drive Dylan to school?"

Something that had started as a chore and now was one of the highlights of his day. "Sure," he said, pushing off the pillow and throwing back the covers.

She grinned at his morning erection. "Thought we took care of that last night?"

"All I have to do is think of you."

"Idiot." She started pulling clothes out of drawers. "He's waiting," she said. "You need any help getting dressed?"

He sat up slowly. He'd learned not to leap up the hard way, back when he was such a macho cop that nothing could keep him down. Leapt up more than once and fallen on his ass, making the hurt worse. Now, sometimes at least, he was smart enough to take help when it was offered. He sat on the edge of the bed and put his shoulder through its paces. Not good. It was a miserable fact of aging that he didn't heal as fast as he used to.

"Help," he said.

He felt like a toddler, having his arm threaded through his tee shirt, his vest strapped on and his arm worked through his shirt sleeve, but it meant he wouldn't use up energy he'd need later, trying to put himself together without help.

She pulled his jacket from the closet, shaking her head as she passed it to him. "Somebody I know needs a new wardrobe."

"I was waiting 'til I lost some weight."

"Cold day in hell," she muttered.

"Not fair," he protested. "I've lost almost twenty pounds."

"So go buy yourself some clothes."

"No time."

"Make time. Not long now 'til people start giving you money on the street, you're getting that shabby."

"I hear they make good money, those beggars at all the intersections. Maybe it's time for a job change?"

"There's December," she said. "And January, February, March, and April. And don't forget November."

"So I'll only work six months a year."

He unlocked his gun, checked it, grabbed his badge, cuffs and flashlight, and shuffled into the kitchen, remembering the days when the house, and his mornings were his own. Nina was already gone, taking Neddy with her. Dylan was lounging against the counter. He held out a go cup of coffee. "Gotta go, dad, I'm going to be late."

"Gotta run," Chris said, giving him a quick kiss and rushing down the stairs. He and Dylan followed. It was another gray day, though a lighter gray than yesterday.

"You sure you should be working today?" his son said, making him feel about a thousand years old.

"Somebody has to catch the bad guys."

"Right." Dylan was about to put in earbuds and disappear into his music, then he dragged his backpack onto his lap, fished around, and pulled out a sheet of paper. "My English teacher wants to know if you'll come in and talk to some of the kids about what it's like to be a cop. She says there's no rush, we've got the rest of the year, she knows you're pretty busy right now. Just when you can."

"Nobody at your school wants to be a cop. And their parents definitely don't want them to join the police."

"I want to be a cop."

Burgess put a finger to his lips. "Shh. Don't tell anyone."

"Seriously. She's a great person and she wouldn't ask if she didn't mean it. She not one of those nicey-nice bullshit you types."

"Language," Burgess said. "What's her name?"

"Well…" Dylan said. "Marcia. And I'm sure she has a last name…it's probably on the note…but she just says to call her Marcia the Magnanimous. I think it's to make us ask what that means, but maybe it's just because she really is magnanimous. You play fair with her and she'll give you a break nearly every time. Which is not how most of them are."

There was a dark note in his son's voice. Dylan was settling in well, but he'd already had a run-in with a couple of the teachers for coming to the defense of a Muslim girl who was being picked on. Burgess saw history repeating itself. Saw his son, partly because of his size as well as his personality, being a defender of those who were weaker or smaller.

"Tell her I'm not sure I've got anything English students will be interested in, but I'm happy to do it once we get through this…" He searched for words. Clusterfuck wasn't a word he wanted his son to be using, and he was supposed to be a role model. Shitstorm wasn't any better. He settled for case, though it felt like too small a word for what was happening.

Burgess was watching the street. It was a habit. It was also a sensible thing to do when there were bad guys out there gunning for cops.

His son was watching him. "What are you looking for, dad?"

It wasn't a snarky 'why aren't you paying attention to me' comment. Dylan was curious.

"Anything out of the ordinary," Burgess said. "Who's on the street. How people are driving. Someone who might have a gun. The way people are interacting. People in trouble. Bad guys I recognize. We like to give them a friendly little wave, just to let them know we've seen them." He shrugged. "All the stuff I've learned from doing this for thirty years."

"Okay," Dylan said, still not disappearing into his music. "Show me something."

"All right."

Burgess studied the street. It was early in the day for bad guys to be out, but some of them might still be up. He pointed to a ragged man who staggered slightly as he walked. "That man there has been living on the streets for about fifteen years. He lost his wife and daughter in a truck crash. He was driving and he was drunk. He killed them and he's never gotten over it. We've put him in shelters. He's been through programs. People have done everything they can for him, but he can't get past his guilt over what he did. It's kind of a long, slow form of suicide."

He realized that what was part of normal for him was awfully dark for a teenage kid on his way to Catholic school. He looked around for something else, something more positive. But what he'd learned to spot wasn't the positive. It was the negative, the damaged, the dark, the potentially explosive.

Even as he thought that, something small and fast and pink dashed between two parked cars and right out in front of him. He jammed on his brakes, the Explorer shuddering and skidding as it came to a stop just inches from the tiny girl who'd run into the street. Heart pounding, he jammed the truck into park and hurried to where a toddler girl in footie pajamas lay in the street, crying.

He picked her up, checking her for injuries, and carried her to the sidewalk, looking around for a parent. Except for two boys in uniforms that matched Dylan's, there was no one on the street.

Holding her gingerly, as her diaper was badly in need of changing, he turned to his son, who stood beside him, a shocked expression on his face.

"This is what I look for," he said.

They were a few blocks from Dylan's school. "You'd better walk," he said. "I'm going to have to stay here and find out who this child belongs to."

Dylan went back to the truck and grabbed his backpack. As he passed, he put a hand on Burgess's good shoulder. "Jeez, and you think you have nothing to talk about?" He swung the pack onto his back and hurried away.

CHAPTER 25

Still holding the girl, expecting at any moment that a hysterical mother would burst out of a nearby door in anxious search of her missing child, he went to the back of the truck, where he kept emergency supplies, and fumbled, one handed, for a blanket. He wrapped it around the sodden girl, a probably futile effort to comfort her and save his last jacket. Then he dialed his phone, one handed, and asked for some backup from patrol.

He couldn't leave her unattended and he didn't have time to sort this out.

First on the scene, bandbox perfect as always, was the woman they called their "kiddie cop," Andrea Dwyer. Dwyer worked with the city's teens, and she was amazingly good at it. Amazingly good to look at, too. Something Burgess always appreciated. He wasn't a sexist pig, he just liked beauty. Dwyer, tall, lean, and fit, was beautiful.

She swung to the curb, jumped out of her cruiser, and came up to him with a big grin. "Parenthood looks good on you, Joe."

"Don't even joke about it, Dwyer. I think three is enough."

"I heard. So much for the monkish life, huh?" Dwyer held out her arms for the child. "She's awfully cute, though. How old do you think? Eighteen months? Two?"

Burgess had no idea.

As he passed the child to her, she wrinkled her nose. "Somebody needs a diaper change."

"It's not me," he said.

"Fill me in," she said, as she reached in through her passenger window, into her bag, and brought out a green rubber frog, which she gave to the child. A small, dirty hand gripped the frog and the little girl stuffed one dangling leg into her mouth, while solemn brown eyes stared at Dwyer.

He told her what had happened. "No sign of a parent. I hate to do this to you, but I've got a team meeting and—"

"You don't have to explain to me. We all want that shooter caught. Anxiety among patrol is off the charts, as I guess you know. You call Human Services yet?"

He shook his head. He'd been expecting a parent to appear.

"Okay. I'll take care of it." She made a shooing motion with her free hand. "Go on. Get out of here. I'll let you know what happens."

When he hesitated, she said, "Joe. Trust me. I'll let you know what happens. Go catch bad guys."

Feeling like he'd just added another unfinished thing to his too full plate, he climbed back in the truck and headed for 109.

It was after nine when he reached the conference room, and a room full of disapproving eyes watched his entrance like he'd been out eating donuts and making daisy chains. There were donuts on the table—he figured Sage Prentiss for those, guilt for being unavailable yesterday—and a large Dunkin's coffee sat before his empty chair.

"Sorry," he said. "Escaped toddler ran out in front of my car and I couldn't find a parent."

"So you left the kid on the sidewalk?" Kyle said.

"I left her with Dwyer."

He dropped into his chair and snagged a donut, then looked around the table. Stan Perry was vibrating in his chair, so Burgess figured the lad had another rabbit for them. He let Perry cool his heels while he filled them in on what he'd learned from Maddie Morris, Lucille Radstein, and Jared Laukka.

"Once I got the parents out of the way, the kid opened up. Right down to a nose stud, three ear piercings, and a chipped front tooth."

Then he let Kyle describe their interview with Kendall Whorter.

He told them Dani's theory about the shoe impressions, and how it fit with the possibility of two shooters and the witnesses' statements about two people and a big black truck.

"I don't know if we're being jerked around, like Dani's theory about the shoes suggests. I don't know if there are two shooters and whether those shooters are using two different vehicles or if that car on Melia's street is even connected. We don't know if it even existed. But we need to carry Stan's surveillance pictures around to Maddie Morris, and see if the woman looks like the one she saw at Gina Melia's soccer games. Track down the kids who were with Laukka in the car and get their stories."

He looked around and realized that Rocky Jordan hadn't joined them. Figured he could put Rocky on the task of looking for a vanity plate on a black Ford F-150 with the letters T, D, O, and G on it. Or the word dog. It was just the kind of needle in a haystack task that Rocky liked. Once Rocky gave them the data on Melia's phone, that was. He still needed to know what had taken Melia down there, had sent him purposefully, if reluctantly, to meet someone in such an out of the way place.

He had more to cover but figured he'd made Perry wait long enough. "Stan? You've got something for us?"

Perry grinned, showing the special pleasure he always did when he'd put something together, and flipped open a folder. He took out some pages and passed them around.

Burgess looked at it. A booking photo of a man, and a booking sheet, with some other pages attached. On one of the back pages, there was a photo of the same guy, this time with a black eye patch.

"This guy," Perry said. "Karl Maloof. Got out of Warren about a month ago. Did six years for molesting a four-year-old child, taking nasty pictures of it, and sharing them on the net. It was one of Vince's cases. Guy was a photographer. Rather a brilliant one, from what I read. Now maybe not so much. He doesn't see so well since he got into with someone inside over whether it was okay to take naked pictures of other people's children and sell them to perverts. Other guy rather strongly reinforced his negative opinion of that behavior with a pen in Maloof's eye."

Burgess looked at the photos. No way this was their shooter. None of their wits had mentioned an eye patch. And no one could have missed it. He waited impatiently for Perry to get to the point. When Perry had something, he liked to amp up the drama by stringing it out.

"We're not getting any younger here, Stan," Kyle said. "You wanna make this relevant?"

Though they already had copies, Perry now gave them new copies of the woman from the surveillance video, the one who had impersonated Sheryl Timmons at the hospital. Then he waited for them to see it.

"Brother and sister?" Burgess said.

"Twins," Perry said. "Karla and Karl."

"We know where Karla can be found?"

Perry shook his head.

"And this is relevant because?"

"Karl Maloof had the sister, Karla, and a brother, Kris. The three of them were very tight. You said look into people who might have a hard-on for Vince, and this trio definitely does. At the time of her twin's arrest and during the trial, Karla Maloof was very vocal about her brother being innocent, railroaded by the cops, and that what police were labeling pornography were just art shots. She told the paper that her brother was a brilliant artist being targeted by philistines who couldn't understand what he was doing so they had to destroy him."

He put down his papers. "First I ever heard that photos of a four-year-old sucking some guy's dick is art. Anyway, Karla and her little brother Kris made no bones about being angry and much of that anger was directed very specifically at Vince. It seems unlikely that their views have been improved by what happened to Karl in prison."

"So you think this might be revenge? The brother and sister, if not Maloof himself?"

Perry nodded.

"But," Burgess said, "we don't know where Karla Maloof is these days?"

"Nope."

"What about the brother? Kris?"

"I'm working on it."

"Got a photo, at least?" Burgess leaned forward. If Perry had a picture, it was something else to show their witnesses.

"I'm working on it."

So Perry had jumped the gun. Brought out the hat before stocking it with bunnies.

"And Karl?"

"That's what got me interested," Perry said. "When I spoke with his PO, it turns out he hasn't been checking in. Karl Maloof, out of prison only a month, is in the wind."

"Friends? Relatives? Wife? Ex-wife? Have you got anything to help locate him?"

Perry looked deflated, like his rabbit should have been enough. "Still working on that, Joe. I'll swing by the address Maloof gave his PO when we're done here. Get Rocky working on seeing if he can find the twin, Karla, or Kris Maloof. I'm working off recent stuff and old newspaper reports. Case file's in storage. Maybe we can get it sometime in the next year or so."

"Well, keep working. It looks like a good lead."

Perry nodded and moved to the edge of his chair, vibrating like a hunting dog on a scent. He couldn't wait to be let off leash and sent out to chase more rabbits. Burgess let him go. Gave Kyle the names of Jared Laukka's friends to follow up with. He lumbered back to his desk to write some reports, update the case files, and check in with Lt. Shaheen and see if the canvass of Melia's street had yielded any results.

The Maloofs looked like a good lead, if they could be found. But what could she, or anyone, possibly have said that would have made Vince go down to that factory building alone? What threat or plea or ploy could someone have used? Melia was a careful, thorough cop. He didn't do careless or impulsive things.

So much about this case was a puzzle. If someone wanted to target Melia, why shoot other cops? If someone wanted to kill cops, why kill Richard Pelham, and why in such a dramatic way? Could they possibly have thought the cops would buy the scenario left at the warehouse? And if they were supposed to believe that Pelham had done the killings, why shoot at him at the hospital? Were they smart and cagy or crazy and impulsive? Had they planned the first op and then gotten some kind of blood lust? Had killing cops been so exciting they wanted to go on doing it?

Or what if that had been plan A, and then Burgess had pushed some button that made them think he needed to be gotten out of the way? Too bad he didn't know what button.

Back at his desk, he checked his phone and his message slips. Plenty of people wanted to see him. None of them was Captain Paul Cote. He went out to the small office where their assistants sat. They were usually up to date on department gossip. "What's up with Captain Cote?" he said.

Both women shrugged.

"You want me to call down, see what's going on?" one of them offered. Janice, the new girl. Bright brown eyes and a cute sprinkling of freckles that had patrol guys hanging around her desk like flies around honey.

"Sure. That would be good. It's just odd, you know. He hasn't called me since yesterday morning. I thought he might be sick or something."

"Or something would be my guess. But he's always something." Janice was new, still getting used to their ways, but she'd caught onto Cote right away. "I'll see what I can find out."

Burgess thanked her and went to find Shaheen. Not hearing from Cote left him vaguely uneasy. Cote was a bureaucrat. A number cruncher. Paper pusher. But someone targeting cops might not know that. Might have seen the captain at the hospital acting important, or on the news, and decided he'd make a good target.

The captain didn't live in Portland. He lived in Falmouth. It could be something as ordinary as one of Cote's pet dogs being sick or despite multiple attacks on cops, Cote had taken a sick day. Depending on what Janice learned, Burgess thought he might take a ride up there later and check things out.

Shaheen was his usual genial self, but he didn't look rested. "It's bad out there, Joe," he said. "My guys are jumpy. We don't catch the shooter soon, I'm afraid there's gonna be an incident. Somebody going off half-cocked and shooting before they think. I've warned them. Be careful. Follow protocol. Call for backup if anything seems off. But with one of their own dead and two still in the hospital, I don't blame them for being antsy."

"It's in the air, Jim. Everybody's feeling it. This damned fog isn't helping, either. Harder to do the job when you can't see what's coming at you."

Shaheen was sorting thought some papers on his desk. "You're here about the canvass? It's the usual. Mostly a whole lot of nothing. A couple of complaints about that guy with the fence—Radstein—acting weird, moving cars around, people coming and going at strange hours, yelling at people who park near his house, but that's par for the course over there. Radstein's always at war with his neighbors."

He handed Burgess a stack of papers. "Maybe you'll find something in here that I'm not seeing." He sighed and asked the question he'd been trying not to ask. "You guys close?"

Burgess shrugged, and then regretted it as his shoulder reminded him it wanted peace and quiet. "Closer than we were yesterday. We've stirred up some wits who may put us on a good track."

He changed the subject, because it was still on his mind, and maybe to put off going back out into the fog a bit longer. "You hear anything about that little girl who ran into the street this morning?"

Shaheen shook his head like the incident amazed him. He was a bullet-headed man with a military gray crew-cut. Mostly he was genial, but responding to Burgess's question, his face tightened in anger. "People ought to have to get a license before they're allowed to have kids."

"So you found the parents?"

"Found the dad, if you can call him that. Mom was at work, dad was supposed to get the girl up and dressed and give her breakfast, then take her to daycare on his way to work. Only dad decided it would be more fun to smoke a little weed with his friends and blow off work, and forgot there was even a kid in the house. She hadn't been fed or dressed or had her diaper changed from the night before. Seems after they'd smoked a while he and his buddies decided they were hungry, so they went out for breakfast, leaving the door open and the baby behind."

Shaheen ran a hand over his bristly hair. "You shoulda seen Dwyer. She was livid. I tell you. I would never want her mad at me. She looks so nice, you know, and she's so calm and easy to work with. Well, I guess she rang doorbells until someone told her who the kid belonged to, then she tracked him down and gave him what for."

"Do tell," Burgess said, because he loved Dwyer stories. Loved the way she cared about Portland's kids.

"Well, maybe this shouldn't get around, 'cuz you know how everyone these days is crying police brutality, but the guys who were there said it was pretty funny. I guess she musta taken the time to change that poor little thing, cleaned her up and then handed her off to human services. Once the kid was safe, she went down to the donut shop where the dad and his friends were hanging, and she took that dirty diaper with her. Seems she marched in there and called out his name, and when the guy says, in that charming way our youth have of responding to authority, 'what the fuck do you want?' Dwyer shoved that shitty diaper right in the guy's face and rubbed it around 'til he opened his mouth to shout for help."

"I wish I'd seen it."

"Me, too. Then she cuffed him and arrested him, and brought him in with that mess all over his face, him going on the whole time asking what was it about. Guess the diaper wasn't a good enough clue. I tell you, Joe. I wouldn't mess with Dwyer."

Shaheen went solemn, thinking about his own kids. "Sad for the kid, though."

Burgess thought about his kids, how hard he and Chris worked to undo the damage that had been done. How easy it was to slip and forget, as Chris had reminded him last night. About so many kids over the years. Beaten kids. Exploited kids. Murdered kids. Little Timmy Watts and Kristin Marks. It was such a rough world to be a kid in.

Burgess picked up the printout, thinking there might still be something there. Like Shaheen said, his guys didn't know all the facts.

His phone buzzed. He pulled it out and looked at it. Janice, so he answered.

"I checked downstairs. No one has heard from him, Joe," she said.

Burgess went cold all over.

CHAPTER 26

Back in the detective's bay, Kyle was bent over, making come-hither gestures as he tried to coax the world's slowest printer to spit out addresses and other information for the names Burgess had gotten from Jared Laukka.

Burgess spread Shaheen's printout on his desk, but he couldn't concentrate. "Shaheen says the patrol guys are jumpy as crickets."

Kyle nodded. "I'm thinking it's only a matter of time before shots are fired. By us. By someone who's so spooked he or she forgets all their training. Too bad we can't get that message out to the bad guys. Tell 'em to lay low for a while."

"The bad guys are always laying low. That's why we call 'em low lifes."

Kyle spread his hands. "Still. Be nice to catch our bad guys. Bring the anxiety levels back down. Bring Terry Kyle's anxiety level back down. That damned fog doesn't help. Makes people a lot more nervous when they can't see anything and don't know where what they're hearing is coming from. The girls are doing okay but Michelle is a basket case. This goes on much longer, I think she'll pull the girls out of school and get out of town for a while."

Burgess was still thinking about Cote. "I haven't had any calls or messages from Cote since yesterday, Ter, and he didn't come in today."

"You sound worried. I should think that was good news?"

"Ordinarily, it would be. But right now, with someone targeting cops, I have to wonder: what if something's happened to him?"

Kyle snatched up the emerging papers and reached for his jacket. "Why would someone target him? He's not a detective. He's not even a cop. He's a pencil pusher. A number cruncher. He's so out of practice at being a policeman he wouldn't notice a bad guy camped on his own front steps."

"True. But he's such a media hound that he's stamped his face all over this thing. In the paper, at news conferences, at the hospital. If the bad guys didn't know, they'd think he was the lead detective. He's made himself a perfect target."

"So if you're worried, get Falmouth cops to do a wellness check."

It was the sensible thing to do. They had too much on their plates to take time out for a field trip to Falmouth. But Burgess was a control freak. If something had happened to Captain Cote, he wanted to be first on the scene. He didn't want to arrive after a bunch of Lookie Loos had already tromped through it. And crazy as it was, he had a strong sense that something was wrong. He'd learned to trust his instincts when they were this strong.

"Look. If it's bothering you, call downstairs and get his landline number," Kyle said. "Then you can have the pleasure of calling up and disturbing him at home, which will endear you to him even more than you already are. It's probably something wrong with one of those rats that he thinks are dogs. One of the little darlings is sickypoo and daddy had to take it to the vet."

Cote had a pair of tiny dogs that did look like rats, animals he treated far better than the police officers he was in charge of who put their lives on the line every day. CID had had a photo of Cote kissing one of the disgusting creatures up on their bulletin board until Melia made them take it down. Melia was just trying to keep them out of trouble. The photo had migrated to the men's room on their floor, a place that Cote had never yet entered. Once it was out of public view, Melia had given up.

Kyle's advice was good, so Burgess called the captain's assistant.

"Normally, I wouldn't give this out, Joe. He's particular about that. But he hasn't called in, and he always calls when he's going to be out. Or late. Or is delayed. You know how he is. Look, will you let me know if you reach him? We're feeling kind of spooked down here."

He wrote down the number and picked up the phone. The phone rang ten times without an answering machine picking up. Cote didn't answer. Then Burgess tried his cell and went straight to voicemail.

Burgess's uneasiness increased. He stared at the printout without seeing it. Finally he gave up. "I'm driving out there, Ter. I'll be useless until I know for sure that he's okay."

"You don't even like him."

"That's putting it mildly. It's not about him, Ter. It's about what he represents. The uniform. The rank. That's part of us. If something has happened, that's what they'd be attacking."

"Then I'm coming with you." Kyle grabbed his jacket, checking for his badge, his gun, and his cuffs. A gesture as automatic as a Catholic crossing himself. Then they headed out into the gray day.

The unending fog must have been having a negative effect on people's charitable impulses. As they turned left on the Franklin Arterial, Burgess noticed that there were far fewer people begging at the intersection.

Kyle, good at reading his mind, said, "Maybe there's a beggars' convention. Strategies for Successful Panhandling. You know, they all gather in some church hall and expert speakers come in and talk to them about how best to word their signs, good materials to use to make durable signs, and the dress code to adopt to appeal the widest number of donors. Urge them to wrap duct tape around their perfectly good shoes. To go out of sight when they want to smoke."

"You are such a cynic, Terry."

"I am such a realist, Joe. That's all. So since we're going for a ride and we don't want to talk about people shooting cops, or speculate about our theories of this freakin' case, maybe you can tell me a story?"

"Got a good one that involves the divine Andrea Dwyer."

"She is divine." Kyle settled back in his seat. "Do tell."

"Okay. So this morning, I was driving Dylan to school…"

"Don't tell me your son is in trouble with the kiddie cop?"

"My son is an exemplary human being—this week— except for a recently expressed desire to become a cop like his dad. So we're driving down the street and suddenly there's this moving blur of pink and a tiny kid comes darting out between two cars. I think I missed her by inches. Little girl, toddler, in pink footie pajamas. So I picked up her, all reeking and soggy—the poor thing obviously hadn't been changed in hours—and looked around for a parent. No one in sight. I sent Dylan on to school and called patrol to come and handle it. Dwyer was first on the scene."

"A lovely sight on a lousy morning."

"Too true. So I wrapped the little girl in a blanket and handed her off to Dwyer. I got the rest of the story from Shaheen. Seems Dwyer beats on doors until she finds out who the kid belongs to, cleans her up and hands her off to Human Services. Then she takes that reeking, shitty diaper down to the coffee shop where the dad who forgot he had a kid is hanging with his homies—and she rubs his face in it. Literally."

Kyle sighed. "I so wish I had seen that."

"So do we all."

They were silent after that. Enjoying one of those moments suspended in time, where they were between tasks and could just breathe, and think, and watch the world go by. What little of it they could see. Normally, Burgess liked driving, it was good thinking time, and he was always comfortable in Kyle's company. But today, despite the respite from to do lists and phone calls, he couldn't fall into his easy flow.

After a few miles, Kyle said, "You really think something's wrong, don't you."

Not a question. A statement. Then they were off the highway and looking for Cote's street. Then for his house. The ebbing and flowing fog was socking in again, so dense they couldn't see from one mailbox to another as they crawled down a deserted suburban street.

"Here," Kyle said.

Burgess pulled to the curb.

A long, curved driveway snaked away from them through immaculate green lawn and disappeared behind some evergreens.

"Great setup for privacy," Kyle said.

"Great setup for bad guys."

"Right. How you want to do this?"

Burgess had no idea. If they just went up the drive and the bad guys were there, they were too exposed to people who were very adept with rifles. That wasn't a good plan. If they went up the driveway and Cote was home and he was fine, Burgess would look like a fool, which was leverage he never wanted to give the man. He sat in the car and stared at the house and decided maybe he *was* a fool and should have sent Falmouth PD just to do a wellness check.

But if he sent another department's officers in and something happened to them?

He was way over-thinking this. But over-think or under-think, he couldn't seem to get a handle on what to do. Not because he was scared for himself or Kyle, but because there seemed to be no careful approach.

"Let's drive around a little," Kyle said. "See if there's another street parallel to this. A back way we can come in."

It wasn't much of a plan, but it was better than anything Burgess had thought of and it was good to know the lay of the land. Not so easy when you couldn't see the goddamned land.

He put the car in gear and started down the street. They hadn't gone twenty feet before an anxious-looking elderly woman standing by the side of the road flagged them down. She had a raincoat over a housecoat and slippers, and one of those clear, accordion-pleated rain bonnets his mother used to wear to protect her perm. The house behind her, closer to the road than Cote's, looked nice and well-kept, but she looked shabby and neglected.

"Help," she said. She was breathless, one pale, age-spotted hand clutching the other. "I think…I'm afraid. Oh. I'm sorry…to bother you…" Her words came in short bursts. "But I don't know…what to do."

"About what, ma'am?" Burgess said.

She unclenched her hands and gripped the edge of his open window. "About…my neighbor…he's a policeman…and…" Another pause for breath.

Burgess wanted to hear what she had to say, but he was concerned that she might collapse. She obviously had received some kind of shock and needed medical attention. "Ma'am, do you need me to call you an ambulance?" he asked.

"Not for me," she said, swaying unsteadily. "For him. For my neighbor. For Captain Cote. I think…he's been shot."

Burgess wanted to ask her a dozen questions, but what he needed to do was get her back inside her house and call the EMTs. At the same time, he needed to be next door, seeing if Cote was alive.

He looked across at Kyle. Kyle already had his phone out and was calling for an ambulance and police backup. He turned back to the woman. "We've got help on the way. Did you say you heard gunshots?"

She nodded.

"You're certain they were gunshots?"

Another nod.

"How long ago?"

"What time…is it'?"

He checked his watch. "Ten."

"Maybe twenty minutes ago?"

Jesus. He needed to be moving.

"Did you see any unfamiliar vehicles at Captain Cote's house?"

Could she have seen anything at Cote's house? Maybe. The fog came and went.

She nodded. "Black. Truck."

"Did you see it leave?"

"I waited until…it left…before I came out."

Why hadn't she just picked up the phone and called 911?

"Do you have a working telephone, ma'am?"

She shook her head. "It's not…My son is supposed to…come tonight…fix it."

"Are you here alone?"

She nodded. "Alone."

He said, "I'm going to open my door now, and walk you back inside. You need to stay there until the ambulance arrives. Can you do that?"

It seemed to take a very long time to walk her back to her house, but he couldn't hurry her. She was old and frail and very frightened.

As soon as he had her safely inside, he sprinted for the truck, and they went up the drive to Cote's house. No sense in walking there. His skin crawled at the memory of Randy Crossman lying in the road. The rookie had been a perfect target for a hidden shooter.

It was a small white cape with black shutters and an attached garage. When they were past the row of privacy trees, he got out, Kyle right behind him. Guns out and ready, they crisscrossed their way up to Cote's front door.

There were no signs of a struggle. No vehicles in the drive. He slipped over to the garage and looked in the window. Cote's official vehicle was there.

Despite what the woman had told them, Burgess rang the bell. No one answered. He tried the knob. Unlocked. He turned it and went in.

He'd never been in Cote's house, but wasn't surprised to find it as neat and devoid of personality as the man's office. There was no one in the living room. And no sign of yipping dogs. No signs of life at all. No books. No clutter. No newspapers. No knickknacks. No photographs except two official portraits of Cote in uniform. Burgess figured they were from when Cote became a lieutenant and when he became a captain.

"Captain Cote?" he called. "Paul? It's Burgess and Kyle. Are you here?"

They tagged each other as they cleared the house room by room. Living room. Empty. Kitchen. Empty. Dining room. Empty. Bathroom. Empty. Home office. Empty. They checked closets and behind furniture where someone might be concealed.

No blood. No signs of a struggle. No signs that the place was occupied at all. The furniture was newish, in good condition, and didn't seem to have been used. It wasn't a big house. There was just one more room to check, what he assumed was the master bedroom, and a basement if the house had one. The bedroom door was closed.

Burgess took a breath, and another, to slow his racing heart, then, standing away from the doorframe, he reached out and turned the knob. He opened the door quickly so he could see into the room. Then he and Kyle stepped in, Burgess doing a crisscross maneuver, Kyle doing a buttonhook. The shades were drawn. The bed unmade. A quick glance showed a man in uniform standing just inside the open closet door.

"Captain? Paul?"

As his eyes adjusted to the gloom, he saw it was only the captain's dress uniform, already out and ready for Crossman's funeral tomorrow.

A pair of striped pajamas and leather slippers lay on the floor.

The unmade bed and clothing on the floor were the only signs of disorder. The room was empty.

CHAPTER 27

"Basement?" Kyle mouthed.

They retraced their steps along the hall to a door they'd opened earlier that led to stairs going down into darkness. Burgess hated searching basements. The lighting was always poor and there were usually stacks of stuff and all sorts of nooks and crannies for bad guys to hide. He'd once found a guy who'd slipped into a woman's winter coat and was standing among a bunch of other stored clothes. Burgess had almost missed him and only found him when dust made the man sneeze.

Another time, a guy shot at him right through a hot water tank. That did not turn out too well for the shooter. Once a crazed woman covered in dust and cobwebs had thrown herself on an officer standing on the stairs and stabbed him with a pair of scissors.

He expected Cote's basement to be a cobweb free, dust-free model of neatness. He was more worried about things that might be out-of-place, like bodies or Cote's little rat dogs.

It might be a good idea to get your heart rate up at the gym, but the intensity of the adrenaline rush that came with encountering bad guys in a dark basement was the stuff of heart attacks. The effects of fear and anxiety on the body in any search situation took a toll on response time and awareness—what his long ago training officer called muscle confusion, as well as causing tunnel vision. Burgess was not as young as he used to be. It was getting to be time to send the kids into basements and stay at a desk doing paperwork.

But would he? Heck no. That was the trouble with being an *aging* control freak.

Burgess snapped on his flashlight and started down the stairs. There was no safe way to do this, you just moved fast and kept looking and when there were two of you, you spaced it tactically so that if one of you got shot, the other could return fire. But there was always danger. They had the advantage of having worked together often. He and Kyle each knew where the other would be without needing to check. Could communicate without speaking.

The stairs ended in the middle of a dark room and they quickly moved apart, one going left and the other right, getting out of what that training officer had called "the fatal funnel." As a rookie, even though he had been a tough army veteran, often enduring whole days in situations that could be called fatal funnels, that phrase had given him chills. He was chilled now.

He and Kyle stood in the dark, breathing quietly, listening for anything other than the usual utility sounds. There was nothing. He began moving, gun in his right hand and flashlight in his left, clearing the right hand side of the room. Nothing but a neat row of utility cupboards, and washer and dryer and a counter for folding laundry. Just empty, sterile space except for a half-folded basket of laundry. He'd reached the corner and was turning back into the area behind the stairs when his foot came down on something other than hard cement floor. Something small and soft. Even before he lowered his light to examine it, he knew what he would find.

Until that moment, if the elderly neighbor hadn't claimed she'd heard a gunshot, he would have thought this was a futile errand. A complete waste of time that should have been spent elsewhere. He had been questioning the cop's gut that had led them here. Now, though he didn't know the scope of it yet, he had confirmation that something had happened here.

Just ahead of his toe, beyond a streak of blood along the floor where his shoe had moved it, was one of Cote's pets. Very small and very dead. Burgess didn't like yippy little pocket dogs, but many people did, and Cote had loved this little animal. The poor creature had given joy and acceptance to an unlikeable man, and come to this hateful end. His anger spiked at the senselessness of it.

Burgess's sense of the bad amped up. He stepped over it, moving even more cautiously now, and finished the room without finding anything else. He met Kyle back at the bottom of the steps.

"You find anything?" Kyle whispered.

"Small dog. Dead."

"Me, too. Poor thing. Now I'm hoping that we don't find a large, dead police captain."

Burgess was getting colder. "We'd better check the garage. The yard."

Just because a house is empty doesn't mean you let down your guard. Too many cops have gotten killed that way. Finished the careful house search, then stepped out the door and into a bullet. They went up the stairs and back through the house as carefully as they'd come in. Used the same positioning to open the door from the kitchen to the garage that they'd used on the interior doors, and stepped into the chilly gloom.

It was a two-car garage with only one bay occupied. But the absence of tire tread marks and impeccable cleanliness of the empty bay suggested that there hadn't been another car. Wherever Cote had gone, he hadn't left in his own car. They examined Cote's department-issued car. Immaculate. No stuff, no clutter, no hastily scribbled note that he'd been taken by a man and a woman driving a black truck.

Nothing.

Dammit. He was a cop, however much he'd forgotten about the job. He should have left them something. Were the unmade bed and pajamas on the floor a message?

They returned to the kitchen, which had a window above the sink that looked out into the rear yard. The fog was lifting again and they could see the yard was a large, neatly mowed expanse of green that dropped down to the blown brown heads of last year's cattails, bordering what Burgess assumed was a small pond. It was a pretty yard, fenced on both sides with shiny white plastic fencing. Directly behind the house was a stone patio with a grill and a love seat and two chairs around a fire-pit. Burgess wondered who Cote entertained there?

Between the patio and the stream, breaking up the smooth green expanse were two clusters of white birches with small, yellowish-green leaves. Burgess was thinking it looked peaceful and bucolic and wondered where else to look for Cote when Kyle said, "Oh shit, Joe. Look."

Burgess realized he hadn't spotted it at first because Cote's naked body was as white as the tree trunks surrounding him. From this distance, they couldn't tell whether the man was alive. He was bound to the thickest trunk with duct tape, his hands tied to a branch over his head. If he was alive, it was an excruciatingly painful position to be in.

"You think they're out there, Ter?" he asked. "Using Cote as bait?"

"I wouldn't be surprised. Except how did they know we were coming?"

Kyle shrugged. "Maybe they thought he'd be missed. In a good way. Remember that when they developed their hatred for Vince, Vince had your job and Cote was doing his brief stint as CID lieutenant. They might still think Cote is in charge. We'd better clue in Falmouth PD, before some eager beaver goes racing into the back yard and gets shot."

He moved away from the window and made the call.

Burgess thought it was taking the local cops and that ambulance for the woman next door an awfully long time to arrive, so long he wondered if their bad guys had created some kind of a diversion to slow them down?

He looked out at the fence, and beyond it, at the indistinct outline of the house next door. Was the woman okay? He was sure she hadn't been lying to them when she flagged them down on the street. But what if the bad guys were at her house? It would be a good place to hang out and watch the action over here. The fence wasn't that tall—it looked like its purpose had been to keep the dogs in, not observers out.

Burgess had binoculars in the truck that would let him get a better look at the situation. But now that they knew they were in a situation, he'd wait for Kyle to get off the phone. He wasn't going out to get them without cover.

When Kyle disconnected, he'd gone very pale and was shaking his head. "This is so fucking bad, Joe," he said.

"Bad how? What's bad?" But he knew, even before Kyle started to explain. Why no local police had responded. Why there was no ambulance. Because the bad guys were winning every round.

Kyle didn't answer, he just stared out into the yard. At last he turned. "The responding cops were shot as they turned into this neighborhood. Two down. On their way to the hospital now. That's why there's no ambulance. Because it was right behind the police car. Conveniently there to transport them from the shooting scene. So Falmouth PD is all caught up with that. And I expect they're going to be blaming us for not giving them more of a head's up about what they were getting into."

"As if we knew," Burgess said. "You'd have to be freakin' psychic to figure out where these bastards will strike next."

"Or a police officer. That part's pretty predictable," Kyle said. "So now what do we do?"

"Wish we could know whether that shooting means they've moved on, because I am not going out into that yard and risking getting shot again just to test the waters."

"Call SRT?" Kyle suggested. "Isn't this what they're supposed to be good at?"

But this wasn't Portland. "Can you cover me while I get my binoculars from the truck?" Burgess said. "See if I can learn anything more about Cote's situation?"

"I'm right behind you."

The news that more cops had been shot made him explosive. "I want to kill those bastards with my bare hands, Terry," he said. "I want to tear out their throats with my teeth. This has got to stop."

He had to get a grip on himself. Going off half-cocked and acting out of anger instead of caution was a good way to get himself, or Kyle, killed. There had been enough killing. Enough damage. He took a moment, in the kitchen, arms braced against the counter, until he'd slowed himself down.

"Okay," he said, pushing off. "Let's go."

He had a bunch of questions, among them how two people could wreak so much havoc and do so much harm and not be caught. Were there only two? Was Karl Maloof working with them? Maybe others? Were they dealing with two angry siblings or a whole conspiracy? Were there mommy and daddy Maloofs as well? He wondered what Perry had learned about the family and realized, with a sickening sense that he might already be too late, that he should have told Perry to take someone with him when he called at Karl Maloof's last known address. Would Perry be sensible or would his youthful sense of invincibility make him careless?

Worrying about that twisted his already knotted gut. Too often these days it felt like he'd swallowed a knife and it had become permanently wedged in his stomach. Along with the other tolls it took on the body, police work was not good for the digestion.

He pushed his questions away and brought his focus back to awareness and survival. Back to making the necessary tactical decisions to get Cote down from that tree. Then finding the Maloofs and putting an end to this thing.

Even with Kyle standing watch, the seconds he spent with his back to the world, bending over his gear bag, felt endless and icy waves of fear traveled up his exposed spine. Then he had them and they were back inside the house.

In the kitchen, he focused the binoculars and studied Cote through the window. He wasn't sure, but he thought the captain's eyes were open. He couldn't see any signs of breathing, though. He handed them to Kyle. "What do you think? Is he alive?"

Kyle looked for a long time, then lowered the glasses. "Honestly, Joe? I can't tell. I don't see any blood, but I also don't see any movement."

"We have to call the chief," Burgess said. "Give him a heads up about this."

Kyle nodded. "Right. Only what do you tell him? That one of his captains is naked and tied to a tree in his own yard and you don't even know if he's dead or alive? What's he supposed to do with that information?"

Kyle was right. Their intel wasn't very useful, but the chief needed to be kept informed about the details of an investigation into the shooting of several of his officers, and this development was definitely something he needed to know about. One of the many things he needed to know about. Burgess should have briefed him after the meeting about their suspicions that they were looking at two shooters, shared the evidence they had to back those suspicions, and the names of their persons of interest. The stuff Vince Melia would have taken care of.

Melia. He hadn't called the hospital or checked in with Gina. Thought of all the other calls he should make. Stalling. He didn't want to make this call.

Hell. This was never going to get any easier. He took a few of those useless calming breaths and dialed the chief.

"Chief? It's Burgess. Detective Kyle and I are out at Captain Cote's house, and we've got a situation."

The chief's sigh was heartfelt, and Burgess, up to his ears in his own concerns, was reminded that the chief was in the middle of planning the logistics for Randy Crosssman's funeral tomorrow. A police funeral was a big deal, and in a matter like this—several cops wounded and one killed in what looked like a deliberate action to kill cops—a bigger deal. The whole city would be swarming with officers from other departments, come to lay one of their own to rest.

The knife in his gut shifted and stabbed more deeply as the implications went home. If they didn't get the shooters today, tomorrow there would be hundreds of new targets and many, many opportunities for someone with a grudge to be shooting. With two, possibly three, shooters acting, it could be a massacre. He didn't know how they were going to stop it. But they had to.

Even before the chief had answered, Burgess had begun formulating a plan for how they might get to Cote. As soon as he was off the phone—which he didn't expect to happen very quickly—he'd share it with Kyle and see if Kyle thought he'd lost his mind.

He'd also call Sage Prentiss, Rocky Jordan, and Stan Perry, and remind them that they were seriously under the gun both in a time and danger sense—and the potential consequences for tomorrow if they didn't catch the bad guys soon.

He hoped the chief was thinking about police safety as well as how to organize, feed, house, and otherwise entertain their many out-of-town guests.

He pushed away the contrast between the grieving that would be done for Crossman, and the fact that Richard Pelham seemed to have nobody who cared at all. He couldn't get distracted by emotion. But tortoise, not hare, wasn't working for him anymore. They needed to be tireless greyhounds until this thing was put to bed.

It was a good twenty minutes later, a grueling twenty minutes trying to answer a thousand questions and to dissuade the chief from jumping in a car and bringing half the Portland police force with him, before he could start carrying out his crazy plan.

CHAPTER 28

"It could work," Kyle said, when Burgess laid out his plan.

It wasn't much of a plan, really. The section of fence that stretched from the side of the garage to the border of the property had a gate that opened to allow landscapers or equipment into the rear yard. If they opened the gate, they could drive right up to that clump of trees, and one of them provide cover while the other cut Cote down. Cut him down if he was alive. Otherwise it was a crime scene. Burgess figured they'd use two cars—the Explorer and Cote's vehicle—for greater mobility and protection.

They found Cote's keys in a tray on his dresser. Burgess got down his long gun from the rack, and backed up, providing cover while Kyle backed Cote's vehicle out of the garage. The gate was locked, and there was an anxious moment while Burgess clutched the gun, scanning the neighboring house and that damned privacy hedge while Kyle fumbled to find the key that would open it. His skin crawled as he waited for a shot to come out of nowhere. Cote must have thought those trees gave him privacy without considering that they also gave thieves and other bad guys privacy as well.

The temperature was only in the fifties, and depending on how long he'd been there, Cote was going to be hypothermic along with any other injuries he had. If he was alive. Burgess hoped the man still stocked his trunk like a cop and not like an anal compulsive who liked to stare into pristine black emptiness. They'd need a blanket and his had been left behind this morning, wrapped around a child.

Kyle drove through the gate and into Cote's yard, heading for the clump of birches, Burgess right behind him, praying that they didn't get shot as they slithered across the grass. Both of them praying that the yard was well-drained and they didn't fall into a ditch or get bogged down in a patch of mud. This was Maine, not Scarsdale. In the past, he'd discovered to his detriment that seemingly smooth expanses of green could harbor swales, old wells, and other pitfalls.

Their tires made dark ruts in the soggy turf. Entertaining one of those crazy thoughts that intrude at times of almost unbearable tension, Burgess knew that at some point, assuming the man was alive, Cote would be complaining about the damage to his yard.

Given the danger of the situation, one of them should have been providing cover throughout the operation, but there was no way one of them could cut Cote down and carry him to a vehicle alone. The captain was a stout fellow and Burgess had a bad shoulder. Burgess swung around and backed up as close to the trees as he could get, then waited, his gun up and ready, for Kyle to determine whether the man was alive. If Cote was deceased, they would back off and leave it for the state police.

The fog was doing its 'now you see me, now you don't' dance again, floating in a ghostly gray wave over the lawn until Cote's house was almost invisible, and coating them with clammy moisture. The gun in his hands was slippery and cold. The day felt like November.

The world was silent except for the sound of dripping, so silent he found he was holding his breath, listening as Kyle's feet squelched over the grass, scraped on tree roots and crunched through last fall's leaves. He heard the rustle of sleeves as Kyle reached out to check Cote for signs of life. More rustling, a grunt, and then, "Bring a knife, Joe. He's alive."

Without cover, it felt risky bending to get the tool from his bag, even though any bad guys out there couldn't see any more than he could. He took off his jacket, which restricted mobility, and when he bent, his shirt rode up and tongues of icy fog licked right up his spine.

He hesitated, listening. The only sound was Kyle, breathing.

He joined Kyle and stretched up, using the knife to cut the rope holding Cote's hands to the overhead branch, expecting every second that a bullet would come flying out of nowhere. Cote's assailants had used some thick nylon rope that took forever to saw through. His shoulder protested and, as he sawed, he felt a couple stitches let go.

Burgess couldn't see any gunshot wounds, but they'd beaten Cote badly. Where he wasn't bruised, his skin was pale blue and waxy and frighteningly cold. When his hands were freed, Cote's unconscious body folded forward like he was bowing to them, the tape around his waist that still fastened him to the tree holding the lower half of his body upright.

Kyle supported him while Burgess sawed through the tape, and they caught him together as he sagged forward. Burgess felt his own hot blood ooze through his bandages. Cote carried a lot of weight, and trying to lift his slippery, blubbery body was like trying to heft a small whale. They half carried, half dragged him to Burgess's car, the toes of his trailing bare feet catching leaves, pebbles, and grass. Burgess had left the rear door open and they squeezed him into the back seat. The engine was on and the heat was running. Burgess kept the gun at the ready as Kyle checked Cote's trunk for a blanket. He came up empty.

Cote's refusal to act or think like a cop was so often infuriating, this time to his own detriment.

"Never mind. We'll stop back at the house and grab something," Burgess said.

"No." Kyle was firm. "We're getting the hell out of here before something else happens."

"What about the lady next door?"

"I'll call Falmouth PD again and remind them," Kyle said. "I think riding in back in Paul would do her more harm than good. I'll let 'em know we're coming through with the captain, too, so they won't think we're the bad guys."

Burgess had a raincoat in the back. They tucked that around Cote as best they could. Burgess backed around, creating more ruts in the yard, and they headed for Portland. They left Cote's car where it was. On the way out of the neighborhood, they passed a cruiser with shot out windows surrounded by what looked like the entire Falmouth police department. It took a few minutes and some badges and explanations to get past that.

"You'd think they could spare one car for that poor old woman," Kyle said.

"But we know how they feel," Burgess said. Assaulted. Threatened. Under attack.

Beside him, Kyle shivered. "What I wouldn't give for some hot coffee. Hot soup. A hot shower. I'm freezing."

Burgess turned up the heat. He wanted those things, too, but there was no time. Beside him, Kyle was on the phone to Falmouth again, and it sounded like he was getting a ration of crap he didn't need.

As soon as they were back on the highway, and he wasn't navigating unfamiliar roads through the fog, he got on his own phone and started making calls. First to the chief, to tell him they had Cote and were on their way to the hospital. The chief had a dozen questions Burgess didn't have answers to. He couldn't even describe Cote's injuries, because they'd established that the man was breathing and not bleeding but that was as far as their examination had gone. He thought it might be internal injuries from a brutal beating. They'd seen no wounds. That didn't mean there were none.

The chief said he'd meet them at the hospital and get someone to make calls to secure the scene at Cote's house, get the local police in to investigate. Burgess told him that two Falmouth officers had been shot, and they suspected, because of the proximity to Cote's place, that it was the Portland shooters.

Once he'd made that call, Burgess moved along to his real to-do list. Call Rocky Jordan and see if they were close to finding that damned truck. Call Stan Perry and get an update. If Perry hadn't had any luck, he'd call Sage Prentiss off looking at Richard Pelham and get him working with Perry on locating any of the Maloofs.

No one was answering their phones and his anxiety level rose. Though the chief hadn't mentioned it, Burgess wondered if the world had ended, at least within the city of Portland, while they were engaged in rescuing Cote. Where the hell was everybody? If it was possible to get more anxious, he was. Getting nowhere with that, and feeling like a human pressure cooker just about to blow a gasket, he began making a mental list of other things to attend to.

Go over the paperwork from the canvass that was waiting on his desk and see if there were any leads or witnesses.

Locate Rufus Radstein's business and pay him a visit. With photos. Lucille Radstein said her husband did customizing. He couldn't help thinking there was some connection between Radstein and that tricked-out black truck. Even if Radstein's instinctive reaction would be to lie about knowing any of the Maloofs, his demeanor might give him away. If he'd worked on that truck, there would be records.

If Rocky's search hadn't found the plate or narrowed the field, might one of Jared Laukka's passengers remember the plate?

Had Rocky finished the search of Melia's phone records, and was there anything there that might lead them to the Maloofs? To what had drawn Melia down to that site?

It all had to be done fast. Faster than fast.

His inability to make anything happen was threatening to make his head explode. He dropped the phone and rubbed his forehead, where a massive headache was building. A too little sleep, too little food, desperate need for caffeine headache. His wounded shoulder was growling like a feral cat.

"We'll get this sorted, Joe," Kyle said, "because we have to."

Where Burgess got angry, Kyle got cold. A clear, efficient, dangerous cold. He wished he could infuse some of that. Anger just got in the way. "But where the fuck is everybody?"

"Hot coffee? Hot soup?"

Was it lunch time? Burgess had no idea. He'd lost track of time. It seemed like they'd been at Cote's for hours. He thought it was later. The gray seemed to be taking on a late afternoon hue. "How about some hot tips? Hot witnesses? Hot data?"

"In the fullness of time." But Kyle's calm voice had notes of suppressed anxiety that matched his own. "You think the chief is aware of the threat?"

The threat. The thing they were rushing desperately to avert.

"He should be. We'll ask him when we see him." Burgess suppressed the unwanted vision of uniformed cops lying bleeding on the sidewalks as Crossman's funeral cortege passed by. "No more we can do, except catch the bad guys."

"You're bleeding, you know."

"I know. Busted some stitches shifting the whale." He was glad the oozing blood didn't show much through his dark plaid shirt. He didn't have time to change.

"The word blubber did come to mind. That why you took off your jacket?"

"It's my last one."

He'd turned the heat down to make his calls, now he turned it back up. It helped mask Cote's labored breathing. It was strange to be going to these extremes to save a man so dedicated to making his life a misery. But as he'd told Kyle, this wasn't about the man, it was about the job. About not letting anyone get away with targeting cops.

Burgess was going 80. He barely slowed to take the turn off the highway. He had lights on and sirens flashing and right now, if some ignorant asshat stepped out in front of him, as the city's denizens were wont to do, he'd just flatten the sucker and keep on going. Taking this much time out of an investigation to go rescue Cote pissed him off, the more so because the man hadn't known enough to be careful and didn't possess the ability to be grateful.

Right now, he looked more dead than alive, but Captain Paul Cote was a survivor of the worst sort. He'd live to fight another day and the fight he'd be conducting would the same one he always fought—a campaign to make the working cop's life as overworked and underpaid as possible.

Kyle, the mind reader, said, "You're right. He won't be grateful."

Burgess blew though a traffic light, missing an oblivious blonde in a BMW by maybe an inch, catching a peripheral glimpse of her open-mouthed shock. If he'd taken a year off her life, she deserved it.

He wove around cars that scattered helter-skelter to get out of his way, and swerved around a guy in a motorized wheelchair so abruptly Cote slipped off the back seat and slid onto the floor. Then it was winding through the streets and up to the Emergency Room door.

Kyle was out of the truck before they'd rocked to a stop, calling for help, and seconds later, a gurney appeared, and a black and blue, blubbery Cote was extracted and wheeled inside.

"Wasn't that fun!" Kyle put a hand under his elbow. "Let's go inside. Check on Vince, and grab some coffee."

When Burgess didn't move, Kyle said, "Joe. They have your messages. They'll call. We need to get warmed up."

"Vince, first," he agreed.

He wanted coffee. A carb infusion. Between the pucker factor of the last couple hours, and rescuing Cote in the cold fog, he had the kind of bone-deep chill that takes hours to let go and was in that post-adrenaline state that leaves you sleepy and exhausted. He had no time for either, nor for the "poor me" side of him that had a pounding headache and a reopened, bloody wound.

He pushed himself forward, using his anger to keep him going. Drawing on the Burgess who wanted to tear someone's throat out with his teeth.

They found the same tableau in Melia's room as the day before, Vince utterly still and Gina holding his hand. But Melia's color was better and she didn't seem so tense. She smiled when she saw them. "Just the guys I wanted to see. Terry, can you sit with Vince for a minute? I need to talk to Joe."

Kyle slipped into the chair she vacated and leaned in toward the still form on the bed. "Hey, Vince, it's Terry. Have I got a story for you…"

As Burgess followed Gina to the lounge, he heard Terry launching into the story of their adventures rescuing Cote. It was a story Vince would love and somehow, despite the stillness, Burgess had the feeling Vince was listening and the story would be good for him. Kyle would embellish the story with them getting spooked by the hanging uniform, the sad fate of the rat dogs, the humorous side of wrestling Cote's slippery whale of a body into the car. So often, Kyle seemed to know exactly what to do.

Gina led the way to the place they'd sat the day before, claiming it like it was their space. "He looks better," Burgess said.

She nodded. "He is better. But that's not what I wanted to talk with you about. It's something Linc said. You know they were here, and they were both…I don't know, maybe you'll understand this better than I do. I thought they'd be in such a state about Vince, about their dad, that that's all they'd focus on. I forgot, I guess," she gave a self-deprecating smile, "forgot they're a cop's kids. Anyway, at one point, Lucas asked what was going on with the investigation, and I told them about the mystery car on our street, and about that odd pair who had been at a couple of the soccer games. And one of them, I think it was Linc, because he hasn't been playing, just sitting on the bench—the mono, you know—said he knew who those people at the game were."

Burgess felt a peculiar tingling, like something very significant was about to happen. He waited, wanting to rush her, knowing he had to let her take her time.

"I figured, you know, that he was thinking about someone different. Some other set of parents. Because I hadn't noticed them, this strange man and woman who'd been watching us. But you know how I told you Vince was teaching them to be observant?"

He nodded.

"So what Linc said was they were brother and sister and they were visiting their mom who lived somewhere on the street."

"How does he know that? Did you ask?"

Calm down, he told himself. Don't spook her. She's exhausted. Just let her tell the story her way. He wrapped his hands around the edge of the sofa cushion, felt the corded edge pressing into this palm. Tortoise. Tortoise.

The freakin' hare wanted to jump and run.

He didn't have enough yet.

"He wasn't sure why he remembered them. He thinks he must have spoken with them. I think he said one of them had a dog. Cute little dog, some kind of Sheltie or something, and he asked if he could pat it. The boys really want a dog, so they notice other people's. I think they're scouting, getting ready to make a case for one of their own."

The hare leapt. "Give me more, Gina. Anything. Or let me talk to Linc. Please. I need to find these people. I need to find them before Crossman's funeral tomorrow."

He didn't have to say any more. She got it immediately. "Oh dear, Joe. No! Not more shooting. Not more killing."

Her hand went to her chest, and she leaned back in her chair, closing her eyes against the horror.

"We have to find them. Today. Tonight. What else did Linc tell you? Does he have any idea whose children they are? Which house they belong to?"

She shook her head. "That's all he said. That he'd seen them getting out of a car with that dog. But you could ask him. Ask them. Maybe they know more than they told me."

"They're still at Vince's parents?"

She nodded.

"Did you ask about the strange car?"

"I mentioned it, but they didn't respond and I didn't follow up. You've got to understand, Joe. They were seeing Vince for the first time. I barely had time to ask what I already told you. They're pretty upset. I wasn't going to push them about anything."

He understood. He also understood that under circumstances like these, so much hanging in the balance, the normal rules of human interaction like patience, tact, kindness, and consideration went out the window. "When do they get out of school?"

She considered. "Linc is done at three. Lucas at four-thirty."

It was almost three.

He wondered if someone was still guarding the Melia boys, or if that had fallen off the minute he stopped pushing for it. The department was short on staff. At least there was someone guarding Melia.

"Can you call Vince's parents, let them know I'll be talking to Linc?"

"Glad to," she said, though she didn't sound like she was glad about anything.

"I'm sorry, Gina. I hate to push you like this, but—"

She raised a hand to fend off his words. "Don't, Joe. I understand."

As they walked back to the ICU, he asked his usual question. "Have you eaten today?"

"The nurse brought me a meal. It was…well, it was nasty. All the time and energy they put into planning food for patients, you'd think they could do better." She shrugged. "Guess I shouldn't complain, but I definitely preferred that croissant sandwich."

"I'll bet."

She patted his shoulder, then drew her hand back, staring at the bloody smudges. "Joe?"

"Tore my stitches. Haven't had time to get them fixed. Or change my shirt."

She shook her head. "Vince's sister is coming in a bit. I think I'll stop at the chapel and pray. For all of us."

"From your lips to God's ears," he said. They could use all the help they could get.

His phone was buzzing. Perry. He needed to take this. In flagrant violation of the signs all around that said no cell phones, he answered.

"Stan? Are you all right?"

"Frustrated as hell. Otherwise fine."

"No leads on these people? What about their parents? Former addresses?"

"No one at the address Karl Maloof gave his PO knows anything about him. Now I'm waiting for the file to come from storage, Joe, and Rocky is running Maloofs. But they aren't that rare."

Stan Perry sounded angry. "Are we the only ones around here who understand the word urgent? I've been thinking that if those fuckers still have a hard-on for cops, tomorrow could be a bloodbath."

"What Terry and I are thinking, too. Give me a call when you get that file. Kyle and I are coming back to 109. We can help you go through it."

"Right," Perry said. "Where are you?"

"Hospital."

"You guys okay?"

"Cote. Bad guys hurt him and hung him from a tree."

There was silence. A long silence. "I don't know whether to be happy or sad. He alive?"

"So far."

Perry said something very un-Perrylike. "Sometimes a terrible experience can be transformative."

"Why don't you pray for that? I'm grabbing coffee and then coming to 109. You there?"

"Yeah."

"Rocky run those vanity plates?"

"Another stack of paper, Joe."

"What about Vince's phone records? Rocky go through them?"

"That's more paper. Sage is working on the vanity plates. We could use some more hands."

"Pull anyone you can and put them to work. We've got a bunch of ways into this thing and every one of them takes time."

He disconnected, grabbed Kyle, and they headed for the cafeteria for that badly needed coffee.

They didn't get that far before they ran into Deputy Chief Longley and were dragged off to a conference room to brief the chief in person. They didn't know any more that they'd already told him, and had more pressing things to do, but this was the chief.

As they entered the room past a gaggle of eager newshounds, Burgess was feeling like he was moving in slow motion through sludge, and begrudged every second they'd waste telling the chief in person what they'd already reported over the phone. None of the time spent would advance their investigation.

He managed to get the chief to send someone for coffee, curbing his impatience to be gone so badly he probably looked like a little kid who had to pee. At the end, the chief patted him on the shoulder and came away with a bloody hand, just like Gina had. At least the chief had the grace not to suggest he take himself to the ER. Burgess had no time to get mended right now.

Before they left, because the chief hadn't raised it, Burgess reminded him of the risks to everyone at tomorrow's funeral if they didn't get these shooters. Even if the chief had already thought of it, bringing it into the open still shocked him.

Finally released, and leaving the stunned chief adding a major security task to his own to-do list, Burgess and Kyle literally sprinted for the truck.

CHAPTER 29

Perry, Prentiss, and some detectives they'd grabbed to help out were in the conference room, huddled over computer printouts. Perry gave them a bleary-eyed look when they entered. "Any idea how many black Ford F-150 trucks with vanity plates there are in Maine?"

"Six?" Kyle said brightly.

Perry snarled and bent to his work.

"Sage," Burgess said, "you get anything from the VA on Pelham?"

Prentiss shook his head. "I figure they'll get around to calling the day before I retire. If they call back at all."

It wasn't urgent. Not at the top of his list at all, but being unable to get cooperation from people when they were working a homicide always pushed his buttons. That and the fact that Pelham's death seemed so utterly senseless unless there was a connection. And it saddened him to think of the man lying unclaimed in a morgue. Those who'd given so much for their country deserved better.

He knew someone at the VA who might have some leverage. Figured it was worth a call.

"How are we doing on the Maloof file?" he asked.

Another snarl from Perry that Burgess took to mean the file hadn't arrived yet.

Court papers, he thought. There might be affidavits, applications for warrants, or other filings that would give them something. "Where's Rocky?" he said.

"I think he went to shoot someone at the phone company," Perry said. "At least that's what he was muttering when he went out the door."

The procedure was simple. You needed someone's phone records, you sent the phone company a subpoena and an affidavit and you got the records. Or you didn't get the records, in which case, you went through the BS all over again. Or, in a case where time mattered, you took your gun and paid someone a visit. Unfortunately, the people who had the authority to compile and release records were rarely close by. Burgess wondered who Rocky was going to threaten? Since Rocky was an even-tempered, desk-bound computer jockey, something must have set him off.

Burgess called over to the court clerk's office and got someone to agree to look for the Maloof case file. He asked for a call back if they found it. He figured he'd go over there himself and see what they had. He gobbled some painkillers, thinking they should just be added to food as a supplement like other vitamins, and carefully flexed his sticky shoulder. If pain spoke in obscenities, he was roundly cursed.

Then he grabbed the canvass reports and started reading. Except for the Radsteins, no one on the street had observed the Charger with the odd paint parked near the Melia's house. Nor had anyone noticed someone watching the Melia's house or any other suspicious activity with respect to the Melias.

His impatience made careful reading difficult. His concentration was shot to hell, and it took concentration to read through these notes carefully. Sometimes it would be a very small thing that would be the tip. An off-hand comment, a closing observation, something the interviewee said that wasn't responsive to the question asked. So far, the lack of information about that suspicious car was the most interesting thing he'd found. No one but the Radsteins had seen it.

He was on the cusp of tossing the whole mess in the trash when he found his tiny jewel. A neighbor had commented that while she hadn't seen any suspicious car with a homemade paint job, if they were going to talk about cars, how about someone in the police department doing something about the Radstein's damned black trucks and the way they parked everywhere including in front of hydrants and drove like the street was a raceway instead of a residential area.

Once he'd spotted it, the phrase jumped right off the page: Radstein's damned black trucks. Trucks plural? The report included the neighbor's name and phone number. Burgess reached for the phone.

Someone else who wasn't home. He left a message, saying it was urgent, and thought about who else might know about those trucks. The Melia twins. They were being trained by their father to be observant, and one thing their dad was sure to start them with was the vehicles on the street.

He checked his watch. Lucas wouldn't be home yet, and he wanted to talk to them both together. He also didn't want to leave here until he knew whether one of the files on Karl Maloof's case had been located.

As if by magic, his assistant put a pink slip on his desk. "You were on the phone," she said. "They've got that file, if you want to go look at it."

He wanted.

He stuck his head into the conference room, told them where he was going, and headed for the stairs. Maybe when he got back, he'd have something. Time felt like it was rushing at him, flying like those calendar pages in old movies. Tonight, the city would be filling up with cops coming for Crossman's funeral. By morning, the number of blue targets would be innumerable. And vulnerable. And it fell to his team to make sure they were safe.

* * *

Forty minutes later, various formal papers filed in the matter of State of Maine v. Karl Maloof—including some sealed files he'd had to have a judge give him access to— had yielded up a gold mine of information and connected a bunch of missing dots. He still didn't have everything he needed, but the murky picture he'd been staring at was getting clearer.

He stopped at the street and called Vince Melia's parents. Got his mother, explained why he was calling, and asked to speak with Lincoln.

"Detective Burgess? This is Lincoln Melia. Grandma said you wanted to speak with me?" There was so much fear in the boy's voice Burgess realized Lincoln thought he was calling to say that their dad had died.

"It's not about your dad," he said. "That is, nothing has happened with your dad. He's getting better and he's going to be okay."

The boy didn't say anything, but his breathing, coming down the line, said relief.

"I'm calling because your mom says that your dad is teaching you and Lucas to see like cops. To be observant."

"It's really cool," the boy said, "and he says we're getting pretty good at it."

"I hope you are, because I need some information and I'm hoping you have it. It's about the Radsteins."

"They hate us," the boy said matter-of-factly.

"Yes, I've heard. Well, this is about their trucks."

"Mmhmm. What about their trucks?"

"A couple of witnesses we've spoken with have mentioned seeing customized black Ford F-150 trucks. And someone on your street mentioned there had been trucks, plural, parked near the Radsteins, and being driven dangerously on the street." He let that sink in, then said, "What can you tell me about those trucks?"

The boy was silent for so long Burgess thought the call might have been dropped. "Linc?" he nudged. "The trucks?"

"Oh, sorry. I thought you were going to ask me specific questions about them."

"How many trucks are we talking about?"

"Three."

"All black? All Fords? All customized?"

"Yup. I mean, yes, sir."

"Who drives them?"

"There's one of the daughters. Karla. She's the one with the Sheltie. She and her husband drive one. That's the one with the HOTDOG license plate, which is funny because their dog, Sasha, is very good."

Thank you, Lord, Burgess thought. *Thank you, Vince Melia, for raising such an observant kid.*

"Mr. Radstein has one, but I guess you already know that. He's got TOPDOG."

"And the third?"

"I don't know who drives that one, Detective Burgess. It used to be the one who is Karla's brother, which I know because he also has a Sheltie, named Masha, and they were joking one day about brother and sister having brother and sister dogs. Only the last time I saw it, the day Lucas and I were getting our stuff to come here to grandma's, the guy with the eye patch was driving."

The boy broke off, like he wasn't sure whether he was giving the right answers or not, then asked, "Is this going to help you find the person who shot my dad?"

"It absolutely is, Linc. Just one more question. Do you remember the tag on the third truck?"

"Sure," the boy said, without hesitation, "it's BADDOG. That's with two D's."

"This is very helpful. Your dad has taught you well," Burgess said. "I'll call you if I have more questions."

He wanted to say be careful. He wanted to say, "Spend the next twenty-four hours inside an armored truck or get out of town." But he was supposed to be being the grownup, protecting them from how ugly the world really was. Not, having had their father shot, that they were probably viewing the world as benign right now.

"You've been a great help to the investigation, Lincoln. Your dad is going to be very proud of you."

There was a choking sound, and the phone went dead.

Burgess headed back down the street to 109. Pissed as hell at how he'd been played by the Radsteins, though even the best cops got played sometimes. Already making calls to dispatch about those license plates. By the time he was back upstairs, he was armed with a real breakthrough.

His team was still in the conference room. He went to the white board and started writing.

Karl Maloof: convicted child molester.

Karla Maloof Tucker: his twin sister. Vowed revenge on Vince Melia and the police for ruining her brother's life.

Then he added in the connective tissue, the information he'd gotten from court records.

Kris Radstein: Brother of Karl and Karla, also vowed revenge.

Lucille Maloof Radstein: wife of Rufus Radstein and mother of Karl, Karla, and Kris.

As he wrote, he realized he didn't know about Karla's husband. Tucker.

"Seriously?" Kyle said.

"This is only the beginning."

He waited until they'd absorbed that.

He wrote: Rufus Radstein—has a body shop where he customizes trucks, cars, and motorcycles.

Three customized black Ford F150 trucks, vanity plates:

HOTDOG
TOPDOG
BADDOG

"How'd you get those plates?" Prentiss asked, frustrated that Burgess had gotten the answers so fast when he'd been staring at lists for hours.

"Melia's son. Lincoln. He's seen them on the street. Vince is training them to be observant and it's paid off."

Finally, from the courthouse records of Karl Maloof's case, he put a vital piece into the puzzle.

Karl Maloof's victim was Linnette Pelham—daughter of Richard and Maryann Pelham.

Burgess wondered if having his daughter molested and the trauma of a trial had put Pelham over the edge? Whether it had caused the marriage to fray? He wondered if Maryann Pelham still lived around here? If she'd care about what had happened to her husband. Ex-husband? If she'd step forward to bury him? He hadn't taken the time to explore how Maloof had gotten access to the child. Had there been some relationship between Maloof and Pelham, something Pelham blamed himself for so he had sent himself into exile?

So many more avenues to be explored. But they now had the vital information they needed to hunt for the shooters. Names. Connections. That was where their focus had to be.

Perry, who'd been hunched over his computer, typing like crazy, now sat back and waved a piece of paper.

"Registrations for those three trucks," he said.

HOTDOG was registered to Karla Tucker, BADDOG to Kristin Collins Radstein, and TOPDOG to Rufus Radstein, with an address on Warren Avenue. Interesting that two of the trucks were registered to the women. Burgess felt grateful for their lucky break. They could have searched for Maloofs until the cows came home and not found these.

Perry was still typing away. Burgess figured he was looking for background on Tucker and Collins. Seeing what other vehicles were registered at those addresses, and whether Tucker or Collins, or anyone else at those addresses had any arrest records.

The next time he picked his head up, Perry said, "Karla Tucker is a weapons instructor."

"A dish best served cold," Burgess said.

Kyle nodded.

Perry raised his head, shook it, and muttered, "You old farts."

Kyle was pulling up drivers' licenses. Karla Tucker was definitely the woman who'd impersonated Sheryl Timmons at the hospital. From the photos, it looked like the three—Karla, Kris, and Karl—were siblings. None bore any resemblance to rusty, belligerent Rufus Radstein. Maybe Kris had changed his name at some point?

The next step was to grab any of these people that they could and get them off the street. No time for careful surveillance and planning. It had to happen tonight.

"What have we got on these people that we can pull them in on right now?" Burgess said, wishing that lying to the police was a crime. He'd love to get that sweet, timid, manipulative, lying bitch Lucille Radstein in a cell. Maybe because he'd been sympathetic. He hated to be played. And because he now knew that she'd raised a pack of monsters.

"One at a time, while we get our warrants to search. See if we can grab their guns. Get their prints to Dani for matches."

When they looked at him blankly, because they were tired and distracted, he reminded them why speed was essential. "Now. Tonight. Before Crossman's funeral."

He'd discussed this with Kyle, and Perry had guessed it, but he realized that Prentiss wasn't on the same wavelength, that the others didn't yet share his sense of urgency. "If they're looking for a big, splashy revenge on the Portland police, or on police in general, it's possible they'll try something during the funeral tomorrow. Someone out there with a rifle? All those cops who've come to honor Randy? Be like shooting fish in a barrel."

The knife in his stomach twisted.

He had to bring the chief in one this. Lt. Coakley and SRT. Like those wildly spinning hands on a cartoon clock, time seemed to keep speeding up.

"What have we got on them?" Kyle said. "Karla Tucker for false impersonation. Assuming it was Kris Radstein in that truck waving a gun, we've got criminal threatening. She was driving, so you've probably got both of them from that. It's a BS charge, but you've also got her for driving without lights and eluding a police officer. You'll need Bill Thornton's statement and an ID from Jared Laukka, which you can get now that you've got the licenses. I'll make up six-packs for Karla and for Kris."

Kyle made some notes. "If we can find him, we've got Karl Maloof for parole violations—giving a false address and failing to report. I don't see that we've got anything on Kristin Radstein."

"You got her picture?" Burgess said.

Kyle pointed to his screen. "I'm printing her now."

Burgess looked over Kyle's shoulder. It was the woman from the surveillance pictures Lucille Radstein had given him. He had nothing on her except a bad feeling and a whole lot of pissed off. He had no idea who the man was. But if this was a family thing, maybe it was Karla Tucker's husband.

"I want all the vehicles registered to any of these people, including Lucille Radstein. She may have played the timid, abused wife card, but she deliberately steered us in false directions. She's in this up to her ears, and the shooters are her kids."

Burgess leaned back in his chair and closed his eyes, summoning clarity and strength for the evening ahead. He wanted Melia here, to consult with, coordinate their actions, work with SRT, make sure the affidavits and search warrants were written, reviewed, and signed. He'd been doing this forever, but tonight he felt very exposed. They'd always been his people—his team—but he'd gotten to used to having Melia there, as a sounding board, to cross the "t's and dot the "i's", ask the hard questions and back them when they needed it.

If ever there was a cloud with a silver lining, though, it was that he wouldn't have Cote meddling. He wouldn't miss that pursed mouthed martinet trying to under-staff everything to save on overtime. He really ought to call the hospital and see how Cote was doing.

He was jerked back into the room, and the mess they were facing, by Rocky Jordan's noisy return.

Jordan was carrying a large cardboard box, and in his hand, a stack of papers.

"Sandwiches, cookies, coffee, and phone numbers," he said, sliding the box onto the table. "And I didn't have to shoot anyone."

CHAPTER 30

It had been an intense five hours of planning, scoping out their targets, getting arrest warrants and search warrants.

An hour ago, during a search of Radstein's Warren Avenue garage, a cache of illegal weapons had been found and seized, along with three stolen vehicles in a locked garage at the rear of the lot. Both Lucille and Rufus Radstein had been arrested. The operation had been swift and silent, and the team now waiting outside Kris Radstein's farmhouse in Gray thought no one would have had an opportunity to alert other family members about the search or the arrest.

During the arrest, officers had found two vehicles at the Radstein's, a Toyota Corolla in the driveway, and a Plymouth Fury in the garage with a black matte paint job and one white door. That discovery had sent Burgess's temper through the roof as he pictured Lucille Radstein, eyes downcast, reporting a suspicious vehicle on the street. An entire family of monsters, it seemed.

There were no black Ford trucks at either property or on the street.

The weight of this operation sat heavily on all of them. There's always weight when an investigation involves someone who has harmed others. They always carried that.

There's always a fear factor when you go into the unknown—a bar, a building, a home, or stop a car when you're after someone with a known propensity for violence. Fear can make you vulnerable, you have to manage it. Channel it and it can give you a valuable edge.

Tonight both weight and fear were amped up to almost unbearable levels. This was about a lot of human lives and the whole damned department. Not only about doing the job but about the honor and reputation of the department. They always needed to win when they went up against bad guys; they needed to win this one even more.

They'd had to say no to a lot of people who wanted in on tonight's operation. This was everyone's fight and everyone wanted a piece of it. But both Burgess and SRT's Lt. Coakley were about keeping it lean and mean. Now they stood in the dark, running the what if's and doing the second guessing, hoping the people they needed to catch were below them in that farmhouse.

From their vantage point on a hill, they could see two black trucks and three other vehicles parked in the yard. The large barn might have held the third truck. Or it might be somewhere else. SRT was using night vision goggles to move closer to the house, where, if possible, they would employ thermal imaging to determine how many people were inside and where they were.

There were several reasons for the timing. First, because moving in at night gave them the element of surprise and might make the people inside easier to control, resulting in less risk for the officers involved. Second, they wanted this over before morning, with all of their suspects secured before police started assembling for Crossman's funeral. Third, and most practical, was that it had taken this long to do all the paperwork and find a judge to sign it.

They had a broad, no knock warrant, a team experienced in dynamic entries. Now they had to hope that finding the trucks did mean they'd find some, or all, of the Maloof siblings inside. It was common for a family, when threatened, to circle the wagons and protect their own. No less common when the family had a criminal bent and the one who was threatened was threatened because of illegal activity. Blood was indeed a strong tie. Burgess had rarely seen it taken this far.

As if it wanted to give them clarity, the fog had lifted and blown away, leaving a crisp dark night with no visible moon. The special reaction team, in their black tactical uniforms, were almost invisible.

Burgess, hanging back with his team, who were there to identify the suspects and conduct the building search, was as close to praying as a lapsed Catholic could come. Enough good officers had died or been injured at the hands of these people. Lt. Coakley, the SRT commander, put a hand on his uninjured shoulder. "Nobody's going to get killed tonight, Sergeant."

Burgess wanted to believe that.

A man in black materialized out of the darkness so quietly Burgess never heard him coming, and spoke very quietly to Coakley. Burgess figured, from the way he moved and how comfortable he was in the dark, that this might be the same guy who'd spotted where their shooter had been standing, and those rifle marks on the tree down by the old factory.

Coakley and the silent man stepped away and conferred. Then Coakley came back to Burgess. "He thinks there are four people inside. And a couple dogs. Do we know if there are any children?"

They didn't. All he could hope was these people wouldn't put their children at risk. But who knew what someone as coldblooded and vengeful as they'd shown themselves to be might do? Certainly, if he was among them, children's well being didn't matter to Karl Maloof.

Up at the street, at the end of the long drive, the SRT tactical vehicle blocked any chances of escape, and a quiet team had rendered the vehicles parked around the house inoperable. It was time for Coakley to move in.

Flanked by Perry and Kyle, Burgess waited for the fireworks to begin, all three of them frustrated at not being a part of the operation, and fully aware that this was better handled by SRT. "I feel like the cowboy whose horse has been replaced by a bicycle and he's been given a cap gun," Kyle whispered.

"Cheer up," Burgess whispered back. "We get to shoot the ones who get through their lines."

"You think that's gonna happen?" Perry sounded hopeful.

"Anything can happen when you've got gun loving bad guys who don't care about human life, Stan." But Burgess didn't want to talk. He wanted to watch, and wait, and hope things went smoothly. Remember to keep breathing.

He jumped at the first bang, even though he knew it was a flashbang they were using to disorient the people inside. It was followed by gunfire. A lot of gunfire and dogs barking and voices yelling, "Police. Police. Drop your weapons." So much for hoping to catch them asleep.

The whole thing, the noises, the muzzle flashes, the yelling, felt like half an hour and probably lasted less than two minutes. Orders were barked, flashlights moved about, then the team vehicle's lights came on and it came slowly down the hill, a thuggish dark shape like some giant caterpillar from a horror movie descending toward them.

A minute later, Coakley materialized out of the darkness and said, "House is clear. We've got four people down here. You want to come take a look, see who we've got?"

Burgess and his team moved down toward the circle of light that illuminated four people, three men and a woman, lying on the ground, their hands cuffed behind their backs. Kneeling down and shining a light onto each face, Burgess confirmed that they had Karl Maloof, Kris Radstein, the man from Lucille Radstein's surveillance photo who he assumed was Karla Radstein Tucker's husband, and Kris Radstein's wife, Kristin.

Karla Maloof Tucker, expert riflewoman, was still in the wind.

Burgess gave instructions about taking them in and keeping them separated, then asked Coakley, "You did the other buildings?"

Coakley cocked an eyebrow. "What, you old fart, you think I was born yesterday?"

"I think I've got the most dangerous one of this group still in the wind, and I was hoping for a break."

"Oh yeah, Burgess." Coakley tilted his pelvis forward and swayed his hips. "It's not about me, it's about you, right?" He jerked his chin toward the farmhouse. "Maybe they left you a note?"

"Everyone's okay? That was a lot of shooting."

"Couple wounded lamps and a dead sofa. The dogs were Shelties, noisy, but they were non-threatening so we didn't have to shoot any, thank God. All kenneled, now. As for the people, one of 'em grabbed a cell phone instead of a gun, but we took her down before she could do anything with it." Coakley pulled it from his pocket. "Maybe you'll get lucky, your bad guy will be on speed dial."

"Bad gal," Burgess said. "Karla Maloof Tucker. Guy with the eye patch, Karl Maloof? She's his twin sister. Believes that Vince, and Portland PD, ruined her brother's life when they busted him for sharing photos of a four-year-old girl sucking his dick. In her twisted mind, that was just art and we destroyed a great artist."

"That's what this is about?" Coakley sounded incredulous.

"Hard to believe."

"People," Coakley said. "I'm leaving a couple guys. They'll have your back while you do the house. But your shooter isn't in there, I guarantee it."

"Thanks, Lieutenant. You did good work tonight."

As Burgess and his team headed for the house, Coakley said, "If there's another one out there, tonight's not over. We're here if you need us."

It was as comforting as anything could be in these circumstances.

As they walked past the commotion in the driveway, SRT sorting out the suspects and sending them down to Portland in cars, he took out the phone Coakley had given him. Rocky had done the warrant and it was his usual careful document. It had given them phones and the contents of those phones. These days, you couldn't be too careful. Some bad guys had the technical ability to wipe a phone remotely. He wasn't waiting around 'til he got back to headquarters.

He scrolled through the recent calls, found one number that had been called frequently. He called Sage Prentiss, who was waiting back at 109 to start interviewing, gave him the number, and asked him to see if it appeared on Rocky's lists, and if so, whose number it was. Something had to lead them to Karla Tucker. Otherwise, bad things were going to happen.

"Rocky's here. I'll give it to him."

Tonight it didn't matter whether they got overtime or not. They were working because this was *their* case. The victims were *their* people.

"There are four suspects en route," Burgess said. "See if any of them will talk. Tell you where she is."

But it would be a slow process. They wanted intel. They wanted prints to match to their initial crime scene. They wanted DNA. They wanted, no, badly needed, to find Karla.

Searching the house took too long but had to be done. Slowly. Methodically. Tortoise, not hare. They all felt it. All vibrating with impatience, struggling with the physical effort it took to not blow this off. Small things could be important and were so easy to overlook when you were impatient. That cartoon clock hung over his head, the hands spinning wildly. Soon the first signs of morning light would appear in the sky.

Room by room. Nothing. Drawer by drawer. Nothing. Kristin's purse. Nothing. Nothing. Nothing that looked like it would lead them to Karla.

"We'll check the vehicles," Kyle said.

An hour wearier, empty-handed, and feeling a decade older, Burgess was standing in the kitchen, staring at dirty dishes in the sink, a bunch of empty Moxie cans, and an overflowing ashtray on the table holding a lot of half-smoked filter cigarettes like the ones at the factory, wondering what to do next. He figured Prentiss would have called if he'd gotten anything from the interviews. He bagged the contents of the ashtray and the cans, and was staring at a hot pink plastic lighter like the one Kendall Whorter had used the other night at the VFW. He recalled Whorter's whimsical comment. "Pink, right? Too damned girly for me, but if they wanna give 'em out free, I ain't gonna say no."

He crossed to the table and bent so he could read the name of the gas station, and that reminded him of the gas station receipt Dani had found where the shooter had been standing. This was a giveaway lighter. Now he needed to know whether this lighter was from the same place as the receipt. Whether it might be from someplace near where Karla lived? Small things were so easily overlooked. The gas slip hadn't been useful when they had nothing to match it to and they'd been too busy to go back when they had that photo of Karla Tucker.

He called Prentiss again. "Need you to do something for me. Right away. In evidence, we've got a gas station receipt, cash sale, dated the day of the shooting. Can you grab it for me? I need that address."

Something he should have noticed earlier. People were creatures of habit and they often bought gas at the same places. He flipped the seized phone open again. The number he'd given Prentiss to check against Rocky's list had been called several times over the course of the evening. What were the chances they could ping it? That that phone, and the third black truck, were somewhere in the vicinity of that gas station?

"Call me back when you know, Sage," he said, and called Rocky.

They'd go back to 109, take another run at Clan Maloof—maybe Kyle's cold eye could succeed where Prentiss could not—and if that fell flat, and Burgess suspected it would, they'd see what phone pings, or that gas station, might bring them.

It was a hell of a long shot, driving around in what remained of the night, looking for a big black truck, especially as the Maloofs seemed to have an unlimited supply of vehicles at their disposal. But she seemed to like that truck, and anyway, it was what detectives did when they'd run out of options. He called Rocky and asked about pinging the phone.

Sometimes it worked. Depended on a lot of things. If Rocky could get them a location, that would be great. If not, Burgess was willing to do some driving around. The funeral was at ten. Right now it was three-thirty. They still had some time.

Before they disconnected, Rocky gave him a possible answer to the question that had bothered him from the beginning—what had drawn Melia to that location and why he hadn't called for backup. In doing a phone tree among the Maloof and Radstein phones and Vince Melia's, Rocky had found a call on that Friday afternoon from what they now knew was Karla Tucker's phone to Melia's. They'd have to do cell tower locations to confirm it—Richard Pelham was dead, and he suspected Karla Maloof Tucker would never tell—but he speculated that Karla and Kris Radstein had forced Richard Pelham to make that call, and the connection to Karl Maloof's recent parole, a case involving a molested child, and the concerns of a still anxious parent had dragged a reluctant Melia to a meeting with Pelham.

CHAPTER 31

E ven with the eye patch, Karl Maloof was a handsome man, buff with prison muscle, black haired, dark eyed, and intense. He was also about as helpful as a stone. He sat across from Burgess, arms folded, an infuriating smirk on his face, and in response to Burgess's first question, said, "I want to call a lawyer."

Burgess had no idea what a lawyer could do for him. He'd violated conditions of his parole and been found in possession of a gun. Someone else, under these circumstances, might have wanted to cut a deal. It seemed that pigheadedness and a kind of misguided, but righteous indignation, ran in the family.

He wondered if that streak of pigheaded, righteous, anti-social thought was what had drawn Lucille and Rufus together?

Burgess gave it a couple minutes, made the suggestion about cutting a deal, and got nothing in return except another smirk and Maloof's promise that Portland's cops were in for a very bad day.

He watched Stan Perry on the monitor, trying a different tack—charm—on Kris Radstein's wife, Kristin, and getting a similar result. In a third room, Kyle was striking out with Karla Tucker's husband, though he seemed the most likely of the quartet to fold. The problem was that it might take hours to get him to that point, hours they didn't have.

Burgess figured the effort was probably wasted, but he took a run at Karl and Karla's brother Kris, having saved him for last. Kris was likely the second shooter down at the abandoned factory, and seemed to be very close to his sister, so Burgess didn't have much to make a deal with. With the clock running, he got straight to the point.

"Maybe you care, maybe you don't, but your sister Karla's going to get herself killed today. We know your plan is to stage a mass killing during Officer Crossman's funeral. That's not going to happen. But if we don't find your sister before ten, she's going to die at the hands of the police you and she have been targeting."

Like his brother Karl, Kris was a big, handsome, dark-haired man, though he lacked the prison muscle and was going soft in the middle. Burgess assessed him as the weaker brother, likely to have been taking orders from Karla. A follower, not a leader. Unlike the others, who'd been spitting defiance, this man seemed to be a little scared. He nervously fingered the silver medal on a chain around his neck and Burgess realized that it was St. Hubert, like the one on the ground where the shooters' car had been parked. Hunters or metal workers? Or both? He tried to remember whether Karl Maloof wore one. Whether it might be some kind of family thing.

Burgess was wondering what had Kris so nervous when Perry summoned him out of the room.

"Found this in Kristin's wallet." He handed Burgess a photo of Kris and Kristin Radstein holding a baby. "She won't say a word about it. Doesn't admit to having a child. Maybe, if it is their child, he gives a damn even if she doesn't, and you can make some headway with him."

Perry swung around to leave, then turned back. "Can you believe it? They have a kid and they're mixed up in this? I saw the preliminary SRT reports, and she fired on an officer after he announced he was police and told her to drop the gun, so she's looking at some serous time. Maybe her parents have the kid? We know his parents don't. I mean, we have to hope they didn't just leave it in a room somewhere, because they're going nowhere from here but to jail, with no possibility of parole."

With a kid of his own on the way, Stan Perry, formerly one of Portland's hottest bachelors, seemed to be coming around. Burgess thought about how all of their lives were being complicated by fatherhood.

He headed back into the interview room, holding the photo.

He slapped it down on the table in front of Kris. "This your kid?"

The younger Maloof brother stared at him, jaw thrust out pugnaciously.

"I asked you a question. Is this your kid?"

"So what if it is?"

"So I'm just wondering, while you're sitting here stonewalling us, and your wife's in another interview room telling a detective to piss up a rope, and your mother and stepdad are over at the jail, who is taking care of your kid?"

"It's none of your business."

But there was something in the voice, something under the defiance. Just a faint tremble and hesitation, like maybe this guy did care about his kid and was concerned about where it was.

"Maybe. Maybe not. Depends on what we find out. We find out that while you and your wife are off plotting to murder police officers, you left your child in an unsafe situation, it absolutely becomes our business. Pretty soon your child is gonna be the State of Maine's child. That means foster care. Maybe termination of parental rights and adoption, depending on what you and Kristin end up being charged with." He touched the picture. "Cute little guy. Be unfortunate if something bad happened to him 'cuz his parents wouldn't keep him safe." In the photo, the smiling baby was dark haired and dark eyed and looked to be about six months old. Burgess didn't know how old the photo was.

Burgess moved his chair closer, so he was invading the man's personal space. Kris was already in a corner and against a wall. He had no place to go. He leaned away as Burgess leaned in, raising his voice. "Is this your kid?"

"None of your fucking business." There it was again, the words defiant, but the tone uncertain.

"You know what it's like for a kid growing up, knowing mom and dad are in prison for murder and attempted murder?"

"Kristin didn't do any—" He stopped abruptly.

"Really?" Burgess said, making his tone conversational. "What didn't your wife do? I have a report on my desk that says after she was told to drop the gun by a uniformed police officer, who had identified himself as a police officer, your wife fired at that officer. Maybe you play by different rules, but in our world, Kris, that is called attempted murder."

Burgess watched the younger brother. The outward demeanor still hadn't changed much, but there was a panicked look in the man's eyes, a growing realization that maybe he hadn't thought this through very well. That he was in well over his head.

"So, I don't know what's gonna happen with Karla's husband. Depends on what SRT says went down in the farmhouse. I don't have the full report yet. But the rest of you? Karl is going back to prison, with new charges that will keep him there for a long time. We connect you to those shootings down at the old factory—which I guarantee we will—and you're looking at life with no possibility of parole. So who does that leave?"

He waited a minute. "Oh yeah, and Karla's going to die, because if she starts a gun battle with the cops, that's how it's going to end. Very Bonnie and Clyde. Except there will be no Clyde, because you aren't there."

He waited for a response. Kris was only half listening, his mind was working on something. So Burgess pushed a little bit more.

"The only one of you who has a chance to get a good deal, a chance to raise your kid instead of him being raised by strangers, is Kristin. And the only way she's getting that deal is if she, or you, give us Karla before all hell breaks loose."

Kris squirmed on his chair like a man being fought over by a devil and an angel, his look growing utterly hopeless. It was the look of man who knew whichever way it came out, he couldn't win. And then Burgess knew with ugly certainty what the man's quandary was. Why the younger, apparently weaker brother wasn't willing to make a deal. And how truly sick and twisted the whole lot of them were. Or how helpless in the face of Karla's quest for revenge.

He looked at Kris, shaking his head in disbelief, and said it aloud. "Karla has your baby, doesn't she? She has your baby and she's going to use the baby as a shield today so that when she shoots at cops, they won't be able to shoot back."

He jumped out of his chair, knocking it over, grabbed Kris by the shirt and hauled him up. "Kris Maloof, or Radstein, or whatever the hell the you call yourself, you are the sickest, most pathetic, and twisted parent I've seen in thirty years. And I've seen the worst."

He threw the man back in the chair.

"Karla wouldn't—" Kris muttered.

"Karla's gonna die, and your helpless, innocent baby's probably gonna die with her. I will personally make sure you have lots of nice colored pictures of his poor, bullet-ridden body to look at. And you can sit in a cell and live with that for the next sixty years."

He left the room.

Kyle and Perry were in Melia's office, where they'd been watching the interview on a monitor.

Perry looked sick.

Kyle said, "Sheesh, Joe, if what you said is true, that is the sickest thing I've ever heard."

"You don't think it's true?"

Burgess tried to calm down. This wasn't something to take out on them. But he was absolutely explosive. If it wouldn't have screwed up the cases against them, he'd go beat the information they needed out of one of these people and even if he got fired, he'd consider it work well done.

"Breathe, Joe," Kyle said. "None of these pieces of crap are worth blowing a thirty year career for."

Burgess tried, but he was so full of rage his lungs couldn't expand.

"We should give him a few minutes," Perry said. "I think he's close to breaking. I think maybe Joe was onto something with the bullet-ridden body stuff. I know it sounds sick as hell, but can either of you think of a case where we had a baby get shot?"

"Why?" Kyle said.

"Because I want to show that fucker the pictures. Now. Before it's too late."

"Think his lawyer could get any charges thrown out on the basis of cruel and unusual interrogation?" Kyle said.

Burgess was already at his desk, digging through his bottom drawer, where he kept his personal file of horrors, the worst of man's inhumanity to man. The photos he looked at some days when he found he was forgetting why he did this job. The photos he longed to show the assholes who asked a million stupid questions about the job and then said, "Come on. That really doesn't happen."

It really happened. All of it. When this was over, he'd add pictures of Randy Crossman and Remy Aucoin and Vince Melia. Pictures he'd long to show to those asshats who said, of situations where cops faced bad guys with guns or knives: Why didn't he just shoot it out of the guy's hand? Because doing that that was foolish and impossible and got cops killed.

He sifted through one grotesque thing after another until he found what he was looking for. He pulled out a fan of photos and handed them to Perry. "This what you wanted?"

Stan Perry, the tough guy who'd thought this was a good idea, stared at the pictures, slapped a hand over his mouth, and ran for the restroom.

Burgess looked at Kyle. "I never expected that."

"Give the kid a break, Joe. He's having a baby. He goes home tonight and puts his hand on Lily's belly and feels his kid kick, this isn't what he wants in his mind."

"It was a good idea, though," Burgess said. He took the pictures and went back into the interview room.

He righted his overturned chair, moved it close to Kris, and sat. He stared at the man without speaking for so long the prisoner finally said, "What the fuck do you want? I thought we were done here."

"Oh, you're done, all right. I just thought I'd give you one more chance to do the decent thing before we send you over to the jail."

"I ain't doin' shit, so ship me out already."

"Right."

Burgess gave him a friendly smile. "Your baby have a name?"

Kris looked at the floor and didn't answer.

"My son's name is Dylan," Burgess said, and slowly started laying the pictures out on the table. Taken in a long ago case where a man got pissed off because he wanted his wife to come to bed and she was trying to get their fussy baby settled first. His solution had been to take his handgun and shoot the baby. Burgess had been a patrol officer back then, and he'd been first on the scene. Kept the father at gunpoint while the screaming mother held her dying baby.

He'd puked his guts out when he got home, and every damned day for a month.

"This is what's going to happen to your little boy unless you tell us where to find him. This…" Burgess stabbed one of the photos, "…is what you'll be living with for the rest of your life. Don't think you won't. Don't think for a second that we're going to let you forget you had a chance to stop this. You know what a piece of shit you're going to be inside? You think that pen in your brother's eye was bad? Nothing to what's going to happen to you. So just remember…in the years to come, when you're locked up with very bad people who are also fathers, when you get what's coming to you. Remember. You had a choice. You had a chance to save your child's life and you didn't take it."

He stood again, more quietly. "Your last chance," he said.

He waited.

When the man didn't say anything, he left the room, leaving Kris Maloof Radstein staring at the pictures.

The knife in his gut felt like it was going to punch right through his stomach. He followed Stan Perry's example. Went to the men's room and tried to heave it up. Then he stuck his head under the cold water tap and tried to cool himself down before he went back in there and took the man apart with his bare hands. He rested his head against the cold tile, eyes shut. He felt hollow and spent. Couldn't think what else he might have tried to bring Kris around. He'd given it his best shot. He'd failed.

Out in the hallway, closing the door on the sour smelling bathroom, he bent down, his hands on his knees, trying to get his breathing back under control. Monsters and the monstrous things they did were a part of his life. But children? God. He hated it when there were children. Now a helpless baby was going to die and there wasn't anything more he could do to stop it.

Moments like this were when he needed Melia most. Melia could help him get his balance back. Yell at him a little about the job they still had to do. Sometimes Burgess thought of himself as Melia's pitbull. Kept on a tight leash, occasionally let off to go bite someone who really needed biting. Radstein needed biting. A mad dog like Karla Tucker just needed to be put down.

He shouldn't think like this. A lot of cops, Catholic cops especially, always clung to the possibility of redemption. Burgess thought there was some evil in the world that was beyond redemption.

Kyle put a hand under his elbow, gently guiding him up, then stuck a can of Coke his hand. "We've got to see if we can find her."

Stan Perry was pacing the detective's bay, looking dangerously explosive, one hand on his gun, the other rubbing his shaved head, muttering, "Killing a fucking baby," over and over like a mantra.

Burgess had to get this back under control. He was supposed to be in charge here. He did no one any good being out of control himself. "Thanks, Terry. Let's see if Rocky has anything for us."

He jerked his chin toward the room where Kris sat, staring at the photos. "Give that piece of crap five minutes and then have patrol take them all over to the jail. I want to two officers on every one of them. And tell them to watch their backs. There's still a cop killer out there."

He just had to call the chief, deliver this latest piece of bad news, and he was going out there to find Karla Maloof Tucker.

Rocky Jordan hunched over his computer. The room was dim and the bluish glow from the screen made him unearthly. He looked up when they came in.

"Got an address for Karla Tucker's phone number?"

"Nothing. Nada. Can't get anything from the frigging phone company. So sorry, but there's no one who can help us, please call again in the morning. Never mind that people are gonna die, right?"

He looked exhausted, and like he was on the verge of tears. Making technology work was his specialty. It hurt when he couldn't make things happen when so much was riding on him.

Kyle patted him on the back. "Don't take it personally, Rocky. Nothing's breaking for any of us tonight. If you want to get away from that terminal for a while, we're gonna go drive around and look for bad guys."

Jordan reached for his jacket.

"Vest," Burgess said. "No one is going out there without a vest."

Before they left to rendezvous at the garage where their killers had bought gas on the day of the shooting, Burgess took one more look at Kris Maloof Radstein. He had no words. Then he headed out into the city.

He stopped in the courtyard and studied the sky. It was getting lighter. He longed to push back the day, give them more time to seek out the creatures that lived in darkness. He looked at his team, up almost twenty-four hours, the weight of the world and the fate of their brother and sister officers on their shoulders. Silently, they walked to their cars, pulled out of the garage, and onto Portland's empty streets.

CHAPTER 32

The city was so quiet he thought he could hear sleeping people breathing over the sound of his tires on the damp pavement. It was only about seven minutes to that gas station, a slightly dingy building at an intersection where two streets met at an oblique angle, in a part of the city with small houses and marginal businesses in small strip malls. No views. No shopping malls. Not much to recommend it other than being a place where someone could maybe own their own home if both partners worked.

The gas station was a 24-hour place, with a sad sack middle-aged man who could barely keep his eyes open perched warily on a stool behind the counter. His hands fluttered to his chest when Burgess and his team entered. Mostly, when groups of men entered a place like this at odd hours, it meant trouble.

Burgess slapped photos of Karla Tucker and one of the black trucks down in front of him. "Burgess. Portland police. Ever see this woman around?"

The man fished some cheaters from his pocket and bent over the picture. Then nodded. "Yeah. She buys gas here sometimes."

"Cash or credit?" Burgess was hoping for a charge slip, something that could lead to an address. Though time was getting short for that.

"Cash. Always cash."

"What about the truck?"

The man raised his eyes to Kyle, Perry, and Jordan, standing in a semi-circle behind Burgess, then looked back down at the truck. "Yeah. That's her usual ride. Kinda stands out, you know, a woman with a truck like that."

"How often does she stop in?"

"Once, maybe twice a week. Truck like that, it eats gas."

"When's the last time you remember seeing her?"

"Midnight, maybe?"

"Last night? A few hours ago?"

The man nodded.

"She alone?"

"She had a kid with her. Uh. Baby. Like, I don't know, like maybe not walking yet. In a blue blanket, so I figured it was a boy. Baby was asleep. She paid for the gas. Got some diapers and milk. First time I ever saw her with a baby, though."

Even half asleep, the man was a good witness.

"Ever see her around the neighborhood when she wasn't buy gas. Driving? Parked?" He figured it was worth explaining, that getting the man on their side might help trigger something. "Baby's not hers. We're trying to find her before something happens to him."

The man flapped a hand at the store. "I'm not out and about much. Mostly I'm here. I did watch her leave last night. Her with a baby was kinda odd, ya know? She's never seemed like the maternal type. She's not bad looking but hard, if you know what I mean. All edgy and businesslike. Fierce, like she'd just as soon shoot you as talk to you. Not that she talks. She don't use many words and those she does, she sorta spits 'em. And she's always got them guns in the truck."

"When she left, did you notice which way she went?"

The man pointed down the street that was heading out of town. "That way. I seen her go maybe ten blocks or so, then she turned right." He shrugged. "I dunno what's down there. Like I said, mostly I'm in here."

When no one said anything, the man tried again, like he wanted to be helpful. Burgess wondered if their desperation showed.

"Seen her turn that way before, if that helps."

Burgess thanked him.

"You want some coffee, help yourself. It's fresh," the man said. A small kindness that meant a lot right now.

Coffees in hand, they gathered in the parking lot and scoped out their plan, if you could call deciding which streets to drive a plan.

"Anyone spots that truck, call. Don't even think about tackling her alone."

Burgess wasn't getting any of his people shot. He thought if they found the truck, if they thought they had Karla Tucker, he'd get Coakley in. SRT was good at this stuff and they had the protective gear. The baby was the big question mark. But that meant that Coakley's guys, with sniper training, might be essential.

Around them, despite the urban landscape, birds were waking up and having their morning conversations. It seemed so peaceful. So normal. Their world so anything but. All over the city, cops from everywhere would soon be waking, showering, putting on their dress blues, pinning on badges banded in black, lacing up freshly shined shoes. Coming forth into the clear morning to pay tribute the job, and the toll it took, and a fallen brother.

Burgess filled the empty morning, quiet but for the birds, with the bagpipes that were always at a police funeral, with the words that would be said. In service to justice and in defense of the innocent. Final roll call. End of watch. The lovely sadness of Amazing Grace. He filled the silence with the rumble of motorcycles escorting the hearse, saw those ranks of white gloved hands raised in a final salute.

All that stood between those who came to honor Crossman and more death directed at the badge, at the job, was his exhausted, ragtag crew, with little intel and a ticking clock.

"Stay alert," Burgess said. No good way to say "watch out for the bullet from nowhere." You couldn't protect yourself from that, as he knew too well. Silently, they filed to their cars.

What you saw from a car at that time of day was a world waking up, scratching its balls, and sleepily grasping for coffee. Cats skulking home after a night on the town, husbands sneaking home after a night out tomcatting. Newspaper delivery. A woman in curlers and a housecoat, standing on her porch, performing the ritual of the day's first cigarette. Workmen with long commutes slamming tools into their truck beds and firing up the diesel.

Mostly it was still and sleepy.

One day, when they were driving, back before the kids, Chris had told him of something she and a girlfriend used to do, years ago. They'd drive around at dusk, as the lights were coming on, giving them glimpses into people's houses, and see what the world was up to. She'd called it life-shopping.

He'd thought of that often since.

The monotony of slow travel, the engine sounds, and the rush of the heater was lulling him, making his eyes heavy. He was past the point where coffee could make much difference. He turned off the heat, and rolled down his window, hoping cold air might help keep him awake.

He was braking for a cat that broke from between two trashcans when he saw it. Just a tip of shiny black and chrome parked behind a small house with a neat front porch and a flowering tree in the yard that looked just like all the other small houses on the street. Silently thanking the cat, he kept driving, keeping his speed steady, until he'd reached the end of the block. He pulled to the curb and called the others.

"I think I've got her."

It could be a different black truck. She could have swapped vehicles. It could mean nothing. But his heart was racing. He called dispatch for information about the owners. They might be able to track it down. Find a city record that might be right or wrong. Meanwhile, they had to figure out an approach.

First they needed to get closer, get a better look at that truck. Kyle would park on the parallel street, see if he could get into the house that abutted the lot, confirm that it was the truck they were looking for.

Perry would park down the street where he could keep an eye on the house, alert them if lights came on or if anyone moved, Rocky would be at the other end of the street, ready to block her escape in case she left in a hurry. Burgess was the floater, left to coordinate. As soon as they had confirmation on that truck, he'd call Coakley.

Alone in his truck, waiting for Kyle's confirmation, he could feel the clock ticking. Every minute that passed, more people were waking up, there were more cars on the streets, more joggers, more potential targets. More Lookie Loos who'd have to be moved out of the way.

"Come on," he muttered, gripping the wheel. Irrational. Kyle probably had to wake the people in that house, explain his mission, and get permission to enter. There might be children. Nothing was ever as simple as walking in and getting it done.

Five minutes ticked by.

Six.

Finally his phone rang. Kyle. "It's her truck. People here say she lives there. Say they heard her come in around midnight. They were wondering what was going on, since they heard a baby crying. They're getting dressed now and they'll be leaving in a few. They say the houses are identical, so we've got a floor plan. Hold on."

Burgess heard the murmur of voices, then Kyle was back. "Guy lives here says she has an arsenal. Hold on."

More murmuring voices, and Kyle says, "Wife says Karla is mean as a snake."

That was news, wasn't it?

Could tension ratchet down and ratchet up at the same time?

He called Coakley. It rang five times before the lieutenant's sleepy voice said, "Coakley."

"It's Burgess. We've found our missing shooter." He gave the address. "And there's a problem. She's got a baby. Her brother's kid. We figure she's planning to use it as a shield. And a lot of guns."

"Shit." Coakley was silent, though Burgess could hear the sounds of the man getting dressed. "Where are you?"

Burgess said where he was parked and what street to avoid.

"Be there in twenty."

Twenty minutes. Insanely fast for Coakley to assemble his team.

An eternity for Burgess and his.

He wondered how they would do this. With or without Coakley.

He called the others, said SRT was on the way.

Waiting was a big part of the job. Waiting when you felt like you were sitting on needles, when the chances of a good result were slim, was impossible. Leaving the windows down so he could hear his radio, he tucked his phone into his pocket and got out, pacing the sidewalk beside his truck.

His phone vibrated. "There are lights on. She's moving around, and the kid is screaming. My people just left. I'm watching through the kitchen window."

Burgess heard Kyle catch his breath. "She's coming out. Carrying the baby. Putting him in the truck. Oh…"

Burgess gripped the phone tighter as if that gave him a stronger connection to Kyle, as Kyle said, "She's left the kid and is going back inside."

Burgess knew what Kyle was going to do before he said it. Kyle was the father of two. The devoted father of two.

The idea of a child in jeopardy was painful to him. Now he was staring at the reality.

Burgess was already moving when Kyle said, "I'll call you back."

He called Perry. "She just put the kid in the truck. Terry's going to try and grab the kid while she's inside." He grabbed a breath. "Get there. Go through the yard next door. Give him some backup."

He called Rocky, told him what was happening. "Move in closer, get ready to block the driveway. She may be about to leave."

He grabbed his shotgun and started weaving his way through backyards toward Karla Tucker's house. Probably someone would spot him and call the police and the whole thing would blow up. He called dispatch, explained what was happening. "No patrol cars. No lights, no sirens or they'll blow this whole thing wide open. If someone calls it in, say it's a police operation and tell them to stay in their houses."

He was breathless by the time he reached the adjacent yard. Over the short hedge that separated the properties, he had a clear view of the truck. Of the back door. Of crazy, brave Terry Kyle reaching up to open the truck door.

What part of go home alive didn't Kyle understand?

Pot calling kettle black.

He heard the creak of a wooden door open. Karla Tucker, carrying two rifles and a diaper bag, stepped out. He raised his gun. "Kyle, watch out!"

Beyond her, he could see Stan Perry, gun raised. The moment when they had to stop her without shooting each other.

"Portland police," he yelled. "Drop the guns and put your hands on your head."

She turned toward him, smiling, insanely fast on her feet. She'd dropped the bag and one of the guns before he'd stopped speaking. Raised the second gun and fired. Who was crazy now? Who'd gotten so caught up in the operation he'd forgotten the difference between cover and concealment. All he had between himself and a crack shot was a bunch of vegetation. As Burgess ducked down behind the hedge and scrambled toward the edge of a garage, he heard the boom of Perry's shotgun and the crack of a rifle.

He raised his gun again, edging it around the side of the garage. She was looking toward the spot where Perry had been. Praying that Perry wasn't hit, that he'd only disappeared from view because he'd taken cover, Burgess sighted on her and pulled the trigger. Once. Twice. The shotgun blasts shatteringly loud in the morning quiet. At exactly that moment, there was the crack of a handgun from Rocky Jordan in the driveway.

From the corner of his eye, he saw Terry Kyle disappearing into the house, baby in his arms.

He ran forward to where Karla Maloof Tucker lay bleeding on her driveway. She was on her back, her dark eyes staring up at him, her clothes so soaked with blood it looked like she was dressed in red. She wasn't dead, but even as Jordan, beside him, called for an ambulance, Burgess knew she would be by the time one arrived.

He stared down at her, wishing she'd lived long enough so he could ask why. Then, heart in his throat, he stepped past her and went to look for Perry. Got to the body sprawled in the grass, head a bloody mess, and knelt beside it.

"Oh, God, Stanley, no!"

He stretched a shaking hand, feeling for a pulse.

Perry's eye opened. He groaned and pawed at the blood. Burgess pulled out a handkerchief and mopped his face. "Stay down, Stan, Keep still. You've been shot."

"Shit that hurts, Joe."

He pulled out another handkerchief and patted Perry's head, trying to get a look at the wound. His relief was so visceral a shudder ran right through him. Perry was okay. Would be okay. He had a nasty head wound. Probably a concussion. But the bullet hadn't penetrated the skull.

"Joe? It is bad?" Perry's voice drowsy, like he was falling asleep.

Burgess squeezed his hand. "Head wound. It's not pretty, Stan, but you'll live to fight another day."

"Doesn't feel like…" Perry groaned and closed his eyes.

"You're going to be okay, Stan," he said. "We've got an ambulance en route." He took off his last good coat and spread it over Perry, then stayed with him while he and Jordan made all the necessary calls.

Burgess's own face felt hot. He swiped at it. Tears. Not blood. The meanest cop in Portland was crying because a baby would live. Because Stan Perry might have an ugly scar on his head but his own baby would know its father. Crying because now Randy Crossman's funeral could be about Crossman and the sacrifice he'd made. About the thin blue line and what it meant and how they had each other's backs. Today could be about a higher calling and not about twisted evil and a lust for revenge.

CHAPTER 33

Once they'd told Coakley to stand down, and got a medical examiner and their forensics people en route, and found someone in the food chain to do the necessary notifications for an officer involved shooting, Burgess made the most necessary call. To Chris.

"Hey," she said. "The bed was cold last night."

"It was a long night, Chris."

"Are you alive?" she said. "Not shot?"

"Not shot. Stan's a little shot up. Looks pretty awful but he'll be okay. And we got the bad guys. I…"

He couldn't quite say it. "There was a baby at risk. I had to shoot someone."

He sighed. "It's a long ugly story."

"I've put out your uniform," she said. "It's hanging on the closet door."

He had a quick vision of Cote's bedroom. Being spooked by a uniform hanging on a closet door.

"Are you…"

Why was he having such a hard time talking? "Everyone okay?"

"We're fine, Joe."

Stunned by how much he meant it, he said, "I want to come home. I want to hold you. Look at you and our kids.

See the good in the world. But this thing…it's going to be a while."

"Where are you?" she said.

He couldn't have them coming to a crime scene. Cops didn't have their families come to crime scenes. He thought about a day recently. A day when he was sure he was going to die. How it felt to walk away without getting blown up and find his family waiting for him. Who the hell made the rules anyway, rules that forced families into the margins of their lives?

"I'll meet you at my car." It was down the street, away from all this. He gave her address. "You all coming? Don't the kids have school?"

"They can be late. The kids have a dad they've been worrying about. They need eyes on you. What's more important, that or school?"

"You're more important. Than anything."

"You going to go all mushy on me, Burgess?"

"Bring my uniform, okay."

"See you in twenty."

What Coakley had said. The echoes of this thing. He wanted to go home. Pull the shades. Sleep for a month without dreams. Sleep with Chris. But even without Cote to nag and complain about reports, they'd be doing the interviews and paperwork on this thing until sometime just before hell froze over.

He thought this had been kind of a hell, this past week, living with the kind of uncertainty the case had created. He'd been in a war and had lived with that uncertainty. Knew the toll it took. He'd been a young man then. Had felt the adrenaline more than the weight. Now he felt the weight. His years. All today's ugly images he'd file in his brain with the others.

They'd done their best. A baby was alive. But Randy Crossman and Richard Pelham were dead and Remy Aucoin and Stan Perry were wounded, and Vince Melia refused to wake up.

With an effort, he dragged himself back to the present. They were loading a gory, protesting Detective Stan Perry into an ambulance. "Don't let them keep me, Joe," he begged. "I've got a funeral to go to."

Then, with a scared glance at the news trucks that had piled up in the street, he said, "Oh, jeez. Joe, you've got to call Lily. Tell her I'm okay." Trying to sound normal. He looked like hell.

"I'll call her." He plugged the number Perry recited into his phone.

Kyle appeared, carrying the baby. The small creature, wrapped in a blue blanket, was sound asleep on Kyle's shoulder. Kyle was wearing a 'Don't mess with me, I'm a crazy fucker,' look. "See what you've got to look forward to, Stan?" he said.

Perry looked at all the people milling around, at the sheet covering Karla Tucker's body. He closed his eyes and leaned back against the pillows. "I hope it's not going to be like this."

"Not every day," Kyle said reassuringly.

As they watched the ambo rattling away, Kyle held out the baby to Burgess. "You hold him. Social services are taking their sweet time and I gotta call my family."

"Give me one minute to call Lily, and I'll take him," Burgess said. "Chris and the kids are coming here. Bringing my uniform."

"Need to see that you're alive. I'm going to swing home. Rocky's arranged for South Portland to send people to guard the scene during the funeral."

Burgess made the call, doing his best reassuring "It's not serious," number that did nothing to reassure Perry's weeping girlfriend. Then he disconnected and held out his arms for the baby. Stood holding a sturdy little guy with a puzzled face and serious dark eyes as he watched Kyle disappear into the empty house again, phone pressed against his ear.

Two hours later, showered and dressed, they joined the rest of the department in saying a formal goodbye to

Officer Randall Crossman. Remy Aucoin and Stan Perry, wheelchairs and all, were there.

Lt. Vincent Melia returned to the world of the living the evening of the day they buried Randy Crossman. Weak and monosyllabic, but back. Burgess, responding to Gina's excited call, swung by the hospital to see for himself. With great restraint, he didn't take an hour to tell Melia to get out of bed and come back to work because they couldn't do this without him. He figured he'd give the man a day to recover first. He did briefly explain how Melia's own son, Lincoln, had provided the vital clues that had led to the arrest of his assailants.

The next morning, media-loving Captain Paul Cote, recovering from surgery and far from the spotlight after being saved by his arch-nemesis Joe Burgess, got to enjoy his bland morning hospital breakfast while glaring at newspaper coverage of a police funeral. That coverage included a photograph of said Burgess and his family. Smiling, curvy wife holding his dress uniform, while his tall, handsome son and his willowy, heartbreaking daughter embraced him, and his smaller impish son presented him with a huge cup of Dunkin' Donuts coffee. The picture, and the story of how close police officers had come to a bloody massacre that day, was in every paper in the country.

Later that day, Burgess himself appeared for a visit, carrying a small, mysterious box. In response to Cote's sullen greeting, Burgess pulled up a visitor's chair and sat. "You watch the funeral? Poor Randy got a superb send-off."

Cote stared past him. It couldn't be easy to have been rescued by a man he'd tried to destroy, especially under such ugly circumstances.

"Deputy Chief says you're going home in a few days."

Cote ignored him.

"You have someone to look after you, Paul?"

"My sisters," Cote said, "Why, were you going to volunteer?"

"I don't think that would work out very well, do you? You hear about Vince? He woke up yesterday."

When Cote didn't respond, Burgess said, "Come on, Paul. You don't hate him. Just me. Anyway, this isn't personal. The investigation, what we did for Randy, for Vince, for Remy. For you. This whole damned thing has been about the badge. The department. The job. So, in case you were going to brood about it, about what Terry and I did, forget it. No one is keeping score. You don't owe us...me...anything."

Cote looked like hell. Burgess figured he should go. Stop bothering the man. He'd offered a truce. It was a one-time offer. If Cote blew him off, so be it. He held out the box.

"Brought you something."

"Whatever it is, I don't want it. I can't eat anything but this hospital crap. Can't keep my eyes open long enough to read, and I'm allergic to flowers."

Well on his way to recovery, Burgess thought. Cote was absolutely his usual, charming self. Burgess didn't know if what he was doing made any sense, but he'd come here to make the gesture, so he very gently shook the box. "Sure you don't even want to have a look?"

"If I look, you'll go?"

"Absolutely."

Carefully, Burgess slid the box onto the man's lap. Stepped back and waited for Cote to lift the lid. It was such a corny gesture. Way too stupid and sentimental for the robotic man who they all believed had been made in a factory where they'd failed to install humanity.

But as Perry had observed when he heard about the rescue and their rushing Cote to the hospital, sometimes a terrible experience could be transformative.

So he waited while Cote loosened the tape and lifted the lid. Peered into the box at the tiny animal inside.

"Oh. Oh my God!"

The man's trembling hands lifted out a dog small enough to fit in their palms. The tiny creature, not knowing any better, stuck out a teeny pink tongue and licked Cote's hand.

Captain Paul Cote, inhuman martinet extraordinaire, started leaking tears.

"Maybe one of your sisters can keep her until you go home," Burgess said. "Gotta run. Lot of paperwork to do. Reports to write. You know how it is. You take care."

The meanest cop in Portland left his archenemy crooning to a dog the size of teacup, and headed back to 109. And he felt good about it.

Perry might be right. Traumatic experiences might be transformative. He just might have been wrong about who was transformed.

THE
JOE BURGESS
MYSTERY SERIES

Playing God
The Angel of Knowlton Park
Redemption
And Grant You Peace
Led Astray

Turn the page for an
excerpt from

CHOSEN

FOR

DEATH

A Thea Kozak Mystery

Book One

———————◆———————

Kate Flora

New England weather can be very unpredictable in September. Mornings that start off crisp and cold can be steaming hot by noon. That was how I found myself sitting in the sweltering church slowly baking in a jacket I couldn't take off. I couldn't take it off because the matching dress was sleeveless and I'd been raised by a mother who knew to the depths of her soul that you couldn't wear a sleeveless dress in church. Everyone else in the Boston area was spending that glorious Saturday outside. Not that I would have been. With the private school year just getting started, the consulting business I worked for had work stacked up like planes at Logan Airport at five p.m. But I wasn't at the beach or at work.

I was at my sister Carrie's funeral.

It was ironic and unfair. Carrie had always loved flowers. Now she had more flowers surrounding her than she ever could have imagined, heaped everywhere around her small white coffin. Be neither the flowers nor the carefully chosen container meant anything to her now. Inside, no less dead for all the pink satin frills and tucks that embraced her, lay my little sister Carrie. My little sister Carrie, who was always a lost soul. Carrie, who had never quite accepted our love, who had never believed she belonged. And now there was no way we could ever persuade her. They talk about people with an amazing capacity for alcohol as having a hollow leg; well, Carrie had a hollow leg for love.

No matter what we did or said to convince her she was loved, it was never enough. It must have been hard for her, growing up. Our family was anything but peaceful. Every meal was filled with cheerful, noisy bickering, impassioned political arguments, loud jokes, and everyone's simultaneous reports about their day. No matter what we did to include her, Carrie was never quite a part of it. She drifted on the fringes like a waif, watching and waiting for her chance to speak. We learned to build in pauses, making spaces in our conversations so she could talk. Still, it must have been overwhelming being a small golden presence among the dark, noisy giants.

Reverend Miller paused in his eulogy and looked down at us with sad eyes. The pulpit was very high. I would have felt too vulnerable and exposed up there, but I suppose he was used to. He looked down at Carrie, lying there in her small white cradle, banked by a million flowers. "I baptized Carolyn McKusick," he said, "the week after Tom and Linda brought her home. She was beautiful. Even as a baby, she had that direct, questioning stare that let no one off the hook, a looked that seemed to ask, 'Who are you? Who am I, and what are we doing here?'"

He was right. Carrie's questioning, demanding gaze had followed all of us, seeking answers. Attention. Love. No matter what we gave her, it was never enough. She could never be satisfied.

He looked like he might cry. "Now she is with God," he said. "For all her questions, Carrie believed in God and in his goodness. So, while for all of us who loved Carrie, our sorrow is great that she is no longer with us, we can take comfort from the knowledge that she has now found peace and perfect happiness. Let us pray." Under the trained ministerial cadence, I could hear his sadness.

Dutifully, I bowed my head, but I didn't follow Reverend Miller's prayer, and I didn't pray the sort of prayer he and God would have approved of. I prayed, as I sat there bent

Kate Flora

over my clenched hands, that today or tomorrow, or someday very soon, the police would call and tell us they had found Carrie's killer. I prayed that he would be tried and convicted of first-degree murder. I hoped he fried. I didn't know if Maine had a death penalty, but I hoped so. By the time the prayer was over, my stomach was in knots and sweat was trickling down inside my black dress.

CHOSEN FOR DEATH

available in print and ebook

Kate Flora is the author of 15 books. Her titles include the star-reviewed Joe Burgess police series. *And Grant You Peace* won the 2015 Maine Literary Award for Crime Fiction. *Redemption* won in 2013. Her nonfiction includes the Agatha and Anthony nominated true crime *Death Dealer*, and *Finding Amy*, co-written with Portland, Maine deputy chief Joseph Loughlin, which was a 2007 Edgar nominee. With retired Maine game warden Roger Guay, she has co-written a memoir, *A Good Man with a Dog*. Her next Thea Kozak mystery, *Death Warmed Over*, will be published in 2017.

A former Maine assistant attorney general in the areas of battered children and employment discrimination, she's a founding member the New England Crime Bake, the Maine Crime Wave, and a founder of Level Best Books. She served as international president of Sisters in Crime. Flora teaches writing for Grub Street in Boston.

CPSIA information can be obtained
at www.ICGtesting.com
Printed in the USA
LVOW10s162015 0517
534583LV00001B/28/P